REFULGENT EYRE

TOME ONE OF THE SOGA ARCHIVES

TERIL SHERMAN

ECCENTRIC GOAT PUBLICATIONS LLC

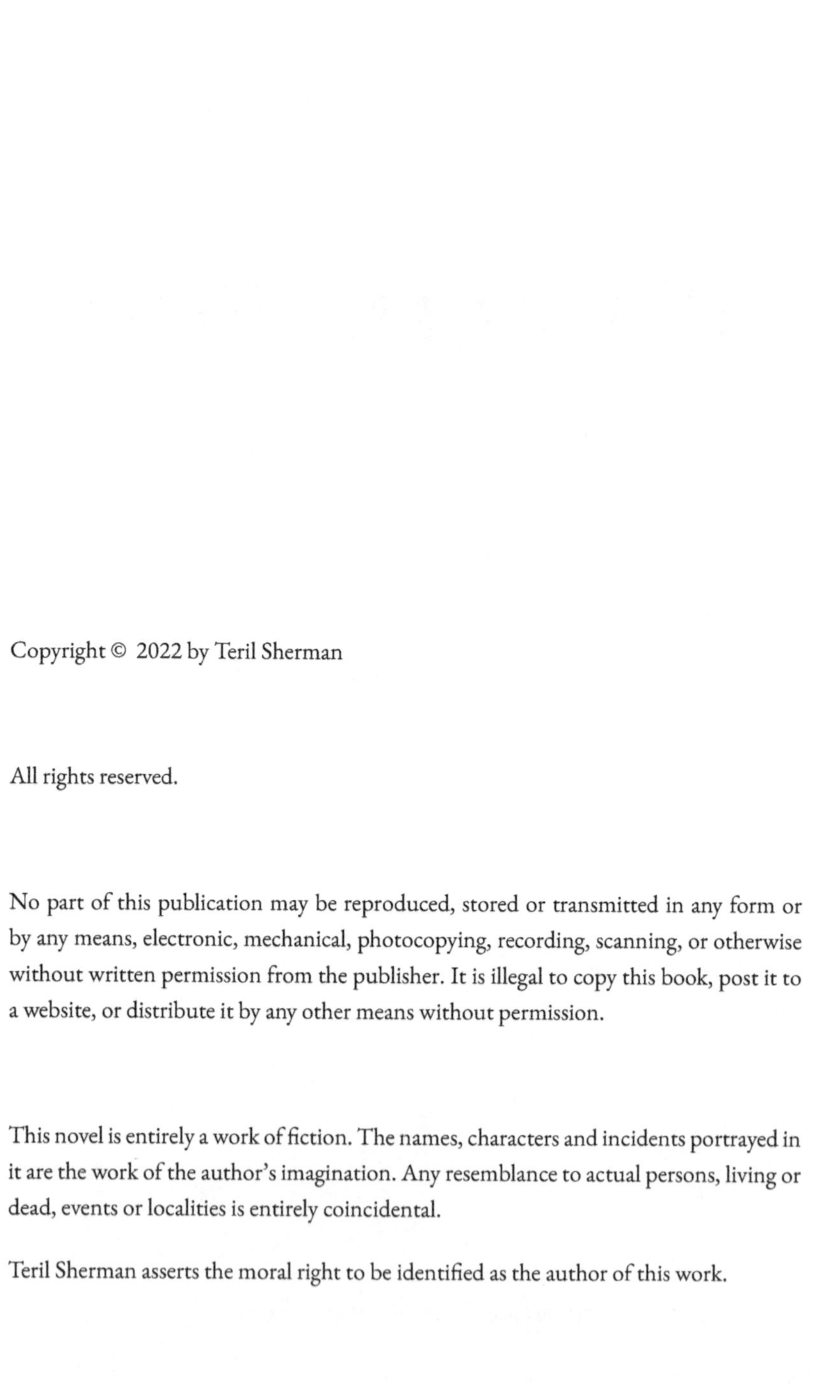

CONTENTS

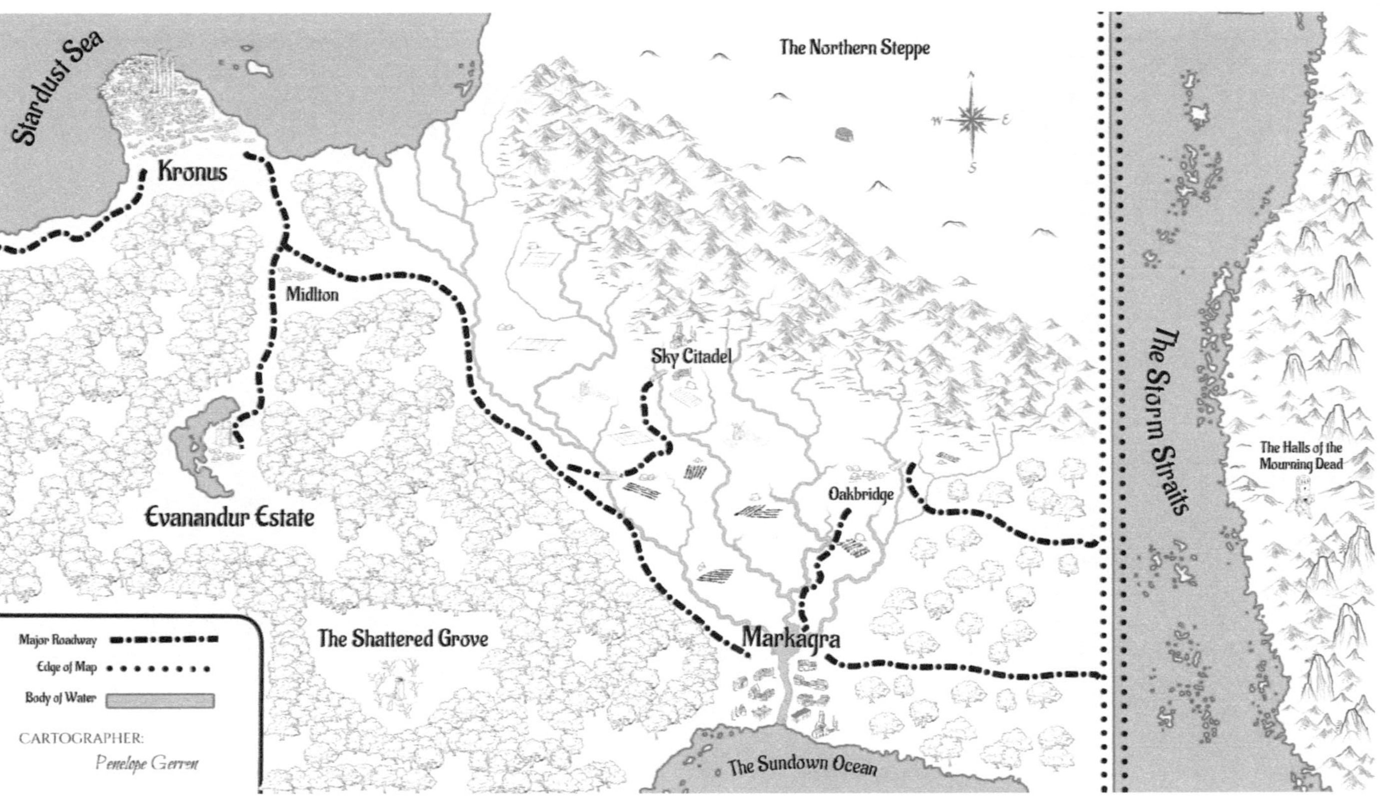

Stardust Sea
The Northern Steppe
Kronus
Midlton
Sky Citadel
The Storm Straits
Evanandur Estate
Oakbridge
The Halls of the
Mourning Dead
The Shattered Grove
Markaqra
The Sundown Ocean
Major Roadway
Edge of Map
Body of Water
CARTOGRAPHER:
Penelope Gerren

Chapter One

Leianna beamed to herself as she effortlessly leaped over a small gray boulder. Her surroundings were a blur of orange, yellow, and red, with a slight touch of green as she sped through the trees. Every year she came just short of winning the Chasing of the Hare event, during her village of Oakbridge's harvest festival.

Every year Dugan would snatch victory out of her grasp. This year would be different. She had been practicing her spell mastery in secret. Even now she had called forth the wind to speed her along. Dugan did not stand a chance.

It was just last year she had captured the rabbit, only to have it wriggle free and jump straight into the arms of Dugan. That braggart would not let anyone hear the end of it. She was not about to listen to another year of that dolt's self-proclaimed superior talent, physic, and intellect. She shuddered at the possibility of that brute winning the chase for yet another year in a row.

She refused to give it any further thought as she focused on the goal in front of her. Leianna's breathing was heavy, and her heart was beating fast with excitement as she ran. The red ribbon flitted about as the hare scurried away from all the young adults eagerly pursuing their prey. She watched as the little rascal raced into some underbrush.

A familiar voice rang out in a labored wheezing, "Leianna... wait up!"

Leianna instinctively turned her head to look back. Espying her lifelong companion, struggling to keep up with her. His pale freckled face was beet red and covered in sweat, the curly scarlet hair matted to his forehead as he desperately tried to not fall behind her.

"We can't slow down now, Peter. We practically have it!"

The rabbit was showing exhaustion after being pursued for the whole first part of the day. She would be the one to seize it up as soon as it gave her any kind of opportunity to do so. She took a sharp turn around a bend in the trees. Focusing on the rabbit, she could tell that it was presenting signs of slowing down. She redoubled her efforts and pushed harder, her focus on the animal absolute.

All at once, she projected herself forward. With a force of will like that of an arrow released from a bow. The world seemed to slow almost to a standstill. The beating of her heart rang in her ears as if it was the loudest noise in the forest. Strange blue and bright yellow lines of light seemed to outline her surroundings. Her movement was undeterred by this occurrence as she wrapped the magic inside to propel herself forward. It was becoming more natural each time she used it.

Her thoughts blazed with excitement; she was getting better at using magic like the Magi. This would be the year she was accepted into the tower for training.

The only thing standing in her way was this little elusive ball of fur. She reached forward to grab hold of the rabbit as if it was standing still. Her eyes widened as she felt her fingers close in on the tiny beast. The animal was captured before it had even realized what had happened.

Once she perceived her grip tighten on the rabbit and it was secure in her hands, time caught up all at once. The world shocked itself back into place. For a moment, she couldn't breathe as the magic dissipated around her. Her heart swelled with pride. She had finally done it!

She turned joyfully toward Peter to proclaim her victory. Only to see that he was face first in the leaves, with Dugan standing above him and right behind her. She let out a frightful yelp as Dugan grabbed the rabbit from her while simultaneously pushing her to the ground in a swift, fluid motion.

He let out a barrel deep laugh as he stared down at the two friends. "You two are as slow as syrup on a winter's night," still laughing as he pulled the red ribbon from the rabbit and raised it above his head.

Dugan let out a yell, "Looks like I win again."

His announcement was met with various cheers, moans, and sighs from the other race participants as they finally caught up.

None of them had seen him take the rabbit from her grasp. It would not have mattered, anyway. The ribbon was the true prize. With it in his hands, he was once again the winner of the chase.

Leianna disdainfully watched Dugan march pridefully toward the village as if he had slayed a dragon. She faintly heard his boasting as the others gathered around him. She clenched down on the dry leaves as she saw them disappear down the hill. Everyone in Oakbridge, especially Dugan, would be talking about how wonderful he was, yet again. She felt her face flush with anger.

She let out a sigh as she muttered, "What a bull's ass," from under her breath.

She glanced over to see Peter still face down in the leaves. Upon taking a closer inspection, she saw he was not moving. In a surge, she jumped to her feet and ran to her friend. She was moving so fast she slid into him, and she spun him over.

His eyes were closed, and a bit of blood was smeared under his nose.

She felt a sense of panic take over as she began to gently shake him. "Peter, Peter, wake up!" She quickly lowered her head down to his mouth and pulled him closer to examine his breathing.

As if on cue, Peter began to whisper faintly, "A kiss... a kiss to save this brave soul."

Leianna rolled her eyes as she dropped him back into the leaves. Reaching down, she grabbed a handful of the dry leaves and threw them into Peter's face. "Hey, I could've died just then", he chuckled as he sat up.

She smirked as she shook her head, "Only in your wildest Dreams".

He was beaming as he showed her his wide smile while he wiggled his eyebrows, "Oh, so you have them too, huh?"

Leianna narrowed her eyes and glared at him as she picked up another handful of leaves and hurled them into his face.

Peter chuckled as he sputtered leaf bits from his mouth and brushed the dirt from his face.

She sighed as she looked toward the direction of Oakbridge, "Dugan snatched the rabbit straight out of my grasp."

She said dryly, "He cheated to win this year. How is that even remotely fair?" her voice almost cracked with her irritation.

Peter smugly glanced over, "Oh, about as fair as using magic, I suppose," he stated in a mocking, matter-of-fact tone.

Leianna sensed herself turn a bright red in embarrassment. She hadn't thought he could see any difference in her when she was using magic.

"H-how did you-?"

Peter cut her off, "I knew it!" he exclaimed in loud delight, "So, you have been going through the village Elders' personal library and-!"

She quickly put her hand over his mouth. "Don't shout it out for everyone to know you idiot!" softly yelling at him through clenched teeth.

Peter's eyes widened in surprise. Leianna slowly removed her hand.

"You know that magic is illegal for anyone not trained by the Magi. I want to get into the tower. They only accept those with the utmost potential and talent for magic," Leianna leaned back.

She glanced around to make sure no one was eavesdropping. Magic was illegal for most adults not formally trained by the Magi. However, an exception was made for those underaged looking to become Magi themselves. It was a blurry line that was as confusing as it was easy to cross.

Peter shook his head, "Magic is dangerous. The Elder only studied at the tower for a year and is always telling people that no good can come from it."

She expelled a deep breath, "Magic is only what we make it. I plan on utilizing my magic only for the highest good." Furrowing her brow in concern, she turned to look Peter in the eyes, "Please don't tell anyone, Peter."

Peter smirked and in a strong voice, "As if I would ever tell on my best friend."

He reached down to cover his heart with his right hand as he stood tall, "As a future Warden of Auldryche, in the order of the Bronzehand, as my grandfather before me, I pledge to never reveal your secret." Peter would have appeared as a picturesque Warden if it were not for his gangly body, spindly limbs, and the gap in his front teeth.

Leianna laughed, "I plan on holding you to it, then."

Peter looked disappointed, "Hey don't laugh, I will be a Warden exactly like my Grandad Lamar was."

She smiled softly. "I know you will, Peter. You will be a great Warden at that."

Peter's face immediately lit up as a smile crossed his face.

Leianna stood up as she brushed the dry leaves and mud from her wool tunic. She glanced down, only to realize that she was practically coated in layers of mud and dead leaves. Peter had fared scant better.

"Well, we better get back to Oakbridge. Get cleaned up before tonight's celebration." The Harvest Festival looked to be the largest she had ever seen.

She examined Peter as he enthusiastically commenced marching assertively, as if he was a banner herald in a parade. "I can't wait for the pies and the honey glazed hog!"

She cracked a grin as she shook her head. Peter had always been the one to go straight to the food. She could not help but laugh a little as she joined in on his marching. It was not long before she had become distracted by his humor and the two of them were joking and laughing. Her best friend had a way of making her smile.

Chapter Two

The long hike back gave her way too much time to think about how Dugan had stolen the win from her. Their fun had distracted her at first, but she could not prevent herself from mulling over the previous events. Once she had her mind set on something, there was no giving it up. Peter had tried to divert her thoughts from it with talk of the festival, but her thoughts had mostly drowned him out.

They arrived in Oakbridge as the sun was beginning to set. Her sour mood faded and was soon completely forgotten as the smell of various types of meats, loaves of breads, and pies greeted her. All these delicious smells and delightful sights made her mouth water. At this moment, she did not differ from Peter.

The vendors from Markagra, a city to the south, had already arrived the day before and set up. They offered assorted baubles for purchase or various games to win prizes. Laughter and jovial voices saturated the village. Young children darted about playfully.

Old men boasted exaggerated achievements of seasons past while sipping on huckleberry mead. The entire village was caught up in the excitement.

Leianna loved harvest season. People came from all around the area to take part in the festivities. She always enjoyed the food. Hearing stories from people of other towns. However, this year she was looking for something specific.

This year she surveyed with anticipation from vendor to vendor. Inspecting for any sign that a Magi Recruiter had arrived from the tower. All her life, she dreamed of being a Magi. This year, she had a real possibility of being chosen. The mere thought of it gave her butterflies and made her bite her lips.

"Hey Leianna, are you with me?" Peter was smiling as he was waving his hand at her.

Leianna smiled back, "Sorry Peter, I am simply excited and lost in my own thoughts."

Peter paid it no attention and immediately started up with questions, "Do you think the vendor with the spicy sweets is here again? Or that dwarf lady that baked all those strange fruit bread things? Oh, or the booth that had the knife throwing?" He made a motion with his arm that gave off the appearance he was throwing knives.

Leianna almost couldn't keep up with the rushed number of questions. "I am certain they are all here. If not, I am confident there is something even better waiting for us."

Peter turned his head rapidly to scrutinize Leianna.

"Something better?" he said with a puzzled tone before whipping his head from one direction to another. Looking about the vendors for whatever that might be.

Leianna chuckled, "Don't forget to go home and get cleaned up. I will meet you over by Old Mary's pie stand when we get back."

Peter mumbled in agreement before hurriedly wandering in a random direction. She was certain that he had not heard a word she said as he darted away.

Leianna shook her head before heading for home to clean up, intent on looking presentable for the Tower recruiter. She needed to make sure that she gave off a superb first impression. Right now, she looked like she lived in a dirt hovel on the outside of town.

She passed by a couple, giggling and kissing. They had not even noticed her or even realized she was there. Looks like Rodrick and Elisse are back at it again. They've always been crazy about one another.

For a moment, she pondered having someone like that herself. The image of Peter popped into her mind, and she laughed at the idea of it. He was like a brother to her, an awkward, clumsy brother. Sure, he was funny, reliable, loyal, and always had encouraged her to pursue her dreams but... She grimaced and dismissed the idea. The thought of it was starting to make her uncomfortable. On top of that, she had the Tower and her dreams of becoming a Magi to think about.

She looked up as she neared her family's cottage. It wasn't anything special, but it was where she experienced many of her most cherished childhood memories. The thatched roof was in much need of repair and the dull gray stone walls had seen their fair share of winters, but it was home, nonetheless.

She thought about telling her father about pursuing her goals of becoming a Magi, but she was positive she would absolutely get another speech about finding something more secure or closer to home instead. Her father, after all, was the one to arrange for her to work for the Village Elder in the first place. She could hear the speech already; he would go on about how it was a good and reliable job to work for the Elder and that she should feel lucky to get such an opportunity. Whenever she talked about the Magi or going to learn at the tower, he would become withdrawn.

She could not help but feel a little guilty. Her work was very light. It helped support her family, but she did not like the thought of being trapped in Oakbridge forever. Her body shivered at the thought of the Elder. She could never place her finger on what was off about him. The Elder had a darkness that followed him around. It was as though he was hiding a dark secret that left her feeling on edge around him.

Elder Garlan had done great things for the village. He had been an outstanding teacher for the children regarding the history of Auldryche. Proficiently teaching the art of reading and writing. Garlan was responsible for the ever-burning lanterns that hovered over the streets. He had also been crucial in educating the locals about ways to improve farming.

Before he had arrived, the village had been poor and isolated. Everyone in Oakbridge deeply loved him. With all of that, she still felt off about the man. He felt hollow and sad, even when he smiled.

She approached the door to her house and gently pushed it open to the sight of her older brother and her father laughing. Their cheeks and nose were a red hue. They clearly had been drinking mead.

Her father, Roland, immediately got up and gave her a big hug. "I heard what happened and for what it's worth, you're twice the man that Dugan is."

"He ish nothin but a Bull's ass", her brother Argus proclaimed, stammering over his words. The alcohol that he had been consuming was clearly causing him to slur his speech.

Leianna felt loved but would not let the opportunity pass by, "So if I am twice the man and he is nothing more than a bull's ass... then are you saying I am doubly a bull's ass?"

Argus looked confused, "Wait... thas not wat I meant," the concern on his face was genuine.

Leianna doubled down, trying to maintain an angry demeanor. "So, are you saying I am fatter than the asses of two bulls?" She held out her hands to elaborate on her false sense of being insulted.

Roland let out a hearty laugh as Argus stammered to save face and correct his statement. "Leave your poor brother be. This is the first year I have let him drink this much."

Argus slouched into his chair in relief. His eyes were wide as he let out a heavy breath of air.

Leianna giggled at the tormenting of her brother. She had always delighted in tormenting him, as he always took everything so literally.

Roland turned to her with a much more somber face, "I have something to give you. My beloved daughter. It belonged to your mother. You're old enough now that you are going to start living your life as you see fit. Your mother and I set some things aside for such a time."

Leianna froze and merely stared at her father. He had never talked about her mother since her passing. She passed away when Leianna was only 9 and he had to work twice as hard to guarantee she was always taken care of. For the first time, she noticed the age and hard lines on her father's face. He had worked so hard for her brother and herself, but she always felt he tried to work twice as hard for her. It was as though he was trying to compensate for the loss of her mother.

He had always been oafish when it came to trying to raise a daughter. It may have not been what she wanted and growing up without a mother was difficult, but she always appreciated his effort. This ox of a man played both the role of her father as well as her mother.

She could see the tears he tried all too desperately to hold back. Roland turned to pull a simple wood box from the table and handed it to her. "She would have wanted you to have these now.", he took a deep breath as he looked at the ceiling, as if the motion of holding his head back would hold the tears in, "Now you have a great time tonight and I will tend to your brother."

Roland turned and sat down, a sign she knew all too well signaled the conversation was over.

Argus waved with an awkward smile in complete obliviousness to the situation, a combination of his straightforward nature and the mead. She hugged her brother, then her father, as she thanked him. She shuffled quickly into her room, clutching the wooden box close. Her mind raced with all the possibilities of what secrets this box held for her.

In a way, she was glad that the talk was over as quickly as it started. Otherwise, she would have been the one to break down into tears. She was never good at acknowledging her own feelings, and she wasn't about to start today.

She lit a candle, quickly closed the door to her small room, and stared at the box for only a moment before trying to open it. She struggled for a moment before realizing that they had sealed it with wax to preserve it. Placing her hand on the box, she envisioned the warmth of a hot midsummer day. She immediately felt the warmth emanate from her hand as the spell took effect. Once the wax melted away, she took a deep breath before slowly opening it.

Upon looking within at its contents, the first thing she noticed folded gently inside was a light blue dress. She lifted it out with care, as if lifting a newborn babe. It was very plain in its style, yet it was one of the most beautiful dresses she had ever seen. She held it close as if by some chance she could feel her mother through it. The dress smelled like lavender.

Tears began to well up in her eyes, but she quickly shook her head and smiled at the gift. A glint caught her eye from the box, and upon closer inspection, revealed a detailed bronze necklace with a small pendant in the form of an ivy in a spiral. She had never seen such a design, nor had she ever owned any jewelry of any kind. Her mouth dropped open as she held it up in the candlelight. It was beautiful.

Leianna used the wash basin by her bed to wash up before she quickly donned the necklace and changed into the dress. She picked a small mirror and admired herself. She had never felt so beautiful. The light blue of the dress stood in contrast to her dark coffee-colored skin and raven-black hair. She couldn't help thinking to herself that this was truly the greatest harvest festival she would ever experience, yet in the back of her mind she couldn't help but feel like this would be her last. If they accepted her into the Magi, would she be able to see her family again? The thought made her frown, but the thought of the festival brought her back into high spirits. She made her quick goodbyes to her father and Argus before rushing back to the village center and its festivities.

Chapter Three

P ETER TURNED AROUND AND watched as Leianna headed for her home. He let out a sigh as he watched her disappear around a corner. A smile crept out on the corner of his mouth. Leianna was so beautiful and amazing. *I hope she becomes the Magi she always hoped to become. If not,* thinking to himself with a shrug, *they could always get married, have lots of kids, and he could become a baker like his parents.*

Peter wrinkled his nose as if contemplating a complex problem. *Though if that happened, he wouldn't be able to become the Warden he had always wanted to be.*

"Sorry Leianna," Peter whispered to himself, "Looks like you will have to wait for the love of this Warden to return after his Heroic adventures."

He blew an invisible kiss in the direction of Leianna as he stood smiling, his hands firmly on his hips.

Excitement soon overcame him as the scent of the festival reached his nostrils. Peter raised his eyebrows as he breathed in deeply. He absolutely loved the Harvest Festival. This year looked to be the biggest yet. The smells emanating from the food vendors had him unconsciously licking his lips in preparation for all the fantastic food he planned to devour. His stomach growled in agreement.

He found his feet had a mind of their own as he again resumed his path toward all the fun to be had. The first vendor's booth he arrived at was selling various honeyed nuts and breaded sweet squares. He stopped dead in his tracks and eyed the treats just as a wolf eyes its prey.

He stepped forward as he reached for his coin purse, only to be met with an empty hand grasping his belt. He looked down to see his hands still covered in mud and a little dried blood on his fingers from his bloody nose earlier. *Dugan had hit him pretty hard in the pursuit of that ribboned rabbit. It was a good thing Leianna hadn't seen it, or she may have tried fighting him yet again and then they would both have bloody noses.*

Peter gave a slight shrug. Dugan was just throwing his weight around. It bothered him very little. *One day I will be the greatest Warden in all of Auldryche. I will marry Leianna and I will tell my grandchildren stories of my adventures, just as my grandfather did for me.* Peter thought proudly to himself as he smiled a big, opened mouth smile.

As he stood there daydreaming, reality returned him to his senses. *I should definitely hurry home.* He needed to clean up so he could meet back up with Leianna by the maple meats vendor they had seen earlier... or was it the hoop ring toss booth? Peter shrugged. He would find her eventually and there was so much to do while he explored.

With that, he broke into a full run towards his home in the center of the village. His home was right on the main way through the village and was connected to his family's bakery. He was quickly reminded of how hard he had run in the Chasing of the Hare. His legs ached, but he considered that a result of the fun he had experienced.

A short distance and a couple of near misses with festival attendees found Peter standing before the bakery. He stopped to catch his breath as he was already breathing hard. Resting his hands on his knees as he looked up. His father was jovially selling baked goods as his older siblings ran back and forth behind him.

His father's beard was a giant red bundle of hair with parts messily covered in flour. Peter could hear his father's boisterous laugh, even from where he was standing. His father's big gut bounced as he laughed, handing another customer what appeared to be a seemingly large round loaf of oat bread.

Peter nodded in silent agreement; his father was always extra generous during the festival. He stood up straight and approached his father with a giant grin on his face.

"Peter Finley!" his father bellowed with pride in his voice, "Come over here and tell me about the chase." He could not help but feel proud upon walking up to his father, who was clearly happy to hear of his participation in the chase.

The Chase of the Hare had no trophy as a prize, only the prestige gained from participating. Dugan had the ribbon to flaunt of course, which he undoubtedly would. All of the youth in Oakbridge that partook in this time honored tradition` would talk about it for the rest of the season. Although it would have been great to claim the ribbon for himself this year. He was still satisfied with how close he and Leianna got to catching that rabbit.

Peter strolled up with his shoulders held high. He gave his family an elaborately detailed summary of the events that transpired during the Chase of the Hare. Leaving out only the part about Leianna using magic, of course. He took his promises to her seriously. His younger brothers and sisters listened with wide-eyed wonder. His father grabbed his shoulder and patted his back in affection.

His younger brother Liam chirped up, "I am going to go kick Dugan's butt right now!"

Peter laughed as he grabbed his younger brother, ruffling his already messy hair. "There is no need for that." Liam was not that much younger than himself, but still had a lot of maturing to do.

Peter said with care in his voice, "Dugan is not so bad of a guy, he is just really competitive. Plus, don't forget what our Grandfather Lamar always told us; the fight isn't with each other, but with the darkness that would bring evil to the doorstep of the common folk."

Upon hearing this, Liam immediately stood up straight. Giving his best impression of a Warden's salute. Liam's shoulders then slumped a little as his head drooped. It had not been that long ago that their grandfather had passed away. It was still hard for even him to believe that he was gone.

"I miss Grandpa," Liam's voice quivered a little as he spoke.

Peter smiled and ruffled his hair again. "We all do, Liam. He also said crying was for girls!"

Peter laughed as Liam looked shocked at first, then looked forward with a look of discipline that marveled that of the most well-trained soldier.

"Mom's waiting for you inside", Peter looked up to see his eldest sister Verna looking at him with a warm smile. She had always been the anchor of the family alongside his mother. The two of them kept the family well cared for.

Peter looked at his younger siblings and gave them a Warden's salute, placing his right hand in a fist over his heart. His younger brothers and sisters giggled as they all did various poses and mockery of salutes in playful fun. Liam alone stood like a stone facing forward in picturesque form. Peter could not help but smile as his heart filled with pride. It appeared he would not be the only Warden for this generation.

Peter rushed inside to see his mother hastily gathering the various items needed for the excursion of taking the little ones out to the festival. He did not know how she did it, but he could not ask for a better mother.

"Peter, you're home. I was afraid we would be out at the festival by the time you found your way back." Peter's mother reached forward and gave him a big hug. "I am glad you have returned. Your father and I decided that even though you don't turn 18 until next month, we still think it is only right you have this," reaching behind a pile of assorted bakery pots and pans to grab something wrapped haphazardly in hempen cloth. She handed it over to him with care. A big smile beamed on her face.

Peter looked at the cloth puzzled, but the heft of the weight in his hands let him know it was more than another wooden sword. He usually got those on his birthday. He loved playing with his siblings in between chores as they practiced the sword techniques their grandfather had practiced with them. Peter pulled back the cloth to reveal a hilt of a sword. Peter's eyes widened and his mouth dropped open at the sight of it, shooting his gaze back to his mother.

"This is mine, like... for real... mine?", Peter asked in complete amazement as his mother silently nodded.

"YES!" Peter yelled in excitement, "I knew it. This was going to be the best festival EVER!"

Peter raised the sword still in its scabbard above his head, "Grandpa Lamar's sword!" His body surged with adrenaline as pure excitement overtook him.

Peter only just barely heard his father behind him through the astonishment in his own mind. "Peter, your Grandpa Lamar only had daughters, and I clearly chose the best one," his dad shot his mother a wink, "and he had always told us it was you he wanted to pass the sword to."

His father walked around the room to hold his mother in his arms. The giant round figure of his father dwarfed her short stature.

His mother gave his dad a playful glare, as he said, "At least I think I chose the best one." His mother poked his father's gut as he let out a deep laugh. He wrapped his arms around her as he showered her in quick kisses.

Peter paid them no attention as he stared at the sword. He was handling it as if it were made of gold, "I can't wait to show Leianna."

Liam pipped up from behind him in a mockery of a girl's voice, "Oh Peter, you are so manly. Give us a kiss." Liam could barely hold back the laughter in his voice as he teased Peter.

Peter grinned mischievously, "One day we will be married, and you can babysit our many, many children."

Liam made a face as if he was about to puke and stuck out his tongue. He knew how to get back at his brother but knew it would not be long before a girl caught his brother's eye. Just as Leianna had caught his.

Everyone was laughing as his father and older siblings returned to their tasks of running the bakery while Peter's mother went to rounding up all the little ones to take to the night's fun and events. The younger ones giggled as they attempted to run from her.

Peter went to his room with all the boy's bunk beds and reached under to gather a clean pair of clothes. He decided on his favorite green wool tunic that his mother had sewn for him. It was a little baggy on him, but he loved the color. He strapped the sword to his belt and swelled with pride.

This year would be the year he became a hero of legend. "I promise you, grandpa, I will make you proud by being the best

Warden ever." Peter stood there in the imagination of his own mind, smiling and thinking of all the monsters and villains he would defeat.

Liam snapped his attention back to reality, "You look like you are ready to slay a dragon." Peter turned to his brother, who now had jelly, most likely from a pastry smeared all around his mouth.

"You know that when I retire, this sword passes to you, right?" Liam's eyes widened with excitement.

Peter used his sleeve to clean his brother's mouth. "You and I will be Wardens that they sing songs about, Liam." He smiled as he watched his younger brother light up.

Liam hugged his brother, and Peter hugged him in return. Peter ruffled Liam's messy hair before heading out the door to find Leianna. "Come tomorrow. I will let you use the sword while we practice!" He did not turn around to see his brother's reaction to his statement, but his brother was a lot like him and he knew he could not wait to try it out.

Peter held his head high with his hand resting on the hilt of his grandfather's sword. Imagining himself in all sorts of adventures as he headed toward the noise of the festival. With a devious smile, he thought to himself that maybe just a couple of those adventures ended with him kissing Leianna, too.

Chapter Four

L EIANNA SIGHED AS SHE stood waiting, arms crossed by Old Mary's pie stand. She had been impatiently waiting for Peter. He is probably stuck at one of the sweet stands, thinking to herself as she shook her head. She observed her foot tapping on the ground in agitation and made a conscious effort to stop herself.

"You look absolutely beautiful deary," Mary from the pie stand was barely audible. If she had not been standing so close to her, she probably would have missed what the gentle old woman had stated.

Leianna did a hasty and half-hearted bow, "Thank You, Mary." Compliments were something that she had never quite gotten comfortable with.

Old Mary gave her a mostly toothless smile. "You resemble your mother when she was your age."

Leianna choked down a moment of sadness or happiness. She didn't know which, but she didn't want to deal with the tears, regardless of whether or not they were happy.

"Your mother was a magical woman, she was too good for this little village and this place became darker without her here," Mary placed her hand on her chest, "But deary me she left an even brighter version of herself for this little village."

Leianna found it very difficult to hold back the flood of emotions when Mary started speaking again, "You should wear more dresses though deary, you look comparable to a boy when you wear those wool trousers."

Leianna chuckled, "I will do Mary", giving her the most dramatic curtsy she could muster, which just left Old Mary smiling and nodding her head.

Leianna smiled to herself as she turned around to see Peter staring at her with his mouth half open.

Leianna lowered her brow, looking back at him, "What?" she stated sternly.

Peter mumbled through half-eaten honeyed nuts, "You are the most beautiful woman I have ever seen in my whole life." Peter's voice almost sounded as if he was in a trance.

"You act like you have never seen me in a dress before, you idiot," Leianna quickly turned away to hide her blushing.

She could hear Peter behind her. "Leianna, check out my sword!"

Leianna's feelings turned from embarrassment to anger. She whirled around, intending to sock him right in the mouth.

She was shocked to see Peter holding up an actual sword. "Where did you get that?" Her voice gave away her obvious state of confusion.

Peter smiled, probably the biggest smile she had ever seen on his face, which still had crumbs from the sweets he was eating stuck all over his cheeks. "It's grandpa Lamar's sword. He passed it on to me." Peter held the blade aloft as if he intended to signal a cavalry charge. "He wanted me to have it on my eighteenth birthday."

"Deary, you better put that away before someone gets hurt," Old Mary spoke nervously. The look on her face shows her lack of confidence in Peter's ability to not hurt himself.

Peter exhibited shock at realizing he was holding a weapon up in the air in the middle of a festival and fumbled awkwardly as he attempted to put it back into its scabbard.

Leianna gaped at him, shaking her head, "You can't just go around waving a sword like that, Peter. You'll get in trouble."

Peter nervously nodded his head in agreement as he finally got the sword back in its scabbard, spilling what was left of his honey nuts in the process. "Aw man," Peter let out a disappointed huff before shrugging and turning to Leianna, "So what do you want to do first?"

Leianna knew right away what she wanted to do. There was supposed to be an announcement by the Magi to the village, and she hoped they had not already missed it. She grabbed Peter by the hand and immediately headed toward the platform where the music was originating from. If there is going to be an announcement, they would make it there.

They swiftly worked their way through the crowd. It was clearly busier this year than the last few years, Leianna thought to herself. They passed by all forms of merriment as they navigated their way through the crowds. Many people she recognized from the village and many she did not. Strangers alongside familiar faces laughed, danced, and ate their worries away. The Harvest Festival was in full swing.

Her ears picked up a pleasant sound and soon she made out the melody as they neared the platform. The moment she caught a glimpse of the band, she became almost entranced by the hypnotic tone of the female Elven vocalists. The way the performers danced and sang was ethereal, as it was captivating. Wanting to get closer to the stage, she pushed her way past the crowd of people that were listening and dancing to the enchanting music. She dragged Peter right behind her.

As she worked her way through the crowd, she nearly ran into a stocky dwarf with a large ornately braided beard, loudly discussing the fine art of brewing with an elven trader that had clearly drunk too much already. She bowed her head in apology as he smiled and raised his mug as if to say no harm done.

After successfully navigating the cramped mass of attendees, she finally found a spot that was less congested to the right of the stage and planted her feet as if to claim this location as hers.

She turned to face Peter. "I want to be sure that I don't miss the announcement by the Magi."

Peter nodded, but she could tell he wasn't listening. His attention was entirely fixated on the melody. She turned toward the stage and decided that wasn't such a bad idea. While she waited for the announcement, she might as well enjoy the show.

As Leianna listened, she realized she did not know what the singer was saying, as she did not recognize the language. She gently bit her top lip as she focused on the words. It didn't resonate the same as the pleasant elvish tones of the river elves. Nor did it boom anything like the deep Stonespeak of the dwarves.

She looked on at the band in puzzled contemplation, as her thoughts were suspended by the older gentlemen to her right. She almost jumped as she had not even noticed him when Peter and herself claimed this spot by the stage. His arrival had made it past her awareness.

"I have not heard this song in a very long time", he said as if he conversed with himself. He stood with his head bent slightly back and his eyes were closed. His body swayed ever so slightly to the beat of the song.

Leianna curiously studied the old fellow. "What language is it?" He seemed to understand the words, and she thought no harm in asking if he knew the origin.

"It is the ancient tongue; some suggest it is the language of the trees," the elderly man stated softly. "It is a lament song about the fall of the Grove of Light and the last of the Do'earee."

Such topics were taboo. The Magi had outlawed any manuscript with teachings of the long-lost Do'earee. Knowing this, the song lost much of its enjoyment. It seemed like an awful choice for a Harvest festival. Leianna was about to ask how he possibly came to such a conclusion when an all too familiar voice grumbled behind her.

"Do'earee were nothing but evil sorcerers and blood drinkers," Dugan proclaimed with disdain in his statement. "They were destroyed by the Magi for their cruelty and practice of the evil arts," Dugan stated in confidence.

Leianna glanced back at him as she watched him take a big bite out of a turkey leg. He examined the old stranger with a smug expression on his face. Leianna, having Dugan right behind her, reminded her of his size. She always considered herself as his equal, but standing here and being so close, it was a confirmation of the grim reality that she was small when compared to his immense physical stature.

Dugan resembled a figure carved from wood, from his short dark hair all the way to his overly defined muscles. Dugan's light olive skin, in combination with his handsome looks, always seemed to grab the attention of the girls in the village.

All the girls apart from Leianna, of course. She viewed him more as competition than as any kind of romantic interest. She gave Dugan a sharp glance of irritation. The memory of earlier in the day was all too fresh in her mind. Her hands gripped into tight fists at her side.

Dugan met her stare and gave a wintry smile before pursing his lips as if to kiss her before taking another messy bite of his turkey leg. The mere implication of a kiss from him made her blood boil.

Leianna scowled and shook her head before turning her attention back toward the stranger. As much as she hated it, Dugan was right. The Do'earee had been eliminated by the Magi during the war at the time of the Cataclysm. The great war left the nation in ruins.

"History teaches us that the Do'earee embodied evil and that the Magi saved us from a cruel fate under their rule," Leianna said. It was just as much a question as it was a statement. Her reading of some of the village Elders' personal books had portrayed the Do'earee in an entirely different light. This had only increased her desire to know more. It was as though the history was missing key information. The way they had taught the history of Auldryche to her had always seemed inconsistent and incomplete.

She had read some books in the Elder's personal collection that had snippets that reflected the statement of the stranger. This conversation had completely piqued her curiosity. She could not help but press for more insight from this stranger.

"According to the history of the Magi... then yes, what you say is true", the elderly man formed a smirk under his large and mostly silver beard with very few patches of black hair peeking through.

Dugan let out a cocky-sounding scoff before letting out a "Told ya". His arrogance threatened to derail her curiosity. Luckily, she was proficient at tuning him out.

Leianna could hear him taking another bite out of the turkey leg. She rolled her eyes and wished he were somewhere else. She had questions she wanted to ask this stranger and Dugan's presence was reminding her how much she disliked his annoying manners.

Peter chimed up with a question that surprised Leianna. "What if the Magi were the bad guys?" His voice was teeming with sarcasm.

Leianna looked at Peter and could tell he was only playfully mocking her. She shook her head and shot him a sideways glare.

Dugan snorted a short laugh. "For once, the twerp is right."

Peter's demeanor became almost cold as he turned to Dugan to show the sword strapped on his belt. He gave the hilt a couple of pats to indicate that he was armed as a half-hearted attempt at intimidation.

Dugan raised his eyebrows and let a smile that curled his top hip cross his face. Dugan turned to show the curve-handed ax on his belt, "Only difference is that I know how to use mine twerp."

Peter shrugged, retiring back to listening to the music.

Leianna turned to the old man. His attention was on the stage as he leaned on a beautifully carved ornate wooden staff that resembled mahogany. "If what you say is true, then how did you come to such knowledge?" Leianna asked, as she focused all her interest on the stranger.

He spoke slow and soft, "I know nothing child, I am merely a wandering old man telling stories."

Leianna was completely dissatisfied with the answer he gave her. "Who are you, old man?"

The old man adjusted the heavy brown wool robe around his left wrist, giving Leianna just a glimpse of what seemed to be a wooden torque similar to the staff he carried.

"I am no one child, I am a ghost of a forgotten past..." The aged man's face turned from apathy to concern as he spoke to Leianna, his eyes fixed on her necklace. "Child, I would be careful wearing such things," motioning towards her mother's necklace. The old man's expression changed from soft to stern and dark. "The symbol about your neck is that of the Do'earee."

Leianna stood in disbelief, "This is my mother's necklace", angry defiance creeping into her tone.

The old man shifted his gaze from her necklace to scrutinize her straight in the eyes. "Then it appears your mother has some questions to answer."

Leianna began to respond and was promptly interrupted by a voice booming on the stage. She had been so focused on her conversation that she had not even been aware that the music had stopped. The band had disappeared only to have been replaced by a Magi in ornately decorated purple robes standing at the front and center of the stage.

The man arched his arms up and motioned to the crowd to gather around. His well-shaven face was aglow with a smile that was welcoming. He spoke casually, as with a friend face to face over lunch, but his voice boomed through the crowd as if it were echoing through a valley.

"Hello all and welcome," he paused for a moment as if scanning the crowd, "I bring absolutely wonderful news for you all."

Leianna's heart jumped in excitement. Not only at the Magi using magic in such a simple and useful way, but at the opportunity of becoming a Magi herself. He used magic to carry his speech through the crowd for all to understand his message.

For a moment she saw herself upon the stage wearing the same decorated robes, making likewise festivity announcements at villages not unlike her own.

The Magi spoke with conviction, "From this day forward the Harvest Festival will henceforth be called..." the Magi spokesman paused for obvious dramatic effect, "*The Festival of Liberation*, this will be done in honor of the Magi who freed the lower citizenry from evil during the cataclysm."

The crowd clapped and cheered so loud that it reverberated throughout the village. Hearing the Magi's statement had forced Leianna to take pause. This is a time-honored tradition. What good was meant to come from changing the name? Not only that, he had referred to them as the lower citizenry. This felt more like a backhanded insult rather than a cause for celebration. She furrowed her brow and turned to Peter, who was not clapping, nor was he showing any signs of joy. She was taken aback as Peter looked angry, and he never looked angry.

She understood why. Peter's ancestors settled in Oakbridge and had been a key component of creating the Harvest Festival as a twofold event. The first is the obvious harvest season, revelries with crops at full yield, and everyone coming together to reap the season's bounties. The second is that it marked not only the end of the war, but signaled to all that the Cataclysm was over. They all knew that the Harvest Festival was meant as a time of healing for the people. It was a time to lay down arms against each other and unite as a nation. From her perspective, it appeared more like the Magi wanted all the credit.

Leianna turned to peer back at Dugan, who had his head tilted, not unlike that of a dog straining to listen with the presence of confusion painted across his face. She looked about the crowd behind her and almost everyone engaged in clapping or rejoicing in one way or another. Most of the people sounded in favor of the change, while others seemed to be as upset at this announcement as she was.

She turned to consider the old man's reaction, but he had disappeared. Replaced by some woman with a mug of mead, cheering at the stage.

She caught the glimpse of a very faint green glow coming from below her. Upon searching for the source of this light, she discerned it was emanating from the pendant at the end of her necklace. In a panic, she quickly slipped the necklace into her dress and looked around to make sure no one witnessed the magical glow.

She took a deep breath. She had not garnered any unwanted attention. Everyone's focus was entirely overcome by the charismatic Magi to witness the soft glow of her pendant. Wide-eyed, she remembered the elderly man's words that it is a symbol of the Do'earee. She shivered at the thought of a Magi witnessing such an item.

Realization hit her by what was implied by wearing her mother's necklace. It was apparently an evil amulet that glowed with illegal magic. She took a deep breath and reassured herself that no one had discovered her hiding illegal Do'earee artifacts. She attempted to calm all the questions racing through her mind. Was her mother unknowingly in the possession of a forbidden item? What had caused it to glow?

She searched toward the stage, immediately connecting to the icy stare of the Magi in the center. She felt her heart in her throat, and she immediately became ill. Her stomach twisted in knots as she stared back at him. How long had he been looking at her and did he see the glow of her mother's pendant?

Time seemed to stop entirely, and she experienced a magic she had never encountered before. Everyone halted in time, and there was complete silence. The ever-burning lanterns darkened as if only a spark remained. Though surrounded by people, she had the sensation that they were thousands of miles away. The Magi's eyes seemed to darken and pull in the surrounding light, soon his eyes became an empty hollow void. His gaze rendered an impression within of peering right through her soul.

The pendant grew hot on her chest with an uncomfortable heat as the immediate area around her flickered in a soft, green glow out of the corner of her eye. She could sense her chest tightening with fear as the Magi's glare turned to a scowl writhing in hatred. The Magi raised his arm rapidly and pointed directly at her before holding his hand open and upward.

The Magi began to close his hand slowly while Leianna experienced a stinging cold in her chest. It was as if the Magi were reaching inside her chest and encasing her heart in solid ice. Leianna was experiencing shortness of breath. Her breathing was becoming short and shallow as her vision became increasingly blurry. The pain was verging on unbearable. It was as though at any second, she was going to pass out. She panicked as fear overtook her, still unable to move. She thought to herself that she was going to die.

The instant the darkness took over her vision, she almost missed a soft and soothing voice that was like a whisper in the wind at the back of her mind. The sound of it was comforting and not at all unfamiliar. She knew this voice... from somewhere...

"Leianna, do not fear... Let the light protect you."

Leianna's vision went from being submerged in total darkness to a blinding light. The sensation of weightlessness flowed through every part of her. It was as though she was floating in the air, suspended by unseen hands. The sudden shock of collapsing on the ground shortly followed it. She found herself on the cold dirt coughing, but not where she had just been.

Chapter Five

As her sight cleared, she took note of her surroundings. She was in a clearing near the village by a small hot spring. She recognized this place immediately as Peter and herself would come here to swim and play when they were children.

The clearing was filled with strange enigmatic engravings with chairs carved from small boulders into the shape of thrones laid out in a circle as hot water flowed between the smooth stone outcroppings into a large, natural river rock-like basin. This clearing was considered haunted by the people of Oakbridge, but to her, this place had always given her a strange sort of comfort. She stood on shaky legs, still bewildered at how she had arrived here.

As she looked about, a feeble glow caught her attention. Just above the still water carved into the rock was a rough and worn silhouette of a spiraling ivy, just like the pendant on her necklace. The carving glowed with a faint green and yellow before dissipating as she watched.

She pulled out her mother's pendant to see it shimmer with the same fading light. She choked up for a moment. Was the voice her mother's? Had her mother somehow saved her from the Magi? Why was the Magi trying to kill her? Her head hurt from the rush of questions filling her mind.

"Are you alright?" A deep voice from behind her startled her back into the moment.

Leianna whirled around, ready to fight, when she saw the elderly man from earlier sitting on a large stone, his hands using the staff for balance. His face was devoid of any emotion.

Leianna looked at him, baffled. She managed to stammer out, "How did I get here?" Her nerves caused her voice to shake.

"If I had to guess, I would say your Do'earee pendant had a lot to do with it," the old man said calmly, with a nod motioning toward the necklace.

Leianna, still in shock, "This doesn't make any sense... Why would he try to kill me?"

The old man looked at her plainly, "He wasn't trying to kill you, child, he was trying to tear the magic from your soul. Although, from what I have seen in my lifetime, death would have been the result regardless of his intent," the old man spoke as if completely unbothered by the events that had just unfolded.

Leianna stared at him in disbelief, "He wanted to remove my... magic?"

The old man nodded subtly. "They seek to remove the magic from those who they do not deem worthy of it or from those they see as potential problems. If it had worked, you would have had no memory of the event and would have no further ability to call upon magic as you do. However, child, you have a gift. I suspect it is from your mother. Magic is in every part of your being and trying to remove it would... simply put, leave you hollow and lifeless."

Leianna gulped in confusion and fear. Shaking her head as she struggled to push out the negative emotions. She began focusing on her breathing, just as her father had taught her to do when she became angry. Closing her eyes as she took a deep breath, attempting to relax and concentrate on the moment at hand.

She shook her hands, realizing she had been clenching them into fists before turning to the old man with a sense of determination, "So, who are you, old man?" Leianna shot him a cold, hard look.

The old man grinned from under his beard, "I haven't told anyone my name in... well, more seasons than I can remember." The old man's gaze drifted up toward the tops of the trees and the stars in the sky. A slight frown formed on his lips, as if he was recalling an unpleasant memory. "You may call me Da'ragh."

Leianna felt a slight comfort in knowing the old man's name. He was giving her a focal point to use in order to avoid becoming overwhelmed.

"My name is Leianna Braun", she felt it was only right that he know her name in return.

Da'ragh turned to her and smiled warmly. "I know your name, child, and I should have greeted you differently before. I am quite familiar with your family. Well, on your mother's side. I know quite little of your father." the old man spoke warmly, as if he were an old friend.

Leianna went to ask how he knew of her mother's family before Da'ragh interrupted her. "Looks like we better be on our way before that wolf in sheep's clothing finds you. You are no longer safe here in Oakbridge. Lucky for you, I know of a brilliant spot to hide."

Leianna was confused. "You mean that Magi is looking for me? Wait... I can't just leave my family behind."

Da'ragh seemed unmoved. "If you stay, the Magi will find you and they will kill you. If you come with me, I can teach you the ways of your ancestors. The way of the Do'earee."

Leianna gave him a skeptical stare, "So you can teach me Magic just like my mother used?" Leianna asked, as if to trick him. Her mother had never used magic as far as she knew.

Da'ragh spoke with unwavering confidence. "I will teach you what I taught Merra and so much more. I know this is a lot to take in, but you must understand we need to make haste. To you, I am a stranger, but to Merra, I was a friend."

Leianna's mouth dropped open in shock. She had never told this stranger her mother's name.

"If you want to learn, that is. However, I suspect that you have already decided what you are going to do," Da'ragh said, as a grin crept over his face.

Leianna was still in confusion about what had just happened to her. She couldn't see where she had any choice in the matter. If she stayed, she risked not only her own life but the lives of her friends and family. If what this man said was true, then this Magi would never stop in his hunt for her.

She thought of her father and her brother. "I need to warn my family!"

Da'ragh shook his head. "By this time, the Magi have already found them. Undoubtedly, they have questioned them and erased any memories that they find as a threat."

Leianna looked at Da'ragh with doubt clearly painted on her face. "I just got here moments ago. How could they have possibly tracked down my family already?"

Da'ragh merely looked up at the star-filled night sky and pointed towards the two moons. "You may have just arrived, but I assure you, it has been hours since you disappeared."

Leianna looked skyward to see that Da'ragh was indeed telling the truth, "How?", her question was barely a whisper as it passed her lips.

Da'ragh looked over his shoulder, then back to Leianna. "We must really be going as the magic in this place will only keep you hidden for so long, especially from prying eyes. This place has power, but it is old and tired."

Leianna was at a loss for words as she turned her back to Da'ragh. "I don't know what to believe in all this."

She stared into the moonlight-filled forest as if she might find an explanation there. Things had happened so quickly, and she had not yet regained her bearings. She let out a long sigh as she tried to decide what to do next.

"Over here!"

Leianna turned to see Peter and Dugan running towards her from around a bend in the path through the dark gray stone that led to the hot spring.

Peter was out of breath as he spoke, "We have been looking everywhere for you-"

Dugan interrupted, "Why are you here... and with him?"

Leianna couldn't tell if he was asking out of concern or out of irritation. Leianna looked at Dugan with confusion, but her voice was that of assertion, "Why are YOU here?"

Dugan looked dazed, as if she had asked him a cherished secret. He was only stunned for a moment as he immediately regained his composure and motioned toward Peter, who was still wheezing. "The twerp practically begged me to help find you", Dugan's voice was defensive but still exuded confidence.

Peter looked up at him with a look of bewilderment before Dugan shot him a glare. Peter raised his eyebrows and looked away, maintaining silence.

Leianna gave a slight frown. She really didn't care why he was here. She turned her attention toward Peter. "How did you find me?"

Peter was smiling, "First of all, I am happy you are safe." He inhaled before giving a long explanation of the various locations and areas they had searched for her.

Leianna listened as he delved into every excruciating detail of their search for her.

Da'ragh let out a cough from behind her. "I must insist that we get moving. The longer we delay, the longer we risk being captured... or worse."

Peter squinted as he stared over at Da'ragh in disbelief. "Captured? What do you mean by worse? What kind of danger is she in?"

Dugan interrupted again, the tone in his voice thick with annoyance, "No one risks imprisonment. The Magi Acolyte was the one who helped us look for you. He assured us he has only a few questions before accepting you into the tower."

Leianna stared at Dugan, panic clearly forming on her face. "Did he follow you?"

Dugan just scoffed and shook his head. "No, he said to come find him once we found out you were safe. He was even expressing concern for your well-being."

Peter smiled and chimed in, "He said that you show promising signs of being a great Magi someday and that you were an exceptional candidate for guidance at the tower." He was clearly excited to tell her what she would have received as fantastic news earlier. Now she had some serious doubts that being brought to the Tower as a student was the case.

Leianna couldn't help but frown. That is what she had invariably wanted, but after tonight, her mind was full of mistrust and fear. It had turned her entire reality upside down.

Peter's face turned from joy for his friend to obvious concern. "Leianna, I don't understand. I thought you would be happy about being chosen for training at the tower. Isn't this what you wanted?"

Dugan shot Peter a look of frustration. "This old fool has clearly rattled her brain with lies about the Do'earee."

Dugan glared at Da'ragh before looking back to Leianna. "Let's get you back to the Magi Acolyte. He will know what to do."

Da'ragh moved with a speed that did not match that of an old man. In a blur, he was up standing in front of Dugan. Da'ragh thrust his staff inches from the young man's face with such speed that Dugan had barely the time to realize what had just happened. Da'ragh stood motionless as Dugan stared at him, wide-eyed. He was clearly unsure of what to do next.

Leianna went to declare that Dugan was not an enemy when she noticed a shadowy figure at the end of Da'ragh's staff. It wriggled, unable to free itself. Leianna gasped, "What is that thing!?"

Da'ragh was speaking in a language that was unfamiliar to her, as a soft white light left his mouth like a fine mist in the moonlight. The mist reached out like hands to envelop the shadowy figure and in moments; the mist dissipated along with the shadow. A disembodied shriek echoed in the clearing as Da'ragh lowered his staff.

Da'ragh spoke clearly and firmly. "That was a shade attached to you, like a parasite. They are used to spy on their hosts and relay information back to their masters. Not only that, but they are often implemented in killing their hosts when necessary."

Dugan nervously gulped, "Who would have attached that thing to me?" The look of shock on his face let Leianna know he knew exactly who had attached the shade to him the moment the question passed his lips.

Da'ragh turned to Leianna. "We really must be going. There is no time to waste. That Magi Acolyte that sent these two to look for you now knows exactly where we are and is most assuredly on his way here."

Leianna found herself speaking before she had time to think, "Alright, let's go." By saying the phrase out loud, she knew she was taking a path that would not so easily be undone.

Peter stepped forward with an enthusiasm that appeared misplaced. "I am coming with you! I can't let you go with this stranger unprotected."

Leianna went to protest, but she could already tell Peter had made up his mind, and truthfully, she felt a lot better with the idea of her best friend coming with her.

Dugan rolled his eyes. "You guys have fun and count me out." Dugan turned and started walking out of the clearing toward the village, "Don't worry, I won't tell the Magi anything, and good luck with all your craziness."

Peter, not giving any thought to Dugan's words, looked at Da'ragh and held out his hand. "Sir, my name is Peter Finley, and it is a pleasure to meet you... uh, what is your name?"

Da'ragh turned to face Peter, "My name is Da'ragh." Da'ragh cleared his throat "I must warn you though that by following your friend here that the path will be hard and-"

Peter interrupted, his face stoic and resolute, "Now mister Da'ragh, I must warn you, if any harm befalls Leianna, it is I you will answer to."

Leianna watched as Da'ragh's eyebrows lifted in what seemed to be amusement. Da'ragh's tone turned warm, "I understand completely Sir Peter Finley and I will be on my best behavior." Da'ragh gave Peter a small bow as Peter's face glowed with a smile like he had just won a pie-eating contest.

Peter, still smiling, turned to Leianna. "There are some horses we can get from the stables near the outside of town. That should be our best bet on covering the most ground."

Da'ragh, in one swift motion, pushed Peter, knocking him off his feet and throwing him a good way away. Da'ragh almost seemed to hover as he dashed backwards away from Peter.

It startled Leianna as a large blade slashed through the darkness, striking the ground where the two had just been standing. She stared in amazement as a giant-like skeleton with what seemed like armor plating grafted onto it stepped out of the shadows with eerie silence. Its hollow eye sockets set on Leianna from under its heavy-looking helm as it began to move forward with the speed of a fox on the hunt.

Leianna found herself frozen in place. The thing before her was terrifying. It was clearly 3 heads taller than herself and looked like it could throw a horse. Its bones were bleach-white in the moonlight. The dark armor pieces adorning most of its body seemed to absorb the light around it as it raised its massive claymore above its head. The skeleton warrior was about to perform an overhead strike, intended to be a killing blow. Leianna could not coax her arms or legs into moving. She stood stunned; her gaze transfixed on this monstrous being before her.

Leianna was snapped out of her stupor when she heard a large twang of steel striking the undead creature's armor from behind. She blinked as she heard yet another loud twang. She could see Peter behind the large skeleton, swinging his sword for all he was worth into the back of the thing with little effect. The skeleton seemed to look back over its shoulder to see what was causing the annoyance. In a flash, the undead giant spun in place, bringing its blade down in one hand toward Peter.

Leianna reflexively moved her hands forward, as if to grasp at a falling dish. The giant slowed as if moving in cold water, its blade barely moving at a snail's pace toward Peter. In a movement made entirely by reflex, she had conjured forth a type of magic she had never used before.

She found herself focusing on the creature. She felt herself projecting the feeling of stopping the thing from hurting Peter in every part of her being. It immediately became clear how taxing this was as she found a bead of sweat dripping down her brow and her breath had quickened. She felt tired, like after a hard day's work. Yet she wasn't even moving.

She watched as Peter moved to the side of the skeleton to bring his blade down hard into the thing's exposed elbow joint of its sword-wielding arm with devastating results. The joint shattered from the impact, sending the forearm and hand still attached to the claymore crashing into the ground. Leianna felt a burst of excitement mixed with relief, but that feeling immediately turned to panic.

In watching Peter strike the skeleton, she had lost her concentration; in return, she was forced to watch as the undead regained its freedom of motion and without missing a step reached out with its still-intact arm to grab Peter by the head. Throw him with ease into the rock wall on the other side of the clearing.

She tried to refocus on holding it in place, but she still felt fatigued and found that her mind was cloudy, making it difficult to concentrate. The skeleton spun in place and reached out to grab her with a giant, boney-clawed hand. She barely managed to avoid its grasp by jumping sideways to the ground.

She scrambled backwards onto the cold rocky soil, trying to gain her footing to run as the creature made another swipe. However, the undead thing's grip would not find its mark. Leianna saw as the giant's taloned hand in full swing met that of a big knot-ridden wooden club in the opposite motion.

She watched as Dugan leaped from the clearing's edge, swinging this large tree branch right into the hand of the skeleton. Bone shards and wooden splinters flew in every direction as the force of the two connected. The armless giant skeleton lost its footing and fell to a knee. The brunt of the impact had rattled the thing. Leianna could only watch in stunned disbelief.

Dugan had lost no momentum as he picked up a big gray rock and slammed it into the face of the giant undead. Dugan let out a growl-like yell as he slammed the rock repeatedly until nothing was left of the skeleton's skull. The helm it was wearing almost flat from the flurry of slams Dugan had brought down on it.

Dugan sounded angry, "Stay down filth, you never stood a chance."

Leianna was relieved by his aid, but she was still in awe of his prideful nature. He was showing arrogance even at a time like this.

Leianna remembered Peter and was instantly jumping to her feet in worry as she looked about the clearing for him. She saw Peter on shaky legs, holding his sword in both hands while staring at the skeleton. He had blood dripping down the side of his face.

All in all, she was surprised to see him standing at all. Peter had always been able to take a hit, but that throw by the skeleton was something else entirely. Peter saw Leianna and immediately smiled, letting out an enthusiastic, "That was outstanding! Good strike Dugan!"

Dugan sneered over at Peter with resentment, "If it wasn't for me, you two idiots would both be dead."

Peter shrugged. "We had it handled." He did not sound all that sure of himself as he awkwardly sheathed his sword and began touching his head, grimacing in pain.

Peter then looked to Dugan, "Thank you though... that was the toughest fight I have ever been in."

Dugan had inadvertently let a grin cross his face. "Whatever twerp."

Leianna gave a pause and looked about. Where was Da'ragh? He had not been of any help during the conflict.

"Fascinating." A cold and confident voice came from the path of the clearing.

Leianna recognized the handsome look and well-kept vibrant robes of the Magi from the stage immediately. The Magi Acolyte's face had a sinister smile as he examined Leianna.

The Acolyte had what looked like wisps of shimmery dark hair coming from his left hand. The wisps were wrapped around Da'ragh, pinning his arms to his side. Da'ragh seemed paralyzed in the same spot he was in earlier when the skeleton had attacked. Da'ragh was not moving, his eyes looking straight forward as if frozen in time.

"So... little girl, how is it that someone such as yourself came across a blasphemous artifact of the Do'earee?", the man seemed to be making more of a statement rather than asking a question. His voice was rife with venom.

Leianna went to answer, but she could tell the man had not come for an explanation at all, but rather for an execution.

The man's upper lip curled into a snarl-like smile. "Imagine my surprise in coming to snuff out yet another would be Do'earee and finding such a prize."

The Acolyte turned to look at Da'ragh. "You have been hiding for far too long brother, it's about time you came home."

The Acolyte took his right hand and pointed two fingers upward, making a slow arc of a circle in the air before pointing toward the unmoving body of the skeleton. Black mist swirled around the bone fragments as they began to roll across the ground and reform on its body. The skeleton was being made whole again by the Acolyte.

Dugan bared his teeth and picked up the rock he had used earlier and began smashing immediately.

Leianna watched as the thing formed just as fast as he could break the undead giant apart.

"Do something, you idiots!" Dugan yelled in anger as he continually hurled the rock into the skeleton.

Leianna looked to see that the Acolyte was laughing in delight at Dugan struggling with the undead thing. She strained to come up with ideas as to what she should do. She took a deep breath and looked at the Acolyte. Leianna focused again on her breathing, then she reached forth all at once, projecting the sensation of freedom directed at the wisps around Da'ragh. She felt time almost stand still as wisps of light-like roots shoot forward like lightning and wrap around the dark wisps holding Da'ragh frozen in place.

Just as she saw the wisps breaking apart, a giant ebony snake the size of a horse snapped at her face, causing her to recoil and fall to the ground. She looked up with panic on her face, only to see that the snake had never been there. The Acolyte was laughing almost hysterically.

There was a snide arrogance in his voice as he spoke, "I have not had this much fun in quite some time, oh please do go on."

Leianna cursed under her breath. There was never a snake, but merely an illusion to break her concentration. She found that her breathing was becoming more labored. The taxing effect of using so much magic, all in a short time, had left her feeling heavy. The sound of cracking bone and crushing rock let her know Dugan was still furiously smashing the skeleton behind her.

Leianna turned to where Peter was, but he was missing. As if to answer the question of where he had wandered off to, she saw the glint of his sword arc toward the Acolyte's face. Her eyes widened as she watched the blade slash across the Acolyte's cheek spraying blood on the ground, but she felt her heart sink as she watched the Magi with ease catch the blade between the fingers of his right hand.

Peter had sneakily worked his way closer to the Acolyte and had thrown his sword at him once he was close enough. Peter had a shocked look of disbelief on his face as the Acolyte slowly turned to face him, tossing the sword to the ground in disgust. The Acolyte's eyes blazed red for just a moment as he took his palm across his face and the wound disappeared as if it had never happened.

The acolyte spoke much more seriously now, "No more games children, it is now time for your untimely and horrendous deaths." The acolyte brushed his robes as if clearing dust from them. "It is such a sad thing to see such young men and women with such potential meet with an early grave, but what am I to do?"

Leianna could tell that the question was rhetorical as the acolyte lifted his hand in a claw-like grasp. Black shadowy mist swirled down his arm and around his hand, forming a whirlwind of inky black that quickly grew in depth and size. Just as panic was beginning to overtake her, time stopped and a bright light above her head flashed like a beacon. It was an orb no larger than that of an apple, but it was as bright as a sun at midday.

She could barely see through the brightness to witness Da'ragh break free of his bounds. Sending the wisps of black scattering like leaves in the wind to dissipate in the air. Leianna could barely believe her eyes, one moment he was breaking free of his bonds and the next he was standing in front of the Magi Acolyte.

She watched as Da'ragh gently reached out and placed his hand on the Acolyte's chest roughly where his heart would reside. The Acolyte seemed unable to move, as the area was still caught in this magical stasis. Da'ragh was completely unaffected by this paralyzing light that saturated the clearing.

Leianna should not have been able to hear what he said, but it came through clearly.

Da'ragh leaned in and whispered into the ear of the Acolyte, "Dear brother, I grant you the gift to witness... and feel... the pain you have inflicted through the eyes of those you have wronged."

Da'ragh's voice was full of sadness when he spoke. Leianna watched as tears streamed down the face of the Acolyte. His once cocky demeanor was now replaced by pure fear.

The acolyte cried out, his voice full of panic and sorrow, "What have you done?!"

Da'ragh stood stoically, no effort made to answer the Acolyte's demand. Leianna watched as the Acolyte gradually disintegrated. Bright orange and red light coursed its way through the Acolyte's body, making it glow sharply, as if being consumed by flame. His body filled with light then fragmented, cracked, and broke away as fireflies in the night. Leaving Da'ragh standing there alone.

The orb above her gently faded out and all at once time resumed its march. Reality was shocked back into its rightful place. The magic that had warped it just moments ago faded into memory. The clearing is back to being lit only by the stars and moons above. Leianna took a deep breath.

As she stood up, she heard Dugan yell out in anger and confusion behind her, "What in the... How did..."

She turned to look at Dugan, who was obviously agitated by the actions that had just transpired.

Dugan let out an exasperated comment from under his breath. "This is insane."

She turned back toward Da'ragh to see Peter had clambered over to retrieve his sword. He had a slight limp in his step. It was a wonder as to how he was able to walk at all after that impact he had experienced from the giant skeleton's throw earlier.

Da'ragh slowly turned toward Leianna. "They will never stop hunting you now. I am truly sorry for that. It appears they have made the choice for you."

Leianna didn't seem very surprised by this statement. After all that had transpired this evening, she couldn't see the Magi just letting her go. Leianna looked to Da'ragh understandingly. "I don't like it, but I understand what you are saying. I will go with you, Da'ragh."

Leianna looked over to Dugan, who had walked around and was now standing by Peter. He was holding the claymore of the skeleton balanced on his shoulder.

Dugan spoke to Peter with what sounded like a cross between concern and agitation, "Throwing your weapon like that was foolish. Disarming yourself is a great way to get yourself killed."

Peter paid Dugan's warning no heed as he looked to Da'ragh hopefully. "I can still come to help protect her, right Da'ragh?"

Dugan gave a small slap to the back of Peter's head. "He was talking to all of us twerp. None of us will be able to stay here."

Peter grimaced and hunched over a little, still in pain from the skeleton's toss.

Dugan looked at Da'ragh. "I didn't want to be a wealthy landowner and farmer like the rest of my family, anyway. It appears that I am destined for an interesting, yet short, life."

Leianna could clearly hear the sarcasm in his voice, but he looked nervous in his attempt at being indifferent to the circumstances. This was a lot for all of them to take in. Tonight's events had set the path for the rest of their lives.

Da'ragh nodded and a small solemn grin crossed his lips, "So it's settled then, no time to waste."

Da'ragh reached into his pocket as Leianna walked closer. He produced an acorn that looked carved from wood rather than an actual seed. Presenting it to Leianna in his open palm, "We will take the old skein pathways."

Leianna cautiously picked up the acorn and gave Da'ragh a puzzled look.

Da'ragh gave her a warm smile, "Your training starts now... Just toss it on the ground over there", Da'ragh pointed his staff to a spot in the clearing that seemed of little consequence to Leianna.

She looked at the acorn carving before gently tossing it onto the ground, but to her amazement, nothing happened other than the sound of it thudding in the dirt. She looked back to see Dugan chuckling and Peter staring at the ground where the acorn had struck with raised eyebrows and a puzzled look on his face. Leianna turned to Da'ragh for guidance. She raised her arms questioningly.

Da'ragh looked at her simply, "Now reach out and envision it growing. Give it a little love, just like a seed in your garden."

He tapped his staff on the ground. "Just like most things in this life, it only takes a little love from others to grow into something great." Da'ragh had a warm and patient smile on his face.

Encouraged, she turned toward the acorn in the dirt. Leianna could barely see it in the moonlight as she focused and thought of the love she had for her family. She thought of the way her father had tried to teach her patience plenty of times and she couldn't help but let a smile slip across her face. Leianna then projected all those feelings forward toward the acorn and in a flash of brilliant green, vines burst from the carving to sprout into the shape of an arched doorway. She was stunned and stared forward in wide-eyed amazement.

She heard a surprised Dugan mumble a curse as Peter spoke in awe, "That was incredible, Leianna."

Da'ragh began walking forward toward the arch, which then filled with a soft blue glow like that of a clear sky in the early morning. "This will take us to one of my burrows. It is protected and should hide us from the Magi for the time being." Da'ragh motioned toward the arch. "Merely walk through the arch and you will find yourself safely hidden on the old pathways. Walk straight and you will emerge in my little sanctuary."

Peter asked curiously, "Burrow, like in a rabbit burrow?"

Da'ragh let out a low chuckle. "Not quite, more like a place of learning that has been long forgotten."

Dugan was shaking his head as he eyed the archway nervously. Then, as if struck by a brilliant idea, his eyebrows raised, "You first twerp, unless you're not brave enough."

Dugan turned to witness that Peter was already walking through the glow of the arch as he let out an excited, "Woo-hoo!"

Dugan frowned, then stepped forward through the arch with his eyes closed tightly shut. His body language showed that he was not happy to walk through the pathway in the slightest.

Leianna could hear he was mumbling something nervously under his breath as she watched him disappear through the arch. Leianna took a step forward and felt Da'ragh's hand on her shoulder. She stopped to look up at him.

Da'ragh smiled but his face looked sad and tired, "If it wasn't for your magic weakening the bonds surrounding me, I would have never broken free." He squeezed her shoulder gently, "You did really great Leianna. Your mother would have been proud of your innate talent and magical ability."

Da'ragh let go of her shoulder and motioned toward the archway. Leianna turned to stare into the soft blue light, and as she stepped forward, she couldn't help but feel a sense of accomplishment and excitement as to what would happen next.

Chapter Six

So'baka leaned forward, balancing as he reached down to slap the neck of his dragon Grymsnar. Grymsnar was as black as midnight. The only other color on his scales was an ivory-white streak that went from the left of his jaw down his neck to his chest.

So'baka spoke with agitation, "I have no desire for this summons, I yearn for west land blood."

Grymsnar let out a low growl as he spoke, "This House seeks to use us in their schemes. Do not be fooled, pale skin."

So'baka nodded silently, then leaped from his mount's neck with ease. His bare feet landed on the cold ground in silence. So'baka looked forward with contempt. He had been called to the convening of the members of Great House Sher'Atul with no idea of the reason for his summoning.

He took his dark magic lance firmly in his hand and whispered a command of sizing to it. Shard, as he had always called it, obeyed, and shrank to the size of a toothpick, which So'baka promptly pushed through the piercing in the top of his ear. Shard looked no more than a mere bauble, not standing out from the others in both his ears and down the bridge of his nose.

So'baka moved aggressively forward toward the Great House's main hall, his movements not unlike that of a wild animal. He walked almost bow-legged and hunched over. He had a look that at any moment, he would drop to all fours and sprint like a wolf after its prey.

So'baka looked about the dragon perches. There were many. The Great House of Sher'Atul rested at the top of craggy mountain peaks that never saw sunlight through the gloomy, cloudy skies overhead. As he walked toward the massive doors that led inside, he glanced at the massive castle walls, made from melted and molten glass with the aid of the dragons. Everything was a dark grey or black ebony, light reflected from fire bowls hanging from chains off the blackened molten glass walls.

A couple of Bloodbound knights, clad in Ebony plate, stood on either side of the doors. Their armor was thick and covered in wild spikes that jutted out, the armor was just as much a weapon as the long axes they held by their sides.

So'baka scoffed, "Slow and heavy, like a rock sinking into the water. A corpse that doesn't know it's dead yet."

The Bloodbound Knights did not pay his words any heed as one stepped forward to open the door, allowing entrance to the main hall. As he stepped inside, he looked down at his own armor with pride; A making of his own creation. His armor was light and had very few ebony parts left.

Ebony was an almost indestructible metal used by all the Great Houses of the Tal'Kor. Most of the original ebony of his armor had been scrapped in favor of the scales given to him by Grymsnar himself. He opted into not wearing gauntlets, nor did he wear shoes of any kind. He had made an Oathpact with his dragon mount. The dark magic had hardened not only his skin but his heart as well.

He passed by some slaves toiling away at washing the blood from the floor, which So'baka glared at as he passed. Naturally, he despised the weak and the cowardly. He would never fall to such lows; he would sooner die before ever serving another like a dog.

So'baka found himself reflexively baring his teeth as the thought of servitude crossed his mind. All too aware, he had been called here against his free will. He made his way down the large and snake-like hallway before reaching the throne chamber.

So'baka took a moment to temper his anger before opening the door. It was inevitable that his orders would be to patrol the edges of the Tal'Kor lands yet again. He wanted to wage war on the weaklings in the west and the south. His heart desired bloodshed. Yet the Lord of the Great House of Sher'Atul would tell him to wait, to show restraint until the time was right.

So'baka was done with waiting. He pushed the door open angrily, causing it to slam open. The sound reverberated throughout the throne room.

To his surprise, the room was eerily quiet and almost entirely empty. No other Dragon Oath Riders, no General of the Bloodbound Knights, no Blood Pact Summoners, and no War Hound Chiefs. So'baka stopped in his tracks and scanned the room. Every fiber of his being said trap, and he was no prey for the taking.

The Lord of the Great House Sher'Atul let out a booming laugh that shook the walls, "Come forward, Little Monkey ."

So'baka snarled, revealing his teeth filed to sharp points. He hated being called Monkey. If it were not the lord of the house saying such insults, he would have killed the man on the spot.

So'baka ran forward with frightening speed and leaped up into the air, landing directly in front of Lord Kull of Sher'Atul at the top of the steps to the throne. So'baka was taken aback to see his lord lean forward without even a flinch so that his face was mere inches away from his own when he landed. Lord Kull had a square face with a large black beard, his hair was long and draped over his shoulders like a raven's wings. Lord Kull was a muscle-covered giant of a Tal'Kor. With frighteningly heartless intelligence.

So'baka took a couple of steps back, overwhelmed by the power of his Lord. Lord Kull's eyes flashed red before turning back to a deep black. He leaned back in his death motif ebony throne, simultaneously placing his hands on a cleaver-looking sword resting on his lap.

The throne was a disturbing thing to behold. It appeared as many souls, trapped and writhing in agony, had been carved straight from dark, molten glass. So'baka looked at the blade in

Kull's lap cautiously. He had never seen his lord even draw the blade. He forced down a gulp as he stared down at the gruesome weapon. His lord had drawn the blade without him even noticing. It was there as a sign of power and as a warning.

So'baka was grimly reminded why Kull was the Lord of House Sher'Atul and why house Sher'Atul ruled over all the Great Houses. The strong ruled all and the weak simply died. This was the rule of law in the lands of the Tal'Kor.

This made So'baka smile, the grin coming across as more of a snarl of a wild animal or the nightmare imagination of a child.

Kull tapped his fingers on the blade in his lap. "We have an opportunity, So'baka, an opportunity beyond the understanding of that monkey brain of yours, but perfect for your abilities."

So'baka listened intently, doing his best to ignore the insult, as the only other option left to him would be a quick death.

"I will have my son explain it... in smaller words so that you can understand", Lord Kull stated as cruelty permeated his voice, clearly amused by the anger he caused in So'baka.

So'baka could feel the corner of his upper lip twitch at the strain to contain his fuming annoyance from the constant string of insults.

So'baka found himself reflexively reaching for Shard in his ear when a figure stepped out of a cloud of shadowy red mist to the right of Kull's throne. So'baka let out a loud breath as he lowered his hand as the figure materialized out of nowhere. The blood mist dissipated like fog in the sunlight.

The man had snow-white hair and skin. His eyes were the color of milk, and he was wearing armor that looked like smooth polished white ivory. The man looked like he had been carved from white marble stone, with no rough edges and only smooth contours. This was in direct contrast to the normal sharp edges of the Tal'Kor ebony armor. This man's appearance stood out like a sore thumb within the throne room.

So'baka couldn't help himself and growled. The man he looked upon was Vilak, Kull's son. So'baka glared at him, for Vilak had done the unthinkable. He had sacrificed his dragon in a pact with a demon. The ivory-white armor he wore was made from his former mount's bones. So'baka watched as an emotionless Vilak turned toward him.

"Hello old friend."

The voice was an eerie combination of two distinct tones, as if two people were speaking in unison. It sent shivers down So'baka's spine as he realized what he was hearing. The demon and its host were speaking as one, their voices overlapping and merging into a single unnerving sound. Vilak gave a hollow grin.

"We are going to give you what you always wanted. We are giving you a war."

So'baka found himself in awe. Had he heard correctly? So'baka turned to his Lord wide eyed. Excitement clearly covering his face.

Lord Kull was slouching on his throne with his hand on his chin. A large sinister smile beaming from the shadows.

So'baka found himself thinking this a cruel joke. This was too good to be true. He turned to look at Vilak, who had now turned to look toward the doors of the throne room. So'baka heard Vilak speak, but his mouth didn't even move.

"It looks like my dear sister has finally arrived."

So'baka furrowed his brow in confusion as the doors remained closed and the throne room remained silent. With the only exception being Kull rapping his fingers on his sword blade. So'baka looked at the doors and then back to Vilak with confusion.

Had Vilak lost his mind when he made the blood pact with that demon? It would not be the first time he had heard of such things. Whisperings of demon pacts driving the host insane with indecipherable visions and nightmares were the bedtime stories for the children of the Tal'Kor. So'baka found himself staring at Vilak. He had sacrificed his mount for a power that was so dark and unnatural that even someone as heartless as himself shunned such paths.

He heard the heavy throne room doors slam open. Heavy footsteps entered the room, the sound echoing around him. So'baka turned with surprise to see Kull's daughter, Xanaphia striding into the room. A terrifying sight for any westerner or southerner to behold for sure.

Xanaphia was the Heiress and Keeper of the Dragon Oath Riders. Her Dragon Kerrungull was twice the size of his Grymsnar and a potent magic caster. Some dragons used magic in their pursuit of power, but both So'baka and Grymsnar had always chosen skill and speed in combat over spells and blood magic incantations.

Xanaphia walked forward with confidence, with her hair trailing behind her. It was just as raven black as her father's. The dragon oath tattoos were clearly visible on the side of her shaved temples, not unlike that of So'baka's own oath tattoos. So'baka, however, was entirely bald, and his tattoos went all the way down his back. He had fully bound himself to Grymsnar and Grymsnar had fully bound himself to him. Xanaphia stopped next to her brother on the steps to Kull's throne. She had a look of contempt on her face as she glanced over at So'baka with disgust.

"Who invited the Monkey?"

So'baka could contain his rage no longer and, in a feral-like fury, he spun in the air as he pulled Shard from his ear, thrusting it forward toward Xanaphia. Shard enlarged to its lance-like size and shot forward with the speed of lightning. A loud, high-pitched twang rang through the air as the tip of Shard hit a large ax-like blade floating in the air in front of Xanaphia.

Xanaphia had malice on her breath as she spoke, "So you choose death then... Little Monkey."

So'baka growled through his sharpened teeth, "You will bleed."

So'baka pulled back Shard as he did a flip and sent the lance-like weapon forward in a flurry of thrusts. Each thrust was met with a deflection of the ax-like weapon Xanaphia wielded. She stood motionless as the wide handless blade arced through the air as if of its own volition. Her eyes were like daggers as she glared at him.

So'baka grinned in delight. She was not fast enough; he thought to himself. He breathed deep as he readied himself to double his speed. The muscles rippled through his body as he exhaled.

He felt the dragon oath power surge through him as he lurched forward, sending Shard forward like light across glass. Xanaphia's eyes widened as she realized her ax would not block the strike in time. She was only able to watch as the lance moved toward her throat.

So'baka found his precious Shard had stopped short of its target. The momentum of his strike suddenly halted. The complete and abrupt stop had sent him stumbling.

He looked up in anger to see that Lord Kull was holding Xanaphia off the ground by her throat with one hand. His other hand had a firm grip around Shard. So'baka barely had time to think before Kull yanked Shard from him, hurling it towards a wall to stick in a pillar-like an arrow would stick in the hay.

In the same motion, Kull had stepped forward. His dark lord moved with blinding speed; catching So'baka off guard and lifting him up by his neck before he could even attempt to dodge. Kull's eyes were glowing a deep red from the blood magic coursing through him.

"I will say this once, and only once."

So'baka could feel the cold and powerful grip of his lord tighten around his neck. He looked over to see Xanaphia hanging from Kull's other clenched hand, but she was glaring at him. So'baka was taken aback as she made no effort to resist her father and instead was staring at him with hateful malice.

Kull's voice boomed and echoed in the throne room, "If you ever fight before me again, I will add your souls to my collection and feed your bones to the slaves."

So'baka found himself on the verge of passing out, as Kull dropped him to the ground. So'baka coughed as he rubbed his neck. He looked up to see Xanaphia land on her feet and go back to standing by her brother as if nothing had happened. A second axe blade that he had not even seen disappeared behind her. He knew that the first blade was just a defensive distraction, and this second blade would have decapitated him without his ever knowing that it was there.

So'baka let out a low growl as he stood back up. He clearly had underestimated his opponent. So'baka watched as Kull took a step back and looked him over.

Kull let out an amused laugh, "You are quite dangerous for being so small."

So'baka was reminded that he was by far the smallest in the room. Even Xanaphia stood a good head and a half above him. He looked up at Kull. The full height of his lord towered above him. So'baka took an uncomfortable step back.

Kull walked slowly back over to his throne and sat down, resuming his slouch from earlier. His lord seemed lost in a constant state of contemplation.

Vilak started speaking the moment Kull had taken his seat, *"As I was saying earlier, we have a plan for you, So'baka. You will get your war."*

Vilak raised his hand and red mist erupted from the floor to take the shape of a landscape all too familiar to So'baka. This was the coast that was due west from the island of the Tal'Kor and the beginning of the kingdom known as Auldryche. Vilak continued pointing towards a large castle keep on the coast of his manifested replica.

"This will be your target, So'baka. An empty throne makes the kingdom weak. The Magi stewards squabble over politics and gold. The kingdom remains stagnant and falls into disarray. Various houses ruled by so-called lords debate and negotiate for the throne that they will never have."

Vilak turned as he moved floating in the air, *"We have garnered the support of the House Sha'Asson and their slave yards. They have already started work on the war barges that will transport our armies west."*

Vilak was so intent on his own droning that So'baka tuned him out. He could hardly contain his exhilaration. This was real, and it was happening. He only caught bits and pieces of Vilak's speech as to what So'baka was supposed to be doing in the upcoming siege. Vilak looked over at So'baka and must have noticed he wasn't listening.

"So'baka."

So'baka looked up at him, still eagerly thinking of the blood Grymsnar and he would spill.

Vilak hovered over the ground as he floated silently toward him with his hands resting behind his back, *"I forget who I am speaking to, clearly I need to make this simpler."*

Xanaphia let out a bitter chuckle and raised her eyebrows while staring him down.

So'baka had heard Vilak and seen Xanaphia's mocking glare, but the slights were ignored. He was anticipating the end of this meeting so that he may begin his murderous rampage. He could feel the beat of his heart thump in his chest like a war drum and the quickening of his breathing, like the cold wind of the mountain peaks.

Vilak again interrupted his thoughts, *"You need to kill everyone here."*

So'baka followed his hand to see him pointing at the coastline fortress on his red mist-manifested table.

"You will need to secure that keep within the next two seasons in time for our great house to take its first steps in conquering these lands." Vilak stepped back and waved the mist away. It faded and promptly disappeared.

So'baka turned to Kull. He could not hide his enthusiasm if he had wanted to. "I will have this keep taken by winter's end. I will take a thousand skulls and a thousand slaves for house Sher'Atul."

So'baka grinned as his lord Kull smiled from the shadow of his throne, "I will bring fear to these people and show them the power that is the Tal'Kor."

Kull motioned gravely toward the door, "Then do as you have promised, little beast."

So'baka headed toward the door. Without missing a beat, holding his hand above his head as he walked, the sharp whistle of Shard returning to his hand brought joy to his cold heart. He whispered to shard and returned the shrunken lance to the piercing in his ear as he strode back down the halls. He was eager to share the wonderful news with Grymsnar.

So'baka found himself running out of the large doors leading to the dragon perches. He quickened his pace to a full sprint, yelling out to his dragon, "Grymsnar, we go to war!"

Grymsnar, who was curled up like a sleeping beast, immediately unfurled his wings to their full breadth and lifted his head high in the air to let out a guttural roar that echoed through the peaks and vibrated the ground beneath So'baka's feet.

So'baka had barely grabbed onto Grymsnar's harness before the dragon launched itself from the perch landing. Flying with great speed toward the craggy, sharpened rocks below. So'baka pulled himself up to balance at the base of the dragon's neck.

Grymsnar, at the last possible moment, pulled them away from the ground in rapid ascent.

So'baka yelled at the sky, "We will have blood!"

In response, Grymsnar let out a roar of flames, "We will feast!"

CHAPTER SEVEN

L EIANNA RUBBED HER EYES and rolled over in her makeshift cot. The flickering and soft glow of fairy light from floating glass orbs hovered lazily about the room. She sat up as she yawned and looked over at the other two empty cots where Dugan and Peter slept. They must have woken up earlier than herself. It had been that way the last couple of days.

Da'ragh's burrow was underground, making the passage of time difficult to keep track of. The only way to access this massive underground structure was by using the old pathways, as Da'ragh had called them. Magic paths led to these hidden libraries and places of magical study, with no conventional windows or doorways to or from the outside. They had been staying in this burrow of Da'ragh's for a few days now as they tended to Peter's wounds. He had given her a crash course in a multitude of magic lessons that had left her exhausted by the end of each training session.

Her legs complained as she stood up and stretched out her arms. Her sight drifted down when she noticed a tear on the left side of her mothers dress. A frown formed on her lips as she changed her clothes into those provided by Da'ragh. She folded the dress neatly before sliding it under her cot. Given the chance she would be sure to mend it. The pendant arround her neck and this dress were her most prized posessions. Another yawn escaped her mouth before she collected herself and wandered toward the table that Da'ragh had cleared off for them. They had been using it as a place to eat and converse.

Upon sitting down, she found various fruits and vegetables, as well as some dried meats, waiting to be devoured. She was still half awake when she had begun eating what looked like a pear but tasted more like a honeydew melon mixed with an apple. She shook her head; the food grew all around this place with no water or gardeners to tend to them.

She found herself examining the grandiosity of the structure she had been living in these last few days. Massive intricately carved wooden pillars dotted the incredibly expansive area that looked Elven in design but seemed to have no end. She could see books and scrolls on massive bookshelves spiraling upwards. Massive stone tables and chairs presumably carved in the style of dwarves lay strewn with various magical implements and coated in dust. She still had not come to grips with how this place could even exist and remain secret. This underground location seemed to span on for days. It was easily larger than the city of Markagra, south of her village.

She continued to eat as she looked around for the others. They were the only ones in this structure, which still left her completely baffled. Da'ragh had told her that this burrow was one of the few that remained untouched by the Magi and their hunt to exterminate all traces of the Do'earee. She let out a loud, wide-eyed sigh. Her entire reality had been turned upside down.

She was always taught that the Do'earee were evil, and the Magi were the saviors of the people, but now she was not so sure. Da'ragh had only been teaching her the basics, but none of the magic she had learned so far had been evil or harmful in any way. She shivered as she thought of the magic used by the Magi Acolyte in the clearing. "Now that was dark magic," she whispered to herself. Da'ragh had explained to her that some of the Magi still practiced an art known as Necromancy. The thought of using such magics made her feel ill. It felt wrong, clear to her core.

She finished her strange fruit and grabbed up a piece of peppered jerky before heading out to find the others. She wandered over toward some tables where she knew Dugan had been spending his time. His love of history had honestly surprised her. She walked a good while before finding Dugan buried in a pile of various books and tomes.

"Find anything interesting?"

Dugan's head shot up from behind the pile of dusty tomes that seemed far too large for an average-sized person.

"Did you know that only half of the Noble families of Auldryche survived the Cataclysm? The Do'earee were mediators and peacekeepers, as well as teachers and advisors?"

Dugan hectically added even more questions, leaving Leianna with no time to respond.

"Did you know that there was an event known as the Black Sky War before the Cataclysm? The Houses of the Tal'Kor invaded! They nearly conquered the western continent! Until the dwarven armies of the Crimson King aided Auldryche in pushing them back!"

Leianna sheepishly responded, "I did not know that—"

Dugan interrupted, "Our history has been completely rewritten. I am going to try to find out why." Dugan clambered up a carved wooden ladder to pull down a massive tome. He set it on a table with a slam, sending dust up in the air. Leianna realized at this moment he had not actually been speaking to her directly, but rather he was speaking his mind out loud.

Dugan had a look of frustration as he exasperatedly pointed toward the cover of the tome. "What in all the realms is an Anduli? This book is titled *A Warning for Arcane Practitioners: Anduli the Magic Cursed*." Dugan shook his head as he looked up at all the bookshelves.

Leianna let out a laugh. "Looks like you have a lot to read about."

Dugan furrowed his brows but said nothing as he opened the pages of the tome and began reading once more. She was quite positive that he was not aware of her presence in the slightest.

Leianna looked at the pile of books and realized that Dugan had not moved from his spot since yesterday. "You may want to start thinking about getting some sleep, Dugan. Or at least getting a bite to eat."

Dugan didn't even look up as he dismissed her away with an agitated wave of his hand. He was clearly consumed by soaking up the knowledge in front of him.

Leianna shook her head and wandered toward the spot Da'ragh had claimed as his own.

As she wandered around the gigantic pillars, she again found herself amazed by the sight of this place. She would have never imagined a place like this in all her life and to think that Da'ragh had said that this had been one of the smaller Burrows that the Do'earee had utilized. Her mind was ablaze, pondering over the unknown mysteries of this place. The size of a small city in its prime. All the various races sharing knowledge and wisdom, but now lying empty and abandoned. It was tragic to have something as amazing as this, lost and forgotten.

She looked up to the little cottage that Da'ragh must have built for himself at some point in the past. It resembled that of a normal cottage you might find in the middle of a forest village like her own, however this one sat in the middle of an enormous library. She could see light coming from within the small round windows as she made her way to the door, giving it a gentle knock.

She waited a moment. Upon hearing no response, she pushed it open slowly to see that no one was inside. She could see various instruments of unknown purposes. Scrolls and books in haphazard piles. As well as mysterious substances in jars and bottles in a clutter against the one wall. Leianna gave a frown. This looked more like the home of a hoarder.

Leianna closed the door and resumed her wandering deeper into the library. When she first arrived, she was afraid of getting lost, but soon found out that the fairy orbs seemed to know what she was thinking and would lead her to whatever she was looking for. She decided to give it another try. She focused her thoughts on where Peter might be off to. Without delay, the orbs all shifted to her left and lit the path before her.

As she moved in the presented direction, she skipped now and again. Taking her time as she looked about in wonder as she went. This place had kept her in a state of such amazement since their arrival, she had not given her family much thought. She stopped in her tracks and thought of her brother and her father. She hoped they were doing well and not too worried about her. Da'ragh had assured her they were safe so long as she did not attempt to make any contact with them. She could not help but frown when reminded of their minds being erased of anything deemed dangerous by the Magi. One day, she would set things right.

A couple of the smaller fairy orbs floated down and hovered right in front of her chest, where her heart would be. She wondered what it was doing when she realized her thoughts were on her family. She smiled and focused again on Peter and the lights again, all in a uniform pattern, lit the path ahead of her.

She wondered for quite some time before she began thinking to herself if the lights might be lost themselves. She passed by what looked like a large stone dwarven forge and various desk-like stations that looked like they were designed for the writing and copying of books. Most of this burrow remained dark other than the few fairy light orbs that Da'ragh had lit for them. This must have been quite the sight to see when it was all lit up and full of people, but now the darkness and the expansiveness of it made it feel like more of a long-forgotten tomb. It felt lonely.

She shivered when she noticed footprints in the dust. Upon looking where the footprints led, she saw Peter humming to himself in the middle of bolts of cloth and various fabrics. Peter's fairy lights seemed to sway to the tempo of his humming. Leianna let out a giggle. Peter was sewing something.

She walked casually over toward him before loudly getting his attention, "Hey Peter, what are you working on?"

Her yell startled Peter as he jumped and let out an "Ow" followed by him promptly shaking his hand.

Leianna laughed as Peter placed the needle-pricked finger in his mouth.

Peter let out a quick chuckle as he mumbled past the finger in his mouth, "You got me there."

Leianna took a seat on a pile of old dusty cloth that had been stacked in large squares before noticing Peter had hidden something behind his back. "So, what is it you got there?"

Peter sighed and shrugged as he pulled the finger out of his mouth to inspect the damage from the needle before turning his gaze to her. "Well, I was going to give this to you later as a gift, but I suppose now is as good a time as any." Peter pulled a bright yellow length of cloth from behind his back and presented it to her.

Leianna nodded and unfolded it as Peter blurted out, "It's a scarf... for you."

Leianna looked at the cloth fully unfolded; It was more of an oversized handkerchief than a scarf. The cloth had been cut into a distorted rectangle. The front of it was adorned with awkward and misshapen green stitching that read "*Leianna Peter Forever.*"

She smiled as she hugged him. It was the effort he put into it that counted.

Leianna spoke sincerely, "I am lucky to have a friend like you looking out for me."

Peter took a step back after the hug while looking at the ground, "Yup... Friends forever."

Peter picked his head up with a big smile. "You can count on me to have your back, Leianna." He moved up his arm, giving her the Warden salute.

Leianna laughed, appreciating her friend's gift. She attempted to wear it around her neck and found it was too small.

Peter scratched his head. "I'm not the best at sewing. My grandfather tried to teach me, but I never got the hang of it. He always said it was equally important to teach the mental skills as it was to learn how to defend oneself."

Leianna just smiled back at him, "Hey, now I have a handkerchief."

Peter laughed, "That is the best handkerchief I have ever made." Peter stood up and brushed the dust off the back of his pants. She noticed he was still a little stiff in his movement.

Leianna could tell he was still sore from the fight in the clearing. However, she was impressed by how quickly he was recovering from it.

Peter grunted and held his side. "This stuff Da'ragh gave me is really helping with the healing. Where is he, by the way?"

Leianna shrugged. Da'ragh was not the most organized. Some days, he would cram as much knowledge as he could into her head. Other days, he would give her a simple task, then disappear for the rest of the day... or night. She really had a hard time telling in a place like this.

When she had inquired as to why most of the library was dark. Da'ragh had told her it was like a living thing and was sleeping to prevent its discovery. She hoped secretly that one day this place would be full of scholars, historians, and followers of the arcane arts once again.

Leianna's attention was diverted to a light coming from behind a pillar. It was a soft pulse of green. She watched as Peter moved to stand beside her. He had apparently noticed the light as well.

Leianna lifted her eyebrows as she looked to Peter, who met her gaze with a shrug, and the two tip-toed toward the mysterious light. It was silent except for her and Peters breathing in combination with their quiet shuffled footsteps. Leianna peered around the corner to see what looked like a man sitting on the ground with his back to the pillar.

She motioned to Peter to be quiet by placing a finger in front of her lips as she noticed Peter place a hand on the hilt of his sword. She leaned to look around the corner and covered her mouth as she tried to contain her shrill gasp.

Peter had pulled his sword and jumped around in front of Leianna, pushing her behind him. He relaxed as he turned to

Leianna. "He's dead… I think." By the time he stepped aside for her, he already had his sword sheathed.

Leianna shook her head and pushed by Peter. Her reaction embarrassed her at the sight of the body. She inspected the body, which seemed to be an elf. The odd thing was that it appeared like its skin had become petrified wood. She tilted her head as she kneeled to get a closer look. He had long deep slashes in his robes with what appeared to be a severely broken ankle and a deep jagged wound on his face through his jaw. She noticed the green pulsing light was coming from his staff. It looked to be made of a delicately carved Birchwood. It looked very similar to that of Da'ragh's mahogany staff, although sizably smaller.

Leianna let out a scream and scrambled backwards when she noticed that the body's eyes had opened and had started watching her.

The mouth of the petrified body opened. A voice echoed as if straight from a forgotten distant past. "*I am not long for this world, but I am not afraid. My wounds are too severe to go on, and my soul will soon join that of my brothers and sisters. If you are hearing this, then you must be Do'earee. I have hidden this burrow from the Magi Reaper Lorcan. My heart is elated for we are not lost. Pass my staff on to an eager apprentice and may our story never be forgotten.*"

Leianna watched as the body became dark and fell to dust. She slowly reached out and picked up the staff, which felt warm in her hands. Her mind raced with memories that were not her own before quickly flickering away. She knew that the knowledge was there somehow, but for the life of her, she could not recall them again. An ocean of lost memory and secrets danced barely outside of her reach. The more she tried to recall what she had seen, the more it evaded her.

Peter watched her in awe. "Do you think he was from the time of the Cataclysm?"

Leianna looked back down to the dust. "He had to be." His question brought her back to the present, and she decided to let it be for now.

She turned to look at Peter. "We have to set things right and let the people know the truth."

Peter nodded in agreement; his eyes still transfixed on where the body was just moments ago.

She kneeled again to say a quick prayer over the fallen Do'earee in hopes that he found peace.

Peter turned away from the dust to look at Leianna. "We should go let Dugan and Da'ragh know what we found."

Leianna smiled as she started walking back to where she had left Dugan. "That's if we can pry Dugan away from those books."

Peter followed closely behind her as she found her thoughts back to that of the fallen elf. What was a Magi Reaper? She had never heard of a Reaper before. This Lorcan seemed to be one of them during the time of the Cataclysm. She let out a soft sigh as she walked. It seemed that the more she learned of the war and the Cataclysm the more she was made aware of how little she knew. Peter was fiddling with something behind her as they walked, but she was too lost in her own thoughts to notice what it was.

Before she had even realized they had arrived at Dugan's pile of books to find him snoring loudly while lying on a book in front of him. Leianna glanced back at Peter to see he had a puzzled look on his face and was scratching his head again.

He had a slight twinge of jealousy as he spoke softly so as not to wake Dugan. "Is he just good at everything? He is even fast at reading."

Leianna thought of the way he was during their childhood together. She recalled his bullying, intimidation, and arrogance. "I wouldn't say he is good at everything, Peter; he doesn't have half the heart that you do."

Leianna turned and started to walk in the direction of Da'ragh's little hut and had been completely oblivious to the bright red Peter had turned as a result of her compliment.

She looked to find her bearings as to which direction Da'ragh's hut stood when the fairy lights shifted and lit the path forward for her.

It was not long before she was stopped in her tracks upon hearing Peter's stomach grumble, "Did you not eat breakfast?"

Peter nodded his head. "I ate breakfast twice while I waited for you to wake up and I brought extra snacks with me when I explored. Can you believe the size of this place?" She could tell he was just as amazed as she was at the sight of it. His excitement to explore it had not dwindled since their arrival.

Leianna raised her eyebrows, "Two breakfasts? Are you still hungry?"

Peter just nodded as he averted his gaze. "Yes."

Leianna shook her head, "Well, you better go get some more to eat then. You are no good at protecting me if you're hungry."

Peter gave some mumbled response that she took as agreement, and then he was off toward the table with all the food.

Leianna lifted the handkerchief that he had made for her and found herself blushing. She shook her head and convinced herself that there were things that demanded her attention right now. Her thoughts focused on her training, and she then took off toward Da'ragh's hut with new found determination in her step. She had questions for Da'ragh, as well as wanting to show him the staff. The thoughts from earlier still tickling the back of her mind.

CHAPTER EIGHT

S o'baka leaned back as he held tightly to Grymsnar's harness. Using his bare feet against the scales for balance. Grymsnar accelerated as he flew with determination back toward their stronghold. He thought of how the other dragon riders used saddles on their mounts and how he would never insult Grymsnar with such a degradation. They were equals as well as brothers.

The sky was a dull dark gray, and the wind was cold. The frigid currents of air biting into the skin on his face. By this time next year, the west lands would be under the control of the Tal'Kor, and nothing would stand in his way. He made a promise to himself that he would bring death to the kingdom of Auldryche, sparing no one on his rampage.

He smiled, thinking of the resentment this would bring to the slave traders. That was House Sha'Asson. After Auldryche lay in ruins, he would turn his Shard toward the lesser houses. He would bring back war to the lands of the Tal'Kor. Not this time of treaty and cooperation. Words were for weak men and cowards. He would prove his worth by the number of the slain in his wake. Exactly how things were meant to be. So'baka had been so lost in thought for hours that he had not noticed they were closing in on his stronghold.

The Halls of the Mourning Dead were barely more than ruins. This had once been the seat of a former Great House of the Tal'Kor, but the name of the house had been lost to history. It had been too weak to maintain its control and so it fell like many before it. He thought it amusing he had chosen such a place to call his own.

Grymsnar let out a low roar, signaling their approach. The bellowing of the stronghold's horns heralded their arrival. The horns sounded deep, like the moaning of a great and dying beast. Echoes of the sorrowful wail reverberated through the surrounding peaks.

So'baka felt the momentum as Grymsnar dove downwards towards the main keep, which had been rebuilt, in the middle of the stronghold's ruins. The tower-like keep jutted up towards the sky like the head of a spear. Drakes with their goblin riders flew around the spires, like that of vultures circling a corpse. The drakes made wide arcs and moved away to avoid getting in the path of Grymsnar's landing. The dragon settled with ease on a part of the spire that had a large stone landing easily three times the size of the dragon.

So'baka slapped Grymsnar's neck before jumping down to the landing. So'baka strode forward with confidence as Grymsnar took back to the air. Most likely, he was off to devour some unsuspecting beast. He knew his mount would return the moment he was called upon. They were bound and linked through the Oath.

So'baka entered the archway, which led directly into his sanctum. The wide pillar supporting the room was just how he had left it. Desiccated bodies of the defeated dead hung from rusted cages and chains from the ceiling. Long tables covered with rotten meat and scattered rubbish of past meals lay unoccupied.

He walked to the back of the room, past the staircases leading below, and moved toward the throne of his own creation. The throne to an outsider would resemble little more than a pile of bones and an ensemble of mismatched and damaged armor pieces, but to So'baka, each piece of the throne came from a foe he had defeated in battle. To the right of the throne sat the goblin known as Snixx. Her gaze fixed upon So'baka as he approached. She glared at him from behind her messy, tangled black hair, coated in oil so much so that it looked damp with swamp water.

Snixx poured poison into hollow-tipped arrows. He frowned as he watched her fill arrow after arrow with the deadly mixture. He had always thought of poison as a coward's weapon. A tool to be used by the weak, but he understood its uses when necessary. So'baka sat on his haunches upon the top of his bone throne and turned to Snixx with a dark joy in his heart. His mouth formed a wide-fanged smile.

"We go to war."

He spoke the words nonchalantly, as if he was teasing a friend.

Snixx froze in place, then turned slowly to So'baka. Her voice was barely more than a whisper and grated like that of someone who had just inhaled smoke.

"We go to war?"

So'baka nodded in feverish enthusiasm. He had planned on tormenting the goblin but found it impossible to hide his own excitement.

Snixx jumped up in the air screeching akin to that of a dying bird, her pointed teeth filled mouth twisted into a terrifyingly broad grin.

"We feast on the flesh of the west men!?"

So'baka hopped forward to the edge of the bone throne, his laughter that of a madman.

"We feast, and we take, and we kill!"

Snixx made a noise that sounded like giggling. To anyone else outside of Tal'Kor, the sound would have been frightening as well as disturbing.

"We leave now?"

She tilted her head and was looking at So'baka with her one good eye, the other eye cloudy and dead within. A deep scar ran down the length of her face.

So'baka remembered giving her that scar as a message when she tried to poison him. It was at that time all the goblin clans swore an oath to serve him and she had taken offense to being usurped. She wore the dull brown chitin of the giant centipedes from her home in the eastern swamps of Tal'Kor. All the goblins wore the chitin armor and harvested their poison to use as they saw fit.

Her pale teal-green skin looked damp like that of a frog. So'baka admired the cunning of the goblins, but to the great houses, they were little more than unwanted pests at worst and poison peddlers at best. So'baka met the gaze of Snixx.

"I want all the goblins ready in six moons' time. I want all the tribes ready. The Muck Crawlers, the Oil Drinkers, the Drake Flyers, the Shadow Hiders... all of them."

Snixx nodded excitedly.

"We will get them all ready. We serve the master."

Snixx hurriedly gathered up her poisons and swamp wood short bow before disappearing into the shadows behind a pillar. So'baka clapped his hands in delight. The goblins were so funny when they were sneaky. It was one of the few things he found pleasing outside of combat.

He stopped and keened his ears in on the stairwell. He heard the slither like that of a giant snake as he watched the Naga Drakamin appear at the top of the steps. Drakamin's approach was almost hypnotic in his movements. His large snake-like tail trailing behind him in curls.

Drakamin was wearing a beast's skull as a helm. Various beads and feathers dangled from its protrusions. His tattered, deep red and black robe covered the top half of his body. So'baka watched his approach. If not for the tail behind him, he would look like a man gracefully walking toward him.

So'baka leaned forward.

"We are going to war."

Drakamin bowed his head.

"As I have foreseen."

So'baka sighed irritably. He wanted nothing to do with magic, but Drakamin had an unnatural gift for seeing the future and had always served him well. The thought of using magic in his planned assault had soured So'baka's mood, but his curiosity got the better of him.

"What do you see now, Drakamin?"

Drakamin did another bow, his voice calm and enticing.

"I see blood spilled, I see war, I see glory."

So'baka felt his excitement rise again.

"Call the tribes together. I will tell them of this war to come myself."

Drakamin nodded before slithering off on his way to the large platform below the spire.

So'baka waited for what seemed like hours before he heard the horns and drums outside. They signaled the gathering and the speaking of their master, and all were to listen. He stood and walked slowly out to the large landing where Grymsnar was waiting.

"We proclaim war today, Grymsnar."

Grymsnar huffed out a plum of black smoke and, with a low growling voice, "I have waited for ages to bring fire to the west lands."

So'baka hoisted himself onto the back of Grymsnar and leaned forward to slap his neck. Grymsnar grinned with teeth like daggers before launching from the perch and landing on the platform far below. So'baka leaped from the back of his mount and took large strides with his arms open wide as a greeting to the yelling and roaring in the crowd assembled before him throughout the ruins. Thousands of Goblins, Naga's, Sher'Atul outcasts, and Amoraug howled, growled, and screeched in praise of their master.

To his right stood his fellow Sher'Atul outcasts and the Chiefs of the Amoraug tribes. To him, the Amoraug looked like a bastardized union between wolves and trolls. They stood two heads taller than the average Olaumen and had their fur painted with various sigils So'baka did not understand. To his left stood Snixx with a murderous sneer on her face in front of the various leaders of the Goblin clans. Beside them was Drakamin, among other Naga seers.

Silence fell as he stepped to the edge of the massive stone platform and shot a glance to Drakamin, who nodded and weaved circles in the air with his hands. So'baka looked to his discarded beast men and outcasts as he screamed, his voice carried throughout the ruins by Drakamin's magic.

"WE GO TO WAR!"

The crowd became a frenzy of howls and screams of bloodlust. The very air and ground under So'baka's feet shook and rumbled from the cacophony below. War drums began beating, and the horns blew loudly at his proclamation. His fanged smile grew and his eyes flashed gold and just as bright as the eyes of Grymsnar. Adrenaline and the dragon oath surged through his body as he looked at his army below. They would have blood; they would take, and they would feast.

CHAPTER NINE

Leianna sat in Da'ragh's hut for what seemed like hours. She had practiced a few of the magics she had learned the day before. She casually thumbed through the book Da'ragh had been reading yesterday, but she had quickly lost interest. It was mostly about navigation, maps, and pathway magics.

She sighed as she looked back at the staff she had found earlier. It had carvings like that of ivy curling around branches of a tree. She reached out and picked up the birch staff, its blonde hue in contrast to her own ebony skin.

Leianna sat up straight and held the staff in front of her. She wondered why Da'ragh had always carried his staff and pondered if all Do'earee had carried similar intricately carved staffs. She stood up and stretched as she wandered outside the hut.

Leianna thought of an idea and pointed the staff toward one of the fairy lights. She focused on the fairy light and thought of illumination, focusing on the warmth that the sun brought to her skin. The staff felt warm in her hand as she looked up in shock at the fairy light. The orb expanded as it floated upwards and the light it gave off grew in its intensity and brightness. It was easily larger than Da'ragh's hut, and she thought she could almost make out a mosaic decoration on the ceiling of the burrow, but the roof was just barely out of sight.

She wanted to see more, but the orb would rise no higher. Her interest piqued as she desired to know more about what was on the roof. She squinted to see if she could get a better look when she heard a noise behind her.

She turned, expecting to see Da'ragh, but what she saw was not a being of this realm. The apparition floated a few feet above the ground and was mostly transparent with a soft green and blue shimmer. It had the appearance of a vaguely womanly shape in a robe, but its face was featureless. Leianna found her mouth was suddenly dry, and she choked down an audibly loud gulp.

She shifted her weight to her other foot in preparation to run, but the specter made no move toward her. Leianna paused as she looked at the glowing being just floating before her. She found herself more confused than afraid. Why was it just floating there? It wasn't really doing anything.

She stared for a moment before she built up the courage to speak to it. "What are you?" her voice was barely a whisper as she forced the words out.

The specter responded with a melodic tone that seemed to resonate from the massive wooden pillars rather from the being itself. *"We are Soga, the assistants to the Do'earee. You summoned us through inquiry."*

Leianna could feel herself crinkle in confusion. "Inquiry?"

The Specter remained silently in place as it pointed upwards with a shimmery blue hand from under the robes.

The melodic sound of the pillars sounded as if speaking again, *"The art piece covering the entirety of the ceiling was created at the beginning of the second age of the Do'earee calendar of learning. They created it as a symbol of harmony within the races. To signify the golden age of peace and sharing of knowledge. They designed this barrow with that aspect of contribution and open knowledge in mind."*

It fascinated Leianna. This being had to be the personification of the library itself. Da'ragh had stated the library was alive, but she did not expect this.

Leianna had so many questions going through her mind, "Where are all the other Do'earee?"

Leianna waited for the specter's response. Surely Da'ragh was not the only one left.

The specter raised its hand and pointed toward her. *"The only known Do'earee at this time is Leianna Braun. No other Do'earee have accessed this library in... quite some time."*

The specter at the end had almost sounded sad, but that was beside the point. She wasn't a Do'earee yet, and what of Da'ragh? Had the library not spoken with him?

Leianna rubbed her chin before turning to the specter. "What about Da'ragh? Have you not seen him? He lives right here."

The specter blinked out of existence before reappearing next to her. *"This is not the home of Do'earee. This is vandalism in the library."*

Leianna jumped and let out a squeal as it appeared by her side. She took a deep breath, "Well you are not wrong Soga, that mess inside is definitely vandalism."

Soga seemed to ignore her comment as it turned toward her. *"Da'ragh is deceased."*

Leianna stared at Soga in disbelief. "But I just saw him yesterday. He was fine. How did he die?" Leianna's voice was shaky as she spoke. How could he be dead? What would they do now without his help?

Soga made no movement of comfort or concern. *"This statement is incorrect. Da'ragh died at the hands of Lorcan, a Magi Reaper."*

Leianna was beginning to wonder if this so-called Soga was messing with her. "What are you talking about?"

The specter Soga floated backwards a few steps.

Leianna stared at it. It did not try to respond. "How do you know Da'ragh is dead?"

Soga responding quickly, *"Da'ragh sealed Soga burrow at the time of his death."*

Leianna felt her face flush red in frustration. "How could you possibly know that?"

The specter seemed to double in size almost instantly as the surrounding pillars boomed, *"Da'ragh was the founding father of the Soga burrow. Da'ragh was a friend of Soga. Da'ragh protected*

Soga from the Magi." The specter shank down to its former size as Leianna stared at the thing in shock.

The specter had resumed its melodic tone through the pillars, *"You now hold Da'ragh's staff, you must be Da'ragh's apprentice."*

Leianna was completely overwhelmed and did not understand any of this specter's statements. She felt her shoulders slump as she tried to work through Soga's explanations. She stared at her newly acquired staff in puzzled reflection.

She lifted her head as she went to ask another question about Da'ragh, when Soga turned from soft blues and greens to bright red.

The tone coming from the pillars sounded like the high-pitched shriek of a frightened child, *"Run and Hide!"*

Leianna barely had time to think before the specter faded. The fairy light that had been so large above her faded out into the darkness above. She stood in confusion as the surrounding area grew silent. The remaining fairy lights hovered about her, just as they always had.

Leianna found herself on the defensive as she listened for any sound that would be out of place or any movement at the edge of her fairy lights. She surveyed her surroundings with absolute focus, but nothing came out of the darkness covering the library.

Leianna found her muscles tense up when a bright green light lit up in front of her. An archway of vines formed by the skein pathway of magic formed out of the ground and filled with the green glow, just like the one they used to arrive here. Da'ragh stepped out of the archway, and it promptly closed behind him as the vines forming the archway withered and faded to a fine dust dispersing in the air. Da'ragh tapped his staff on the ground and around a half a dozen orbs of fairy lights lit up around him.

Leianna looked at him nervously. "Soga said you were dead."

Da'ragh curved his mouth into a frown and raised his eyebrows as he reached up to stroke his beard, "I don't know who this Soga is, but I certainly don't feel very... dead."

Leianna was still confused by all the information the specter had given her. She looked to Da'ragh for answers, "Soga is the burrow... or maybe the library here in the burrow... I'm not sure."

Da'ragh just gave her a chuckle, "I didn't realize the burrows gave themselves names, how did you..." Da'ragh's voice trailed off as his gaze found its way to her birch staff, his voice turned cold and distant, "Where did you get that?"

Leianna looked down to her staff, then back to Da'ragh. "I found it deep in the burrow. Peter was with me."

Leianna felt nervous under Da'ragh's stare. His eyes seemed to pierce right through her. She felt like this had somehow turned into an interrogation. Leianna took a deep breath to calm herself.

"Peter and I found a body sitting against a pillar. It was over near a forge. I think... over that way."

Leianna pointed in the direction where Peter and she had found the body, at least to the best of her recollection.

Da'ragh did not move his cold eyes from her, and she was unsure what to think when his features softened and the mood in his voice gentled, "Forgive me, it has just been a long time since I have seen that staff."

Leianna felt her tenseness relax; she had not realized Da'ragh could be so daunting with so little effort.

Da'ragh shifted his weight onto his staff as he began speaking to her again. "That staff belonged to... well, I guess you could say an old friend."

Leianna found herself looking at the staff held in her hands as Da'ragh continued, "The staff of a Do'earee is a symbol as much as a tool. Use of the staff passes the memories and experiences on from one Do'earee to the next."

Leianna turned and gave him a puzzled look. She wondered if she could access these memories somehow.

Da'ragh cleared his throat. "Think of the staff as a sort of living book that cannot be read until the wielder is ready and willing to understand."

Leianna felt herself frowning and forced the disappointment from her face, "I am ready to learn whatever this staff holds. How do I access the memories?"

Da'ragh smiled. "I do not know. Each staff is as unique as the one who carries it. Normally, the Do'earee spend seasons preparing their apprentice to either carve their own, or they are passed down an existing one."

Da'ragh shrugged. "Think of the staff like a living extension of the Do'earee. Some need the assistance of their teacher more than others and are given a staff, while others forge their own unique paths and carve their own. It is odd that the staff attuned to you like it did. Nonetheless, this is a boon in our favor, as this will help you to focus on your magics and enhance your learning."

Leianna nodded. She was excited to have one of her own if she was going to follow the path of magic that she had always dreamed of. She had always thought she would be a Magi, but the more she learned, the more she started seeing herself as a Do'carce, which in itself was very overwhelming.

Leianna thought of the specter from earlier, "Do you really not know of Soga?"

Da'ragh shook his head. "I am sorry child, but I do not. I try not to spend much time here as it brings back too many terrible memories... and I am sure many spirits of fallen Do'earee haunt this place."

Leianna watched Da'ragh look to the ground. His face had the look of remorse more than that of someone who was mourning.

Leianna's mind wandered. "Did my mother have a staff?"

Da'ragh seemed taken aback by her question. "Your mother? Oh no, she learned very little from me before she fell in love and walked away from the path of the Do'earee."

Da'ragh sat on a stone bench near his hut and motioned for Leianna to take a seat as well. "Your mother showed amazing promise and talent. She was fascinated with magic and sought out knowledge everywhere. However, she found that the life was too dangerous to pursue. Especially when she found out she was pregnant with your brother."

Leianna listened intently to Da'ragh, eager to hear anything about her mother. "Your mother changed the day she met your father. We had traveled to that little village of yours to find an artifact of the Do'earee that would help in our journey. I knew she was lost the moment she beheld your father. She made her home there and put a distance between us and her teachings. I would check on her from time to time, but she didn't want me around and after her passing... I just wandered."

Leianna seemed confused. "Why would she want to stop learning even if she met my father? Why would she not want you around?"

Da'ragh sat silent for a moment before he responded, "I suppose she just wasn't ready to start the path that was before us. The journey that stands before us now."

Da'ragh turned to face Leianna directly. "We must travel to the broken lands to recover a relic that will help us expose the Magi for what they are."

Leianna felt her face turn pale. "The broken lands are ravaged by magical storms, terrifying creatures, and things from nightmares. That place was told to me by traders in my village as scary campfire stories." Her voice was trembling.

Da'ragh nodded. "I will not lie to you. The aftermath of the cataclysm still ravages the place. It is indeed a very dangerous area, but not unscalable."

Leianna looked at him in amazement. "You are serious. We are traveling to the broken lands? I don't think even the Tal'Kor would travel there if they had to."

Da'ragh laughed, "I don't think the Tal'Kor would have any reason to go there... no one to eat or enslave."

Leianna was shocked, "No one to eat?!"

Da'ragh nodded, "They say some Tal'Kor are cannibals and the beast men favor the meat of other races. At the very least, we make a meal for the dragons."

Leianna was wide eyed as she shook her head, "Is this supposed to make me feel better?"

Da'ragh was amused as he chuckled, "At least there are no Tal'Kor in the Broken Lands."

Leianna found she had stood up at some point and sat back down. "I guess there is that."

She didn't feel any better about going there, but she felt very strongly about undoing the deception of the Magi over the people. She wanted to know more about the path her mother had started, but ultimately walked away from. Leianna felt she had to continue where her mother had stopped. She didn't blame her mother, as she had children to worry about.

Leianna couldn't even imagine having kids yet. She didn't even like anybody. Peter came to mind, and she found herself blushing again. She immediately dismissed the thoughts. Peter had always liked her. She was not oblivious to this. He was her friend and she couldn't see it any other way.

Da'ragh spoke up. "We should tell the others and start to prepare for departure. We will go to the city of Kronus and I will hire some Green Cloaks to aid us in crossing the Broken lands."

Leianna couldn't believe what she had just heard. "Kronus is the capital and the seat of the Magi."

Da'ragh nodded. "It is also the one place they will not be looking for you and the others. Along with it also being the location of the Green Cloak center of operations."

Da'ragh stood and stretched his back. "There is an old friend of mine that works there that could aid us in our search."

Leianna did not like the idea of going to Kronus, nor did she like the idea of traveling across the broken lands. It seemed things were going from bad to worse. Not that long ago, she would have been overjoyed at the thought of a trip to the new capital of Kronus. Now she just felt that she was risking her life in just traveling there.

Leianna raised her eyebrows, "What is it that we are looking for in the broken lands?"

Da'ragh started to walk in the direction of the others as he spoke and motioned for her to follow, "There are a couple of things we are looking for and I have found the means to find them. There is a weapon used by the Magi Reapers during the war, as well as the crown of the old king. I was able to travel to a separate burrow and retrieve this."

Da'ragh reached into his pocket and held up a small bronze arrow. "It is a tool of the Do'earee that helps one locate objects. Think of it like a compass." He balanced the small bronze arrow on his palm. It was barely longer than the length of his hand and far too thick to be an actual arrow.

Da'ragh murmured something, and it began to float for a moment before it settled back down on his palm. Da'ragh smiled and handed the bronze arrow to Leianna. She looked at it closely and could see it looked rather plain and heavily worn. She found herself biting her lips as she began to wonder how the device even worked.

She looked back to Da'ragh. "So we need the one thing that can unite the noble houses as well as an evil weapon used to exterminate the Do'earee?"

Da'ragh didn't change his pace and answered with a very simple and straightforward response. "Yes, that is about it."

As they approached the table where Peter and Dugan were sitting, she could overhear what sounded like an argument.

Peter was speaking very passionately. "That's not it at all. The Wardens protect the PEOPLE, not the nobles or the land!"

Dugan had just as much vigor in his speech, "I don't see the difference between them and, say, the Knights of Calembrech. They are just people taking up arms for gold, glory, or honor. A warrior is a warrior, plain and simple."

Leianna could see Peter shaking his head, "The difference is that Wardens are protectors of the people. Not some shiny knight you see in a parade. The Wardens consist of volunteers within the community. Not paid mercenaries holding allegiance to a noble house!"

Leianna coughed to get their attention.

Both Peter and Dugan looked at each other in a silent truce before greeting her and Da'ragh.

Da'ragh turned to her. "Would you want to share the plan with them, or should I?"

Leianna looked toward Peter and Dugan as she took a deep breath. "We are going to the broken lands to find a weapon used by the Reapers, as well as the lost crown."

Simultaneously, the two boys stood up with startling speed.

Peter let out a yell of excitement, "Yes, a real adventure!"

Dugan, however, had a completely different response. "That's signing our own death warrants!"

Dugan shook his head.

His voice was higher pitched than normal. "Do you know the kinds of atrocities and horrors that lurk in the broken lands? I do, because I just read about some particularly nasty ones!"

Leianna was in no argument with his statements and looked again at Da'ragh for support.

Da'ragh was smiling, "Oh, I assure you, boy, that everything you said is quite true and worse. However, no one said you had to go. This journey will test all of your abilities and your resolve. Leianna here needs those willing to brave these obstacles with her. Not those that would try to dissuade her from her path and fill her with doubt."

It did not surprise Leianna to see Peter raise his hand and speak with a giant smile on his face, "Leianna can count me to have her back... always."

Leianna mouthed the words thank you to Peter, to which he turned a bright shade of red and nodded.

Dugan's posture slumped as he leaned forward with both hands on the table. He glanced at Peter, then at her with a defeated look.

Dugan's voice sounded somber, "Well, if you two are set on going, then count me in. Someone has to keep you two idiots alive. Plus, it's not like I can go back home, anyway."

Leianna gave Dugan a soft smile, "Thank You Dugan."

Peter chimed up, "This is going to be amazing, Dugan, you'll see."

Dugan shook his head as he let out a heavy sigh. "Sure, if we survive, I am sure it will be great. Nothing quite like trudging through dangerous territory while we try to hide from magical horrors."

Peter just nodded his head in excitement.

Leianna speculated if he understood the gravity of the situation.

Da'ragh spoke up. "We will leave in the morning, so make sure you have everything you need. I have gathered some various supplies and placed them in packs by my hut for each of you."

Leianna felt nervous, but at the same time, she also felt excitement. She couldn't help but think she was starting down the same path her mother had started, but she planned on finishing the journey.

Leianna woke to Peter talking loudly with Dugan, "I always wondered what the Green Cloaks did."

She could hear Dugan setting down a heavy pack, "Well, they are also a kind of, an exploration and retrieval company. They usually get hired by Magi or wealthy nobles to retrieve items from the broken lands, but also offer their services as scouts and guides for those brave and or stupid enough to explore the broken lands themselves."

Peter sounded a little confused. "So they are paid to go on adventures?"

Dugan huffed, "I guess you could say that."

Peter sounded like he was talking more to himself as Leianna shifted on her cot as she sat up. "I wonder if I could be a Warden and a Green Cloak?"

Dugan laughed mockingly, "Sure, twice the chances of getting yourself killed."

Peter laughed it off. "Hey it sounds like I might have another career path to think about after I become a Warden of Legend."

Dugan shook his head in disbelief, "If you become a legendary Warden, then I will have to reevaluate my entire life and become a warden myself."

Leianna chuckled as she rubbed her eyes.

Peter had just now noticed she was awake and promptly wished her a good morning.

As she was getting up, she stretched and turned to Peter, "Where is Da'ragh?"

Peter shrugged as Dugan responded, "Da'ragh said he needed to get something done before we left and used a pathway out of here. I am sure he will be back soon to lead us to our deaths."

Peter chuckled, "He said we would need some coin to pay for our Green Cloak guides and said he had some put aside."

Leianna washed her face in a small water fountain surrounded by some plants. It still amazed her they grew down here and in the dark, no less.

Dugan called out to her, "I brought your pack over with ours. It's by the table."

Leianna waved her hand to show that she had heard him as she dried her face. She would make sure the pack was in order after she had eaten breakfast.

She looked toward the pitch-black ceiling. If it was even morning, that is. She looked forward to feeling the warmth of the sun on her skin as well as getting some fresh air. As amazing as this place was, she looked forward to being outside again.

She wandered over to the table and joined the other two in, eating breakfast. They mostly talked about the journey ahead. Peter with his enthusiasm and Dugan with his despondency regarding the excursion into the broken lands. Before long, they had finished their meals and began getting their packs together as they awaited Da'ragh's return.

Leianna found herself speaking out loud as she tightened the straps on her pack. "Do you think Da'ragh is lying to us?"

Peter looked puzzled for just a moment before shaking his head, "I don't think so."

Dugan was fiddling with the claymore he had taken from the skeleton. He appeared to be wrapping the blade in what looked like a makeshift scabbard of his creation, "I suppose he could be lying to us, but I don't understand why he would take the time to teach you magic and let me have my way with reading whatever I wanted in a library if his intent was to deceive us. From what I can tell by these books, the Do'earee are nothing like the Magi are telling us."

Leianna nodded in agreement, "I just can't shake this feeling that I am missing something."

She found herself thinking of Soga and what it had said about Da'ragh being dead. She wondered if he was hiding something. Leianna sighed. She believed that he was indeed helping them, but wondered if he was just using them as a means to an end.

A skein archway grew and opened before them. Da'ragh's figure could be seen stepping out of the green light. He was holding what looked like a small wooden barrel coated in dry mud. Da'ragh set it on the table with a large thud. Da'ragh took the tip of his staff and waved it over the top of the small container before the lid shot up in the air like a cork from a bottle.

She felt herself gasp when it popped. The lid clattered on the ground as she leaned forward to look inside. Leianna felt her eyes widen. She had never seen so much gold before. The entire barrel was chock-full of gold coins.

She heard Peter behind her whistle in amazement.

Da'ragh reached in and started placing handfuls in leather pouches for each of them. "This gold is to aid us in our journey. It is not to be spent frivolously."

Dugan accepted his leather pouch and looked closely at one of the coins, "Wait, this is old coin... this is the mark of the old king... this is pre-cataclysm gold..."

Dugan looked shocked as he turned to Da'ragh. "This is worth a fortune. How did you get this?"

Da'ragh smiled. "I used to care about wealth a long time ago. I follow a different path now."

Dugan frowned, "That doesn't answer the question, where-"

Da'ragh interrupted him. "I gathered it up from another burrow. We can use it now to aid us in our journey."

Peter was talking to himself as he looked at the gold filled pouch handed to him. "It's all gold; there are no silver or copper bits..."

Leianna nodded her head. "This is going to seem incredibly suspicious if we start paying for everything in gold. Most people barely see a gold coin in their lifetime. Let alone one of these big gold coins from the old king. They usually use silver and copper to pay for goods." Leianna eyed the gold coins with concern.

Da'ragh looked agitated as he let out a sigh. "I don't keep up with these kinds of things. You two make a good point. We don't want to attract attention."

Dugan spoke up abruptly. "I have an idea! There is a coin exchanger in the trade city of Markagra. They are constantly dealing with high end merchants and traders. Even seafaring ships use the giant rivers as a way to bring goods inland."

Dugan took a breath. "My point is that they see a lot of money and goods being exchanged. If we went there, we could easily exchange our gold for more recognized forms of currency without standing out too much."

Leianna looked to Da'ragh, "It is worth a shot and we could use the pathway skeins without losing time."

Da'ragh nodded. "So it seems we have a detour to take. We take a risk going to a town just south of your village."

Peter exclaimed, "Why do we need gold, anyway? Couldn't we just use a pathway into the broken lands and out again?"

Da'ragh shook his head, "Unfortunately we cannot pathway into the broken lands. The chaos of the residual magic there could send us somewhere else entirely or trap us in the pathways themselves."

Peter looked discouraged, "Well, I would rather not get trapped."

Peter immediately shifted his frown into a smile, "Looks like we are going to have to take the long way."

Leianna couldn't help but smile. It seemed that nothing could keep Peter down.

Dugan began explaining how he had traveled with his father to the town many times and how it was always so busy they would most likely go unnoticed, "That town is always bustling with fresh faces. Even if the Magi are looking for us in Markagra, it would be difficult to find us. The place is a hub for trade in the area. Even dwarves from the north mountains come there for trade." Peter nodded in agreement, "That's saying something. The dwarves from the northern stone halls are not as friendly as their seafaring cousins."

Dugan shot Peter an irritated glare, "That is besides the point."

Dugan took a deep breath before he continued, "If we are going to the broken lands and we can't pathway there, then the choice is obvious. We will need coin for food, supplies, guides... whatever, we will need a lot of coin to grease palms along the way. Especially if the Magi decide to put out a warrant for our arrest... then we will have to worry about bounty hunters and-"

Peter interrupted with a look of disgust, "I am not greasing anyone's hands."

Leianna laughed at Peter's comment.

Da'ragh joined in on the laughter.

Peter and Dugan both looked completely confused.

Dugan soon caught on, "You don't actually grease their hands, twerp. It's a phrase people use when they mean to bribe officials."

Peter looked shocked. "That sounds like what a criminal would do. We are not criminals!"

Dugan looked frustrated and rubbed his hands on his face.

Leianna could barely stop laughing as she tried to explain the situation to Peter, "Peter, we are not on the good side of the Magi. They are the ones looking for us and they are the ones that dictate the laws. So, it may be necessary to bribe people in order for us to go unnoticed."

Peter had a look of horror cross his face, "We need to get this Magi business resolved and fast... How am I supposed to be a Warden if I am a wanted outlaw?"

Leianna watched as his head fell to the table with a loud thunk, "That's why this is important Peter, the Magi determine who is a criminal and who is not. With us returning the old king's crown, they can proclaim a new king for the people. That will strip the Magi of their authority."

Peter's head shot up from the table. He had a red spot on his forehead from hitting the table so hard, "Wait, we would be heroes for helping the new king... from outlaw to hero... to legendary Warden..."

Leianna laughed as she watched Peter drift off into his own imaginary world, where his legend was already being written.

Da'ragh chuckled, "This has been amusing, but I think it's time we travel to Markagra."

Leianna looked to her friends, "I hope you guys are ready."

Peter snapped back to reality and out of his imagination as Leianna spoke to him, "I am so ready for this."

Leianna looked to Dugan, who seemed completely annoyed by the situation.

Dugan picked up his claymore as he stood up from the table, "This is going to be a disaster, I can feel it in my bones."

Da'ragh placed a hand on Dugan's shoulder. "That is one of the key principles taught by the Do'earee. Always trust your instincts."

Dugan looked at Da'ragh skeptically, "My instincts are telling me to run the other way."

Da'ragh went to speak but was interrupted by Peter, "Maybe your instincts are broken, Dugan?"

Peter laughed and barely got out of the way as Dugan went to give him a back-handed slap.

Leianna laughed at the two as Da'ragh turned to her and handed her a tan leather satchel. Leianna stopped and looked to Da'ragh for an explanation.

Da'ragh pointed to the bag. "That is a pathway bag. It slowly grows the seeds needed for the pathways."

Leianna looked inside to see a few of the carved acorns like before, "They looked like they have been carved from wood, not grown like a normal seed."

Leianna looked to Da'ragh as he shrugged, "I suppose it's a little bit of both."

Leianna shook her head. This magic of the Do'earee made no sense to her. The library burrow was alive and spoke. The staff was somehow living memories of its former wielder and seeds, if you could call them that, that grew and carved themselves inside a bag. Leianna let out a deep sigh. She had a lot to learn.

Da'ragh reached into a pouch of his own and threw down a carved acorn. The vines grew instantly from the ground and formed a green, glowing archway. She watched as Da'ragh went through the arch first, followed by Dugan. She went to walk forward as she felt Peter's hand on her shoulder. Looking back, Peter was smiling.

Peter sounded sincere, "I got your back Leianna, you can count on me!"

Leianna nodded and smiled back as she stepped into the archway and into the skein pathways.

Chapter Ten

HYLON COULD BARELY KEEP up with Torin as they ran down one of the back alleys here in Markagra. He had no intention of slowing down, though. He was in no hurry to receive a beating today. The merchant enforcers could be heard behind them, close on their heels. They were screaming threats as they chased after them.

Hylon looked ahead to Torin, who was so much faster than himself. He could never hope to be as fast as his lifelong friend. Torin easily jumped up to grab the top of a low hanging roof and lifted himself up with effortless speed and agility.

He picked up speed and leapt for the edge of the roof and came short a good foot and a half. Just as Hylon felt himself falling towards the ground, he watched as Torin dove and grabbed on to his forearm and hoisted him up. So that they could resume their run from the local authorities.

He could hear the curses of the enforcers behind him. If he were not so out of breath, he would have yelled obscenities back at them. He watched as Torin, in full sprint, jumped from one roof to the next without missing a step. He couldn't help but feel envious of his friend's ability.

Hylon again attempted to make the jump between an enormous gap between roofs and hit the edge of the overhang dead center into his stomach. He felt the impact knock all the air out of him as he tried to scramble and grab at the edges, but he couldn't find a handhold and started to slip backwards. Hylon panicked as he began to fall, and again without fail, Torin dove and yet again saved him.

He could hear Torin laughing under his mask, "Don't worry Hylon, I hear there are birds that can't fly either."

Hylon let out a nervous chuckle as he tried to catch his breath. Torin was always so kind to him, and Hylon was not entirely sure anything could shake him.

They continued their run, going down random alleys and through various corridors until they made their way back to the old docks. The massive stone pillars and long white stone docks were created at the time of the old king during the second age. Nowadays, they were worn from countless seasons of use and trade, but had long been abandoned and remained unused.

Giant stone warehouses and buildings lined this side of the rivers on the north end of the city. Most left abandoned long ago or occupied by squatters and street rabble. Most of the major business was done in the southern end of the city, which made sense as the south side was the part of the city that saw the ships coming in from the ocean for trade.

Hylon recognized the worn building up ahead. It had long sweeping arches that came off the edges of the roof and were made of giant stone blocks of incredible size. This building must have been a wonder for its age, but what was left of the wooden roof was mostly rotten. The building looked no different from the others surrounding it.

They had made a makeshift home for themselves there inside this abandoned warehouse. Their home was barely more than a tarp in the corner among all the debris of old crates, nets, and fish barrels. As they worked their way in through the warehouse, Hylon was met with the familiar smell of dead fish and stagnant pond water.

Hylon watched as Torin closed the creaky wooden door behind them and grinned, "Home sweet home."

Torin took a seat on an empty crate as he took off his monkey mask. They had bought children's masks from the harvest festival to hide their identities. Torin was roughly six feet tall with short, messy blonde hair and green eyes. His stature was lean and muscular, it was as if he was custom made for speed.

Hylon felt he was the exact opposite of Torin. He was easily a foot shorter than his friend and his eyes, as well as his hair, were black as midnight. Hylon took off his Fox mask and adjusted the hair from his eyes.

He kept his hair long to hide his ears. He was a half-breed, half elf and half olaumen. The Elven side of his heritage gave him a thin and graceful frame. He never knew his parents. Torin and he had been like brothers as they grew up together on the streets.

Torin forced a cough and leaned forward, bringing Hylon out of his own head, "Sorry Torin, I was thinking." Torin laughed, then leaned back. "That's weird. I didn't think you ever did any of that. So how did we do?"

Hylon knew Torin was teasing him. It seemed like all Hylon did with most of his time was thinking. He always had great ideas and schemes on how to get what they wanted or needed. That, and he had a natural skill for picking locks.

Hylon reached into the bag tied at his side and felt inside, only to find a large, jagged hole ripped in the sack's bottom. Hylon felt defeated, this always happened to him, "The sack must have ripped while we were being chased. I'm sorry Torin."

Torin looked completely unmoved by the loss of their prize. He simply shrugged while he started laughing again, "You know Hylon, that if you didn't have any bad luck... I am positive that you wouldn't have any luck at all."

Hylon felt himself slump. For once, he had hoped that his bad luck would just sit this one out. His bad luck was always messing things up for them both.

Hylon shook his head. Even this last job should have gone off without a hitch. What are the chances that the merchant would come back to the warehouse after he had already locked up? Hylon had scouted this particular location for weeks and the Merchant locked up and went home at the exact same time every day. All they had to do was slip in and claim their prize and sneak out with no one ever noticing.

Instead, they were caught right in the middle of the act of theft by the very merchant they were trying to steal from. The merchant was a scumbag, anyway. He had shady dealings on the side, all the time, hence the secret cache of coin they had intended to steal.

Torin pulled a couple of apples from under his vest and threw one to Hylon.

Hylon looked at the apple, then back up to Torin, "Where did you get these?"

Torin wiggled his eyebrows. "I found them while you were picking that lock. I also found a couple of other things."

Hylon curiously looked at Torin, "What did you find?"

Torin hopped down from his barrel and sat on the ground in front of Hylon. "These, to be precise", Torin reached into his vest to pull out a couple pieces of silverware.

Hylon's eyes widened in delight, "Those look like solid silver!"

Torin nodded. "Looks like we got really lucky this time around. They should fetch a decent price."

Hylon chuckled. He was relieved they had something to show for their efforts. It had been one day too many since they had had a good, hot meal. Telgrid would maybe show them some leniency. She was kind of like an older sister to them.

Hylon heard the door in the back of the warehouse slam open, he looked over to Torin who was already peaking over the top of the empty crates and old fish barrels.

Torin turned to look back at Hylon, "She doesn't look happy", Torin took another big bite of his apple and shrugged.

Hylon felt his stomach turn to knots as he stood up to watch Telgrid march toward them. Torin had understated her mood. She looked furious. Hylon had always been afraid of Telgrid, and for good reason.

She was one of the orneriest sea dwarfs he had ever met. She stood a good head shorter than himself but her body looked entirely composed of muscles and sinew. The sea dwarfs were not as stocky as their stone mountain cousins. She was lither in her form and had a skin tone more like that of tanned leather with a long black braid hanging to the side of her head.

Hylon forced down a dry gulp as he heard her yell, "Hylon! Torin! I am going to break both of your necks!"

Hylon turned to Torin with open arms. Silently asking what they should do.

Torin merely smiled mischievously as he lowered his monkey mask to cover his face and silently climbed to the top of the crates.

Hylon couldn't believe his eyes. He shook his head and whispered, "Don't do it", but Torin had already found his way to the top.

Hylon turned to see Telgrid standing right in front of him. He couldn't help but let out a squeak as he shuddered. Hylon was sure that if Telgrid could, she would light him ablaze with her glare alone.

Telgrid spoke with a tone so sweet that it sent a shiver down his spine. "Hylon, where is the tall dumb one?"

Hylon gulped nervously. Sweat was forming on his forehead. "Dumb one?", his voice came out all high pitched.

Telgrid's eyes narrowed.

The sweetness she had been faking disappeared. "Torin! I am talking about that beanstalk idiot brother of yours!"

Hylon jumped as she yelled, "He... uh... well, you see..."

Before Hylon could think of an excuse, Torin came screeching down with a tarp spread out like wings right behind her.

Hylon found himself staring in wide-eyed shock as Telgrid screamed and stamped her feet in place like a frightened child. Torin came crashing to the ground and rolled with the momentum and direction of the fall.

Hylon watched Torin leap to his feet and let out a shout, "Welcome home, sis!"

Telgrid turned away from Hylon with rage in her eyes. Hylon found himself feeling grateful that Torin had redirected her fury away from him.

Her voice sounding like that of pure rage, her fists clenched as she took slow and steady steps toward Torin, "I... am... going... to... break... you..."

Torin lifted his mask and took that last bite of his apple as he stood smiling at Telgrid. Hylon wanted to tell him to run or hide, but he found he was too stunned to say anything. He could only think to himself that Torin must want to die. Scaring Telgrid like that was just asking for a beating.

Telgrid started yelling, "Do you know how long it took us to get into that place? I watched as you guys ran like scared rats from the enforcers, spilling OUR coin as you went!"

Telgrid took a deep breath. "Not only did I watch you lose all the coin as you ran, but one enforcer recognized you, Hylon!" She spun and was staring at him with a fiery intensity.

Hylon was at a loss for words. How had they recognized him?

Torin pipped up behind Telgrid, "I can understand why. You had your mask up Hylon", Torin made a motion with his hand above his head as if lifting a mask.

Hylon tried to recall how that could be, and quickly remembered that he had lifted his mask to get a better look at the lock inside the warehouse. Hylon let out a disappointed sigh. He had never pulled the mask back down when they went to make their escape.

Hylon went to apologize to Telgrid but was quickly interrupted by her, "This is the fourth district you two have been spotted in. This time, I am sure, they have made a wanted poster."

Torin seemed to be speaking to himself as he rubbed his chin. "Do you think they will get my chin right this time?"

Telgrid let out a scream. "I can't handle you two! We should be rich by now, but you guys can't appear to keep it together long enough to get us a payday!"

Telgrid sighed, and her shoulders slumped. "We need to at least get enough to eat. I never thought I would say this, but I am starting to get sick of eating fish. The fish in the ports are nasty and I can't be the only one relied on for feeding us."

Telgrid went and sat on crate, "We need just one job to come our way that even you two won't be able to mess up."

Torin sat next to her and smiled as he pulled out another apple from his vest and dropped it into Telgrid's lap.

Telgrid chuckled, "At least it's not fish."

Torin smiled as he pulled out a silver fork and handed it to Telgrid. "You can eat it with this."

Telgrid scoffed, then gave the fork a closer look. "Wait, is this silver?"

Torin nodded as he pulled out the other pieces and handed them to her.

Telgrid examined each one before looking up. "Well, it seems you two are not completely useless. We should be able to turn these into Mr. Sidestreet for a decent price."

Torin frowned as Hylon exhaled loudly, "Why does that fence get like ninety percent of our profit? We did all the work, and he just takes all the money."

Telgrid had a grim look on her face. "You already know why, Hylon. If we try to sell under his nose in this town, we will be killed... or worse."

Hylon nodded, everything went through Mr. Sidestreet if it was criminal in nature and he got a cut or he did some cutting.

Torin looked up towards the rafters of the warehouse. "What if we take him out?"

Telgrid's eyes widened as she shushed him. "Don't say that kind of stuff out loud. Sidestreet's has eyes and ears everywhere."

Torin just smiled as he put his arms behind his head. "It was just an idea."

Hylon spoke up, "We just need to find another job, and I promise I won't mess it up."

Telgrid and Torin looked at each other, then back to Hylon with an unconvincing nod.

He could tell that they were in disbelief, and he didn't blame them. Something always came up when he was doing a job.

He sighed. "I must be cursed."

Torin jumped to his feet and wrapped an arm over his shoulders, "Hey now, all things considered, I would say that none of us has the best of luck." Torin waved his other arm out slowly, bringing attention to their surroundings.

Hylon couldn't help but chuckle, "I suppose you're right."

Telgrid looked at Hylon. "We have seen worse."

Torin chuckled. "We have also seen better. So get to using that brain of yours and find us a way to get rich." Torin slapped his back as he took dramatically long steps before falling backwards into his previous seat.

Telgrid looked as though she was deep in thought, as Hylon spoke up, "What if we joined up with the Green Cloaks?"

He had been toying around with the idea for months now, and it was a great way to use his natural skill without looking over his shoulder all the time.

Telgrid went to yell at him, then stopped herself. "Hylon, that's the dumbest... decent idea you have had yet."

Torin was leaning back on his crates as he spoke. "What about the money we owe Mr. Sidestreet?"

Hylon watched as Telgrid's face went from hopeful to agitated, "He won't let us go without a large sum of money, and even then, he views us as assets... he may not let us go."

Hylon was determined to figure this out, "What if we got him a score so big that he had to let us go? We could give him all the credit and the total profit... most of the profit."

Telgrid sat up straight and looked as if she had remembered something. "This may be a long shot, but I overheard this old guy in the market this morning looking for the currency exchange office."

Telgrid leaned forward as she talked, her hands moving in the air to further push her idea. "This guy paid the vendor with old gold."

Torin sat up with his full attention on Telgrid. "Old gold? Like coins of the dead king? Those big looking ones."

Telgrid looked at Torin as she nodded with a big smile on her face.

Hylon knew that look on her face and knew that she had already made up her mind. When Telgrid had decided something, there was no changing it.

Hylon was going to tell them that this guy had most likely already gone to the exchange office when it hit him, "The exchange office is closed until tomorrow! This is the day that they do inventory counting."

"This old guy you're talking about wouldn't have been able to exchange today!" Torin smiled, "So we have until tomorrow morning to find this guy and steal his gold?"

Telgrid nodded. "This old guy easily looked two hundred years old, at least. We could take the gold even if he tried stopping us."

Torin looked puzzled for a moment, then that grin of his crossed his face. "We don't live as long as dwarves, Telgrid. If he was two hundred, he would be a dusty skeleton at best."

Telgrid looked uncomfortable. "I knew that Torin. I have been taking care of you since you were like this tall."

Telgrid held her hand out in example.

Torin still had that grin. "You mean as tall as you?"

Hylon couldn't help but laugh as she glared at the both of them. Hylon smiled, "We are grateful, you know; you took care of us when no one else would."

Telgrid scoffed, "I just needed help with jobs, and you two were gullible enough to do them."

Torin smiled as he stretched. "You know, without us, you could have gone back to the floating cities to look for your family."

Telgrid seemed to drift into thought for a moment. "Yeah, I could have done that, but I made the mistake of getting attached to two young lads. Who seemed just as lost as I was."

Hylon smiled. If it wasn't for Telgrid, they would have been swallowed by the streets or left to die. Orphans like them were invisible, but not to each other. They were family.

Hylon wondered if her family was even alive. She had washed ashore from a wreck out at sea when they had first met. She did not go into detail about who her family even was. Hylon didn't care, though. They had been together for as long as he could remember.

Torin yawned, "So... where do we start?"

Telgrid bit her top lip, trying to recall the old man's whereabouts, Hylon guessed.

Telgrid nodded as she smiled. "The old guy mentioned to the vendor he was looking for a place to stay the night off the beaten path. I overheard the vendor mention that place over by the rat way."

Hylon crinkled his nose, "That place is disgusting... it's a great place to get stabbed or robbed in your sleep."

Telgrid smiled deviously, "That's right, IT IS a great place to get robbed."

Hylon smiled. He couldn't believe their luck. This was going to be the easiest job he had ever done.

Torin jumped to his feet. "Well then, let's get going before someone beats us to it."

Hylon nodded as he looked at Telgrid. She was staring at him as she was biting the edge of her bottom lip.

Telgrid was speaking softly, "We better go armed."

Torin turned to Telgrid with a puzzled look on his face, then followed her gaze back to Hylon.

Hylon couldn't help but feel a little insulted as Torin nodded his agreement.

Torin looked at him and shrugged, "Just to be on the safe side."

Telgrid must have noticed the disappointed look on his face. Her voice started confident enough but then trailed off as more of an insecure question. "It's just a precaution in case this... really old guy... is dangerous."

Hylon shook his head, "I get it. You guys are worried about my bad luck."

Telgrid and Torin did a quick glance at each other as they mumbled and headed in different directions. Most likely to avoid hurting his feelings as much as to fetch their weapons.

Hylon shrugged it off as he went to his old blankets that he called a bed. He reached under the top corner to produce a curved dagger of Elven design. Hylon looked it over. It was the only thing he had to remind him of the parents he never knew.

He smiled. He liked to think that they were still out there looking for him. That it was all an accident that he had been abandoned. He knew it was probably a lie; he told himself, but it was a pleasant lie and it gave him hope for a better future.

His earliest memory was of Torin grabbing his hand and covering him with an old blanket in a dark alley. He frowned. He never understood why he couldn't remember anything before that.

Torin landed behind him with a loud thump.

Hylon jumped and hid the dagger behind his back reflexively.

Torin just let out a laugh. "You ready for this Hylon?"

Hylon looked to see that Torin was holding a long-bladed half-spear. Hylon nodded as he raised his eyebrows. Torin must be taking this very seriously if he was bringing that.

Torin spoke with a somber tone, "Well, little brother, this is the day things finally start to turn around for us. Today is the day we forge our own path. Bad luck be damned." Hylon smiled.

Torin always had a way of making him feel like things would be alright.

Hylon could hear Telgrid yelling from the other side of the wall like debris, "Are you two coming or should I just do this myself like usual!?"

Torin wiggled his eyebrows, then motioned his head toward Telgrid.

Hylon smiled, this was going to be the best score they had ever had. He followed closely behind Torin as he saw Telgrid over by the doorway. She had her favorite hammer; it was more of a giant iron mallet, really. Hylon shivered at the thought of being hit with the thing, especially if Telgrid was wielding it.

They all headed out the door as the last bit of sunlight dipped past the horizon, giving the rivers below a bright orange hue. Hylon smiled. That's the second most beautiful thing he had seen since arriving in this town.

After the three of them had spent hours looking for this old man, Hylon had just about given up hope of finding him. They had investigated almost all the inns, shanty houses, and dumps along the rat ways with no luck. Hylon sat done on the edge of the street to collect his thoughts.

He looked over to see a drunk passed out by a sewer grating. Hylon was not entirely sure the man was not dead. Hylon let out a deep breath as he looked up at the night sky. It was starting to get late.

He went over the inns and flop houses in his mind, thinking if they had missed anything, when he overheard the conversation of two strangers passing by.

The red-haired one looked like a country kid out of his element and spoke far too loudly with way too much enthusiasm, "Do you think I could use some gold to buy Leianna something nice, like a new dress, or maybe a bracelet?"

The other one looked like pure muscle and murmured enough that if not for his half elven ears, he would have missed it.

The muscular one with olive-colored skin sounded angry, like he was whispering through clenched teeth, "Peter, if you talk any louder about the gold, you are going to get us both mugged. On top of that, Da'ragh doesn't want either of us spending coin on worthless crap."

The one called Peter spoke up defensively. "I don't think Leianna would think it's crap, Dugan."

The big one named Dugan almost sounded like he was growling, "Twerp, if you don't shut up, I am going to give you a beating you will never forget."

Hylon was shocked. He could not believe his luck. These two had to be traveling with the old man. It couldn't be a coincidence that these two country kids would be carrying gold. No one other than nobles and merchants in the high district carried gold.

Hylon stuck to the shadows as he followed them. He was extra careful so that they would not see him, but these two didn't even pay attention to their surroundings. Hylon smiled to himself. Once he found out where these two were headed, he would circle back to get Telgrid and Torin. They were going to be easy marks. These guys were oblivious. Hylon would be in and out before they knew anything was amiss.

Hylon followed them for a good way down the roads of the old rat ways. Hylon found himself looking at the damaged statues and heavily worn stone pathways. The architecture and designs on the street told of a better and more prosperous time. He thought that at one point in the past, this would have been just like the rich districts to the south during the age of the old king.

Hylon shook his head. He was daydreaming again and needed to focus on the task at hand. He listened as the two continued to argue almost the entire way. Hylon was wondering if these two even liked each other at all.

They made a bend and up a short set of stairs toward a giant stone mansion-like building. The building looked like it had been a home of some noble blooded family during the distant past, but now it was little more than a shell of its former grandeur.

Hylon frowned. This was one of Mr. Sidestreets' buildings. It was known as "The Bourbon Lady" and was mostly used as an inn, a brothel and a gamblers' den. This place was used to make some of the shadiest deals he had ever witnessed.

Hylon was crinkling his nose; this would not be as easy as he thought. If the strangers were paying to stay in one of Mr. Sidestreets establishments, then they had also paid for his protection. Hylon watched the two strangers enter the building, unaware of his presence.

To the side of the double doors sat a group of Mr. Sidestreets thugs. On the foot of the stone stairway there sat a couple sea dwarves, a burly looking man with tattoos and a gaunt-looking river elf playing liar's dice. They were drinking, boasting and threatening each other as they played.

Hylon squinted as he watched. Getting past them would be easy. The hard part would be getting the gold to Mr. Sidestreets and then getting clear of town before he found out they had stolen from paying patrons in HIS business. Hylon took a deep breath as he hurried back toward his friends. This would not be the easy score they had originally thought it to be.

Hylon was trying to come up with some ideas on how he and his friends would proceed when he heard a disgruntled voice behind him, "There is the thief! I told you I saw him."

Hylon went to run just a moment too late when he felt a firm grip on his shoulder throw him to the ground. The force of the throw knocked the air out of him. He blinked as he tried to catch his breath.

Three figures stood over him as he laid on the ground, looking at the night sky. They were the merchant enforcers from earlier today. Most likely come down to the rat ways to drink away their coin.

The one with unshaved black stubble growled as he looked down at Hylon, "You cost us our jobs today, petty thief."

The fat looking one had black in his teeth and Hylon could smell his putrid breath as he heaved, "I say we kill him."

The one with stubble spat on him and stared at him right in the eyes. "No, we will not kill him. We will cut off his hands and leave him."

Hylon panicked and tried to look for a way out as the others laughed.

The unassuming one that had remained silent to this point pulled out a large rusty looking butcher's knife and smiled with a mostly toothless grin.

The one with stubble motioned to the dark alleyway behind them. "Grab him up and bring him over here. We are gonna cut you up, boy."

The group of men laughed as they hauled him up and dragged him into the alleyway. Hylon struggled, but the men were twice his size and were out for blood. Hylon tried kicking the one, but came short.

The man just laughed, "Little thief is trying to escape again."

He was desperately trying to think of some way out of this when the man, laughing to his right, started making a strange gurgling noise. Hylon turned to see the point of a spear coming out of the man's mouth. Hylon almost passed out at the sight. Blood had always made him faint.

The death of the man gave him an opportunity to wrench free. He watched as Torin pulled his half spear from the back of the man's neck. Torin looked furious. Hylon nervously watched as the two men turned to face Torin with weapons drawn.

Hylon moved quickly behind Torin as he spoke, his voice low and calm, "If you run now, you will live this night. If you stay, then you will join your friend here in feeding the crows."

The man with stubble barked, "You curs dic tonight!"

The man lunged forward with a dagger when Torin slashed the blade of his short spear across the man's knuckles. This caused the man to cry in pain as he dropped the dagger. His scream was cut short; Torin caught the man's knee with the heel of his boot, causing the man to fall forward as Torin brought up the point of the spearhead into the underside of the man's jaw. The man spasmed for half a breath before Torin ripped the blade free and, in a blink of an eye, drew the blade across the exposed neck of the toothless man.

The toothless one had tried to make a wide stab at him but was stopped in his tracks as the blade of the short spear found its mark. The man fell to his knees as he tried to stop the bleeding from his neck. Torin thrust the spear forward through the man's right eye into his head.

Hylon watched as the man slumped to the ground in a lifeless lump. All three enforcers just moments ago had the intention of killing him. Now were corpses in some unmarked alleyway.

Hylon gulped, if Torin hadn't come when he did... Hylon shuddered at the thought. Torin reached down and used one of the men's coats to clean the blood from his short spear.

Torin turned to look back at him. "Looks like your luck may just be turning for the better Hylon. I came looking for you just in time."

Hylon nodded nervously as he tried to avoid looking at the blood. He already felt faint and nauseous.

Torin looked at Hylon with concern on his face. "You know it was them or us, right?"

Hylon nodded, "Yes, they were out for blood."

Torin had begun to search the bodies for anything valuable. "Good. This realm will not pull any punches. It will eat us up if we let it, and eventually, you will have to use that blade of yours."

Hylon's body sagged as he stared at the ground, "I know, I just... I just don't like hurting people."

Torin turned with a small handful of coins and a smile across his face. "Well, it's a good thing you have me watching out for you, then."

Hylon sighed, "I appreciate you watching my back, but did we have to kill them?"

Torin put the coins into his coin purse on his belt and turned to look at Hylon, "These are not... were not, good men Hylon. That merchant we tried to steal from has ties to the slave trade and other equally nasty dealings. Do you think good men would work for a guy like that? Not to mention they were going to kill you for losing their jobs."

Hylon nodded slightly as he looked up at Torin. He was right. These men were going to kill him for stealing from a man who had gained wealth through unsavory means. Hylon shook it off. Maybe Torin was right and someday he would have to protect himself by way of the blade.

Torin brushed his hands on his trousers and looked at Hylon. "Have you had any luck in finding the old man?"

Hylon had almost forgotten in all the commotion that he had followed the two young men earlier, "I think I found where the old man and his friends are staying. I overheard a couple of young guys talking about gold. I followed them and know where they are staying."

Torin grinned as he slapped Hylon's back. "This is great news! See, I told you your luck is turning around."

Hylon furrowed his brow in concern as he looked back at the lifeless bodies on the ground.

Torin had noticed and waved his hand in the air. "That was a hiccup. Your bad luck getting in its last jabs before your good luck takes over."

Hylon bit his tongue. He was not at all convinced.

Torin was walking toward the street out of the alley, "We better get Telgrid, she was checking around back by the markets for information on the old man."

Hylon took one last look at the men on the ground. They had been cruel and had murderous intent, but he couldn't shake the notion that maybe there could be another way, a better way. Hylon chased after Torin as they headed off to find Telgrid and develop a plan for stealing the gold that would ultimately give them a chance at a better life.

Hopefully, they could convince Mr. Sidestreets to let them go. Hylon didn't want to be a thief forever. He didn't want to get his hopes up, but secretly held out at the idea of joining the Green

Cloaks with Torin and Telgrid. He couldn't help but smile. They would make a great team.

Chapter Eleven

DUGAN COULDN'T BELIEVE WHAT he was hearing. Da'ragh was trying to convince them that with the right team, they could get across the broken lands unscathed and retrieve the crown of the old king. The very same crown that had been lost to the ages, and an item coveted by all the noble houses. He had grown up on the fables of adventurers seeking the crown in the broken lands.

He looked over at Leianna, who was sitting on the edge of her seat, holding onto that stick of hers. She seemed to be eating up this old man's ploy entirely. Dugan shook his head and turned to look at Peter, who was stuffing his face with that odd-smelling cheese he had purchased from the market they had gone to earlier.

Dugan frowned. Peter wasn't even capable of advanced thought. He would just follow Leianna around like usual. Dugan moved his gaze over to Da'ragh, who was discussing in depth their need to take a very specific path in order to find the crown. He was sure that Da'ragh just liked the sound of his own voice.

Dugan laid back on the couch with his arms folded behind his head. This has got to be the worst idea he had ever heard. Dugan tuned out the others as he was lost in his own thoughts.

He thought of his family back in Oakbridge and wished he could return. His father's age was catching up with him, but he was still the strongest man he had ever known. His mother had always told him he had reminded her of his father with his own strength and smarts. They shared a love of books and history. He hoped he was doing well.

His mind moved onto that of his siblings. The three older brothers were the ones who worked on the farm. His older sister would take over the business side of things. Dugan smiled, she was always good at numbers.

He was the youngest of all his siblings and he had always felt like he was constantly underfoot. He had always strived to prove his worth, but it always felt like he wasn't truly needed anywhere on his family's farm. No matter how hard he worked or learned as much as he could, he could never shake the feeling of being an extra wheel on a feed cart.

He let out a soft sigh. Maybe he was supposed to be here helping these two idiots. If not for him, they would have died in that clearing. Peter was worthless in a fight and Leianna was still a novice at that junk Da'ragh was teaching her.

Dugan shook his head as he watched the light from the fireplace's flames danced on the ceiling. A twerp, a Magi reject, and an old man. If not him, then who would keep them from getting killed? He blew air out as he gave it some more thought. For now, he would stay with them, at least until all this trouble with the Magi had been resolved.

He looked up at the others, still discussing their best course of action for the broken lands. He laid his head back down on his hands. This may not be all that bad. How many chances would someone like him get at a chance of traversing the broken lands?

Dugan couldn't help but think that maybe if, by some infinitesimal chance, they found the crown, the prestige of such a thing could bring his family's farming business more publicity. Maybe he could be the mayor of Oakbridge. That would make his father proud.

He found his thoughts wandering to the place they were staying in and shook his head. His father would never stay in a place like this. This place had a stench of ale and loose women he wanted no part of.

Da'ragh had paid a good amount of coin to a group of obvious thugs to keep an eye out for Magi, and he was convinced that this place was not entirely legal. They had to keep their heads down and stay low, but this felt dirty to him. He at least appreciated the space they could stretch out in that Da'ragh's gold had purchased; he had never dreamed of paying for an entire floor of a building before. A precaution Da'ragh had called it. As far as he was concerned, it seemed like a very lavish kind of precaution.

Dugan looked forward to things going back to the way they were and living his life in peace back at Oakbridge. He looked back at Peter and Leianna. Those two had always been friends. He felt a twinge of jealousy before averting his gaze back to the ceiling.

They always had these grandiose ideas with their head in the clouds, they never had their feet on the ground. He couldn't imagine living his life like that. Without proper planning, it would doom them to failure. Even with all that said, he still couldn't help but feel a soft spot for those two, even with them being as obnoxious as they were.

Dugan smiled up at the ceiling when he heard a barely audible clatter from the other room. He leaned up and looked over to the adjacent room as he strained to hear if anything else sounded but heard nothing. He couldn't shake the feeling that something was off and stood up and made his way into the other room, where a few beds were lined up against the wall.

He squinted as he surveyed the room with the light from the fireplace at his back and moonlight coming in through the window. He could not see where anything was out of place. Shrugging, as he must have been hearing something from a lower part of the building. He went to return to the others when he heard a soft creak from the window.

He quickly hid in the shadows next to the doorway and watched as he unhooked his hand ax from its loop on his belt. He waited to call out to the others until he got a closer look at these would-be burglars. Dugan watched as a hand outside the window came from below and slowly pushed the window open.

He watched as a small frame with long black hair lowered themselves in from outside and made no noise as they slipped across the room toward the door that led into the hallway to his right. Dugan smiled. Whoever this girl was that had snuck into their place had no idea he was watching her or the trouble she was in. Dugan was planning to catch her when she passed him to open the door when she stopped in the middle of the room.

Dugan held his breath so that he wouldn't give away his location. The sound of his colleagues discussing their plans could be heard clearly. Dugan squinted as he focused on the figure in the moonlight. He could only make out her outline, even with the moons shining brightly through the windows.

He waited patiently, but the figure took a slow step backwards and turned to face him. Dugan couldn't figure it out. He was in the shadows, and this figure looked like it was staring right at him. It finally hit Dugan like a stack of bricks. It was an elf, and they could see him as clear as day.

Dugan stepped out of the shadows and held his ax at the ready. The figure took several steps back and he could make out the glint of a blade in their hand.

Dugan thought he should give them the chance to leave. "You better go back the way you came. Unless you would rather, I throw you back through it."

He heard the elf girl softly mumble under their breath, "Damn my bad luck."

Dugan smiled, "Unless you want your luck to get any worse, then you better be on your way."

The elf girl seemed to put her blade away and held up her hands. "Alright, I will leave. No reason for anyone to get violent."

Dugan heard the creak of a floorboard behind him. Dugan instinctively jumped to the side to see the glint of a blade flash by in front of his face. That was meant for the back of his head. Dugan spun and swung his ax with incredible force, catching the shaft of a half-spear weapon and knocking a second would-be burglar to the floor. Dugan watched as the figure leaped to their feet from a completely prone position. He was not always impressed, but that was something he could appreciate in a combatant.

The elf girl yelled out, "Don't kill him, Torin, we just need their gold!"

Dugan bared his teeth in a menacing grin. "So, Torin, do you intend to kill me and take my gold?"

This Torin laughed as they circled each other in the shadows. "Oh, I intend to take your gold. It's up to you whether or not I take your life."

Dugan squinted as the room filled with light. An orb hung in the air above their heads. He could hear Peter and Leianna enter the room behind him.

He could clearly hear the shock in Leianna's voice. "Who are these people, Dugan?"

Peter let out a yell before he could respond, "Watch out!"

He looked out of the corner of his eye just in time to see Peter run his shoulder into a female sea dwarf and knock her to the ground just as she was about to bring her hammer down on his head. Dugan felt a little impressed by the twerp. Dugan saw a shimmer out of the corner of his eye and was barely able to deflect a jab by this Torin.

Dugan boasted, "You are just too slow, buddy."

Dugan watched as Torin grinned and spun the half spear in his hand, "Oh, I am just getting started."

He watched as Torin pushed the elf girl behind him, but something caught his eye. Dugan looked to see that the elf girl was no girl at all, and he wasn't sure they were an elf either. "You're not a girl!"

The girl with long dark hair turned red and looked completely taken off guard. "Wait, what!? Of course, I'm not a girl!"

Dugan chuckled, "You could have fooled me."

Torin made a twist as he brought the spearhead down with frightening speed.

He scarcely avoided getting skewered. Dugan exhaled sharply as he sidestepped the blow and brought his ax up in an arc that forced Torin back a few paces.

The blonde-haired spear wielder had a smile on his face that made Dugan's blood boil. He felt himself glaring at him as his anger boiled to the surface.

Torin let out some boasting of his own. "Careful, big fella, or you might find yourself with an extra hole."

He growled as he saw Peter getting pummeled by the sea dwarf.

Leianna stepped forward and whispered something just before the sea dwarf was lifted into the air and slammed against the far wall.

The small, long-haired lad yelled out in concern, "Telgrid!"

Dugan had his gaze transfixed on Torin. If he gave this guy any opening, he would find himself stuck with that half-spear for sure.

He watched as Torin's eyes grew wide from Leianna's spell craft.

The dark-haired lad yelled out as he waved his arms, "Truce, please everyone, just wait a moment!"

He refused to take his eyes off this Torin as he heard Leianna talking behind him. "Ok, we are listening."

The sea-dwarf climbed out from behind the furniture, cursing and glaring at what Dugan presumed was Leianna behind him.

The lad took a deep breath. "My name is Hylon, and these are my friends, Telgrid and Torin. We didn't come looking for a fight. We were only looking for gold. No one needs to die."

Dugan watched as Torin maintained eye contact with him and smirked.

His mouth forming a snarl as the spite fueled his voice. "Well, you are not getting any gold this night. So, you all just be on your way."

He noticed as Peter stood up shakily and wiped blood from the corner of his mouth and nose, "Wow, Telgrid, your punch hits like a horse can kick."

She turned a bright red, and her voice sounded agitated and shaky. "Are you complimenting me?"

Dugan shook his head. Peter was clueless about the situation, yet again.

The twerp sounded way too happy as he spoke. "Well, yeah, why wouldn't I? You have a powerful punch."

He watched as her face went from shock to confusion.

Leianna interrupted the conversation, "None of that matters. What matters now is resolving this situation... Dugan."

He was taken off guard. "What do you mean? I didn't start this fight, blondie over there did."

Torin was smiling mischievously as he reached up and ran his fingers through his hair in response.

Dugan was becoming more irritated with this guy by the minute.

The small guy Hylon spoke up again, "We can just leave. No harm done-"

Torin interrupted him, "We are not leaving empty-handed, spell caster or not."

Dugan's muscles tensed. He was going to teach this fool a lesson.

Da'ragh walked into the room and right between Torin and himself.

Dugan went to warn Da'ragh when he watched the old man throw a sack onto the ground in front of Torin. The sack was full of gold coins.

Da'ragh's voice was warm as he spoke to the others. "Is this enough? I am not very good when it comes to money, so if you need more, I can get it for you."

The entire room fell silent in disbelief.

Dugan looked back at Leianna, who was staring at Da'ragh. She looked confused.

The old man smiled as he held out his arms. "No amount of gold is worth someone's life. I hope you can take this and leave in peace."

Dugan could not believe what he was hearing. Da'ragh was just going to give their gold away!

He went to voice his opposition when Peter chimed in, "He is right, you know. We are not your enemy."

Dugan shrugged as Telgrid turned to him. "Is he soft in the head?"

Leianna stepped forward defensively, "No, he is not soft in the head, but you will be if you insult my friend again."

Dugan shook his head. One of these days, she was going to have to let Peter fight his own battles.

The little one spoke up. "Why would you just give us gold?"

Da'ragh chuckled softly, "You seem in desperate need of it and I hope it helps, but in my experience, gold only seems to amplify your problems."

He watched as Hylon hung his head in shame, "Thank you, sir."

Dugan watched Hylon pick up the gold and Torin took a step toward him, "Well Dugan, until next time... it has been a pleasure."

Torin winked, and Dugan bared his teeth at him. Next time he would take this Torin's head.

The sea-dwarf was turning a bright red as she spoke to Peter, "I... I just want to say thank you... and that you can take a hit better than anyone I have ever seen. Usually, I knock the person out after at least the second or even third punch to the face... but your head is like punching rock."

He turned to look at the twerp with that stupid smile on his face.

Peter enthusiastically said thank you.

Dugan shook his head. "I don't think I would say thank you to someone who said my head was like a rock. It's like saying you're dense if you catch my meaning."

Leianna snorted as she held back a laugh. She tried to hide the fact she was going to laugh by again going to Peter's defense. "It was a compliment, Dugan."

Da'ragh motioned for the door as the three would-be thieves cautiously left the room.

Peter was waving as if he was giving a farewell to guests.

After they had gone Dugan forced out an agitated sigh, "Why in all the realms would we give them coin when they had all the intention of killing us for it?"

Da'ragh turned to him and was smiling, "Like you said before, all that coin was a small fortune, and we really don't need that much for our journey. We just need enough."

He couldn't believe what he was hearing. This old man clearly did not know the value of the amount he had just given away.

Leianna came up and grabbed his arm. "They looked down on their luck, plus we have loads of coin to spare. Before yesterday, we hadn't even seen that much gold, let alone find a use for it."

He felt his face flush as Leianna held onto his arm. His thoughts went all fuzzy and his anger washed away. He was trying to think of an argument, but instead found himself agreeing with her. "I suppose you're right Leianna, we really don't need that much gold."

She smiled and went to look after Peter's bleeding nose.

Dugan was irritated with himself; she always had a way of clouding up his thoughts. Dugan shrugged it off as he walked into the other room. He was going to sleep off tonight's brawl and first thing tomorrow, they would leave this city.

He stopped in the doorway to look back and watched as Da'ragh was showing Leianna how to treat Peter's nose. She was applying some type of ointment as Peter smiled at Leianna like he always had. Dugan again felt that twinge of jealousy before turning away and walking toward the couch he was laying on earlier.

He took a breath and told himself that if not for him, they would all be dead. Someone had to keep a clear head around here. He gritted his teeth as he thought of Torin. The next time he saw that blonde-haired punk, he was going to give him a beating he would never forget.

CHAPTER TWELVE

Leianna leaned back after finishing the last of her breakfast. Most of the morning was spent discussing what to expect when they arrived in Kronus.

She was sipping on some dark tea when Peter blurted out in between bites, "Da'ragh has been gone a few hours now. Do you think we should go look for him?"

Dugan shook his head and answered before Leianna could, "The exchange office is incredibly slow. If he gets back before noon, then I would be surprised. They deal with hundreds of merchants throughout the day. Da'ragh is probably waiting in a very long line right now."

Leianna motioned her left hand to Dugan as she spoke to Peter, "See, I am sure he is going to be fine. After last night, he said we should stay put until we head for Kronus."

Dugan nodded his head in agreement. "With the way you talk, everyone in this city probably knows we are here."

Peter frowned. "How can you not be excited? This place is fantastic with all the stores, vendors and food!"

Leianna smiled as she watched as Peter went back to eating. It was astounding how much food he could fit into that skinny body of his.

Leianna was thinking of the three would be burglars last night and the kindness that Da'ragh had shown them. Those three were not so unlike Dugan, Peter, and herself. They looked like they had been on hard times and were trying to change their fates through the actions of their own hands. She couldn't blame them for doing what they did. She was sure that she might do the same in their shoes.

The one with the long, dark hair had something about him that Leianna just could not put her finger on. He seemed to be the voice of reason for the other two, but he had something about him that called out to the magic within her. He was more than he seemed.

Leianna whispered to herself, "Maybe he is Do'earee, too?"

Dugan looked up from his plate. He seemed to be moving the food around despondently more than eating. "What was that Leianna?"

Leianna did a flat grin, "Oh nothing, I was just thinking about the people who broke in last night."

Dugan made a scowl. "They would have tried to kill us for that gold if Da'ragh had not given most of it away. They were no more than thieves looking for an easy score." He let out a deep sigh, "Which Da'ragh handed right over to them."

Peter finished chewing as he smiled. "I thought they were nice."

Leianna laughed as Dugan looked at him with disbelief. "That punch by that sea dwarf was quite the loving embrace."

Dugan paused and shook his head, "Wait, this is my fault... have you convinced yourself that all those beatings I have given you were meant out of love?"

Leianna watched as Dugan and Peter both laughed. She thought it odd that Peter could so easily shrug off all the pain Dugan had caused him throughout their childhood.

Peter was smiling. "Look at it this way, Dugan. We are all on the same side. If it wasn't for you picking fights with me, and barely winning, I might add, then you wouldn't be as strong as you are now."

Dugan scoffed and rolled his eyes.

Peter continued, completely unfazed by Dugan's actions, "With you being as strong as you are, you were able to save Leianna and I from that skeleton thing. Plus, look at us now. We are all friends about to go on an epic adventure! Who knows, maybe those guys from last night will be our friends."

Leianna smiled. Peter's optimism had a way of rubbing off on her. She wondered what it was like to view the world through his eyes. Everything must look brighter and full of potential.

Leianna heard Dugan huff. He looked apathetic.

Dugan leaned forward as he pointed his finger at the table to make his point. "This realm will crush you with the weight of it if you don't take it seriously. They would have killed us given the opportunity."

Peter pursed his lips and squinted as if deep in thought, "But they didn't and they seemed grateful for the gold. I hope it helps them and that we see them again."

Leianna just smiled as she listened to the two go back and forth. Their view of the realm directly opposes each other. She reached down and looked at her mother's pendant. It seemed to shine more and seemed less dull than it had originally appeared.

Leianna smiled as she picked up her staff and made her way over to her pack. "We should be ready to go once Da'ragh returns. I am glad you think well of this place, Peter, but I think Dugan has the right idea on getting out of here before more people arrive looking for free gold."

Dugan leaned back and held his hand out toward Leianna as he looked at Peter. He was behaving as if his argument had just been won by her statement.

Peter just smiled and shrugged as he took another bite from a piece of bread.

Leianna reached down and was adjusting her pack as a loud banging came from the door. She quickly shot a glance back to Dugan and Peter. They were already jumping up and grabbing their weapons.

She stepped up and held her staff in front of her as she faced the door. Focusing in her mind on wind and force to use the magic just as she had done the night before. The loud banging continued, and Leianna looked back at the other two as she motioned to open the door.

Dugan nodded, his face cold and focused as he held his claymore pointed at the door.

Peter stepped slowly on his way over to open the door. He had a chunk of bread sticking out of his mouth as he reached down and slowly turned the door handle.

Leianna shook her head. Peter was going to eat, even at a time like this.

Peter opened the door as he let out a muffled and barely understandable, "Who's there?", the bread wiggling in his mouth as he spoke.

Dugan was obviously agitated and whispered through gritted teeth, "Spit that out!"

No sooner had he said that did the door get forced the rest of the way open and Hylon came bursting inside. Leianna watched as he came stumbling in and out of breath. Hylon had blood coming down his forehead, and his arm looked wounded.

Peter spit out his bread, "Are you ok?"

Dugan interrupted before Hylon could respond. His voice was stern and threatening, "I don't care why you're here, just turn around and go back the way you came."

Hylon looked up as if he were about to cry, "I don't know anyone else I can go to for help. My friends are in danger and you guys have shown us kindness. I beg of you! Please help my friends!"

Leianna took a deep breath. "Calm down and just tell me what happened."

She watched as Dugan went to protest, but she shot him a sharp look that just left him shaking his head.

Hylon held his wounded arm and stared at the floor.

His voice rattled as he spoke. "I have nothing to offer. I am just praying you show us mercy. I don't have much, but I will give you whatever you want if you help them."

Leianna tried to speak as calmly as she could, so she didn't startle him. He seemed so very delicate to her. It was a wonder he was able to survive on the streets at all. She leaned her staff against a nearby table as she stepped toward him. "Don't apologize, just tell us what happened and I will help if I can."

Dugan groan behind her, but she did not pay him any attention.

Hylon's voice was quivering as he spoke, "We took the gold you gave us to Mr. Sidestreets last night. We had hoped that all that gold would pay him off enough to let us leave this city for good. He just laughed at us and had his thugs rough up my friends."

Leianna reached into one of her belt pouches to pull out a cloth and began tending to his head wound.

Hylon winced as she cleaned his wound, but quickly brushed her hands away, "We don't have time to spare. Mr. Sidestreets is hurting my friends. I barely made it out of there..."

Peter nodded. "All right, we will help you save your friends."

Dugan scoffed, "You will do it on your own without me." Dugan lowered the tip of the claymore and shrugged as she looked at him.

She shook her head as she turned to look back at Hylon. "I will do what I can to help your friends as well."

Hylon looked relieved at her response.

Dugan behind her groaned, "This isn't our fight."

Leianna turned to face him again. "They need our help and if Da'ragh was here, he would offer aid."

Dugan looked up at the ceiling. "Fine. I can't let you both go get yourselves killed on behalf of this street trash."

Leianna was grateful he had changed his mind, but as she turned around, she noticed Hylon was again staring at the floor shamefully.

She was reminded how callused Dugan could be and offered reassurance to Hylon, "Don't pay attention to him. He is always an ass."

Hylon let out a nervous chuckle as Peter smiled and stuck his tongue out.

Leianna gently grabbed Hylon's shoulder. "So, where are your friends now?"

Hylon looked up at her, "They are not too far from here. They are at Mr. Sidestreets' personal residence. I can take you there now." He quickly turned and was already out the door. Obviously in a rush to aid his friends with their help. They all followed closely behind him as he rushed out of the building.

Leianna was having trouble keeping up with Hylons' sharp turns through all the alleyways and secret shortcuts. This was clearly his territory. She was witnessing firsthand how he kept out of the grasp of the local law keepers.

Hylon jumped to grab a ledge of a wall and fell backwards onto his back. She heard him yelp in pain and grab at his wounded arm. Leianna rushed over to him and helped him up.

Hylon looked up at her, "Thank You. I am not as good at this as Torin. He is so much faster than I am."

She could tell he was worried. "Don't worry Hylon, I am sure your friends will be fine. How much further until we arrive?"

Hylon hoisted himself painfully up onto the wall and looked back to her, "Not much farther, but just so you know... they will probably try killing us."

Dugan had his claymore resting on his shoulder. "They can try."

Leianna turned to see Peter stand next to Dugan with his arms crossed in front of his chest.

Peter was smiling confidently, "With the four of us, Mr. Sidestreets doesn't stand a chance."

Leianna smiled and turned back to look up at Hylon straddling the wall. He looked nervous.

Leianna lifted herself up onto the wall with him. "We will do our best to get them out safely."

Hylon nodded as his gaze dropped to the ground. His face was hidden beneath his long hair.

She hopped down on the other side and helped him down.

Dugan effortlessly pulled himself over with one hand while balancing the claymore in the other.

Peter clambered over in the way Leianna expected and nearly fell face first into the ground before catching himself.

Hylon led them down a back street that led to a couple of large iron gates that lay unused and rusted open. The gates would have looked beautiful, with their carvings and figures signifying bountiful and prosperous marketplaces. Instead, the gates lie ridden with rust and dilapidated designs looking distorted and the worse for wear.

Hylon held his hand back, letting them know to stop as he surveyed the broken and empty courtyard. She looked around herself to see debris litter the walkways and empty planters filled with refuse and dirt.

Peter whispered behind her, "This Mr. Sidestreets is terrible at cleaning up after himself."

Leianna looked at Hylon. "What now?"

Hylon sounded anxious, "There are no guards... he always has a bunch of thugs watching his place."

Dugan nudged her shoulder. "This looks like a trap."

Leianna did not like the look of it either. "Maybe we should try to sneak in another way."

Hylon nodded as he pointed to the left of the courtyard. "He keeps the cellar access open for deliveries at the back of the building. People like me deliver our stolen goods and information to him through that door. Its usually only got a guard or two and a coin counter to log the items through that entrance."

Peter whispered, "Isn't he worried other thieves will steal from him?"

Hylon did not look back and just shook his head, "No one steals from Mr. Sidestreets and lives to talk about it."

Peter sounded almost unhappy. "Then he is a criminal."

Dugan sighed, "What did you think he was?"

Leianna shushed them both, curbing an argument in the making.

Leianna took another look around the courtyard of this old and worn building. It looked like almost all the other stone buildings in this district. Nothing signified its importance other than the size of it.

Leianna faced Hylon, "Go ahead and lead the way. We will be right behind you."

Hylon carefully made his way along the outside wall over to the cellar entrance. He looked around the back of the building and then motioned for them to follow. Peter and Dugan followed Leianna as they quietly worked their way around to the back of the building.

As she came around the corner, she was startled to see a few men who looked like hired thugs, as well as a stone mountain dwarf who was very well dressed. Behind him, kneeling on the ground, were Torin and Telgrid with their hands tied behind their backs. Both of them looked like they had recently taken a beating.

She looked over in shock to see Hylon standing by the dwarf. He was staring at the ground sheepishly.

Leianna went to tell Peter and Dugan to run, but two more men with weapons were coming up behind them from the front of the building.

The well-dressed dwarf motioned for them to step closer. "Don't be shy now. Come closer so that I can get a closer look at you. My name is Mr. Sidestreets and Hylon here tells me you have a gift of magic."

Leianna gritted her teeth. Dugan was right, and this was a trap.

Mr. Sidestreets took a step closer to her as he spread his arms out, "Oh, don't be so shocked, girl. This is my domain, and I am its king. The thing is, well, to be precise, there is a bit of a buzz going around about a Do'earee renegade. The Magi have put out a sizeable reward for your capture."

Peter moved forward so that he was standing between her and Mr. Sidestreets. "You got the wrong girl, mister, she's not a Do'earee."

Leianna could see Mr. Sidestreets smiling from behind Peter, "I don't care if she is or not, boy. I will get the reward, regardless."

Mr. Sidestreets slowly took steps toward them. "Now, if you give yourself up, the rest of this lot will go free. If not, then I will start by killing these three to get my point across."

Mr. Sidestreets snapped his fingers. One of the men grabbed Hylon.

Leianna watched him struggle against the man, to no avail, as he yelled, "You said you would set my friends free if I brought you the magic user! You lied to me!"

Mr. Sidestreets erupted in laughter. "You street rats are all the same, easily fooled and, well, replaceable, to be honest."

Mr. Sidestreets looked at Leianna with a dead eyed stare, "So what do you say girly? Do you take a walk with me or do my friends here do a little extermination?"

Leianna's mind raced as she tried to come up with a solution. She had an idea and really hoped it would work.

Leianna spun the magic into the tips of her fingers as she thought of the ropes binding Telgrid and Torin. Focusing on releasing the tension on the ropes and setting them free. Whispering to herself. Her full attention was on loosening the bonds of Torin and Telgrid.

She barely noticed Mr. Sidestreet as he watched her closely. His eyes went wide as soon as he realized what she was doing and attempted to yell at his men.

Before he could, Peter lunged forward and caught the dwarf on his right shoulder. Blood sprayed as the dwarf fell to his knees in pain. Peter pointed his sword at the dwarf and demanded he surrender.

Leianna felt the ropes around Torin and Telgrid break free as Mr. Sidestreets spat on the ground and yelled, "Kill them!"

Peter attempted a thrust, but it was deflected by a curved knife that Mr. Sidestreets seemed to pull out of thin air.

Leianna felt nauseous for a moment as the magic set her at unease. She had still not yet grasped its nature and using it, which sometimes brought out various side effects based on the magic she had used. She took a quick mental note that rope manipulation made her motion sick.

She picked up her staff and held it in front of her as she looked back at Dugan. She almost gasped at what she was witnessing. One of the two men that had come up behind them was writhing on the ground as blood poured from his throat.

Dugan brought the claymore down in a large arched swing onto the left shoulder of the other man with violent force. The blade carved down to the midsection of the man with gruesome effect. He struggled to pull his blade from the body of the dying man.

Leianna heard Hylon yell behind her, "Leianna, watch out!"

She spun around to see a man running at her and wielding a large wooden cudgel, intent on knocking her out. She quickly focused on wind and force into the palm of her hand. Directing it at the assailant. The world seemed to slow, and she watched the magical energy form swirls of yellow and blue light that spun and twisted on each other.

She looked at the man as he raised the club over her head and focused on the energy she had accumulated for the spell and released it right into the man's chest. The air sounded like a large drum had just been struck as the man flew backwards through the air and into the opposite wall with a crunch. She felt short of breath and watched as time caught up around her. The man she had sent flying made no attempt to stand. She stared for a moment, wondering if she had accidentally killed him.

It brought Leianna back to reality as she watched Torin leg sweep the hired muscle standing closest to him, bringing the large guy face first into the stone ground. The man cried out in pain and went to stand up, but Torin had jumped on his back, forcing him back onto the ground. She let out a gasp as Torin brought out a knife and slit the man's throat. Leianna was still not used to seeing someone killed, and she stood stunned as she watched.

Telgrid picked up a couple of rocks and hurled one at a gaunt-looking elf with a long knife. The rock caught the elf in the sternum and caused him to wrench over, landing on his knees in agony. Telgrid dashed forward and grabbed the arm holding the knife, hit it with the other rock, knocking the knife from his grasp. The elf reached up and hit her square in the jaw with his fist. Telgrid seemed entirely unaffected as she gave the elf a headbutt that connected with brutal effect. The elf fell backwards unconscious with a nose and part of his cheek bones twisted into a gruesome shape. Telgrid had broken most of the bones in his face with the impact.

Leianna shook her head to clear her mind. She yanked the staff up and held it pointed before her, facing Mr. Sidestreets. Who was currently attempting to dodge and parry the flurry of swings by Peter.

Mr. Sidestreets yelled out to her, "It's not too late to give up, girl! You can walk away and still save your friends!"

Leianna gritted her teeth and glared at him. She had no intention of giving up, now or ever.

She was completely caught off guard as she was knocked from her feet and yanked backwards up into the air. She sat almost frozen as her body refused to respond. She couldn't move as she floated up high above the ground. She was easily outside the reach of her friends, suspended within her arcane entrapment.

Leianna watched in horror as a Magi stepped into the open out of a plume of smoky shadows next to Mr. Sidestreets. She looked appallingly at the markings on his robes and instantly recognized that he was an Exarch. A ranking far higher than the Acolyte they had faced in the clearing. The Magi that had attained the ranking of Exarch were in charge of entire regions for the Molcainan Magi. They were known for their prowess in the arcane arts.

The elderly man stared up at her with cloudy eyes.

His voice was raspy, the sound grated on her ears and sent shivers down her back, "So Mr. Sidestreets, you have come through for me yet again. This is exactly the kind of gift I was looking for."

She could feel the anger growing inside her.

Peter jumped forward and pointed his blade at the Magi. "Let Leianna go right now!"

The old Magi laughed and pointed a finger at Peter. Black smoke blew out and encompassed Peter, but then dissipated around him.

Peter slashed his sword through the smoke as it cleared and then again pointed his sword at the Magi. "I said let her go!"

Leianna could hardly believe what she was seeing. The magic was meant to take Peter's life, yet had no effect on him.

She looked to the Magi, who appeared to be just as puzzled, "Curious... I wonder what sort of abomination you are, boy."

Peter lifted his sword and moved forward as if to strike the Magi. The Magi pointed his fingers at the ground. With a flick of his wrist, he sent a burst of stones from the ground at Peter, like a swarm of bees, knocking him back and onto the ground.

Leianna felt herself try to scream, but was still unable to move from whatever magical prison he had placed her in.

Dugan charged at the Magi with a weapon in each hand. Only to be met with the same black smoke that had been meant for Peter the first time. She watched in terror as Dugan collapsed on the ground. Black smoke coming from his mouth as he went into a coughing fit.

Leianna closed her eyes and tried focusing on magic, but nothing seemed to align for her. She was struggling against bonds that were too strong for her.

She opened her eyes to see Hylon pleading with the Magi, "Please don't do this. We don't want to fight!"

The Magi let out another heartless laugh as Dugan struggled to stay alive on the ground. Telgrid ran forward with her head low like a ram toward the Magi, but came short as the Magi had used the same black smoke to similar results. Telgrid came tumbling to a halt and entered a similar coughing fit as black smoke erupted from her lungs.

The magi looked up at Leianna. He had the look of a sadist, as he was clearly enjoying all of this.

He had a devilish grin as he laughed. "I could kill them outright, you know, but I tend to relish the simple things. Like slowly stealing the breath from others. They are currently experiencing a slow and painful sensation of suffocation and burning..."

Leianna watched as he lowered his gaze down to them. His eyes looked black from where she was.

Peter was bleeding and was having trouble standing. The stones looked as though they had torn through his clothes and he had cuts all over. Leianna felt a small sense of relief that he was not dead. She wanted to tell him to run or stay down so that he would not gain the attention of the Magi again.

She tried to yell out but again was stopped by this Magic holding her in place.

Peter stood up shakily and in obvious pain as he held his sword up and at the Magi, "I... said... let her go..." Peter looked like he was struggling to breathe and the sword looked heavy in his hands.

The Magi let out a giddy laugh. "Oh, how delightful! I do love when the broken toys still want to play!"

Mr. Sidestreets stepped forward and let out a cough. "Not to interrupt you, Caldane, but if you don't mind, I will take my pay and see myself out of here while you have your fun."

The Magi went from a state of euphoria to a state of anger so fierce it caused his body to shake. The Magi, with a flick of his hand, hit Peter with another burst of stone from the ground that sent her friend flying painfully back to the ground.

The Magi Caldane turned with a smile toward Mr. Sidestreets, that made Leianna stare silently in fear.

Caldane's voice sounded patronizing, "Oh, I am dreadfully sorry to keep you waiting. I had totally forgotten about your payment."

Mr. Sidestreets held out a hand coated in blood from his own shoulder with a grin on his face. That grin quickly twisted into terror and anguish as Caldane reached forward with his hand like that of a hawk's talons grabbing at prey. Leianna grimaced as all at once Mr. Sidestreet's body convulsed snapped backwards into itself with a cacophony of sickening snaps and crunching noises that made her sick to her stomach. In mere moments, all that remained of Mr. Sidestreets was a broken pile of torn and twisted flesh on the ground.

Caldane chuckled as he turned back around, "Where were we, ah yes..."

He looked up at Leianna. "The path of the Do'earee is full of sorrow, my child. You follow a path of darkness and evil that I simply cannot allow to exist."

Leianna could not believe what she was hearing. This psychopath actually believed that what he was doing was good. What kind of demented fiend thought like that?

She again tried to reach out and focus the magic on escaping, but his maniacal laughter interrupted her thoughts.

Caldane looked up as spittle dripped from the edge of his mouth, "Oh, you will find the prison you are held by is of Do'earee design, my dear. You will be unable to harm or be harmed while I keep you contained therein. You will be free to watch, however..." He was murmuring to himself something else that Leianna could not quite make out, but gathered enough that it wasn't good.

Hylon stepped forward, his voice was trembling from fear, "Please sir, let my friends go. You can do whatever you want to me as long as you let them go."

Caldane's eyes lit up and he held out his open hand to Hylon, "Ah, a volunteer. Come closer, child, so that I can get a better look."

Hylon slowly walked over to stand before Caldane. His head and shoulders slumped as he stared at the ground. Caldane took a finger under his chin and lifted his head. Leianna felt as though she were witnessing the movements of a cobra ready to strike down its prey. Leianna could only watch as her magical prison kept her held in place.

Caldane had a grin on his face that was anything but comforting. "Let me get a better look at you. It is not often I get a willing volunteer. It takes quite the coward to... to... Wait... You look like..."

His face changed from sadistic pleasure to shock and concern.

His voice turned into a yell filled with anger and disbelief. "This cannot be! I will not allow such a..."

Leianna watched as a point of a blade erupted from the center of Caldane's throat from behind. She stared in complete surprise as Caldane fell to his knees, flailing in a desperate attempt to grasp at the half spear lodged in the back of his neck. Blood flowing down the front of his robes in crimson currents.

As Caldane struggled, she witnessed Torin emerge from the ruins of the rear wall behind where Mr. Sidestreets had been standing earlier. He must have thrown his spear from there. Leianna grimaced as Torin placed his boot on the side of Caldane's temple and tore the spear free, taking most of Caldane's neck with it.

Caldane's head flopped to the side as his body slumped to the ground in a pool of blood. The look on Torin's face was disheartening. He looked cold and distant. Torin looked entirely apathetic with the act of killing he had just performed.

Leianna let out a sigh of relief as Telgrid and Dugan sat up. They were still coughing a little, but neither had any black smoke coming from their mouths. She glanced over at Peter, who was unmoving on the stone ground. She went to yell and found that she still could not move.

Leianna felt panic wash over her as the magical prison she was trapped in had not gone away as the other spells had when Caldane died. She had a terrible thought that he had not been slain and looked to Caldane, who appeared to be very dead. She could not figure out how she was still contained by a spell if the caster was deceased. Spells required constant concentration in order to work.

Telgrid stumbled over to check on Peter. She watched as Telgrid rolled him over and felt tears well up in her eyes. She felt relieved. He was still alive. She could clearly see that he was still breathing.

Her attention was drawn back over to Torin as he shouted, "Hylon, watch out!"

Torin dove and pulled Hylon to cover with him. Caldane's body erupted into black smoke like an explosion. Black fumes and shadowy tendrils reached out in all directions like ash from a fire being blown in the wind. For a moment, she thought she saw a pair of eyes in the shadows, like stars in the night, staring right at her just before the shadows faded.

She looked down to see Dugan approach Caldane's body cautiously. She gasped at the sight of Caldane's body, which looked little more than a dry shriveled husk.

Dugan looked up at her as he spoke. "Leianna, can you hear me?"

Leianna tried to respond, but she could not get the words to come out. She watched as Dugan's mouth turned to a sour frown.

He then walked over and began poking at the body with what looked like a heavy mace.

Torin walked up to him with an inquisitive look on his face. "So, big guy, what exactly are you doing?"

Dugan paid him no attention as she watched him start going through the pockets of Caldane's robes.

He looked up at Torin. "Don't just stare at me. Either help or get away from me."

Leianna hoped the two wouldn't fight after all that had just happened. She was a little surprised to see Torin kneel and help Dugan search what was left of Caldane's body. Leianna watched as Torin lifted what appeared to be a small piece of Amber stone the size of a quail's egg. Torin handed it over to Dugan, who walked over to stand directly below her and began waving the Amber over his head in her direction.

She heard Dugan curse under his breath as Torin laughed at his efforts. Dugan spun around and began yelling at Torin, "I don't know how this magic works! This is ridiculous. That guy is dead. Why is she still floating in the air like that?"

Leianna could make out a familiar voice behind her enter the rear courtyard.

Da'ragh spoke with clear tones. "She is contained in a Do'earee stasis sphere. They were used in transporting and imprisonment of dangerous spell casters during ancient times."

Da'ragh held his hand out to Dugan, who handed him the Amber stone, "These stasis spheres would prevent the captive from harming others while also preventing them from being harmed while they served out their prison term. The only way to release her is by destroying the stone."

She watched as Da'ragh began circling his fingers over the stone as he continued speaking. "There are hundreds, if not thousands, of these types of stasis spheres lost in the broken lands. Entire prisons dedicated to housing the most dangerous and unpredictable evils. That have been lost to time. Their locations are a mystery. Those contained therein are trapped in stasis. Tormented by their own thoughts."

Leianna watched as the stone in Da'ragh's palm turned a bright white and then turned to dust.

Instantly, she felt like she could breathe again and had the sensation of falling. She winced in anticipation of hitting the ground, but was caught in Dugan's arms.

She opened her eyes to see him grinning at her like a fool. His voice was back to its normal cocky tone. "You're welcome."

Leianna shook her head as he sat her on her feet, "Thank You Dugan."

Leianna quickly turned and ran over to Peter to check on him. She knelt next to Telgrid, who was holding his head in her lap.

She looked to Telgrid as she spoke, "He's beat up real good, but there doesn't appear to be any mortal wounds on him."

Leianna felt herself relax a little.

She looked over at Peter and was amazed at the amount of punishment he could take and walk away from. Her attention was caught by his lips moving. She quickly leaned in and tried to listen to what he was saying.

She could barely make out his whisper, "A Kiss... a kiss to save this brave soul."

Leianna chuckled as pulled away, "Nice try, Peter."

Telgrid looked confused. "What did he say?"

Leianna just waved her hand as if it were nothing. "He just needs some healing and he will be fine."

Peter had a devious grin on his face as he struggled to sit up. "Hey it was worth a try to steal a kiss."

Telgrid still looked confused. "You wanted to steal a kiss?"

Peter just nodded with that devious grin still plastered on his face.

Telgrid looked at Peter. "Ok, fair enough."

Leianna watched as Peter's eyes went wide in disbelief, but before he could respond, Telgrid leaned in and gave him a kiss that was a little too intense and passionate for Leianna's liking. When Telgrid finally leaned back, she was smiling from ear to ear. Peter was as red as a tomato.

Peter stuttered as he tried to talk and Leianna felt herself get angry with jealousy, but immediately choked it down. She was lost in her own thoughts. What did she care if someone liked Peter? He was just a friend. She tried to block these uncomfortable feelings and was not sure where they were even coming from.

She looked over at Telgrid, biting her lower lip. Staring far too longingly at Peter still stammering over his words. Leianna could feel the anger make her chest tighten and she huffed. She was just about to express her disapproval when Da'ragh placed a hand on her shoulder.

She looked up to see him smiling down at her. "Do you have a moment where we can talk in private?"

Leianna nodded, and the two made their way over to a corner of the courtyard with some empty planters they used as temporary benches.

Da'ragh had asked her what exactly had happened in his absence. She had explained to him to the best of her knowledge all the events that had transpired. His interest had piqued when she mentioned the eyes in the shadows that had erupted from Caldane's corpse.

Da'ragh's voice sounded somber. "That shadow you saw was his soul. You cannot defeat a Magi with mere steel and iron. His soul is bound by dark ritual magic."

Leianna listened in bewilderment. "So they bind their very souls to this realm?"

Da'ragh nodded. "They give themselves immortality at the cost of their soul. Over time, they lose sight of what it means to be alive. They view people as pawns and vermin. Losing sight of the path they were meant to live in this realm. Existing in a state of a twisted shadow of their former selves. This will not be the last we see of Caldane, I fear."

Leianna was disgusted. "Are all magi bound like this?"

Da'ragh shook his head. "No, thankfully this dark ritual is only shared with those within the Molcainan Magi that have been deemed worthy. Only for those with the darkest of hearts, I am afraid."

Leianna watched as Da'ragh looked at the ground and fiddled with his staff. He seemed lost in thought momentarily before taking a deep breath. He stood up and looked at her with what appeared to be a less than sincere, rather forced smile. She couldn't help but feel he was miles away inside his head.

Leianna stood up next to him, deciding to change the subject in order to bring him back from wherever his mind had run off to. "Were you successful at the exchange office?"

Da'ragh seemed to stand up straight at the question and he seemed to return to the present conversation, "Yes, even with me having to pay off every other person I came across. This place is very much run by bribes, shadow gangs, and those who can afford to pay them."

Leianna looked about the courtyard at what used to be Mr. Sidestreets. "Do you think he was in charge of all the criminal activity here?"

Da'ragh shrugged, "If I was to guess, I would say he was at least one of the major minds behind the crime in this city."

Leianna looked over at the others.

Telgrid was tending to Peter's wounds as the others were all talking in a circle.

Torin and Dugan seemed to reach a decision and headed inside of Mr. Sidestreets building.

Hylon began walking in her direction. She wondered what they were up to when she noticed Hylon waving gently as he approached her.

Da'ragh softly grabbed her shoulder before he started walking toward Telgrid and Peter. Most likely to use magic in aiding the healing of his wounds, she thought to herself.

Leianna could see that Hylon had a look of concern and shame he was trying to hide behind his long black hair.

Hylon went to speak, and she decided to interrupt him, "I am not mad at you. You were only trying to help your friends. I just wish you would have been honest with us in the first place. We came here to help you and your friends, after all."

She watched as Hylon began to cry silently. She watched as tears fell from his eyes onto the stone below.

Hylon was talking in a barely audible hushed whisper. She could scantily hear what he was saying. It was so quiet, "Thank you Leianna."

She went to say there were no hard feelings between them but was taken off guard when Hylon hugged her, "People are not usually kind to people like my friends and I... so thank you."

Leianna did not know what to say, so she just hugged him back.

Hylon stepped back, "I will do whatever it takes to make this up to you and your friends."

Leianna just grinned. "Oh, I expect you will. So I assume you will be getting out of this town as soon as possible?"

Hylon nodded, "There is no way we can stay here now. Mr. Sidestreets associates will be looking for us."

Leianna had an idea that she knew Dugan would be adamantly against. "What if you come with us to Kronus? The city is big enough for you to hide in until you and your friends decide what to do next. Plus, we could use the company. You and your friends seem very capable."

Hylon looked up with his eyes as wide as dinner plates, "Do... do you mean that? After all I have done, you want us to travel with you?"

Leianna just chuckled, "Well, to be honest, you have not done a lot yet. Even leading us straight into a trap, we should have never walked away from, didn't pan out the way you thought it would. Seems you might be suffering from a bit of bad luck."

Hylon grinned and lowered his head, "I suppose so."

Leianna reached down and held his hand. "BUT I can see the way you love and care for your friends, and I hope maybe I can be your friend as well."

Hylon stared at the ground and sheepishly whispered to her, "I would like that."

Leianna smiled, "It is settled! In the words of my best friend Peter, it looks like we are going to be great friends."

She was not sure why, but she wanted to take a risk with Hylon and his friends. They may just need a hand in getting themselves out of the rut they were in. She did not see herself being any different if she had to grow up on the streets without the love of her father and brother.

Leianna looked up as she heard Dugan and Torin cheering as they exited the back of the building. They produced arms filled with sacks and crates stuffed with various goods and supplies. The two went and laid them on the ground near Da'ragh. Leianna looked down at Hylon and nodded in the direction of the others.

Hylon nodded taciturnly in agreement.

The two walked over to join their friends.

Torin and Dugan pulled various items from the crates and sacks. The items consisted of various armors, weapons, and some maps rolled up in leather cases. Torin was the first to speak as the group looked through the pile of goods. "There is a lot more inside. We just grabbed some of the more interesting stuff. It looks like Mr. Sidestreets had a bit of a hoarding problem."

Da'ragh handed some bandages to Telgrid. She addressed the cuts on Peter's left forearm before he leaned in to browse amongst the items.

Leianna decided to take a look at Hylon's wounds as she watched Telgrid wrap the bandages around Peter's arm. She let out a soft huff as she pulled Hylon's arm up to get a better look at it. Hylon let out a soft whimper.

Leianna mouthed an apology, as she was a little rough in picking up his arm. She just didn't like the way Telgrid was pining over Peter like that. She looked down and noticed there was quite a large gouge in Hylons arm and it was filled with dried blood. It looked painful.

Without even thinking, she held her hand over it and focused her mind on mending and healing. She felt her hand grow warm and soft white light fluttered before her eyes and appeared as dancing butterflies all congregating on Hylon's injury. She was amazed that the effort had not winded her like the other magics had done.

Upon closer inspection, she noticed that Hylon's wound had completely disappeared. She smiled to herself at a job well done. It surprised her to see everyone staring.

Da'ragh's eyebrows were raised as he muttered, "That was quite impressive. It usually takes years of study under the teachings of The Sisters of Mercy to attain that level of magical healing."

He stood up looking genuinely impressed. "It looks like you have found your talent. For each of us that uses magic, we usually have a type that comes more naturally to us than others, and for you, that appears to be the healing arts."

Peter looked at her in amazement. "Wow, that was outstanding, Leianna!"

She noticed that Dugan even looked impressed.

Torin, however, seemed completely unfazed by her magic and was still going through the supplies. Laying them out on the ground for the others to see.

Da'ragh smiled, "We will address this further in your trainings but for now it looks like you boys found some interesting items."

Da'ragh reached down and picked up a simple leather scroll case that appeared to be heavily worn and old. Da'ragh smiled and shook his head. "I cannot believe our luck. This is incredible! Someone is looking out for you, Leianna."

Leianna was confused as she leaned in to inspect the top of the leather scroll case Da'ragh was showing her. It had a scarcely visible imprint in the same design as her mother's pendant.

She looked up at Da'ragh, who was already nodding, "Yes, it is Do'earee made. I have an idea of what is inside."

Da'ragh opened it and pulled out a small but sturdy looking map. Rolled it out for everyone to see.

Leianna looked down and saw that it appeared ancient, with writing and markings she did not recognize. She tried to focus on the map, but it seemed to change and shift under her gaze. It seemed the more she tried to concentrate on the map, the more it blurred.

Dugan spoke up, "A lot of good that will do us. It looks like a jumble of nonsense. I can't seem to read any of it."

Peter looked confused as he scratched his chin. He looked over at Dugan. "I don't see anything. It looks blank to me."

Dugan furrowed his brow in disbelief as he spoke. "It looks like a Do'earee map to me, Peter."

Da'ragh turned the map so she could get a better look. "It is indeed a map. However, we will need a Do'earee Cipher Stone in order to use it. They protected the maps with magic to keep them out of the wrong hands. Once we get a hold of a Cipher Stone, we can use this in combination with your Do'earee compass, that small bronze arrow I gave you. We will be able to locate the items in the broken lands with ease."

Dugan raised his hand with a pointed finger, "First off, Broken Lands and with ease, do not belong in the same sentence."

Da'ragh chuckled, "I suppose not, but this will make our journey ten times easier... once we have a Cipher Stone, that is."

Telgrid looked up at Da'ragh. "So, are we going to travel with all of you?" She sounded nervous in her questioning as her cheeks turned red and she looked out of the corner of her eye at Peter.

Da'ragh nodded and went to speak, but was quickly cut off by Dugan.

Dugan looked serious as he spoke. "I need everyone to listen."

Leianna could already tell that he was going to oppose Torin, Hylon and Telgrid joining them on their journey. Probably say something along the lines of them not being trustworthy or something similar.

She was going to say that she had already decided they were going when Dugan interrupted her with a glare and stern voice, "I said for everyone to listen."

She raised her eyebrows and waited for him to finish before she yelled at him for being an ass.

Dugan took a deep breath before he started talking, "We just met you three and we are not friends."

Leianna rolled her eyes. He was going to push them away before even giving them a chance.

Dugan continued, "However, I have decided that you will all come with us to Kronus and I won't hear any arguments to the contrary."

Leianna felt her mouth drop open. She could not hardly believe what she had just heard.

Dugan raised a pointed finger and waved it around to expand his point. "You will not be safe if you stay here and I can't guarantee you will be safe around us, but it will at least get you clear of this city. It is the least I can do for you saving my life." Dugan reached out and slapped Torin on the back.

Torin looked taken off guard. "Yeah... about that Dugan. I was trying to save his life. You just got saved in the process."

Dugan shook his head and grinned, "Doesn't matter, I still owe you my thanks."

Peter let out a yell that took everyone off guard. "Woo-hoo! Looks like we just made some new friends!" Peter was looking at everyone with that usual smile spread across his face. "This is going to be great!"

Chapter Thirteen

V ONDUR PEERED DOWN AT his golden gauntleted right hand and found himself thinking of the war with the Do'earee. He had lost his right hand in the first battle, better known to the average olaumen as the Cataclysm. He brushed his gold and purple robes; sensing the touch of the garments, but the gauntlet did not allow him to feel them. Holding it up before his face and moved the fingers of solid gold. No feeling at all, he reflected to himself.

A voice interrupted his thoughts at the bottom of the steps, "Great Archon, my apologies, but what will you have us do in response?"

Vondur had been absorbed in thought and had not heard a word of his Prelate Adjudicator. Vondur stared down the tall ivory steps at the Adjudicator with his arms behind his back, awaiting an answer.

Vondur lowered his golden hand and rubbed the tip of his tongue along the inside of his teeth. "Execute them."

The Adjudicator glanced about the room nervously before replying, "Execute them? The entire Noble House of Calembrech, Great Archon?"

Vondur let out a laugh that resonated throughout the entire hall as Magi of all ranks joined in the laughter. Vondur snapped his gold fingers on his right hand and employed magic to amplify the sound with an adequate force that the entire hall fell mute.

Vondur leaned forward staring at the Adjudicator, "Of course not, but this House has been a thorn in the side of the Magi for too long. Start using the merchant guilds to leverage pressure on their holdings here in Kronus and increase taxes in the eastern provinces. Let's examine how they struggle to rally the other houses in search of a new heir when they cannot afford to eat."

The Prelate Adjudicator bowed and nodded toward a group of Magi, who in turn bowed to him and scurried off.

Vondur searched around the hall and saw only weakness. These pompous Magi that rested in his hall were nothing like those during the war. They were fat on the wealth he and his fellow circle had accumulated from the conflict with the Do'earee.

He scowled as he peered down his nose at the Magi, discussing business and policies. These so-called Magi were scant more than aristocrats and politicians. Barely any of them were capable of any real magic.

Forcing air out through his nose as he snarled an almost inaudible whisper, "Maggots...."

The Adjudicator once again forced him out of his own thoughts, "Great Archon, the Exarch Caldane has requested your presence down in the Alchemist Wing at your earliest convenience."

Vondur stood up so suddenly the hall echoed with gasps and startled squeaks. "I will leave immediately."

The Prelate Adjudicator tilted his head. "What of today's other orders of business yet to be addressed?"

Vondur felt the drain of fatigue from the monotony that was daily business wash over him just from hearing the question. He took long, slow strides until he was standing right next to the Adjudicator.

The man was sweating slightly and appeared incredibly nervous as Vondur leaned in and whispered, "Let the maggots fight over it."

Vondur did not even wait for a response before turning and walking toward the Alchemy wing of the inner Molcainan Magi Towers.

He scoffed at the Adjudicator's feeble response, "Yes... yes, of course, Great Archon."

He could hear the hall break out in argument before he had even made the bend into the hallway. Vondur shook his head as he whispered to himself, "Vultures fighting over carrion."

Vondur soon found his mind focused on the fact that Caldane had returned after all these many seasons, but for what purpose? Caldane was one of the inner circle and would have only returned if he had acquired something of substance. Caldane was one of the few left who had hated the Do'earee as considerably as himself.

Vondur relished at the thought of a hidden sect of Do'earee that would oblige him to embark on another inquisition.

He noticed that his pace had quickened. He had felt no emotion, let alone excitement, in years. The thought of news from Caldane made his mind ablaze with ideas. Before long, he discovered himself in the Alchemist wing. Various Magi bustled around tables covered in assorted concoctions and implements of experimentation. The hall went from a noisy, chaotic rush to a hushed trickle when everyone noticed his arrival.

Vondur executed a slow look around the wide chamber but did not see Caldane. He inadvertently found himself frowning. Had this been some sort of joke on his behalf? Caldane was not into alchemy of any kind. Why would he be here?

Vondur pivoted on his heel and took one step when he heard a voice behind him. "Great Archon, we have been expecting you."

He turned slowly to see he was being greeted by a Renewal Supplicant from the lower levels. His left eyebrow raised inquisitively. The supplicants had not been used since the last purge. This Renewal Supplicant was garbed in red robes and was bowing with his arm held out to show the way.

Vondur tried to keep his astonishment hidden. If he was being led to the lower levels, that meant Caldane's vessel had expired. Vondur found his pace quickened again as he descended the stairs leading to the renewal sanctum far below. His inner thoughts were overcome with intrigue that increased with each step.

What could have possibly brought about the expiration of Caldane's previous vessel? Caldane was not one to be trifled with, and he was not entirely sure that Caldane's gift of immortality had not driven him insane. Vondur held his hands together behind his back as he walked down the steps leading past floor after floor.

Each level was filled with various dark dealings and unsavory experiments of the Magi. Vondur had a disdain for keeping their works hidden and knew it was only a matter of time before they could operate in the open with no one to oppose them.

Most noble houses had been in silent opposition to the Molcainan Magi. Some had recently become more outspoken in their contempt of the Magi order. These noble houses had called for a new heir to be named and called for an end to the Magi stewardship of the throne.

Vondur scoffed slightly. They would never find an heir. His fellow circle members had eradicated the bloodline of the old king.

For now, they would maintain an appearance of public service. As protectors of the people. They would retain their charade of caretakers for the common good of all while they facilitated their machinations of control and power covertly.

He slowly descended the final steps. Walked into the darkened room. A decoration on the floor of a giant serpent in a circle devouring its own tail surrounding him. The very symbol of the Molcainan Magi, the symbol represented their never-ending immortality.

The Madu had given the symbol to them. A secret race of shapeshifters and magical adepts that had instructed the Magi in the endowment of immortality. The Madu had advised them on many secrets, among them being the arcane arts. If not for the

Madu and their secret font of knowledge, then the Magi would have never been successful in destroying the Do'earee.

Vondur smirked as he thought of the power their teachings had granted him and that almost no one was aware of their existence. He took pride in being one of the select few chosen by the Madu to share their secrets with.

Vondur's attention was lifted from his own internal thoughts to that of the Renewal Supplicants dragging a young man in chains to the center of the room. They fastened the young man's restraints to the strong iron loops on the floor in the middle of the Magi symbol. The man was in a state of fear and Vondur could tell, by the man's gagged muffles, he was pleading and begging for his release with the Supplicants.

Vondur kept his distance from the inside of the circle. He began slowly pacing the perimeter of the room, watching over a dozen Renewal Supplicants. They formed a circle around the young man and began chanting. Vondur observed as the room grew even darker. The very light from the hanging candelabras appeared to be only embers as the room was swallowed into darkness.

The young man began to scream, but the darkness seemed to absorb the very sound of it. The chanting, on the other hand, was getting louder and louder until time seemed to stop and all was silent. Vondur stopped his pacing and watched as a silhouette of soft glowing blue in the shape of the man left his body. His spirit, Vondur thought to himself.

Vondur observed as a shadowy serpent, barely visible, swallowed the spirit whole. Before disappearing back into the shadows as quickly as it had arrived. He continued to watch as the room lightened only marginally, but enough that he could see black smoke coming from the shadows enter the eyes of the soulless body.

After a moment, the light returned to the room and all but two of the Supplicants vacated the area. Vondur observed the remaining supplicants as they unfastened the restraints. Then silently leaving the way the others had gone. Leaving only himself and the young man in the Sanctum.

Vondur took slow strides toward the man and looked down at him. "What brings you home, Caldane?"

The young man had messy black hair and an unusual handsomeness to his appearance. Vondur examined as Caldane adjusted to his new vessel. Caldane's eyes wandered about erratically. Independent of one another inside their sockets. Like they were trying to escape. Until both stared straight forward and locked onto Vondur.

Vondur observed as Caldane stretched in such a fashion that his body appeared as if it was going to snap inwards on itself. He did not as much blink as Caldane lurched upwards onto his feet, right in front of him, like that of a willow bent down and then released. Upon searching past the youthful appearance of Caldane's new vessel, he recognized the old darkness and all too familiar hate projected in his eyes.

Caldane had a smile spread across his face that most would probably find unnerving. "Greetings Vondur, it's been a few seasons since we have last spoken."

Vondur did a brief nod. "Indeed."

Caldane lifted his hands and studied them. "It appears the Supplicants have found me a sufficient vessel. Hopefully, this one lasts longer than the previous one. It was becoming quite frail."

Vondur raised his left eyebrow. "That is because you are overly demanding of your vessels. You draw upon their very life essence when you play around with that inferior Do'earee magic. I will never figure out why you still actively try to understand their dead ways."

Caldane smirked and tipped his head back and extended his arms, "Why not try to better understand the Do'earee blight we so wish to utterly remove from this realm? That way, we can make sure none of it survives."

Vondur scowled. "It is a waste of our time and efforts to understand that which is below us. It is incompatible with our arcane arts. Now I am still awaiting your answer, Caldane."

Caldane tilted his head to his side as he spoke to Vondur, "Why have I returned home?"

Vondur was beginning to tire of Caldane's games. "Yes, why have you returned? Last we spoke, so many seasons ago, you said you would never return unless the Do'earee had returned. So Caldane, have the Do'earee returned, or have you returned to test my patience?"

Caldane stood hunched over and spat, his face contorted in a combination of madness and rage as he growled, "I do not care for your patience, Vondur!"

He made no attempt to move but held his place and stared at Caldane apathetically.

Caldane's features changed in an instant, his face returning to a disturbing smile, "I did, in fact, find a Do'earee, Vondur. She is young and appears to be alone."

Vondur narrowed his eyes at Caldane. "What makes you believe she is Do'earee?"

Caldane screeched and shook his hands violently in the air before him, "She has a staff! She has a skein satchel! She has light magic!"

Caldane all but froze and dropped his voice to a murmur, "She..." He gently tapped the base of his neck with his fingertips. "She wears their symbol." Caldane took a step back as he slowly and repeatedly nodded his head as he lifted his palm up with a single pointed finger, "And where there is one..." His voice became raspy and high-pitched, "There are many," he opened his hands to fan the air and flicker his fingers around him.

Vondur grinned slightly as he glanced down at his golden right hand. "Then we will have some entertainment for once."

Caldane's face twisted in loathing as he pointed at Vondur's golden gauntlet hand. "Why do you keep this vessel? It is not whole, and you have worn it since the wars."

He tightened his right hand into a balled fist. "My right hand was lost. This is true. However, it is a reminder of my hate."

Caldane grinned like a child who had gotten away with mischief. "Hate is good. Hate is strong."

Vondur loosened his fist and turned to ascend the stairs, "On this much, we agree, Caldane. When you are more presentable, find me in my studies. We have much to discuss. Especially regarding these newly found Do'earee."

He could hear Caldane let out what sounded like a joyous howl of a madman as he ascended the stairs leading out of the Sanctum.

Vondur pondered what had caused yet another return of the Do'earee. Each time they would stamp them out, yet others would rise. Vondur thought they had gathered all the remaining Do'earee souls; the Magi Reapers had captured them and prevented them from reentering the cycle of life.

He gritted his teeth. Could it be possible that new Do'earee could rise from the souls of commoners? The idea sickened him, but if that was the case, they would continue to hunt them down and eradicate them. He reflected back to the Madu that had taught him how to entrap the souls to prevent their return. How the Madu explained to him that the soul could never be destroyed, but it could be imprisoned.

Vondur was proud of his creation; he had formed the three Reapers from the most depraved and corrupted of the inner circle of Magi. He had employed them with great success against the Do'earee as each Do'earee slain was absorbed by the Reaper. Their soul was contained in the Reaper, like a prison from which the Reaper could draw upon their power and amplify their own.

Vondur grimaced. After the conclusion of the war and the magical explosion that had produced the cataclysm, his creations disappeared. He had sought to recover them, but to no avail. The Reapers were the embodiments of chaos. He was never fully able to control them. They abhorred Do'earee just as much as himself.

The scythes he had constructed for them were also lost. A weapon terrifying in its capabilities of allowing the user to absorb the souls of others. Vondur did not like the idea of such a weapon being found, let alone being wielded against the Magi; he decided to cross that bridge when it presented itself.

Vondur entered his study only to spy a Magi Acolyte sitting behind his large white marble desk.

He could feel the rage boil up inside, but he kept his voice cold and calm. "Acolyte, I do believe you are relaxing in my chair."

Vondur raised his hand as he warped magic through the air of the Acolyte with the intention of tearing out his spine. Finding himself give pause as the Acolyte began to laugh. He observed purple and black smoke swirling around the acolyte as an elegant woman with long raven black hair clear to the ground slowly and seductively stepped out of the smoke toward him.

She was wearing little more than black gossamer wrappings that flowed over her frame like water and revealed all underneath. Her face was painted with elaborate gold makeup and gold markings covered her body. She traced her fingers up her torso, starting at her hips as she neared him.

Her voice was like honey as she spoke, "Oh, but I do love your chair, Vondur."

Vondur lowered his hand and dispelled the magic he had intended to use earlier, "I will never understand the games that the Madu play."

The woman smiled as she approached him. Raising her arms to wrap around his neck as she looked up at him with a pout, "What games do you want to play, my beloved Vondur?"

Vondur glanced down with little interest in the Madu's attempted seduction, "Maybe another time. For now, we have important matters to discuss."

The Madu stepped back and playfully shrugged. "Fine."

Vondur observed as the air spun again with black and purple, not unlike that of storm clouds. Upon the dispersal of the shroud of smoke, the Madu emerged appearing as his Adjudicator.

The Madu grinned mockingly, "What important matters do we have to discuss this evening, Great Archon?"

Vondur was not affected by the Madu in the slightest, "A young Do'earee has been found."

The Madu's face coiled in disgust and its voice sounded hollow and unnatural, "Then we kill it," a slight hiss escaped its lips.

Vondur smiled. "Now that I have your full attention. I have some questions for you."

The Madu walked through a haze of smoke to sit in a chair across from his desk, taking on the vestige of an old man. The Madu sounded as old as it looked. "What wisdom can I bestow upon you?"

Vondur walked around his desk and sat in his chair with the Madu, watching him closely through its elderly-looking eyes.

He sat for a moment and paused before he spoke. "Why is it that the Do'earee keep returning? We eradicate all semblance of them. Confiscate all items pertaining to their memory however, they always return."

The Madu sounded agitated as it responded, "Why does an old house invariably have rats?"

Vondur lifted his hands in a query of the metaphor.

The Madu, in an instant, changed its form to that of a giant black snake with purple glowing eyes. It slithered around the desk until its head rested on Vondur's shoulder. The snake tongue of the Madu flicked at his ear as it spoke. "An old house will always have rats because it is an old house. Burn the house and then the rats have nowhere to go."

Vondur turned his head slightly toward the Madu. "Are you suggesting we burn the entire realm?"

The giant snake coiled around Vondur as it hissed, "Not burn but reshape to our will. We will change this world to that of the image of the Madu. A world of power and control as the Magi see fit."

Vondur smiled as he whispered, "No house... no rats."

The Madu shifted yet again into the figure of the beautiful woman. She was sitting in his lap with her arms wrapped around his neck.

She was looking up at him as she spoke in sultry tones, "You will rule this domain with power, Vondur. You will remake this realm for the Madu... For me."

The Madu leaned up and kissed him.

He found himself returning the kiss. His mind, however, was a thousand miles elsewhere. The power the Madu had promised him would be his. He would use it to consume the Madu. He would be a God.

Chapter Fourteen

Leianna and the others had arrived back at the Soga Burrow with their new allies. Da'ragh had stated that returning to Mr. Sidestreets' establishment was a bad idea. So he had brought them all back to the burrow before they headed to the city of Kronus. Hylon did not handle the Skein pathways very well and had thrown up upon exiting the arch. Torin had handled the trip very well. He strolled through it as casually as he would any door.

Leianna chuckled, thinking about how Telgrid refused to go through the arch at all until Peter helped her through. Telgrid had turned as pale as snow upon entering the arch. When Leianna glimpsed at her, she still appeared unnerved. She was not clear as to if it was the Skein pathway or the fact they were in a Do'earee burrow that had her so shaken.

Leianna had tried to use her magic to heal Peter, but it hadn't worked on him. She had concluded that no matter the intent of the magic, it would have no effect on him. Da'ragh attempted to use magic on him as well and had failed. Da'ragh had even commented on the circumstance that he had never seen such a thing in his lifetime and that they might find a reason as to why in their quick rest in the Soga Burrow.

Leianna had waited until the others had settled and Da'ragh had wandered off to gather healing herbs from his hut for Peter, before she decided to sneak off. She wanted to see if she could speak to Soga again. Soga had disappeared when Da'ragh had shown up, and she wanted to know why.

She had worked her way down some narrow aisles filled with various books, relics, and ancient implements, for which she could not even begin to guess as to how they would even be used. She continued until she came across a large wooden pergola of beautiful design. Deciding that this was a place as good as any to try to contact Soga.

She peered up at the fairy light orbs floating around her and focused on it, thinking of Soga and the heart of the library. She closed her eyes and concentrated. Once she had done so, she could feel the magic reach out. For a moment, she could feel something.

When Leianna opened her eyes, the specter-like shade of Soga was floating in front of her. Soga had soft hues of blue and green, just like the first time she had spoken with it.

Leianna felt excited that her calling out to it had worked. "Soga! You came."

Soga made no movements, and the sound coming from the pillars was soft and soothing. *"Leianna Braun has called, and we have answered. How may we assist you, Do'earee?"*

Leianna grinned as she studied the shimmer of Soga's form floating before her. "I have questions about Da'ragh."

Soga did not make any movements as the sound from the pillars sounded again. *"What is Leianna Braun's inquiry regarding the Do'earee known as Da'ragh?"*

Leianna chuckled, "It is just Leianna, Soga. You don't have to say my entire name."

Soga replied with melodic tones, *"Incorrect, your name is Leianna Braun, apprentice of Da'ragh. Until you achieve your true name and follow your true path."*

Leianna could tell she wasn't getting anywhere with this. "Ok Soga."

Leianna sat down under the pergola on a wide crescent-shaped bench, "You said that Da'ragh was dead before, but that I am also his apprentice."

She watched as Soga floated and remained silent. She furrowed her brow when she realized she had not asked a question. Leianna bit her top lip as she thought to herself, I have got to keep this simple, otherwise Soga won't answer.

Leianna leaned forward. "Is Da'ragh dead?"

The surrounding pillars sounded sorrowful and low, *"This is correct. Da'ragh has passed into the light."*

Leianna thought of a way to word her question, "Soga, who is the man that is currently teaching me Do'earee magic?"

Soga replied more flatly this time, *"Leianna Braun is the Apprentice to Da'ragh. Leianna Braun wields the birch staff. Leianna Braun is learning the ways of the healer."*

Leianna shook her head. She could not figure out why Soga would not comment on her Da'ragh and would only refer to the one whose staff she had gained. Leianna tapped her fingers on the bench next to her as she thought of her next question.

Leianna thought about Peter and decided to ask Soga about his immunity to magic, "Why does magic not work on my friend, Peter? He is the gangly one with the bright red hair and freckles." She lingered for a moment, thinking of his freckles and how, when she was little, she wanted freckles just like her best friend.

The pillars Soga spoke through brought her to attention. *"Peter Finley is of the Anduli blood lineage. The Anduli lineage comes from the remaining bloodline of the King's sworn guardsman. Anduli bloodlines have the curse gift of the king. Words of deception nor the effects of magic can sway them."*

Leianna peered at Soga with her mouth hanging open. She could barely understand what she had just heard. She smiled to herself. This explains a lot about Peter's sense of duty and his eagerness to serve others. She bet that even Peter himself did not know that he was a descendant of the old king's guardsmen.

Leianna gazed up at Soga, "Thank You, I don't have any other questions for you right now Soga."

Soga blinked out of sight.

For a moment she thought she heard a faint whisper from one of the pillars, *"Beware the Reaper."*

Leianna turned in the whisper's direction, "What Reaper?"

The surrounding area was silent, and she shrugged. She had no concept of what a reaper might look like, but if she came across one, she had no intention of sticking around.

Leianna thought of returning to her friends when the fairy lights lit a path before her in their direction. She took her time in getting back to them as she thought about what Soga had said. She wished that she could have a conversation with Soga, but its ability in the way it conveyed information was limited.

Once Leianna had gotten closer, she could hear a ruckus and the clash of steel. She broke out into a run as her mind raced with all sorts of bad scenarios when she came around the corner of a large bookshelf to see Dugan and Torin circling each other with weapons drawn.

Dugan had a mace in one hand and his hand ax in the other. While Torin held his half spear pointed in front of him at Dugan. She couldn't believe they were fighting again. Especially here of all places.

She went to yell out but was drowned out by the loud clang of Dugan's hand ax being knocked aside by the flat of Torin's spear head. Torin deftly side stepped an overhand swing by Dugan's mace and retaliated by stepping forward and hooking Dugan's forward leg with the haft of his spear and yanking Dugan off his feet. Dugan fell backwards onto his back with a crash.

Leianna went to reach out with magic when she heard them both laughing. Torin was holding his hand out to help Dugan to his feet. Leianna let out a sigh of relief as she listened to them discuss tactics.

Torin was still laughing a little as he spoke. "You have power. I will give you that. You just need to learn how to not project your attacks."

Dugan nodded, "It would help if you weren't so damn fast."

Leianna heard Peter speak up as she approached the table he was sitting at. "I want to go next!"

Leianna shook her head as she sat down to his right. She was going to tell him he was still recovering from his injuries to start sparring just yet, when Telgrid sat down to Peter's left with a thump. Leianna had not even seen where she came from.

Telgrid was shooting her a dirty expression when she peered up at Peter and beamed, "Peter, you are still hurt. You need to rest so that you are ready for when the fighting gets real."

Leianna let out a huff and scooted down the bench away from Peter. Peter looked over at her with that big dumb smile of his. "Hey Leianna, you're back. I was wondering where you had gotten off to."

Peter leaned toward her. "I can't protect you if I am not there. Let me know next time and I will go with you."

Leianna was a little irritable. "I can protect myself, Peter."

She felt a little bad as she watched him frown and then look back toward Torin and Dugan. She didn't even know why she was acting this way. It just bothered her the way Telgrid acted around him.

She glanced over at Telgrid, reaching up and wrapping her arm around his. What was she doing? She bit her tongue as she pushed the thoughts aside. It didn't matter, anyway.

She looked up to see Torin and Dugan looking at her with both their eyebrows raised. "What do you guys want?"

Torin and Dugan both smirked. Glancing at each other before both of them looked back at her and in unison both replied with, "Nothing."

She shook her head and stood up. She was going to go find Da'ragh and help him with whatever he was doing.

As she made her way towards Da'ragh's hut, she heard Peter say, "Leianna, would you like me to go with you?"

She turned and gave him a harsh look that she would later feel embarrassed about.

His voice sounded sad as he gazed at the ground. "Sorry, I just thought... never mind."

She turned and hurried out of the area without saying a word. She felt instant regret. He was always kind and looking out for her and she was being unusually cruel towards him. She promised herself that she would apologize to him later.

Leianna approached Da'ragh's hut within the burrow. Soft orange light could be seen from within.

She heard a crash from inside his hut followed by Da'ragh chuckling and exclaiming, "Well, we won't be using that."

Leianna stopped just short of the door and stood up straight before knocking and heading inside. The hut appeared like its usual mess, with piles of random items cluttered all over.

Da'ragh glanced up from a bottle he was smelling. "Hello Leianna, what can I help you with?"

His nose crinkled as he pushed a cork back into the bottle. "It is not that one either. I should really start labeling these things." He picked up another bottle to smell.

She really didn't have a reason for being here other than to get away from Telgrid, who was making her feel uncomfortable around Peter. Which made her furious because they had been best friends since childhood. Telgrid was trying to wedge between them.

She looked up as Da'ragh winced and tears formed in his eyes, "That smells downright harsh... Woo that burned... You know I am not entirely sure what that is." Da'ragh shrugged as he placed the bottle back on the shelf.

Leianna laughed softly. This old man was as lost as the rest of them. She took a breath and decided to ask him some questions.

Maybe he could enlighten her about the ones Soga could not. "You are Da'ragh, right?"

Da'ragh slipped and dropped another bottle onto the ground upon hearing her question. "Well, I guess we will not be using that one either, will we? But to answer your question, I am Da'ragh, among other things."

Leianna was curious, "What other things?"

Da'ragh sat down on a pile of books. "Many things, some good and some bad. I promise you that my intentions mean well, Leianna. I will do everything in my power to prepare you for the path ahead."

Leianna was beginning to wonder if Da'ragh or Soga had the more cryptic answers.

She thought of another question. "Why are your answers so confusing? You seem to avoid the questions as much as answering them?"

Da'ragh appeared lost in thought. "To be honest, Leianna, things are not as clear as they once were. My mind is full of many things and access to that knowledge is not as easily obtained as it was in my younger years."

Leianna nodded. That made sense. He was aging and who knew how truly old he even was?

Da'ragh smiled softly and picked up his staff. "My purpose now is to help you achieve wonderful things. One day you will be teaching Do'earee and I want to pass as much knowledge onto you as I can."

She smiled. "Thank You for helping me understand."

Da'ragh evaluated the shelf of jumbled bottles. He reached over to pick up a small bottle filled with a greenish brown liquid. "Ah! Here it is!" Da'ragh held out the bottle and handed it to Leianna. "This is a healing concoction that will knock Peter unconscious but will leave him as right as rain by morning."

She reached down and pulled out the cork and leaned down to smell. Da'ragh was slightly shaking his head no as she caught a whiff of the most putrid smell of her life. She recoiled as she hurriedly shoved the cork back in. She coughed, as she could almost taste the smell of it.

She took a step from Da'ragh. "Are you sure this stuff won't just kill him outright?"

Da'ragh chuckled, "No, I am afraid not. Though his breath for the next few days may say otherwise."

Leianna laughed as the two left his hut to go administer the medicine to Peter and speak with the others.

Leianna dragged her feet while returning to the others. She couldn't help but feel like she had treated Peter unfairly, for no fault of his own. She was never good at admitting when she was wrong, but she didn't want to put a distance between them.

Da'ragh had matched her pace on the way back and remained silent as they made their way to give Peter the medicine. Leianna was surprised that Da'ragh had located anything in that disaster he called a hut. She took a deep breath as she got closer to the table where everyone was gathered.

Peter was yet again stuffing his face with fruit harvested from the burrow. Hylon was seated across from him. Torin and Dugan were discussing something as they practiced various combative stances, strikes and parries. Telgrid was sitting to Peter's left, practically in his lap, but she looked busy weaving something.

Daragh walked over and took a seat at the corner of the table with a groan. She could make out part of a low grumble of complaint about his old age. She stepped around Da'ragh and sat next to the right of Peter.

Leianna sat the medicine in front of Peter. "Da'ragh found something that should help you heal, since I can't use my magic to help you."

Peter eyeballed the small bottle filled with the dubious liquid. With a shrug and one swift motion, he popped the cork and downed the medicine faster than a sea dwarf given a bottle of rum. Leianna watched in anticipation for Peter to choke or recoil. Peter did no such thing. Instead, he used his finger to wipe and lick up the remaining medicine from the bottle.

Leianna tried not to gag as she detected the aroma of the medicine.

Peter smiled, "That tastes just like my mom's summer squash and mash soup!" He looked at Da'ragh. "Are you sure that was medicine? It tasted delicious."

Da'ragh merely nodded in awe of Peter's resistance to the putrid smell of the medicine. Peter practically licked the bottle spotless before setting it aside. She was trying to find the courage to apologize when she noticed that Peter was smiling at her.

Peter leaned over and whispered to her, "I am sorry I get so protective of you. I totally get that you are under a lot of pressure. Our realm has been turned upside down. The thing is... I care about you and just want you safe. You are my best friend, Leianna. You have always had my back and I just want to have yours. I know I can be oblivious, but I will try to be better for you."

Leianna was dumbfounded. She had come to apologize, and he was the one apologizing to her. She felt her face flush, and she was having difficulty coming up with a response.

Leianna felt her stomach in knots, "Peter... I..." Leianna was stammering as she took a slow breath to refocus, "The thing is Peter, you are one of the most important-"

Leianna was cut off as Telgrid reached over and handed Peter a woven necklace, "Peter, I made this for you."

Leianna peered down at the leather braided necklace that had a small disk in the shape of a spiral made of what looked like plant fibers.

Telgrid was smiling as she spoke to Peter, who seemed excited to receive the gift. "This is what my people call a dream circle. It helps you to dream of home and your loved ones while you are away at sea. They are made and given to those who we wish to return home safely."

Peter held up the disk in the light of the fairy orbs, "This is amazing! I can't wait to see what kind of dreams I have!"

Leianna felt her heart stuck in her throat as she watched him hurriedly put the necklace on.

Peter sounded grateful as he spoke to Telgrid. "Thank you! I won't ever take it off."

Telgrid was beaming as she peered up at him.

Leianna felt numb. She could only stare at her best friend as he turned around to show her the necklace. She forced a smile and a nod as he repeated to her what Telgrid had told him about the necklace. She hated this feeling in her chest and wanted it to go away. Leianna was about to excuse herself from the table when Dugan tapped the table to get everyone's attention.

Dugan waited for everyone's attention and cleared his throat before speaking, "So what is our next plan of action... exactly?"

Da'ragh laid the map they had acquired from Mr. Sidestreets' estate out on the table. He then held out his hand toward Leianna. "The compass... please."

Leianna reached down into the satchel by her side and pulled out the small bronze arrow and handed it to him. Da'ragh placed the relic next to the map as he addressed the group.

"These items will allow us to traverse the Broken Lands far more safely and efficiently than any number of hired Green Cloaks could ever hope to. We, however, are missing one piece of this navigational puzzle and that is a Cipher Stone."

Hylon raised his hand like a child would in a schoolhouse.

Da'ragh smiled as he spoke to him, "You don't have to wait to speak your mind. You are an equal at this table, Hylon."

Hylon slowly lowered his hand and Leianna could hear the lack of confidence in his voice, "What is a Cipher Stone?"

Da'ragh held a hand up to show the relative size of a small object. "It is a stone enchanted by the Do'earee that allows the use of certain magical devices. Without the stone, the map appears like nonsense to those with magical ability. As blank paper to those without."

Da'ragh motioned to Peter with that last statement as to prove his point.

Da'ragh pointed to the map. "Think of this map as a door and the Cipher Stone as the key. A key that works on many types of doors."

Leianna understood, "So without the stone, then the map won't work?"

Da'ragh nodded. "The compass will still guide us in the direction, but we will be moving forward blindly. The map can reveal what awaits us."

Dugan had his hand on his chin, "Life favors the prepared. Having a map that can literally determine what lies ahead and the path to travel would go a long way in helping to keep us alive."

Telgrid had her head tilted to the side as she stared up at Da'ragh. "So, where do we get one of these stones?"

Da'ragh frowned. "Therein lies the problem. The Magi has confiscated the only Cipher Stones that I am aware of. They hold relics of power taken from the Do'earee within the vault labyrinths underneath the Molcainan Magi's central tower."

Dugan appeared as if he had just been slapped in the face, "Oh, is that all? So what do you propose? We just waltz in through one of the outer six towers through hundreds of Magi? And then what?! We just walk past the most powerful Magi in the entire realm and into the most guarded structure in all of Auldryche?!"

The group was silently staring at Da'ragh. They all seemed incredibly nervous.

Leianna sighed. Even she was not thrilled at the idea. Especially after Dugan had just listed off the obstacles they would have to overcome.

Da'ragh chuckled, "Well, that is one option Dugan, but I was thinking we would sneak in the backdoor."

Da'ragh pulled out a small black rod with a carving of a snake coiled around it and gently placed it on the table beside the map.

Leianna did not know what it was. It looked old. "What is that Da'ragh?"

Da'ragh rubbed the bridge of his nose. "This is something that I was hoping to never use again. It is called a serpent wand, or more commonly referred to as a displacement wand. It makes a small tear in reality to allow movement from one location to another."

Leianna lifted her eyebrows, "Like a Skein pathway?"

Da'ragh shook his head slowly. "No, these magical devices use destructive magic and leave scars when used. The Skeins use natural magic to expedite our trip by means of the wind and trees. Whereas the serpent wands force a hole into this existence. It consumes part of the life essence of the user."

Hylon was concerned, "That sounds dangerous."

Da'ragh nodded. "The Magi have no concern for the natural order of things nor for the life of others. That being said, this wand can successfully transport all of us directly into the vault labyrinths."

Torin was smiling, as he chipped into the conversation, "I am all for stealing from the Magi. While we are down there, why don't we take a few other pieces as well?"

Da'ragh shook his head. "The place is dangerous. The Magi have placed guardian beasts and undead in their vault to kill any would be intruders. We will spend as little time in the labyrinths as necessary and get out as quickly as we can."

Torin shrugged. "That doesn't sound like much fun."

Dugan looked at Torin with disbelief. "This isn't meant to be fun. I don't want to be in there any longer than we have to be. The more I learn about this vault, the more the Broken Lands don't seem to be all that bad."

Telgrid spoke up, "What is it you need from the Broken Lands?"

Da'ragh stroked his beard before responding, "We need two things. The most important being the crown of the old king. With the crown in hand, a new heir can be proclaimed and the Magi will lose their ill-gotten hold of Auldryche. The Magi during the wars wanted the Do'earee and the King out of the way so that they could begin their control over the realm. I cannot do it alone."

Leianna reached over and grabbed hold of his forearm. "You won't have to. I have decided to see this through to the end."

Peter chimed in right after her, "If Leianna is in, then I am as well. People deserve to know the truth about the Magi."

Dugan nodded. "I agree with the twerp. People need to be made aware of the lies they are being fed. The truth of Auldryche and its history needs to be told."

Torin was smirking. "I don't know about all that, but it does sound like it's going to be fun, so count me and Hylon in."

Hylon looked surprised, but nodded in agreement.

Telgrid seemed unconvinced. "I will go along with this just so I can keep these two out of trouble... and it doesn't hurt that I get a splendid view along the way."

Telgrid had turned her gaze toward Peter while fiddling with the dark hair at the end of her braid. She was twirling the hair between her fingers. Leianna shook her head as Peter seemed completely oblivious to her meaning.

Da'ragh appeared sad but forced a smile as he spoke, "I have been trying to fight against the Magi on my own for so long... that I have forgotten what it's like to have support. Thank you."

Hylon raised his hand and sat patiently as everyone stared at him, "Oh, sorry, I forgot." He lowered his hand as he glanced curiously at Da'ragh. "What is the other component we would need from the Broken Lands?"

Leianna observed as Da'ragh placed his hands on the table and cleared his throat, "The second item we need is a weapon of the Magi used by their Reapers. It is a terrifying weapon adept at removing someone's soul from their body."

Torin chuckled as he tapped the end of his half-spear on the table. "My spear is capable of doing the same thing."

Da'ragh began to stroke his beard yet again. "True, but these weapons enable the wielder to absorb the souls they separate from the bodies. Once someone is killed by such a weapon, their soul is imprisoned within the wielder and their powers can be drawn upon."

Telgrid crinkled her nose up. "That sounds disturbing. My people believe that soul's return to the cycle of life to be born anew. To be denied passage into your next life would be an atrocity."

Da'ragh nodded. "You are very right indeed. Magi Reapers do just that. They absorb and draw upon the very souls they have imprisoned."

Da'ragh lifted a pointed hand forward. "This is the reason we need such a weapon. With a Magi Reaper's scythe, we could use it to strike down the Reaper and free all the souls they have imprisoned."

Leianna felt the realization hit her like a brick.

She looked at the others and blurted out, "All of those Do'earee souls would be set free... they would re-enter the cycle of life!"

Da'ragh nodded. "That is exactly the point. They would return and start to offset the balance of dark having its grip on the land."

Dugan huffed, "This is a great idea and all, setting Do'earee souls free, I mean. However, that would involve us finding a reaper *and defeating them.*"

Da'ragh nodded, "Yes, a tremendous obstacle to be sure, but until we have the scythe, there is no reason to go looking for such an opponent."

Torin was scratching at the back of his neck. "Couldn't we use the scythe against the Magi more effectively by using the scythe to absorb souls and use their power against them?"

Peter looked uneasy, "That sounds kind of evil Torin..."

Torin nodded, "Well, ya, sure it isn't good... But it would be like fighting fire with fire."

Da'ragh motioned before him. "Fighting fire with fire, as you put it, would light the whole forest ablaze. In other words, using the dark magic of the Magi would only corrupt and spread their dark arts until all were consumed."

Torin looked skeptical as he shrugged. "Just saying I think it's an option."

Da'ragh shook his head, "Even if we were to try to use the scythe as you suggest, you are not Reapers and absorbing souls would tear you apart. The Reapers performed unholy and blasphemous oaths to the dark in order to use these scythes. They cannot be used as you would propose."

Leianna could not imagine trying to control such a weapon in the way Torin suggested. How could they employ such a weapon for good? She craved the freeing of the spirits of the fallen Do'earee, but would the scythe really help?

Telgrid spoke up, "All right, so do we use this snake wand to leave from here?"

Da'ragh shook his head. "The closer we can get to the tower, the better. To use the wand from here would have the potential to kill the user."

Dugan lifted his head back as he groaned, "So we will have to sneak our way through Kronus and get close to the towers..."

Da'ragh nodded slowly. "Yes, but we only need to get relatively close."

Leianna had a thought, "Why can't we use the Skein to access the Labyrinth Vault?"

Da'ragh sighed. "Unfortunately, they have magical barriers in place to prevent Do'earee magic. Leianna, while we are in the vaults, you will not be able to use magic."

She could hear Dugan grumbling under his breath, "This is getting better and better."

Peter gave Leianna a big smile as he leaned over and whispered, "I will keep you safe while in the vault."

Leianna forced a smile. He had already gotten hurt on her behalf more times than she cared for. She looked over at him. "You need to watch out for yourself too, Peter. I don't want to keep watching you get hurt because of me."

Peter nodded, "You got it."

She knew he was lying; he would throw aside his own self preservation in an instant if it meant protecting her. She still felt a little bit better. Hopefully, he would at least think about it.

Telgrid looked over at Leianna. "I will keep an eye on him."

Leianna was not comforted by the statement at all. She was sure that wasn't the only thing she wanted over him.

Hylon spoke up and grabbed her attention, "So Da'ragh, when do we leave for Kronus?"

Da'ragh shrugged. "As soon as all of you are ready to depart."

Everyone looked at her. She had no notion of what to expect in Kronus, but she knew that staying safely here in the burrow was only delaying the inevitable.

Leianna forced a smile, "Why don't we head out first thing tomorrow?"

Everyone was expressing their agreements when Torin spoke up. "No sense waiting around here any longer. I never was the patient type."

Da'ragh tapped his staff on the floor. "It is settled then. Tomorrow we depart for Kronus."

Leianna could hear Dugan whisper under his breath as he got up from the table, "And our unfortunate demise…"

She could see Torin chuckling as he had heard Dugan's comment as well. Leianna watched until everyone had stood up and walked away from the table.

She reached inside her shirt and pulled out her mother's pendant, "I hope I am doing the right thing." Leianna gripped the pendant firmly, "If only you were here, mom. I hope you would be proud of me and what I am trying to do."

She stood up slowly and followed in the way of the others as they began preparing for their journey the next day.

Chapter Fifteen

Peter was the first one up. He could barely contain his excitement. He couldn't believe how good he felt. Whatever was in that medicine had taken away almost all the aches and pains. Peter could not remember the last time he had slept so deeply.

Capital City of the Magi or not, he was thrilled to be going. He could not wait; he had heard stories of the size and grandeur of the city but had never seen it himself.

He quickly gathered his things and as he picked up his grandfather Lamar's sword. Peter took a pause and sat back down on his cot. He slowly withdrew the sword from its sheath and ran his fingertips down the side of the worn blade. The blade was of a good quality steel and had been custom made. It seemed rather plain and did not have any fancy carvings like some swords he had seen. The hilt was longer than the average arming sword. Peter could grip it with both hands. His grandfather had requested that it have a slightly wider blade than that of the average sword. It was unusual, but Peter had always admired it.

He couldn't help but think of his grandfather and all the adventures he must have been on while protecting people. Grandfather had always told him stories from the east coast and fending off Tal'Kor invaders and slavers. He loved his grandfather's stories and missed hearing them. Peter promised himself that he would become a warden worthy of his grandfather's legacy.

Peter held the sword out in front of him as he repeated softly to himself, "I will protect those who cannot protect themselves. I will fight evil whenever it comes to spread darkness and fear."

Peter slid the sword back into its sheath and strapped the sword onto his hip. Peter glanced around at all his friends still sleeping and couldn't help but feel grateful.

Peter smiled, "I have got to be the luckiest guy in the world to have so many great friends."

Dugan was stirring as he turned over on his cot and peered up at him. "What are you talking about, twerp? Why are you awake so early?"

Peter paid no heed to Dugan's questions. Clearly, this was a sign to get moving.

Peter raised his hands and clapped loudly as dozens of fairy orbs lit up and illuminated the area in which they had been sleeping. "Time to get up everybody!"

Peter was met with groans and moans of protest, but he felt it was important to get an early start on the day with everything they had to accomplish.

Peter chuckled, "Ah, come on, guys. We have a long way to go and a lot to get done today."

Dugan sat up in his cot and stretched. "Well, no sense in trying to sleep in."

Peter couldn't stop thinking about all the sights they were going to see in Kronus. He couldn't wait to see what kind of food they served. Peter studied Dugan as he was collecting his belongings, "Do you think we could check out the market before going to the vault, Dugan?"

Dugan huffed, "Peter, we are going to try to keep a low profile and try to get out of there as quickly as possible. Perusing the food or looking for a gift for Leianna really isn't an option."

Peter hadn't even thought of that. He could surely find her a gift of value in a city of that size, for sure.

Peter could barely contain his imagination. "What if we snuck off for just a minute to find-"

Dugan cut him off, "No Peter, we could not."

Peter noticed that Torin had rolled back over and was snoring.

Hylon was staring forward with a numb gaze that indicated he was not yet awake.

Peter was not entirely sure Hylon was even conscious.

Peter watched as Telgrid had already gathered their packs and was making her way over to him. He was relieved to see someone who appeared as excited as he was. She had a smile on her face as she approached him.

Peter gave her a smile. "How did you sleep, Telgrid? I could barely sleep thinking about our trip today."

Telgrid had a sly smile. "It was really cold last night. Maybe next time I could share your cot with you?"

Peter felt confused as last night didn't feel cold to him at all. It always felt rather pleasant down here in the burrows.

He turned and peered down at his cot before looking back at Telgrid. "I don't think we could both fit on that cot, Telgrid. I am sorry you got cold. Next time, I'll try to find you an extra blanket."

Peter found himself a little puzzled when he heard Torin break out snickering as he rolled over on his cot. He wondered if that was how Torin normally woke up.

Torin was chuckling as he sat up in his cot, "Peter, it's your warmth she is after."

Telgrid marched over and attempted to give Torin a slap, which he quickly evaded. Peter couldn't make out what she was growling at Torin in hushed tones when it hit him. Telgrid liked him.

Peter felt his face go flush. No one had ever been interested in him. He was in love with Leianna, though. He panicked a little, trying to figure out a way to tell Telgrid that Leianna and he would be married someday.

Hylon had broken free of his dazed state and had walked over to stand beside Peter without him realizing it.

He was whispering, "She really likes you... But I see the way you look at Leianna. Just be sure you are honest with her. She's a good person."

Peter looked down at the half elf, he sheepishly smiled up at him.

Hylon moved away and back over to his cot to collect his items.

Peter examined Leianna, who seemed rather distant, and had her back to the rest of the group. Peter decided he would go over to her and make sure everything was alright. She had a lot of responsibility and pressure on her shoulders to think about. He wanted to make sure he was being a good friend. He approached and noticed her shove the handkerchief he had made into her belt pouch.

He smiled. "Hey Leianna, are you ready to go to Kronus? I am excited to see the size of the towers and the..." He trailed off as he noticed that she appeared as if she had been crying, "Are you ok Leianna?"

She only nodded her head, and her voice sounded a little shaky to him. "I am fine, Peter. Just a lot on my mind."

Peter understood, she had a lot to overcome with the Magi trying to kill them. He decided to try to make her feel better. "Don't you worry, Leianna, you will do great. Look at how good you are at magic already!"

Leianna chuckled softly at him, "There is that, at least. Don't worry about me, Peter, I will be fine. We better get going."

She picked up her staff and started walking toward Dugan.

Peter bit his lips as he lowered his brow. Something was off and he couldn't put his finger on it. Leianna had felt distant ever since they had returned to the burrow. It had to be all this Magi stuff she was dealing with. Peter promised himself that he would do whatever it took to help his best friend.

He looked up to see that Da'ragh had made his way over to them. Da'ragh was leaning on his staff and started to speak to Leianna, but Peter could not hear what they were saying. He joined the others as they stood waiting for Da'ragh and Leianna to finish.

Dugan leaned over and slapped him on the back, "So, Peter, are you ready for this?"

Peter smiled back. Of course, he was ready. Peter couldn't wait to see the city. "I am so ready! It's exciting to be able to see the city of Kronus!"

Dugan gave him a dirty look. "Not the city you twerp, the labyrinth vault. The vault is the thing you need to be worried about. Who knows what we will have to deal with down there?"

Peter hadn't really thought about the vault, but he wasn't worried either. "It's not anything we can't handle together."

Dugan scoffed and shook his head. "If you say so, twerp."

Torin was standing on his other side. "Personally, I am curious about what is in the vault. Money exchangers have all sorts of valuables they store in their vaults. I can only imagine the things worth taking in a vault belonging to the Magi."

Hylon's voice was barely a whisper, "Or the things that will try to kill and eat us down there."

Torin chuckled as he grabbed his friend by the shoulder, "Stick close to me and you will be fine. Even if we have to abandon the others to die in order to save ourselves."

Dugan give Torin a sideways glare, "I don't think we will be the ones being left for dead down there."

Peter assessed Torin, who had a mischievous smile on his face as Telgrid spoke up. "No one is being left behind. Torin, stop trying to cause problems."

Telgrid glanced over at Peter with a smile. "I won't leave you behind."

Torin and Dugan both laughed at her statement, but Peter thought her sentiment was sincere.

Peter thought the best way to get through this was all together. "I won't leave you behind either Telgrid. You can count on me."

Peter would make sure everyone got out of this unscathed.

Telgrid had given him a kind smile and was playing with her braid when Torin and Dugan started laughing again. Even Hylon was chuckling. Peter just didn't understand what was so funny, but he decided it wasn't important.

Leianna and Da'ragh came over to stand with the group. Da'ragh was standing behind her, leaning on his staff as she began speaking, "So this is the plan. We are going to use the Skein pathways to get us into the outer edges of the city. Once we have arrived, we will work our way inwards, toward the Magi Towers at the city center. As soon as we are close enough, we will activate the displacement rod, gaining us access to the Labyrinths Vault."

Peter thought it was a great idea. He did not see how any of this could go wrong.

Peter looked over after he heard Hylon make a soft groan. Hylon was more pale than usual. Peter gave him a thumbs up, which Hylon slowly and nervously returned with his own thumbs up.

Torin stretched his neck. "I say it's about time we all just get a move on."

Peter couldn't agree more. He was practically teeming with the anticipation of seeing the giant city of Kronus.

Leianna reached into her satchel and produced a small wooden carving in the shape of an acorn. "Well, in that case... Let's get out of here."

Peter watched as Leianna threw the acorn on to the ground, a few paces from where they were all standing. In moments an archway had formed, soft blue light emanated from within.

Da'ragh was the first to step through.

Peter looked again at Hylon, who looked like he was about to get sick. Hylon was incredibly pale and had a cold sweat forming on his brow. Peter could hear him mumble, "Oh no... not this again..."

Peter was about to say something when Dugan stepped forward and grabbed Hylon by the shoulder. "I find it's easier to stomach if I just close my eyes when going through it."

Dugan was not looking very enthusiastic about going through the archway, either.

Peter decided to try to cheer them up. "I think it's fun! Just think of how far we are traveling and in how short a time. We are traveling thousands of miles by using old Do'earee magic. Who knows what kinds of places we could show up in?" He was confused to see that not only did Hylon not look any better, but Dugan was also starting to look a little pale.

He shrugged and watched as Torin chuckled and clutched Hylon by the hand before passing through the archway portal, basically dragging him behind him.

Dugan closed his eyes and rushed in next.

The moment he was about to step through the archway, he felt Telgrid grab him by the hand.

Peter turned to find her beaming up at him. "This is for good luck, Peter."

Peter could not believe her strength as she pulled him down to give him a kiss. He tried to pull away, but felt like a puppy in the arms of an excited child. There was no way he could pull free. Peter felt his face turn bright red as she let him go, and his mind was a jumble of confusion.

He stammered as he spoke, "Wow... you're strong..."

Telgrid smiled at him as she walked toward the archway. "Thank you."

Peter watched as she flipped her braid before entering the archway and passed through it. Peter paused for just a moment before following behind her. How was he going to get out of this one?

Before entering the portal, he murmured to himself, "I guess I am going to have to find a solution. Who knew being this handsome would be so troublesome?" Peter smirked and stood up straight as he marched through the archway.

Peter used his hand to shield his eyes. The late morning sun was high in the clear blue sky. The sun's rays felt warm on his skin as the crisp fall season air bit at the tip of his nose. Once his eyes adjusted to the brightness of being outside, he could see the others before him.

Hylon was doubled over and heaving as Torin was rubbing his back and laughing. The others were huddling together as they looked off into the distance ahead. He looked up past them and could barely believe his eyes. The city stretched before him as far as he could see. This made Oakbridge look like a mere speck compared to the expansiveness of Kronus that blanketed the area.

Off in the distance, he could make out the Magi towers that rose as high as the clouds. He looked to see that they were in a less populated area, but up ahead, he could see people moving about between the buildings.

Peter yelled out, "This is amazing!"

Dugan spun around and shushed him through gritted teeth, "Keep your voice down twerp. Do you want to announce our arrival to everyone in Kronus?"

Peter mouthed sorry before looking at the horizon littered with buildings of various sizes. He could tell that even from here, the buildings closest to the Magi towers were beautiful in design. They appeared to be what looked like white marble that glinted in the sunlight.

He spoke softly to himself as he stood with his hands on his hips, "One day they will have parades in my honor."

Peter nodded his head as he imagined being a decorated Warden in the new king's forces. He could see it now in his mind; flowers and gifts being showered down around him and his fellow Wardens. They would be greeted by the people with cheers and song.

Peter smiled and nodded his head, thinking of Leianna as his wife. He whispered to himself, "One day, I will be a hero just like my granddad was."

Telgrid gave a sharp whistle and knocked him out of his imaginary parade. Peter looked up to see the others walking toward the city center. He quickly ran to catch up.

Peter thought that this place was marvelous, or at least that is what he had originally thought upon their arrival. He had a much different view now that they had been walking the streets for the last few hours. The smell was unpleasant and homeless and diseased were huddled in almost every alleyway.

Peter could not wrap his mind around why so many people walked around with sour looks on their faces. After being gripped at for saying hello to a few strangers, he had given up trying to be friendly to the city residents. Everyone seemed depressed and agitated. He thought that after being around so many marvelous things, it must leave people jaded. Looking up at the glistening towers as he shook his head. He couldn't imagine ever ceasing to be amazed by such wondrous things.

The group had been rather silent as they marched down the streets. The further they got, the better it looked. People seemed less poor and buildings appeared nicer the closer they got to the city center.

He peered over at a cart that was selling meat chunks on kabobs when he heard his stomach growling. He reached down to grab his coin pouch when he felt someone grab his right hand. Peter turned to see that Hylon was shaking his head while preventing him from getting his coin.

Hylon leaned in and whispered, "I wouldn't eat that if I were you."

Peter lowered his eyebrows in confusion, "Why not? It smells good, and we didn't eat breakfast this morning."

Telgrid leaned in to whisper to the left of him, "That is rat meat, Peter."

Peter was shocked. Why would people eat rats? Didn't they have any pork, beef, or goat?

Peter thought on it for a moment before leaning in to whisper to Telgrid, "Is rat meat really that bad?"

Telgrid turned slowly to stare up at him with a puzzled look on her face, "Yes, Peter, it's that bad."

Peter would take their word for it, but he felt a little curious about what it tasted like.

Peter tapped Leianna on the shoulder, "Do you think we could stop somewhere to get something to eat?"

Leianna nodded, "I am a bit hungry myself."

She nudged Da'ragh before she started speaking, "Is there a place we could go to get some food?"

Leianna looked back at the cart selling rat meat kabobs, "Is that safe to eat?"

Da'ragh's voice was low but he could hear him clearly as he answered Leianna's question, "Up ahead is the Merchants Quarter. We should be able to find a place with a decent hot meal for purchase."

Peter was surprised to see Da'ragh's pace quicken, "It has been quite some time since I was last here, but I knew of a place that served stew inside of big fresh bread bowls."

His stomach growled upon hearing Da'ragh's description of the food. Peter couldn't wait to share this information with his father. They would make a lot of money selling soup inside of bread.

Dugan had moved so that he was walking beside him, "Peter, try not to start a conversation with everyone we meet here. Remember that we are trying to go unnoticed."

Peter nodded, "Doesn't that bread bowl thing sound delicious, Dugan?"

Dugan smiled slightly, "It does, but I still don't think it will be as good as your dad's honey oat loafs, straight from the oven."

Peter chuckled as he heard Dugan let out a low moan. His dad's honey oat was the best. He looked forward to eating a whole loaf of it once they returned to Oakbridge.

They continued to walk for quite some time before Torin had moved his way to walk beside Da'ragh. Peter could scarcely make out part of what Torin was saying.

Torin was speaking in a hushed whisper, "... they have been following us for the last hour or so."

Peter got a little closer so he could hear the conversation more clearly.

Da'ragh was nodding to Torin, "I saw them as well. We should use caution, but for now, we will act like we haven't noticed them."

Peter could see Torin tense up, "There are only two of them. I could take care of them without anyone noticing."

Da'ragh chuckled softly, "We do not even know if they are hostile yet. Let's hold off on killing anyone just yet."

Torin shrugged and resume a more relaxed posture.

Peter looked back behind them and didn't notice anyone following them. There were quite a few people on the street, but it wasn't crowded by any means. Upon examining those near them, he wondered what Torin and Da'ragh were talking about. He couldn't imagine anyone finding them inside a city of this size.

Leianna had started whispering to Da'ragh, "I see another one up ahead."

Hylon was right behind Leianna as he whispered to her, "I see two up ahead."

Peter looked over at Telgrid, who had a focused look about her. Her eyes were intently searching in the same direction as Hylon was.

Peter tilted his head and strained his eyes to see what the others were noticing that he wasn't. He couldn't see anyone or anything out of the ordinary.

Dugan was speaking slowly and softly, "What should we do? This bend up ahead in the street looks unoccupied and a perfect place for an ambush."

Da'ragh just kept his pace steady, "Everyone be prepared for the worst."

Hylon sounded anxious, "I think they are intending to rob us."

Torin was chuckling softly, "It's about time something interesting happened. I was growing tired of walking."

Peter started to look around again but still couldn't see anything out of place or anything that indicated they were being followed, let alone about to be mugged.

Peter rested his hand on the pommel of his sword as they all made their way around the bend in the street. He could barely believe his eyes as a group of men had gathered, blocking the path forward. He looked behind to see more men block the path back the way they had come from.

Da'ragh raised his left hand up in greeting, "How can we help you fine, sirs?"

Peter watched cautiously as one of the men stepped forward. He looked haggard, with a bushy mustache, and was wearing a leather jerkin covered in iron studs. The man had a short sword on his hip and was chewing on a toothpick as he took his time approaching them.

The man had a sharp look in his eyes and a dead smile as he spoke in a hoarse voice, "The thing is, we here are toll collectors and you lot haven't paid your fees."

Da'ragh went to reach for his coin purse when Torin stepped forward with his long-bladed half-spear in hand.

Peter reached over to grab hold of his sword and prepared to draw it at the first sign of violence. The men were fairly well armed, but none of them seemed all that tough. He was sure that he could take any one of them.

The man with the mustache spat out the toothpick, "Listen boy, this is going to go one of two ways. Either you give us coin, or we take the coin... and your lives."

Torin laughed in a way that made Peter a little uncomfortable. Torin spoke assertively at the mugger, who had claimed to be a toll collector. He strolled slowly up towards the man as he spoke, "Actually, there is a third way and it's the one you are going to take if you want to stay alive. You are going to give us YOUR coin and run away like scared little piggies."

The man turned red as his face twisted in anger, and Peter knew that this would not end well.

Da'ragh raised his hands, "Everybody just calm down. We can pay our way. There is no need for bloodshed."

The man with the mustache was baring his teeth as he growled and yelled out, "New offer, the coin and this one's life!"

Peter watched in awe as the man went to draw his sword but was stopped short by the heel of Torin's boot. Torin had kicked the hilt free of the man's hand and knocked the sword back into its scabbard.

Peter drew his blade in preparation for the fight, but before his sword could clear his own scabbard, Torin had swung his half spear at the mustached man. His spear slashed in an upward arch, catching the bottom of the man's chin and splitting his face in two clear up past his eyes. A jet of red blood sprayed outwards as the man attempted to scream but came out in a muffled gurgle.

Peter had barely processed what he was seeing when Torin sidestepped and threw his half-spear through the chest of another mugger that had started running toward him. The blade caught the man square in the chest and knocked him off his feet with the impact. Torin reached down and pulled the short sword from the mustached man's side, dragging the blade along the man's chest and across his neck before kicking the dying man to the ground.

Dugan had already moved forward and caught one of the charging muggers upside his temple with a heavy swing of his mace. Peter grimaced as he heard the crunch and saw the man's teeth scatter on the ground. The man fell down in a slump. He was dead before he hit the ground.

Peter turned with his sword drawn just in time to watch Telgrid swing her giant mallet into the knee of one of the muggers behind them. The man crashed to the ground in a pained scream as Telgrid lifted her hammer and brought it down on the man's head in a sickening smash.

Peter realized Hylon had moved to hide behind him as a rather large mugger took a swing with a wood cutter's ax. Peter leaned back as the edge of the ax head flew right in front of his face. The ax had barely missed by a hair's width.

Peter wasted no time in retaliating and brought the point of his blade upward in a lunge toward the man's stomach. Peter could feel the tip of his sword puncture the man's intestines before withdrawing it and sending another thrust that caught the large man in the ribs. The man grunted and stumbled backwards as Peter slashed his sword forward in a wide arch. The man attempted to stop his sword with the handle of his ax but had misjudged and the edge of Peter's sword drew across the man's forearm, nearly severing it completely. The man screamed and recoiled, but Peter was quick with another slash in the opposite direction. The blade went across the man's throat, sending a spray of red over Peter's face and his clothes. The man flew backwards and spasmed on the ground momentarily before he stopped moving entirely.

He was breathing heavy; this was the first man he had ever killed. He was stunned. This was not how he imagined his first kill would be. He had always thought his first kill would be in a battle against the Tal'Kor.

Peter didn't even notice when the remaining street thugs began running. He turned with his blade pointed forward in a jab when Torin had stepped up behind him. His sword met the cross-guard of Torin's short sword with a loud clang of clashing steel.

Torin smiled, "Not quite fast enough, Peter. Better luck next time."

Peter was still feeling a little out of breath and was trying to process the death of the man he had just killed. "Sorry... I thought... sorry..."

Torin looked over at the body as he knocked the tip of Peter's blade away from him with a simple slap of the flat of the blade of his own sword, "Not bad, Peter, you messed him up pretty good."

Peter tried to respond, but just felt numb.

Torin must have noticed he was uncomfortable because his tone changed completely. He grabbed his shoulder and leaned in, "It was either them or us, Peter. Killing a man is no simple thing, but it gets easier with time."

Peter forced a nervous grin, "I suppose you're right, Torin."

Torin smiled as he nodded and turned around to speak with Hylon, "I see you didn't help with the fight... again."

Hylon looked up shamefully, "I tried, but I jus-"

Torin interrupted him, "I am just giving you a hard time. Leave the killing to me. Fighting is why I am here, that and keeping you safe."

Peter could not understand how Torin took all of this so lightly. They had just killed all these men. They would have killed them for their coin. He just hated how people had to fight. He was supposed to be fighting evil and dragons. Not people down on their luck.

Peter took a deep breath as he cleaned the blood from his sword. His hands were shaking. He felt terrible and was sure that his granddad had never been nervous about going into battle. He promised himself he would steel his resolve. No more would he hesitate. If he was to be a Warden of any worth like his granddad, he would have to come to terms with killing.

Peter sheathed his sword as he noticed Leianna holding her arm. Blood was dripping between her fingers as she applied pressure. Peter felt panic wash over him as he ran and slid over to her side.

Peter could hear the panic in his own voice, "What do you need me to do, Leianna?"

Her face was twisted in pain, "Just apply pressure here Peter."

Peter quickly grabbed her arm and applied pressure as blood tried to pour from a long gash in her bicep. Peter was breathing rapidly as Da'ragh kneeled down next to them.

He was stroking his beard, "What are you doing, Leianna?"

She was speaking through her clenched teeth as she responded, "Trying to stop the bleeding and bandage the wound... care to help."

Peter recognized the tone in her voice. She sounded extremely angry.

Da'ragh shook his head, "Not particularly."

Leianna looked at him in shock, "What?!"

Da'ragh shrugged, "I am still confused as to why you haven't healed yourself yet."

Leianna's face went from anger to confusion, "What in all the realms are you talking about!? Stop babbling and help me stop the bleeding!"

Peter could see that she was losing a lot of blood, "Da'ragh, use your magic to heal her."

Da'ragh smiled and shook his head, "I do not have the ability to use healing magic but Leianna does. Focus, Leianna, and heal yourself."

Leianna looked frustrated as she took a deep breath and closed her eyes. She hovered the palm of her other hand and held it over her wound. He watched as her face relaxed. It was almost as if she was sleeping.

Peter had completely forgotten what he was doing as he stared at her. She was so incredibly beautiful. She had full lips and Peter felt his face flush as she slowly opened her eyes and looked at him.

Leianna started smiling, "You can let go now, Peter."

Peter had not even noticed that she had stopped bleeding. He slowly removed his blood-soaked hands to reveal that her wound had completely healed, with no sign that it had ever existed.

Peter was completely amazed, "Wow, Leianna, that is incredible!"

Da'ragh smirked, "Now that you are healed, we should probably be on our way before the authorities arrive."

Peter couldn't tell by the tone of his voice, but Da'ragh had the look of being bothered.

Peter helped Leianna to her feet, "Are you ok Leianna?"

Leianna nodded, "A guy came at us from the side and I wasn't able to avoid being hit. Torin made short work of him, though."

Peter followed her gaze to one of the bodies on the ground. He shivered a little. The dead man's body on the ground was missing both of his hands and his head was twisted backwards. He dreaded to think of what maneuver Torin had performed that would end in such carnage. Peter looked up to see Hylon looting the bodies as Torin attached the mustached man's sword to his hip and retrieved his spear.

Peter glanced behind him to see Dugan handing Telgrid an iron war hammer. Telgrid swung the hammer a couple of times in the air before tossing aside her large wooden mallet.

Da'ragh let out a sigh, "Now that you got your blood lust sated Torin. I suggest we make haste out of here before the authorities arrive, or the ones who escaped return with friends."

Everybody silently agreed as they hurriedly left the area.

Leianna held out a piece of cloth as the group made their way down the back streets, "Better try to clean up some of that blood, Peter. You are looking rather grisly."

Peter looked at his hands, which were coated in Leianna's blood. He went to clean his hands when Leianna took the cloth back from him and began wiping his face. He remembered the man he had killed earlier and realized the blood must have gotten all over his face. Peter felt glum. He would make sure he was better prepared for the next time he had to take someone's life. He wasn't sure how he would do it, but he would try.

Leianna gave him a halfhearted smile, "Well, you are looking better now."

Peter looked up, "Really?"

Leianna shook her head and laughed, "No, you look terrible. How did you get so much blood on you?"

Peter shrugged. He looked back at Torin and Dugan and neither looked like they had been in a fight. Telgrid barely had any blood on her trousers, and Hylon looked clean. Peter looked down at his own clothes and cringed. He looked like he had been slaughtering livestock all day. He had blood all over his clothes, "This is going to be a lot of work to clean up."

Leianna was laughing softly as she nodded, "I think the best bet is to throw you in the nearest river."

Peter looked over at Leianna, "Does it bother you that people have been dying around us?"

Leianna averted her eyes and looked to the ground, "More than you know, Peter. This is not what I expected it to be. I just hope we are doing the right thing. I want to do the right thing."

Peter nodded, "I think we are. There are bound to be those that can't see what we are trying to do. It's not their fault."

Leianna smiled softly in agreement, but remained silent.

Peter thought to himself that she must be trying to wrap her mind around the deaths as well.

He found that everyone had remained silent for the most part as they worked their way deeper into the city. The closer they got to the towers, the more incredibly immense they appeared. Peter looked up and couldn't make out the top of the towers any longer. He let out a long exhale. He couldn't imagine how many Magi must be inside them and to think that they were all enemies of the Do'earee.

Peter shifted his gaze to Leianna, who was also looking up at the towers. He gritted his teeth. His best friend was Do'earee now. That meant all those Magi wanted her dead.

Peter found himself looking up at the towers with resentment. If they meant to harm Leianna, then every Magi in that tower would have to get past him first. He didn't care who they were. If someone intended to hurt any of his new friends, they would answer to him. Peter felt his hand reflexively grab hold of the hilt of his sword.

He loosened his grip and looked at the horizon. They had been walking for most of their time here in the new capital, and it was now late afternoon. He couldn't believe the size of this city; they had walked for an entire day and still not made their way into the city center where the towers stood.

Da'ragh coughed to get the group's attention before he stopped and turned around to face them.

Da'ragh looked at each of them before speaking, "This is the place that I was speaking of. It is known as the Drunken Roustabout. With any luck, my friend still owns the place. While we are inside, there will be no bloodshed and no fighting." Da'ragh stood staring directly at Torin as he spoke.

Da'ragh continued, "I will inquire within about availability. I alone will speak for our small band of outcasts. Once we have eaten and I have paid for your rooms... you all will retire and rest for the evening. Trust no one and avoid telling anyone where you are from."

Peter could hear groaning from Torin and Hylon. He would have been unhappy to hear this news as well, but after their encounter with the muggers, he was more than just a little relieved to have an excuse to stay off the streets.

Da'ragh looked at Leianna, and Peter could barely hear him. He was speaking so softly, "It is far too risky to use magic. It's highly illegal in this city and people here would not hesitate to turn you in for the reward. Using magic would be the fastest and surest way to bring the Magi down on us."

Da'ragh let everyone know to stay put while he went to go check on the place to see if room and board were indeed available. Peter watched as he headed toward a structure not too much larger than the inn back in his hometown of Oakbridge.

It seemed well cared for and he could smell the very familiar aroma of freshly baked bread emanating from inside the building. Peter could hear his stomach rumbling and he hoped it wouldn't be too much longer until they got a hot meal.

Peter felt someone grab his arm while they waited and was expecting to see Leianna, but instead saw Telgrid smiling up at him. She had a devious look in her eye as she pulled him down to whisper in his ear, "I can think of a few ways we can occupy ourselves for the evening."

Peter nodded, "I agree. It's good to know what we are going to do ahead of time. Our limits and abilities will be tested, and we will need to be prepared for anything. We don't know how long we will have to be here, and we should take advantage of the time we have."

Peter was a little confused and wondered if he had misunderstood her message. She had turned slightly red and looked far too thrilled for just preparation and planning. He couldn't blame her for being excited, though. This would be quite the adventure with their excursion into the Magi's vault.

He tried not to look her in the face because she wouldn't stop smiling and staring at him. He couldn't seem to break free of her grasp, either. Peter looked around him for assistance, but everyone else seemed focused on the door of the Drunken Roustabout, awaiting Da'ragh to emerge.

Da'ragh came out of the entrance and waved the group in.

Peter was relieved and couldn't wait to get something to eat. The moment that Da'ragh had opened the door, Peter was met with a waft of scents, some good and some not so much. The one smell that Peter immediately recognized was the smell of cinnamon.

He remembered having cinnamon bread once as a kid when a trader had come through with a sack of the stuff. His father had baked them bread with cinnamon in it and it was one of the best things he had eaten in his entire life. Peter could feel his mouth water in anticipation. If they had cinnamon, then he could only imagine the quality of food they had inside.

The group drifted their way inside. Peter nearly hit his head on the top of the arch of the doorway and wondered why the door was so short.

Once inside, his question was answered almost immediately. This was a dwarven establishment. It was clear to Peter why the building looked so small from the outside. It was built down into the ground.

He stepped over to the railing and peered down; he could barely believe what he was seeing. It appeared like a small town had been built underneath the city of Kronus. Floor after floor going downward, connected by a complicated network of stairways and ladders. They had placed Glimmerstone within the carved pillars and walls, which illuminated the structure in a soft orange hue.

He had heard stories of such stones when he was a kid. The stone dwarf wizards, known as Stonespeakers, used magic to make the stones sing, which produced light. From where Peter was standing and looking down, the Glimmerstones looked like bright orange jewels that sent light in all directions.

He could hear the busy bustle, singing and hearty laughs of the stone dwarves from below. Peter had always found the stone dwarves fascinating. With their elaborate and decorated stonework, all the way down to their hard work ethic, and devotion to family.

Sometimes dwarf traders would travel south through Oakbridge on their way to Markagra and he would get to hear their stories. The stone dwarves hailed from the Crimson Massif and ruled the area from their massive underground cities. Peter looked in awe. To hear the stories was one thing, but to behold such work had left him in awe.

Dugan let out a sharp whistle of amazement, "Now this is impressive. I have read about places like this but I have never seen stonework like this in person."

Torin shrugged, "Looks about the same as the stonework in Markagra if you ask me. Only difference is that no one has stolen those glowing rocks out of the walls yet."

Da'ragh motioned for them to follow him as he led the group down the steep steps down onto the first floor. Once down, Peter could see that each floor must stretch out in almost every direction under Kronus.

They followed Da'ragh until they stepped up to a long stone counter covered in paperwork and architectural blueprints. An old dwarf with thick, wiry gray hair looked up from behind the counter.

Her voice was deep but soothing, "Well I'll be... I can't imagine what sort of nonsense has dragged you back to the city, old friend."

Peter watched as the dwarf woman walked around the corner to give Da'ragh a firm handshake. She was smiling as she took her other hand and looped a thumb down into the front of her thick leather belt. She was stocky and looked like condensed muscle, only the lines and gray hair giving an indication of old age.

She seemed happy to see Da'ragh, "So how long has it been, old friend?"

Da'ragh chuckled, "Oh, I would say, longer than I care to remember."

The dwarf woman let out a soft laugh before turning to look at the rest of the group, "So what's with all these young folk? You taking to collecting pets now?"

Da'ragh shook his head as he laughed, "Actually, no, we are here in Kronus on official business, Opal."

Peter figured that this must be the host Da'ragh was speaking of. This Opal seemed kind despite her rough looking exterior. Peter thought she looked more like a labor foreman rather than that of an innkeeper. She even had various tools on her belt.

Opal smiled and nodded her head, "I have to admit this group looks of better quality and morals than the usual group you would take company with."

Peter thought that was an odd thing to say before he noticed the tables off to the right filled with all kinds of people and races eating and drinking. This was a much different sight to the streets when they had first arrived in Kronus.

The streets on the outside of the city were impoverished and unkempt. Whereas the people here seemed in uplifted spirits, and the area as a whole appeared to be well maintained. He could smell the food and his stomach growled yet again, letting him know that not eating all day was completely unacceptable.

Opal had apparently heard the grumblings from his stomach, "It looks like your friends could use a good hot meal and some warm beds. Buska!"

She had yelled out and Peter watched as a young dwarf ran from behind the counter. He had a short messy brown beard and mop like hair that was tied behind his head in a thick leather band.

The young dwarf had a big smile and wore an apron covered in flour as he spoke with Opal, "How can I be of service Opal?"

Peter watched as Opal motioned toward him and the rest of his group, "These fine young people are in need of your fine food."

Buska nodded and motioned for them to follow.

Peter looked back as they all made their way toward one of the large tables. Da'ragh had stayed behind to talk with Opal. He shrugged, as he would have done the same if he had been away from Leianna for any amount of time.

Buska led them to a table and told them he would return shortly with food and drink. Peter couldn't wait to partake of the delicious food he was smelling. He noticed that as soon as Telgrid took a seat next to him, Leianna veered away and took a seat at the far end of the table by Hylon.

Peter frowned. He wasn't sure why she had become so distant at times. He was going to say something when Telgrid shivered. Peter looked over to see that Telgrid looked uncomfortable.

He could tell she seemed a little anxious, "What's wrong Telgrid?"

She forced a smile as she looked back at him, "I don't appreciate being underground."

Peter found this odd, "But you're a dwarf, right?"

Telgrid seemed a little irritated by his statement, "I am a sea dwarf Peter. My people find their home on the open seas and traveling the oceans, in exploration. We don't enjoy being underground in caves and hovels."

He had almost forgotten that although the stone and sea dwarves were both dwarves, their cultures could not be any more different.

Telgrid looked at Peter with a grin, "My people are beautiful and graceful while our very distant underground relatives are just a bunch of rock munchers."

Peter chuckled, she wasn't completely wrong. stone dwarfs were stockier and far more muscular than their seafaring cousins. Telgrid appeared to have a far leaner frame. He could tell that her shoulders and hips were not as wide as the stone dwarfs either. sea dwarves were a very hardy people and known for their skill in commerce and naval capabilities. He did not have as much experience with them growing up in Oakbridge as he did with the stone dwarves.

He slowly examined her body and couldn't help but admire the muscular definition when he realized he was staring at her. Telgrid was staring right back at him when she gave him a wink and bit her bottom lip. Peter felt his face flush bright red and quickly looked forward. He hoped she didn't think he was staring on purpose.

Peter forced out an exhale as Buska brought out a giant circular serving tray with giant bread bowls on plates. Buska handed them out to everyone before another dwarf came up with a large iron pot and began pouring a hearty stew into each of the bowls right in front of them.

Peter was ready to dive in when Buska clapped his hands together, "Enjoy my friends! If you need anything, please don't hesitate to ask."

Peter picked up the wide wooden spoon and shoveled in a giant bite. The heat burned his mouth, but the flavor was amazing.

Dugan began laughing, "It's not going anywhere Peter. Maybe you should try cooling it down and tasting it before scarfing the whole thing down."

The group laughed and Peter joined in. He was just so hungry, and it smelled so good.

They spent the first part of the evening eating over meaningless chatter. The group was doing a good job of unwinding after the trouble they had run into earlier. Da'ragh had made his way over to join them after he spent a good portion of time in conversation with Opal.

Peter was wondering what tomorrow would bring when they attempted to access the vault. He couldn't wait to see them himself. Who knew what kinds of wonders they would come across?

After looking around the table, he couldn't imagine anyone else he would rather have by his side. Everyone was skilled in their own way and brought something to the table. Peter felt like he could really count on everyone here. Torin talked tough, but he believed he really cared on the inside. If what Da'ragh was telling them was true, then this place would be quite the test. He couldn't help but feel confident. They had overcome everything so far and he didn't see how this Labyrinth Vault would be any different.

Da'ragh tapped his staff on the ground to grab their attention. Everyone quieted down as he began to speak, "Alright, we should get a good night's rest. We will head out first thing tomorrow. Everyone be here early so that we get a big breakfast before we undertake this endeavor."

Dugan had just finished his drink when he looked over to Da'ragh, "Is there anything we need to expect or prepare for specifically?"

Da'ragh shook his head, "I am not sure what to expect from the vault. The place was created long before the Magi and was merely used by them. The Magi Towers and the Labyrinth Vault beneath them were constructed during the age of the King before the war and the Cataclysm."

Dugan looked baffled, "The Magi have always taught that they constructed the towers. I guess we can notch that up to yet another lie of theirs."

Da'ragh nodded his head, "I am afraid so. They have twisted history to fit their agenda. They have done away with all texts that paint them in any sort of negative connotation. Over the generations people have begun to forget the truth. Those that remember are either too afraid or incapable of doing anything about the fraud that is presented as truth. The Magi seek to control the people of Auldryche entirely through manipulation of the body, mind and soul."

Dugan exhaled sharply, "Well, isn't that just fantastic."

Torin had a smirk on his face, "I fail to see where this changes anything. People have always been out for themselves and I don't see that getting better any time soon."

Peter looked over and could see Leianna was agitated.

She was insistent in her speech, "There has to be a better way Torin. There has to be a way and we will find it."

Torin appeared completely unmoved by her statements, "If you say so, but with what I have seen... people just don't care about anyone but themselves."

Hylon spoke up in an uneasy voice, "I care about you Torin... and Telgrid too. I also care about Da'ragh, Leianna, Dugan and Peter."

Hylon motioned to each one as he spoke, "They forgave me when I led them into an ambush and helped to rescue you and Telgrid when Mr. Sidestreets was trying to use us. They showed all of us kindness without asking anything in return. Now we are friends. So, I would say you are wrong Torin... People do care about others."

Torin stared at Hylon with wide eyes before he shrugged and let out a chuckle, "I guess I am wrong... Wouldn't be the first time."

Peter watched as Hylon hid his face by looking down and letting his hair fall in front. Peter could tell that Hylon was smiling even with him trying to hide his face underneath all that hair.

Peter looked about the table and could see everyone was smiling, "Hylon is right though, we are all friends now and we got each other's backs."

He felt Telgrid hug his arm and saw Leianna avert her gaze. Peter wasn't sure what he said but Leianna seemed upset again. He decided he would try to talk with her later about what was bothering her. Peter hoped he hadn't done something that would trouble her. She was his best friend in the entire realm.

Everyone looked over as Opal walked up and threw a pile of large iron keys on the table. Peter listened intently as she spoke.

He couldn't help but wonder how the Stonespeakers sounded when they sang to the rocks to get them to move. Peter had even heard stories of Stonespeakers entering a trance-like state to put their souls into the bodies of large stone golems in defense of their mountain fortresses. Peter thought that their singing must be amazing to hear firsthand.

Opal looped her thumbs into her thick leather belt, "I expect all of you to be on your best behavior while you are in my halls. The rooms are on the third floor and match the numbers on the keys. You all can decide who stays where. Leave the keys on my counter when you leave in the morning."

Opal turned to walk away when she stopped suddenly, "May the light of the grove guide you home." She then continued on her way and disappeared around a stone column.

Peter noticed Da'ragh was smiling at Leianna, "The Do'earee still have friends. They are merely hiding, but once you expose the darkness for what it is, you will see that you have allies everywhere and in the most unusual of places."

Leianna began smiling again. He loved her smile. He couldn't imagine anyone not liking her smile. It had always improved his days after seeing her happy.

Everyone started grabbing keys and discussing who would stay where. When Telgrid tapped a key on his upper thigh. He turned to see she was smiling suggestively up at him.

Peter went to say he didn't think that was a good idea, when she interrupted, "Looks like we get a room all to ourselves tonight."

Peter went to protest when he noticed Leianna in a huff snatch up a key and march off toward the stairs. Peter narrowed his eyes and frowned a bit; he didn't understand what was going on. Peter turned to face Telgrid whose face looked so deeply flushed red that it drowned out her tanned skin.

Peter stammered, "Telgrid I... well the thing is that... um..."

Dugan interrupted, "Telgrid, Peter is staying in my room tonight. The whole point of getting rested before tomorrow, is actually resting."

Telgrid's face turned from longing to anger almost instantly. He watched as she looked at Dugan with fire in her eyes.

Dugan raised his eyebrows, "I don't know about you, but having everyone refreshed and prepared for tomorrow's unknown dangers would put me at ease."

Telgrid was speaking low and through her teeth, "Oh, I assure you Dugan that Peter will be quite refreshed come tomorrow morning."

Peter tried to calm her down. "I think Dugan is right. We need to prepare ourselves for tomorrow and if I am not rested then how can I protect everyone?"

Telgrid's face relaxed a bit as she looked at him, "Protect everyone?"

Peter nodded his head, "I am going to be a Warden some day and I intend to protect those I care about. Who knows what kind of trouble is waiting for us down there? I want to be at my best when protecting those I love."

Telgrid's eyes widened, and she had a giant smile on her face, "Those you love... I understand Peter. You get rested and I will do the same to make sure I can take care of those I love as well."

Peter nodded his head, "I am happy that you understand, Telgrid. I will see you first thing tomorrow morning."

Dugan and Torin were both laughing. He didn't understand why they were though.

They all got up and walked down to the third floor as they made their way toward their respective rooms. Dugan was still chuckling under his breath. "I was trying to help you back there, but now I am not so sure you want help."

Peter turned his head in confusion, "What do you mean Dugan? I thought I got my point across."

Dugan began laughing again, "I am sure you will figure it out. Eventually."

Dugan used the key to unlock the door and headed inside. Peter stopped in the doorway to look for Leianna but she must have already entered her room by now.

He watched as Hylon and Torin entered another room. Torin sounded like he was still laughing to himself.

Peter looked down the hall and saw that Telgrid had stopped at her door. Peter smiled and waved when Telgrid smiled back.

Then hurriedly walked over to Peter, "I know you need your rest for protecting me and all... but this is for good luck and to give you something to think about for later."

Peter didn't have any time to react when Telgrid reached up to grab his collar and yanked him down. Peter went to pull free when Telgrid kissed him. He was trying to think of what to do when he felt her other hand plant firmly on his butt and squeeze. Peter tried to protest, but it just came out as a mumble with her mouth firmly against his. He did not understand how she could be so small yet so strong at the same time.

Telgrid finally released him and winked at him as she walked away in such a way that her hips swayed. Peter stood there dumbfounded and his head was in a fog. He stared as she got to the door of her room and looked back at him. Peter stood dumbfounded as she blew him a kiss and ran her hand up the side of her hip before she disappeared inside.

He was still in disbelief. Apparently Dugan was right. Whatever he had said had made things worse. He reached up and scratched his head while entering his room. Dugan was sitting on the edge of the bed with a disturbing looking smile on his face.

Peter was completely bewildered as he looked at Dugan, "I must have said or done something... because she... well she put her tongue in my mouth."

Dugan erupted into laughter as he rolled back and forth on his bed.

Peter stood looking at him, "I am serious, Dugan. She put her tongue in my mouth... and she grabbed my butt!"

Dugan was laughing so hard he was having trouble breathing.

His voice came out between struggled gasps for air, "Please Peter... no more... I can't take it..."

Peter lowered his eyebrows down at him. He was not any help, and he didn't seem to understand what he was trying to tell him. He decided he would just go to sleep and try to think of a way to talk with Telgrid and explain to her he was in love with Leianna. Telgrid was pretty and really strong. However, he would not be swayed by her advances. He would be married to Leianna someday... or at least he hoped he would be. He took off his gear and laid down in his bed.

Dugan snapped his fingers, "Peter, I am really looking forward to seeing how you get your way out of this one. My money is on you having little half dwarf babies. I can see them now; little Sea Dwarves with bright orange hair and freckles."

Peter furrowed his brow, "If I am to have anyone's babies, they are going to be Leianna's babies!"

Dugan erupted back into raving laughter. He rolled over and ignored him.

Peter sighed and whispered to himself, "I am sure she will understand once I talk with her. I just need to be forthright and honest about how I feel. No more confusion... I hope."

Peter played out different scenarios in his mind of how to tell Telgrid how he felt about Leianna. But not long after found himself imagining a life with Leianna and how their kids would look. Peter smiled hoping that their kids would look just like her. The most beautiful woman he had ever seen.

Chapter Sixteen

DUGAN FOUND HIMSELF WAKING up fairly early. He hadn't slept very well thinking about what the vault would throw at them. That and the Glimmerstone in the walls had been glowing bright throughout the night. All that light would have made it hard to sleep, even without his mind racing.

His imagination had gotten the better of him as it concocted new and terrible things that would befall them. The place sounded dangerous, and he was not looking forward to traveling through an underground labyrinth. Filled with all kinds of horrors trying to kill and eat them.

Dugan looked over to see that Peter was beginning to stir. He chuckled to himself, thinking of Peter and Telgrid. Dugan could hardly believe how oblivious Peter had been and how unwavering Telgrid was in her pursuit of him. He would need to figure something out soon, otherwise he would be on the sour end of that dwarf if he wasn't there already.

Dugan pulled his boots on as he eyeballed his mace, leaning against his pack. If the labyrinth was really constructed during the reign of the old king, then it would be possible that this mace of his would be lacking. He was glad he had gotten rid of that claymore; it had proved too large and unwieldy once he had actually used it in battle. Hopefully, he wouldn't need to use it at all, and all his worrying would be for naught once they were in the vault, but he wouldn't count on it.

He stood up and walked over to Peter to give him a gentle shake, "Wake up Peter. Today is the day we find out if we are cut out for this... adventuring... burglary... uh, thing."

Dugan was deep in thought. He couldn't believe where he was. Not long ago he was back in Oakbridge thinking about how to make a living on his family's farm, and now he was trying to prepare for breaking into the Magi's vault.

He was a little shocked with himself that he could take a life as easily as he had. The taking of someone's life was not easy, but in the defense of his friends, he had not even hesitated for a moment. Dugan decided he would never hold back when it came to defending his friends. If someone was going to try to take his or his friend's life, then they would get what was coming to them. Anyone willing to murder for coin or gain was an enemy and was undeserving of his mercy.

He kneeled down to gather his pack when he heard Peter yawn behind him. Dugan had started to develop a soft spot for the guy. He was a twerp, for sure, but the kid had heart and never shied away from a fight.

Dugan smirked. No matter how much he had tormented Peter as they were growing up, he had never given any ground willfully. It used to drive him nuts how this twerp would never back down. Now he felt a minor comfort in knowing Peter had his back in all this.

Dugan heard a knocking on his door and got up to check on who was there. He undid the latch and tugged the door open. Telgrid was standing in front of the door smiling.

"Is Peter awake?"

Dugan grinned, "He is still waking up. I can tell him you're looking for him."

Telgrid shook her head, "I will wait for him upstairs and make sure his food is ready for him when he arrives."

Dugan nodded and watched her practically skip down the hall.

He exhaled as he whispered under his breath, "I am glad I am not in your shoes, Peter."

Dugan looked over to see Peter getting dressed in a stupor, with his eyes still closed.

He went back to his pack when Peter mumbled, "Who was that?"

Dugan grinned again, "Oh, just your future wife checking up on you. She is going to make sure breakfast is ready for you when you arrive."

He chuckled as he watched Peter burst to life and, in a flash, had finished getting dressed.

Peter was attempting to put on his pack when he excitedly spoke, "What did Leianna say, exactly?"

Dugan tried not to laugh, "Oh, I haven't seen Leianna. I said your future wife came to check up on you. You remember her? She touched your butt... Telgrid."

He watched as Peter's features turned from excitement to dread, "I had forgotten about that."

Dugan let out a short laugh, "Forgotten? It only happened last night. If I were you, I would set things straight with her before you lead her along any longer and get into some real trouble."

Peter slumped and sat down on his bed, "What do I tell her, Dugan?"

Dugan shrugged, "I always try to let the girls down easy. Just tell her you aren't looking for a relationship right now." Dugan smirked, "Just tell her you don't want anything serious for now. Instead, tell her you are just looking for some fun." Dugan had to bite his tongue to keep from laughing.

Peter was nodding up until that last part, "I am not seeking fun Dugan! This is serious. I don't want to hurt her feelings."

Dugan shrugged, "Then I guess you will just have to take the bull by the horns and tell her the truth. Then pray that she doesn't beat you to death."

He was chuckling when he heard Peter sigh, "Well, I guess that helps, Dugan. Seems like I am going to take my life into my own hands this morning."

Dugan stopped him, "Hey now, I don't mean to tell her this morning. Tell her after you are out of the Labyrinth, otherwise she is likely to leave you for dead down there."

He did not want emotions affecting their chances of survival down in those depths. Telgrid would just have to wait as far as he was concerned.

Peter finished getting his pack on and walked up next to him, "Dugan, so you really think I should wait to tell her?"

Dugan stood up and faced Peter so that he was staring him dead in the eyes, "Peter, I don't want her getting emotional and making mistakes because you let her down. All of our lives are on the line with this. There is absolutely no room for mistakes. Wait until we are safely out of the vault, then you can tell her whatever you want."

Peter had a solemn look on his face as he nodded in agreement.

Dugan grinned, "Until then, you are just going to have to let her touch your butt."

Peter gave him another glare as he laughed.

Dugan hoisted up his pack, "Enough nonsense for now. Let's go get some breakfast before it gets cold. I don't want to be the last ones upstairs."

Dugan exited the door, with Peter on his heels as they went up the stairways, past some dwarves who seemed to be leaving the mess hall. The group of dwarves were heading further down for whatever work they needed to accomplish.

He still felt in awe of the structure they were in. The stone dwarves were skilled artisans. Dugan couldn't help but feel like they were walking through the halls of the dwarven fortresses deep within the Crimson Massif. When they had ascended the stairs to the second floor, Dugan admired the detail the dwarves had carved into some of the statues.

Dugan nudged Peter, "Check this one out, Peter. It almost seems as if it will move at any moment." He looked at the statue of a dwarf with a large shield that looked to be carved from some sort of red marble like stone. His thoughts were interrupted as a bald dwarf with an incredibly long beard came out from behind the statue.

"That's because it can move if it needs to. These statues you are admiring are called Guardians. We can rouse them to defense through song by Stonespeakers such as myself."

Dugan was not sure what to say when Peter spoke up, "So these Guardians help protect you?"

The dwarf nodded, "Yes, however, these in particular have not moved since the time of the great war before the Cataclysm. But I assure you, the stone is eager to protect those who are in need."

Dugan listened as Peter piped up, "That sounds a lot like a Warden, mister."

The dwarf smiled, "It is exactly like a Warden, my boy."

Dugan bumped Peter with his shoulder before glancing back at the Stonespeaker, "Thank you for the information, sir, but we have to get going. Our friends are waiting for us."

The dwarf just smiled and bowed as they made their way upstairs to the first floor.

As they stepped up onto the first floor, Dugan could clearly smell fresh food being served. He motioned for Peter to go on without him as he made his way to the large counter where they had met Opal the day before. No one stood at the counter when Dugan peered behind.

Upon inspection, he saw where others had placed their keys in a pile on the countertop near some architectural diagrams and various paperwork with sketch work. He placed the room key on top of the pile and turned to join the others as he resisted the urge to examine the paperwork in more detail. He loved learning new information and thought back on the burrow and its library. A lifetime spent there would be a life well lived with all of those books. He could not wait until he could spend some serious time there. If only there was a way to get there without the use of magic.

He looked up to see Telgrid smiling and hanging on Peter's arm as Da'ragh sipped from a steaming mug. The others must not be up yet.

He wondered if he should go knock on Leianna's door. She had always been one to sleep all day during their time in the burrow. She would sleep well past the afternoon.

Before he went looking for her, he decided to eat first and give her the benefit of the doubt. He took a seat across from Peter and Telgrid. He snickered to himself as he watched Peter squirm as Telgrid practically mauled him with the way she kept touching him.

Da'ragh seemed deep in thought and was clearly enjoying whatever hot liquid he was drinking.

Dugan signaled Buska when he noticed him serving tables, which were greeted with a nod. Soon after, food was brought over to him. It didn't take him long to finish his breakfast, but it did take him a moment to sip the hot cinnamon tea. Before long, both Torin and Hylon had joined them in eating breakfast.

Dugan was still not convinced that Hylon wasn't a girl. The guy was petite even with his half elven blood and his mannerisms were so submissive. He shook his head; he didn't care as long as Hylon didn't get them into trouble with his cowardice.

Hylon must have noticed Dugan was staring at him. Hylon set his cup down on the edge of his own plate, sending hot tea into his lap.

Torin turned laughing with a tablecloth to help him clean up, "Best get your bad luck out of the way now before we head out. I don't want our bad luck getting us into a spot down there."

Dugan shook his head. Hylon was so incredibly timid. How did he survive on the streets for so long? He was taking the last sip of his tea when he realized that Leianna still hadn't joined them.

Dugan looked to Da'ragh, "I am going to go get Leianna. I am sure she is still asleep."

Da'ragh merely nodded as he took another sip of his drink.

He stood up and saw that Peter was attempting to stand, but Telgrid had a firm grip, "Don't worry, Peter, I will be right back with her."

Dugan couldn't help but smile as he watched Peter's shoulders slump in defeat as Telgrid doted over him.

He made his way down the steps, peering over the railing now and then to take in all the sights. This place was a wonder and made a promise to himself to come back one day to further explore its depths.

Before he knew it, he was standing outside Leianna's door. He knocked but heard no reply. When he tried the door, he found it opened with ease. Upon entering the room, he saw Leianna sitting on the bed with her back to the door.

Dugan went to comment on her sleeping in but it looked like she had been awake and ready to go for a while now, "Everyone is almost finished eating breakfast. You best come up before Peter eats it all."

He moved forward when he thought he heard her sobbing, "Are you ok?"

Leianna jumped up and wiped at her face. She had been startled and probably hadn't even heard him enter the room when he did.

Her voice was shaky, "Oh hey Dugan, I didn't see you there. I was just about to head that way."

Dugan leaned against the door frame, "What has you all upset?"

Dugan watched as Leianna stuffed a bright yellow handkerchief into one of her pockets, "Oh I am just... a little overwhelmed, I think."

Dugan shook his head, "Do you take me for a fool? Everyone can see that you two care about each other."

Leianna stopped where she was standing, "It's not that... I can't see it... I just don't know how to feel."

Dugan walked over to place a hand on her shoulder, "I can see where it might get a little complicated. You two grew up as friends and now that you are both becoming adults. He is quite the strong and handsome man. I can see why you would struggle with your attraction toward him."

Dugan laughed as Leianna punched at his chest, "Ok, ok!"

Leianna was smiling, even though she appeared to have been crying for quite some time.

Dugan smiled back, "I am not great with that sort of thing myself. Feelings are not really my area of expertise. However, you two have been friends as far back as I can remember. I think you will feel better if you two can sit down and have a friendly talk."

Leianna nodded in agreement, "I just don't know what to say, Dugan."

Dugan chuckled, "Well, don't ask me. That's between you two to figure out."

He shifted and crossed his arms, "I need you to focus on the task ahead of us. That place is going to be dangerous; we have no concept of what we are walking into and I don't need you thinking about your feelings when something is trying to eat us."

Leianna nodded, "I agree Dugan, this can all wait until after."

Dugan smiled, "I am glad we are on the same page."

Dugan helped her with her bag, "You realize that Peter is completely in love with you, right?"

Leianna softly nodded her head, but said nothing.

Dugan wanted to be sure that this little love feud would not interfere with their chances of survival, "You know Telgrid is going to be all over Peter, right? Do I need to step in and intervene?"

Leianna shook her head, "I will maintain my focus and keep my emotions under control. At least until we are free of the labyrinth... then I will slap him upside his stupid head."

Dugan chuckled, "Ok good, just make sure I am there when you do. I don't want to miss out on the show."

Leianna smiled, and Dugan took this as a win. They all needed to keep their wits about them and having two love birds figuring out their feelings was not something he wished to deal with. Dugan could tell that Leianna seemed to care about the mission ahead of them as much as himself, so that brought him a little comfort.

She said nothing as they made their way upstairs. Dugan couldn't blame her though. She had a lot to work through, even without working through her feelings. Dugan noticed as they cleared the top of the steps onto the second floor that the Stonespeaker from earlier was approaching them.

The dwarf was polite as he spoke, "Excuse me, miss, pardon my forthcoming, but I just wanted to give you a gift on behalf of the other Stonespeakers and myself."

Dugan watched as the dwarf pulled a small polished Glimmerstone from the pocket of his deep red robes and handed it to Leianna.

He smiled as he looked at her, "When you are lost in the darkness, let this stone shine with your light so that you may find your path made clear once again. Just know that the Do'earee are not without friends in these dark times. When the Do'earee are in need, all you have to do is call and the Stonespeakers will answer."

Leianna awkwardly accepted the gift. Before she could express her gratitude, the two watched as the Stonespeaker disappeared behind one of the guardian statues.

Dugan looked at Leianna, who also had a puzzled look on her face, "What was that about Leianna?"

Leianna smiled as she pocketed the small Glimmerstone. "I think that was a sign that we are on the right path and doing the right thing."

Dugan sighed, "I will have to take your word for it."

As they made their way to join the others, Dugan ran over and dropped off Leianna's room key for her. Once he had rejoined and taken a seat with the rest of the group, they were already in the middle of a discussion about the plan for their next move.

Da'ragh was stroking his beard, "I see what you are trying to say, Peter, but it's not that easy. We will need to get just a little closer in order to use the displacement rod in order to access the vault."

Telgrid spoke up next. Dugan noticed she seemed overeager about something, "I have an idea, Da'ragh. What if we get a cart and dress like tower servants? No one will pay attention to us if we look like we belong, but at the same time, look unimportant. The Magi probably won't even look at us."

Dugan was impressed. The idea sounded really solid to him.

Da'ragh stroked his beard and nodded his head, "That is... actually a great idea, Telgrid."

Dugan watched as Telgrid beamed at the compliment.

Leianna looked like she was deep in thought, "If we do this, then we can practically walk straight up to the front doors without raising suspicion."

Dugan voiced his thoughts, "The only issue is that we will need some of the servants' uniforms."

Hylon raised his hand and Da'ragh chuckled, "Yes, Hylon?"

He spoke quietly, but Dugan could tell he was excited, "I noticed a laundry house on our way here and it looked like it had some of the servants Telgrid is talking about working there. I can sneak into the laundry house, get the uniforms, and be out before anyone is the wiser."

Torin was smiling, "I can go with him, give us an hour, and we will be back with the uniforms."

Telgrid stood up, "I better go to keep an eye out for you. Keep an eye out for trouble."

Torin dismissed her, "No need, this will be an easy in and out. The more of us that are there, the more chances we have of getting caught."

Telgrid shrugged and sat back down, "Ok then, but if you two get in trouble, I will knock both your heads."

Dugan watched as Da'ragh looked like he was about to express concern but ultimately waved them the go ahead to proceed.

Both Torin and Hylon were headed out the door in a matter of moments.

Dugan turned to Da'ragh, "So do we just wait, then?"

Da'ragh nodded, "Those two are trouble, but they are our best bet of getting the uniforms quickly. The longer we stay in this city, the higher our chances of being found."

Da'ragh leaned back and began to slowly stroke his beard again, "Although this branch of stone dwarves is sympathetic to our cause, there are many within the city walls who would happily turn us in for the reward or simply out of spite. The Do'earee have been painted to look evil so that the Magi can appear as the saviors. This is so that they can spread their influence unopposed and without question. We are taking a lot of risk coming here, but the reward of getting our hands on a Cipher Stone will prove invaluable."

Leianna seemed concerned, "I just hope it works and doesn't prove to be too much hassle."

Peter looked over to Leianna, "I will do whatever it takes to help keep you safe while we are in the labyrinth."

Dugan looked over with interest in her response. So far, she had done well in keeping her jealousy in check.

Leianna merely smiled and said a polite "Thank you" to Peter before returning to her breakfast.

It impressed Dugan. He decided he would step in and negotiate for the two if it looked like emotions would interfere. As far as he could tell, Leianna seemed to be keeping her cool. Despite Telgrid having her hands all over Peter.

Dugan frowned as he looked at Telgrid. This girl had no shame in her advances when it came to Peter. Dugan shrugged. At least she was straightforward about what she wanted. He looked at Leianna. He could tell that she had no idea what she wanted when it came to Peter. Dugan ordered another tea while they waited for Torin and Hylon to return with the uniforms.

Dugan was talking with the others when Hylon came back and asked the group to join him and Torin outside. Dugan noticed that Hylon seemed more nervous than usual, but dismissed it due to the fact that Hylon was always apprehensive. They made their way outside as he led them into an alley.

They could see Torin was leading a horse with a wagon behind it. The wagon was filled with folded clothes in baskets and what looked like bed sheets.

Torin was already wearing the brown uniform of a tower servant as he dramatically bowed, "Why good morning, my great lords and ladies. If you would be so kind as to hide yourselves under the garments. I shall lead us to the tower. Do not fret, the laundry was just freshly cleaned."

Telgrid and Leianna laughed at his acting and fake accent, but Dugan had noticed blood on one of the wagon wheels. Everyone hid themselves under the garments and linens as Dugan made his way to stand next to Torin.

Dugan whispered, "How many people did you kill to get this?"

Torin winked, "Just the one, he proved quite stubborn. So I convinced him, the hard way."

Dugan shook his head, "I am sure that was a terse conversation."

Torin grinned as Dugan made his way into the back of the wagon to hide with the others. Dugan disliked that Torin was so quick at turning to violence, but understood the simplicity of it. He had worked his way and was hiding under the sheets with the others when he heard Torin click his tongue at the horse and he could feel the wagon move.

Dugan couldn't judge Torin too harshly. He understood that they had grown up in the shadows of Markagra and that if they didn't steal and kill, they would have gone hungry or worse. No one had looked out for or taken care of them. They had to grow up quick and take care of themselves.

Dugan sighed. Hopefully, everything they were working for would leave the realm a better place than when they arrived.

They huddled silently as they passed through the city, ever closer to the towers. Despite all Torin's setbacks, he was fairly skilled at keeping a low profile when need be. A couple times he could hear people comment, and Torin responded respectfully. If Dugan didn't know any better, he would think that Torin was a decent person under all that rough and troubled exterior.

He did notice that he cared greatly about one thing. He seemed to be overprotective when it came to Hylon. But that came as no shock to him. Leianna was usually the same way with Peter. Dugan was sure that the two had a deep bond because of having grown up together.

Dugan exhaled at the thought of the vault. It was never far from his mind. The more he thought about it, the larger the obstacle became.

He quieted his mind by thinking of the library again and all the books waiting for him there. He thought for a moment about the books and wondered if he would ever write a book himself. He adored history and learning new things about the realm he lived in.

Maybe one day he would become a teacher. The thought made him smile. To think of all the things that he could possibly be and the thought of being a teacher brought him the most joy. One day, he thought to himself, maybe one day I will be a teacher back in our little town of Oakbridge.

Dugan noticed the cart had come to a complete stop and could hear someone talking with Torin.

Their voices sounded agitated, "What do you think you're doing?"

Dugan could hear Torin reply but he sounded very submissive, "Excuse me, sir. I am sorry if I am inconveniencing you."

The other voice was deep, "Servants use the back entrance. We reserve this entrance for visitors to the tower."

Torin had a stammer in his voice, "I am so sorry sir... you see I am brand new and they didn't tell me which entrance to use... please don't tell the head houseman."

Dugan noticed that the deep sounding voice had become arrogant, "Well, I can keep this our little secret if you can pay, that is."

Dugan could hear what sounded like a few coins jingling and Torin sounded defeated, "Here sir, it's all I got. This is my wages for the entire week... I don't have any more."

The deep voice chuckled, "Well, let this be a lesson to you, boy. If I see you again trying to sneak your way through here, then your head houseman will be the first to hear about it."

Torin was speaking quickly, "Thank you sir! Thank you, it won't happen again!"

It impressed Dugan, Torin was quite the actor. He had gotten them past a checkpoint without bloodshed. Dugan smiled. This had to be a first for Torin.

He realized his hand was firmly holding onto his mace. Forcing his hand to relax as the thought that he might be acclimating to violence just a little too easily himself. He could feel the cart move again and before too much longer, they came to an abrupt stop.

Dugan looked up as Torin pulled back the linens as he motioned for the group to be quiet and exit the wagon. Dugan hopped out first. He did a quick survey of his surroundings. They were within the outer walls that enveloped the perimeter of the Magi Towers.

Dugan was relieved. They had made their way right inside and without any trouble. He would have to compliment Torin on his skill when given the chance. He secretly hoped that the rest of this mission would be so smooth.

Dugan could hear the others quietly exit the wagon behind him as he took another look around him. The area seemed eerily empty. The silence in the area was almost deafening.

As he listened intently, he instinctively placed a hand on his mace. He was trying to listen for anything that sounded out of place, but heard nothing. He couldn't imagine the Magi knowing their plan and setting up a trap, but he would not take any risks, either.

Dugan turned around to face Da'ragh, "We should hurry? Something doesn't feel right."

Da'ragh nodded, "Trust your instincts, Dugan. What you are feeling are magical traps and alarms saturating this entire side of the towers."

It surprised Dugan at Da'ragh's response, "How did they know we were coming?"

Da'ragh shook his head, "They didn't. This is just their normal precautions. They set the entire area with deadly traps and magic to notify them of intruders. They made whole areas within the tower walls to look like elaborate garden pathways and decorated buildings. However, they are never used and only there as bait to dispose of unwary trespassers."

Dugan looked up at the white marble building they had stopped by. It had multiple floors and light was emanating from the curtained windows. Dugan looked at Da'ragh and pointed to it.

Da'ragh nodded, "It is a ruse and a tomb for those that would enter."

Dugan shivered. He took another look and could see nothing that indicated a trap. The silence was the only sign that something was amiss.

Dugan looked to Da'ragh, "Looks like I am following right behind you until we enter the labyrinth."

Leianna stepped up next to Da'ragh. Dugan noticed her eyes darting around. She appeared to be very concerned.

Leianna's voice was barely a whisper, "Is all this magic-"

Da'ragh interrupted her, "Yes, it is all deadly magical traps set in place by the Magi to guard against intruders."

Dugan watched Leianna's eyes widened as she exhaled slowly. If she was concerned as well, then Dugan knew it must be terrible.

Da'ragh motioned for everyone to gather around as Torin finished discarding his servant uniform. His voice was hushed and sounded pressing, "I need everyone to stay close. This area is dense with harmful magic. Walk where I walk and don't stray."

Da'ragh pointed over near the right side of one of the lesser towers, "We will make our way over there."

Everyone expressed they understood silently.

Da'ragh led them forward. He was saying something that Dugan did not understand at all. It was in a language completely foreign to him.

Dugan tensed up as he saw the black shapes and forms of what must have been the Magi traps. Some forms resembled what looked like terrible beasts and shadowy creatures from a child's nightmares. The shadowy figures seemed trapped in place and some paced back and forth in angered strides. Da'ragh had used magic to reveal the traps to them.

One resembled a giant maw of an impossibly large fish to Dugan that silently snapped at the air in front of it. Dugan felt uneasy as Da'ragh led them right past it. The figures and shades faded away as they made their way past them on their way to the edge of the tower that Da'ragh had pointed out earlier.

Everyone remained silent as ghosts as they slowly made their way through the maze of deadly magical traps. Dugan could hear Hylon's nervous breathing right behind him. If this imagery of deadly beings was getting under his skin, then he could only imagine the distress that Hylon must be under.

Dugan heard Torin softly whistle as a long coil of thorns made of shadows floated just over the top of the group. Barely missing the top of Dugan's head. For a moment, he thought that he had heard rustling leaves as it passed by.

Torin was whispering from behind Hylon, "That was uncomfortably close there, buddy."

Dugan exhaled sharply as he continued forward, but found that he had unconsciously hunched over as they continued following Da'ragh. He did not like the feeling he was getting off of any of this. It all felt wrong. He was not sure if seeing the traps made him feel better or worse.

He couldn't imagine what Leianna and Da'ragh were seeing, but without the help of Da'ragh, the rest of the group would be blind to the dangers that surrounded them. Dugan felt as if some of these traps must have been living things at one time or at least resembled them. They appeared to be more like that of trapped spirits than mere mindless energy, but maybe that was the point. Dugan shivered at the thought of the Magi instilling the traps with a semblance of a consciousness only to fill that consciousness with pure anger or murderous intent.

Once they reached the outside edge of the tower, Dugan inhaled deeply. Apparently, at some point on their way over here, he had started holding his breath. He looked around the area after Da'ragh had stopped his strange chanting. It had the appearance that nothing had been there to begin with.

He breathed in through his nose. Those traps or things were still out there and no one could even see them. Dugan hoped they would find another way out once they had gained the Cipher Stone. He took no joy in thinking of making their way back through that maze of unseen death.

Dugan glanced up at the sky and could not make out the top of the tower.

Peter was next to him and whispered, "I can hardly believe that this is one of the lesser towers. Can you imagine what it looks like inside?"

Dugan shook his head, "I hope to never find out, Peter. These towers are filled with people who want us dead. If we ever find ourselves inside one of these towers, I am afraid we would never see daylight ever again."

Peter mouth formed a frown, "I didn't think of it like that."

Torin leaned in with a cocky smile, "I can imagine all the wealth we could help ourselves to inside of just one of these towers and the Magi would be none the wiser."

Leianna shushed them as she turned to Da'ragh, "Are we close enough to use the displacement rod?"

Da'ragh nodded as he pulled the strange obsidian carved rod from under his robes, "If we could get any closer, it would be better, but I think we are pushing our luck as it is. Best we take what we can get." He fiddled with the snake effigy rod in his hand.

Dugan could tell he seemed upset just by looking at it.

Da'ragh let out a sigh, "Once I activate the rod, we will have only moments to get inside before we are detected. So be quick about passing through the rift. We should be able to remain hidden while in the labyrinth." He looked at Leianna, "Try not to use your magic while in the labyrinth. There are things down there created to feed on Do'earee and their magic. I cannot imagine that they have eaten in quite some time."

Dugan watched as Leianna nodded grimly to show that she understood.

Da'ragh's shoulders slumped as he stood dejectedly staring down at the rod as though it were an unwanted visitor. "I suppose this is necessary..."

Dugan could not tell if Da'ragh was trying to convince himself or the others. He watched as Da'ragh lifted the rod and pointed it at the wall. In moments, the air around him felt instantly colder.

The rod spewed out black smoke as the colors drained from the surrounding area. Dugan thought that this is what Da'ragh must have meant when he said it warped reality and drained nature. Dugan could hear a crackle like that from a fire as a rift formed before them. It looked like a tear in a cloth as it widened and grew. The smoke looked like a snake spiraling as an entrance formed where there was none before. Dugan could smell death and the dry dust not unlike that of an old grave.

Da'ragh waved them forward, and the group passed through the tear in reality one by one.

As Dugan traveled across the threshold, he could not shake the feeling that they were being watched from the other side.

CHAPTER SEVENTEEN

LEIANNA PASSED THROUGH THE rift as quickly as she could. She winced as the black smoke bit and stung at her skin. Once through, she looked down to see the smoke clinging to her, and in a panic, tried to brush it away. After a few moments, the fumes faded. She felt relief that it did not have more of an effect on her than it did. She had feared the Magi fueled rod would have an ill effect on her. Leianna looked up and could not believe her eyes. She had expected stone tunnels and locked rooms, but what she saw was nothing of the sort. There was no ceiling, instead she saw a sky devoid of a sun. No moon or stars, only a sky that had the hue of a deep red that was uneasy to look upon.

What looked like the portions of giant buildings floated in the air. Stones floated like pathways in multiple directions. What looked like dry, long dead trees and shrubs coated parts of the massive stone areas. Warm, stagnant smelling air hung heavy around her.

Leianna looked back at the others, who were also staring in dismay at the landscape before them. This was not the labyrinth vault she had mentally prepared for. An unsettling feeling fell over her as a distant rock tumbled down the side of one of these ominous structures in a hollow echo. She gulped as she reflected on the absence of life in the area. She wondered if this had been the right decision.

Da'ragh stepped forward, "This place was once a meeting place for prominent leaders, spiritual advisors and practitioners of the arcane. It is... or was connected to areas throughout the realm by the means of Skein Archways. Before the Cataclysm, this place was used to broker treaties and alliances between all the races."

Leianna looked around and could not imagine what it must have been before. Now it only resembled the decay of a tomb for the long-lost dead.

Dugan had stepped forward, "How is it we have never heard of this place?"

Da'ragh leaned on his staff, "Magi have done a thorough job of erasing this place from the history books. All once knew the Labyrinth as a place of peace and understanding. The Magi were all too successful in the corruption of its guardians and the execution of its inhabitants. Now all that remains is a dumping ground for the heretics and the relics they wish to expel from the realm."

Peter turned to Da'ragh, "Was this during the war?"

Da'ragh nodded, "The war completely devastated the land, and the Magi were quick to pick up the pieces and arrange them in the narrative that fit their agenda. Now very few are alive and know of what occurred. The truth has been buried by those that had sought its destruction."

Leianna looked again at the floating ruins that stretched out for as far as she could see around them. How could they possibly hope to find anything within these forgotten structures? She stood for a moment, staring into the expanse of it, when she heard something. It almost sounded like a moan from deep within the debris.

It startled Leianna as Hylon spoke, his voice was wavering, "What was that?"

Dugan stepped forward scanning the ruins from the direction the sound had come from, "I don't know, but with any luck we won't have to find out."

Da'ragh lightly tapped his staff on broken flagstones at his feet to get everyone's attention, "A word of caution. Touch nothing. Take nothing. We are here for the Cipher Stone and nothing else. This place is cursed and filled with all manner of horrors. Stick together, watch your step, and remain quiet."

Everyone nodded in agreement except for Torin, who looked like he was smirking. She hoped they would find a Cipher Stone and be free of this place before Torin could find any trouble to start.

Da'ragh led the group forward across a string of stones, not unlike what she would have used to cross a stream back in Oakbridge. The only difference was that losing your footing back home would merely leave you wet, while losing your footing here would send you spiraling down into the abyss of the ruin's underneath.

She took a deep breath as she took her first step onto one of the stones. It was unnaturally solid for floating in the air like it was. She thought to herself that at least she didn't have to worry about the rocks giving out and sending her into an endless tumble below, or at least she hoped that was the case.

Once across the gap, she found they were all standing in the middle of what looked like an open square. She reflexively lifted a hand to cover her mouth upon seeing the withered corpses strewn about. Most had been placed on iron spikes. The long dead were sprawled out with looks of agony held aloft on the iron skewers.

She felt sorrow for these people and the suffering they must have endured at the hands of the Magi. This did not look like a battlefield from days long forgotten, but rather that of a slaughter performed by the wicked. She felt that this place was indeed a tomb and the sooner they found their way out, the sooner she would be at ease.

Peter spoke up behind her, "This is terrible... Why would the Magi do such a thing?"

Leianna looked behind her and saw Dugan staring at the bodies with clenched teeth. She could tell that it was bothering him, but he remained stoically silent.

Da'ragh was already moving through the square as he looked back, "Do not linger. The longer we remain in one place, the higher the chance we are found."

She watched as Da'ragh walked with a quickened pace. He appeared to be anxious. She could not imagine what would have him this troubled, but if Da'ragh was being this vigilant, then she would be doubly so.

Peter had caught up with her as they carefully made their way through the ruins. He stepped over something that resembled the rotting wood of a table as he moved to her side. Peter was speaking in a quieted voice as he walked beside her, "This place makes me feel uneasy, Leianna. I feel like we are being watched."

Leianna agreed, this place had a way of making you feel like someone was watching you at all times. She took another look and shook her head, "I was expecting more magical traps, like the area outside the towers. I don't feel any magic here. It's as if all the magic has been drained from everything."

Da'ragh interrupted their conversation, "That is because it has. The Magi have stripped this place of its very life essence. What you see before you is the slow rotting of its remains."

Leianna scrunched her nose at the thought. If this place was once alive like the Soga Burrow, then they were basically walking through its rotting body. She felt a twinge of sadness. What wonders were lost at the expense of destroying a place as incredible as this? She frowned as she thought of the Magi finding and taking the life essence from Soga. If she had anything to do with it, she would not allow that to ever come to fruition.

Leianna had her attention grabbed when she thought she saw one corpse move on its own. She dismissed the thought as merely the disturbance of the area by their passing through, which had caused the body to shift. She gasped slightly as she saw yet another skull lift and seemed to watch their passing.

She felt her heart begin to race as Da'ragh whispered to her and the others, "Pay the dead no regard. They are reacting and yearning for the life and heat from our bodies. Do not linger lest you wish to join them."

Leianna looked back to see the dead lay its skull back down on the floor as they got further away from it. It appeared to her as if someone was going back to sleep. This did not make her feel any better. If the dead reacted to them being here, then how long would it be until they tried reacting violently? She shook her head. She hoped that would be the worst thing that they would have to worry about during their trek through these ruins.

Da'ragh held out his hand once they crossed another outcropping of stones leading to the next hovering structure. Da'ragh looked back at them, "Everyone rest here for a moment, I need to investigate this before we proceed."

He stepped forward toward a highly detailed and dark green stone effigy of what looked like a kneeling man holding a staff. He kneeled in front of the carving, slowly reaching out his hand to grasp the hand of the statue. Leianna was not quite sure what Da'ragh was doing. He did not appear to be using any form of magic, but he seemed to be in a deep manner of concentration. After a few moments, Da'ragh stood and returned to the group, looking dour.

She could not figure out what had just transpired, "Da'ragh, what is that?"

Da'ragh had a sting in his voice that she had not heard before, "Who... you mean who is that?"

Leianna averted her eyes when he practically glared at her, "I am sorry, I didn't know."

Da'ragh sighed, "No, I am sorry. This place has a way of getting to you and I have far too many memories for it to prey upon. That is not a statue. He is a Do'earee in a magical hibernation. We cannot interact with him. He will remain in stasis until the enchantment falls away."

Leianna thought of a similar magic used by the Do'earee. The stasis orb that was used on her back in Markagra was far too clear in her mind. She looked at Da'ragh, "Can we free them somehow? The Stasis Orbs are connected to a stone, correct?"

Da'ragh shook his head, "This is not a prison, but a self-induced form of magical sleep. They are not aware like that of the Stasis Orbs, and there is no stone for us to activate in order to free them. They are in a dreamlike state and will awaken to rejoin this realm when certain circumstances or conditions have been met."

Dugan had been listening intently, "But we have no idea of knowing what those situations could possibly be?"

Da'ragh simply nodded, Leianna was wondering what would cause this Do'earee to use such a magic when she remembered where they were.

She looked back to Da'ragh, "So when using this hibernation magic, I would venture to guess the Labyrinth was under attack. He could have made the condition for his release to be a safe environment and by the looks of this place, I don't see that happening anytime soon."

Da'ragh was speaking in a flat tone, "That could be one of the many unknown conditions for his awakening. We may never know."

Leianna was curious, "How can they not be interacted with? I just saw you walk up and touch his hand."

Da'ragh shifted his weight while leaning forward on his staff, "They are in a state of duality, caught somewhere between this realm and the spiritual realm. We can physically see the imprint they left behind, but it is not truly them we are looking at. They cannot be harmed, nor can their state be altered in any way. Magical or otherwise."

Leianna nodded, "I am sorry Da'ragh, he must have meant something to you."

Da'ragh nodded, "He did indeed. He was the first to get me looking inward for answers during a time I thought the realm owed me. He started me down the path of asking questions I did not even realize I wanted answers for."

She looked toward the effigy of the Do'earee. He looked to have been middle-aged. Somehow, he looked familiar to her. Leianna noticed he had sadness in his eyes. She could almost feel the sorrow from just looking at them.

Leianna turned to face Da'ragh, "What was his name?"

He merely smiled and shrugged, "I have no idea, nor do I expect to find out in this lifetime."

Leianna could not help but think the response he had given was a little odd. How could he seem to care so much about someone that he didn't even know? She was convinced that he was not telling her the truth, but decided she would no longer press the issue. They had more important things to worry about.

Torin clicked his tongue to get their attention, "Hey guys, I am pretty sure someone... or something is following us."

Peter turned to look at Torin, "What? We should be alone in the Labyrinth."

Leianna watched Da'ragh scan the ruins behind them with narrowed eyes. He seemed to be intently searching for the person Torin had seen.

Dugan whispered, "Is it possible we were followed?"

Da'ragh shook his head, "Highly unlikely, we used the displacement rod to gain access. It is enchanted with dark magic and used by Magi that wish to remain undetected."

Telgrid was holding her Warhammer at the ready, "I don't like the feeling of this place. It feels like we are in the middle of a busy market with everyone staring at us."

Da'ragh spoke quietly, "Make no mistake, many eyes are upon us. Let us hope that is as far as it goes."

Leianna noticed Da'ragh had never stopped scanning the ruins behind them the entire time he had been talking. She followed his gaze to the edge of a crumbling and deteriorating wall that was part of a rather extensive building they had not gone through. She stared for a moment before she noticed what looked like a pair of eyes in the shadows behind the wall. The shadowy figure moved back behind the wall as she gasped. She turned to Da'ragh, who was already motioning for the others to follow him. Da'ragh had begun to lead them at a fast pace through the ruins ahead of them.

She moved her way, so that she was right behind him as she whispered, "What was that Da'ragh?"

He didn't look back, nor did he slow his pace as he responded, "That is a remnant of the Roka. That is... or was the military branch of the Magi. They have long been disbanded and absorbed into other towers within the Molcainan Magi order. What you saw was a Roka either left behind during the war or discarded to the Labyrinths for disobedience. They are not living anymore... at least in the way we understand. They were once people that have been warped and twisted into a malevolent version of their former selves."

Dugan spoke up, "I read back at the burrow that Roka were actually soldiers under the command of the Magi and had been twisted by so much dark magic that they no longer resemble people anymore. The Magi corrupted their bodies and distorted their minds so that they could be used as disposable shock troops during the war."

Leianna could not imagine what this Roka was exactly, but she could venture to guess what it was after now. She looked back to see the others following Da'ragh silently as he led them single file, further within the Vault Labyrinth's remains.

Leianna looked to Da'ragh as he held out his hand to stop the group from proceeding. She listened as he turned and spoke to them in hushed tones, "I do not see how we can go around this grove cathedral up ahead without crossing the path of our pursuer. So we will have to go straight through. This place was the site of a grievous and devastating battle. This particular Grove Cathedral was the last holdout of the Do'earee here in the Labyrinth. The battle lasted for years before they were finally overrun. Once inside... touch nothing."

She could tell this was serious by the severity of his voice. Da'ragh looked behind them. He was obviously looking for the Roka following them, "I repeat, touch nothing."

Leianna nodded. She had no intention of touching anything while they were here. So far, they had seen only the deteriorating devastation of this labyrinth filled with decay around every corner.

Da'ragh spun back around and marched up and across the stones floating in the air that led to the edge of this grove cathedral. They all quickly fell in behind him and crossed with an underlying urgency. Once across, she noticed something that she did not before. What she had mistaken as ruins were, in fact, the remains of a giant forest which now lay petrified and withered.

The place was filled with charred and broken remains of the long dead trees all around them. She felt a chill go down her spine as she observed all the bodies of the fallen amongst the trees. She looked down at the corpses of Magi and Do'earee alike. These people must have died back in the war and their bodies were never recovered. They laid strewn about and forgotten, their ultimate resting place being the very same spot they had been slain. She frowned as she thought of the carnage that must have transpired here.

They passed thru the lifeless trees in silence. Everyone was in awe of the size of it. She thought that this place must have been beautiful when it was full of life. She started to notice that there were far more Magi and their soldiers on the ground than there were Do'earee.

She looked upon a deceased Do'earee withered like parchment, its face to the sky in a silent scream as its dried hands clutched what was left of a burnt staff. To the front of this Do'earee laid around a dozen corpses. Most were burned to husks, while some she recognized wore the purple robes of the Magi.

As they passed this by, she noticed one of the bodies had long talons on the ends of its fingertips and teeth like that of a shark. She winced at the sight of it and wondered if it was the remains of a Roka she was looking at.

Leianna kept her voice low as she got Da'ragh's attention, "I see more Magi than Do'earee. Were the Do'earee capable of wielding destructive magic?"

Da'ragh paused for just an instant, then quickly resumed his hurried pace forward through the grove. She could tell he had a hint of reverence in his voice as he spoke to her, "The Do'earee are capable of wielding the light. Which means they wield the true power of the realm. However, they only used the magic for defense. So naturally, most spells that are known of and documented are that of healing, protection, discovery, and so on and so forth."

Leianna listened carefully. She wanted to learn as much as she could about the Do'earee.

Da'ragh sighed, "One thing that the Magi never saw taking place was near the end of the war. Some Do'earee showed capabilities beyond normal comprehension. The magic they wielded was terrifying and powerful beyond reasoning."

Leianna was curious, "What brought about these changes in the way they used magic?"

Da'ragh sighed and Leianna could hear sadness in the way he spoke to her, "I believe it came to fruition at the last when Do'earee would give all they had in the defense of families and friends. They would call upon the light in times of desperation and selflessness. They would call and the light would answer, with inconceivable and miraculous results. Sometimes this would cost the Do'earee their life. A price they seemed more than willing to pay to protect those that they loved."

Leianna could not imagine what sort of personal decision that would take place for something like that to occur, to give up one's own life in order to protect those most important to you. Leianna looked back at Peter, who was staring up into the tops of the trees with his mouth open in wonder. She questioned what she would be truly capable of in order to protect her friend.

Da'ragh stopped in his tracks, and the rest of the group quickly did the same. Leianna looked ahead and saw the most amazing structure she had ever laid eyes upon, the building seamlessly intertwined with the surrounding trees. The building was wide with the roof looking like it had been made of leaves and most of its walls had carvings and decorations of growth with various plant life.

The most astonishing thing about it was the sight of the trees within it still had the semblance of life. Leianna could see what looked like a few small sprigs of green at the base of one tree.

Da'ragh was stumbling over his words, "How... this should not be possible..." Da'ragh, who seemed to be awestruck by the sight of life in this place that until now was full of death.

She whispered as she spoke, "Da'ragh, is that the cathedral you spoke of?"

Da'ragh made a slight nod as he began to slowly make his way to the entrance. She motioned for the others to hang back. He looked like he was in a stupor as he stumbled forward and Leianna almost couldn't hear what he was saying to himself, "This cannot be... the last time I was here, this was a pile of ash and bodies. None could have survived yet... the cathedral stands..."

Leianna looked about as they made their way through the massive entrance and noticed that there was an absence of the dead here. She looked around and the cathedral was full of light and life. It was barely an ember in the center of the ruins outside.

She turned to Da'ragh, "Who would've taken the bodies? Did someone rebuild this place?"

Da'ragh was coming out of his stupor and responded with a shaky voice, "They are the cathedral. The bodies of the dead have given life to what you see before you. I was here during the siege, and I heard the last heartbeat of the Labyrinth. I watched as this cathedral burned to nothing... but here we are standing in the great Grove Cathedral of the Labyrinth."

She felt different in this place. It was peaceful and calming.

She jumped as Da'ragh started laughing in a way that made Leianna feel uncomfortable. Da'ragh's voice sounded like that of a madman. "She was right! There was no way we could possibly win this war... Light will always prevail in the end... she was right..."

His laughing became stifled sobs, "How could she know?" He turned to her with tears streaming down his face, "The Magi have a false claim to this realm, and it is about time that they lost their stranglehold. You have to help people see the light again."

Leianna could not make sense of his previous statement, "Da'ragh, you said that you heard the heartbeat of the last Do'earee..."

Da'ragh forced a grim smile, "That is because I am no Do'earee child."

Leianna could not believe what she was hearing, "But I have seen you use their magic... You have taught me their ways. How could you not be one?"

He stood up straight and wiped his eyes, "They knew me as Lorcan the Reaper. Do'earee would tremble in fear upon hearing my name and there was once a time that brought joy to my dark heart. That is until I met her... She awakened the Do'earee souls I had consumed. The result of this was my turning from the dark and towards the light. The light trapped within me has changed me. I am no longer the dark instrument of death that I was designed to be. My purpose and my very being yearns to undo the damage I have caused."

Leianna took a step backwards, "You are Magi? You killed the real Da'ragh?" She could hear the fear in her voice despite her trying to stand firm.

Da'ragh let his staff slide into the crook of his elbow as he held out his open hands, "Yes and yes. However, I would never harm you, Leianna. You are my hope. With teaching and guiding you, I hope to atone and hopefully undo some of my past wrongs. I know I cannot be forgiven for my wickedness, but I don't need forgiveness. What I hope to accomplish is to bring some of that good back into the realm I heedlessly stole from it."

Leianna was breathing heavily, "So your real name is Lorcan?"

Da'ragh nodded, "I was one of the three from the inner circle of Magi who were chosen to become Reapers. I was the first of the three and sought the complete and utter annihilation of the Do'earee order. I have done terrible things, Leianna, but like I said, I hope to make amends for them. My hope is that you will one day teach others a better way."

Leianna tried to calm herself down by focusing on her breathing. How could he have lied to her like this? Leianna turned to him with anger in her voice, "Why did you lie to me? Why did you lie to all of us?" She waved her arm toward the others outside.

Da'ragh smiled, "Would you have come with me if I told you the truth? You would have thought me a madman." Da'ragh was chuckling, "Hello there, my name is Lorcan, but I go by the title of Da'ragh in honor of the man whose life I needlessly took. I am a Magi Reaper who looks to bring down his own order, because now I can clearly see the darkness in my own heart and the evil that the Magi and Madu spread. Would you like to come with me to learn the ways of the Do'earee hoping we can undo the evil that they and myself have sown throughout all of Auldryche?"

Leianna stared at him with her mouth open in befuddlement. She did not know what to say, but she felt like he was telling her the truth. She lifted her eyebrows as she questioned him, "So, are you telling me the truth about our reasons for being here... for going to the Broken Lands?"

Da'ragh nodded, "Yes, I pray that with your help I can expel at least some of the darkness I have brought into this realm."

Leianna felt her heart get heavier, "So you have killed some of those people out in the Labyrinth?"

Da'ragh lowered his gaze to the floor, "Yes, and there is not a day that goes by that I do not regret it. That is why I need your help so badly. I cannot make these amends on my own. Please Leianna, I hope the truth of me does not tear you from the path of the Do'earee."

Leianna looked at him, his face appeared sincere and full of regret, "Was this the reason my mother kept her distance from you? Was it because she found out who you really were?"

Da'ragh nodded, "Yes, in a way... She found out the truth and from that day forward I have walked this path alone. I hold your mother in great esteem, and I will not hold it against you if you don't want to continue. That being said, please... please, help me in helping everyone else... I am incapable of doing it myself, otherwise it would already be done."

She glanced back out the entrance to see the rest of her friends standing guard over the perimeter of the cathedral.

Leianna stomped over to stand eye to eye with Da'ragh, "There are three things you need to understand and rules you will need to follow if you want my help. First, I am not my mother. I am Do'earee, and you will treat me as such. Second, you will not lie to me ever again. You will be honest with me about all things. Third, you are my mentor... and my friend."

She reached out and hugged Da'ragh, "Everyone makes mistakes, yours are just... well... terrible. I will help you Da'ragh, no matter what it takes. We will bring the light back." She felt reassured as Da'ragh hugged her back. He was trying to say something, but he was too busy trying to hold back tears. She stepped back, "I expect you to follow these rules without fail."

Da'ragh's voice was uplifted, and he sounded hopeful as he repeated what she had just said, "Without fail, Leianna, without fail."

Leianna let out a hefty exhale as she once again looked outside to the others, "I know I said no lying, but I think we should wait to tell the others about all of this. I don't think they will be very understanding of you being a Reaper for the Magi."

Da'ragh nodded, "I would expect not. I will leave the time for revelation up to you." Da'ragh had moved to stand beside her next to the entrance, "Thank You Leianna."

She just smiled. She was not yet comfortable with all this newly acquired information about her friend and mentor. Leianna felt strongly that there had to be a better way. She was going to find out what that was. She believed that helping Da'ragh with this was the first step and the right move from now on. However, she hoped she was making the right decision.

Leianna looked to Da'ragh, "What do we do now?"

Da'ragh stroked his beard, "We will make our way to the rear of the cathedral and find a path that will hopefully lead us to the Magi vault that should be here deep in the Labyrinth. Once there, we will hopefully find a Cipher Stone locked away inside."

Leianna silently agreed, "Let's get the others and make our way out of here. Hopefully, our pursuer is content with merely following us."

She headed out the large archway leading out of the Cathedral and approached her friends, "Alright, we have our next plan of action. We will make our way deeper into this Labyrinth and hopefully find this vault without too much trouble."

Leianna looked over to see Hylon staring out into the ruins. He appeared to be transfixed by a particular building. She made her way over and sat next to him, "What is it you are looking at Hylon, is the Roka still behind us?"

Hylon made a slow nod with his head and then pointed at the third floor of a crumbling building that was slowly floating in lopsided circles over the tops of the dead trees. As she watched the building slowly turn in the red sky, she still couldn't believe that such a place existed. She tried to focus on the spot he was pointing at and could not see any movement at first. When she tried to look inside the windows, she saw something move. She did not get a very good look but guessed that it was the Roka still hot on their heels. She turned to glance back at Hylon, who was still staring at the awkwardly floating structure.

She took a breath, "Do you think it will try anything?"

Hylon shrugged, "I have been watching it go between the buildings and shadows. What I find odd is that I don't actually see it move from building to building. If I didn't know any better, I would say it is using the shadows as a way to instantly travel from place to place."

Hylon looked over at her, "Do you think it is using magic to walk through the shadows?"

Leianna hated the thought, but she did not put it past something made by the Magi. If they infused it with dark magic, walking through shadows seemed entirely possible. It was probably a type of magic that she would not exclude from the scope of Magi abilities.

She stood up, "Alright Hylon, let's get moving. I would rather not hang around the Labyrinth any longer than we need to."

Hylon got up and brushed off the dust from his pants.

She turned to look back at Peter and Telgrid talking and pointing up at the Cathedral. She huffed lightly before turning and walking toward Dugan, who was in a conversation with Torin. They both greeted her as she approached.

She waved and motioned for them to follow, "We better get going, Da'ragh thinks the vault entrance is deeper within the area ahead."

Torin smirked, "With any luck, we will find some additional treasures contained within."

Dugan shook his head, "I wouldn't touch anything if I were you. This place looks cursed, and just being here makes me wonder if we risk catching some of that darkness ourselves." Dugan crinkled his nose then made his way toward Da'ragh, Leianna looked to Torin who looked unconvinced.

She narrowed her eyes at him, "Don't get any ideas about collecting anything while we are down here Torin. We don't know what kinds of magic still linger and what those magics will do once disturbed."

Torin shrugged, "We will see. We already plan on stealing a magic rock. What harm will come in taking a couple of other items on top of that?"

She went to protest, but he just turned and walked away from her. She just hoped that nothing would be shiny enough to get his attention until after they had escaped the Labyrinth.

She turned to get Peter's attention, but Telgrid was already pulling him behind her toward Da'ragh. She took a deep breath; with everything she had just learned about Da'ragh, there was no time to worry about emotions. She gripped her staff tightly as she made her way to Da'ragh and the rest of the group.

Da'ragh looked at everyone as he spoke, "I apologize for the delay. This cathedral was not supposed to be here. The memories of it shook me at my core. Leianna helped me to focus on the more important task at hand. We will push forward. With a little luck, find the entrance to the vault."

Torin chuckled, "Sounds fun."

Dugan looked over his shoulder as he spoke, "I don't like that thing following us like it has been. I keep expecting something to happen, but that thing just watches. It has me on edge."

Da'ragh nodded, "All the more reason to hasten our way to the vault."

Everybody seemed to agree and followed behind Da'ragh as he led them along the outer wall of the Cathedral.

Leianna looked ahead to what seemed like more of the same; a damaged and lifeless forest filled with bodies left behind from the war. She looked around and saw more of the ravaged forest spread out in all directions. She tried not to pay much attention to the dead. Every now and then, one of them would watch her from its eyeless sockets. This place was warped and wrong. The whole feeling caused her insides to twist into knots.

Da'ragh motioned for her to watch her step. She glanced down to see a terrible sight. A giant pool of black liquid spread out in a large radius with what looked like skeletal hands reaching up and outwards from within. She shivered. The skeletons and bodies trapped within looked like they had been melted in place. This war must have been a horrible sight to behold.

She looked over at Peter as she heard him scoff. He had a look of disapproving anger, while his hand had a firm grip on his sword's hilt. He looked like she felt.

Da'ragh stopped abruptly in front of her. When she leaned over to see what had made him stop so suddenly, she gasped and covered her mouth. The Roka was blocking their path. It stood unmoving and silent as it faced them.

Leianna could make out where it had once been olaumen, but its limbs were far too elongated and gaunt. It looked pale and emaciated, with an unnatural grin far too wide for its narrow features. The Roka's eyes looked far too small and were barely the size of peas. Its eyes were black as pitch and stared right through her. Dark, disheveled hair hung loosely about its shoulders and its clothing looked like black leather that tightly fit its slender frame. The Roka's hands ended in fingers that unfolded with far too many joints and ended in long sharp black talons.

The sight of it transfixed Leianna as Da'ragh whispered to her, "Do not use your magic, Leianna. I will try to speak with it."

Leianna shook her head disapprovingly but remained silent as she watched Da'ragh approach the Roka slowly.

Da'ragh spoke slowly, "We are not here to fight. We are not Magi. We are not Do'earee. We are travelers who seek the tower."

She watched as the Roka tilted its head to the side and hissed. She listened as the Roka struggled to speak and stumbled over its words and showed clear signs of trouble in trying to speak.

The Roka hissed in between its words, "Zradsi does not care for Do'earee... for Magi... for tower... Zradsi seeks Madu flesh..."

Leianna gulped as she heard the Roka's last statement.

Da'ragh bowed slightly, "We ask that you let us pass in peace."

The Roka hissed, "Zradsi cannot find the way... show Zradsi... show Zradsi or die..."

Leianna was not sure why, but this Roka seemed to address itself in third person. Its name must be Zradsi.

Da'ragh gripped his staff and slowly moved it between him and the Roka, "We do not know the way Zradsi."

The Roka unhinged its jaw like that of a snake and screeched so loudly that it made Leianna's ears hurt. She watched as the Roka unfurled its multi-jointed fingers and stretched them out in a way that made her feel uneasy.

Leianna didn't even have time to react as Zradsi slashed forward at Da'ragh faster than that of a cat snatching up a mouse. She could do no more than watch as its clawed hand made its way toward Da'ragh's throat, as it shifted and changed momentum mid swing. She barely had time to process what had just happened.

She watched as Torin struggled to free his half spear from the clutches of the Roka's grip. Torin must have snuck behind it to strike it, but the Roka had proven to be far too fast for Torin.

She barely saw Dugan out of the corner of her eye as he charged with his mace drawn in front of him. Peter and Telgrid had also wasted no time and were charging the thing with their weapons drawn. She watched as the Roka slashed with its free hand and Torin fell backwards.

The thing spun and caught Dugan in his right leg, sending blood spraying and sending him crashing to the ground. She ran forward as she watched Telgrid go flying backwards. The Roka took a slash at Peter only to have its claws stop mere inches short of his face. The Roka howled and reared back to swing again, only to have the same result of its claws.

Peter counter attacked after the Roka's second failed strike. His blade bit into the creature's abdomen, but Leianna saw no blood. The Roka grabbed hold of Peter's sword blade and threw it aside, sending Peter with it. The Roka was unnaturally strong for its thin physique.

She swung her staff as hard as she could muster at the creature's head. With all the chaos, she had gone unnoticed and felt her staff connect with its skull. She could feel the impact of her staff as the Roka was knocked to its knees. It screeched out in pain as it ran backwards on all fours. Its forearm was emitting steam where her staff had just struck.

It pointed at her and screamed, "You lie! Do'earee! You lie!"

The thing sprung upwards into the air, similar to that of a frog toward her. She lifted her staff and winced in anticipation of the impact. She watched as the creature stopped in midair. Black smoke swirled around it as it struggled to rip free of its magical bonds.

She looked over at Da'ragh, who had a look of anger on his face. He was using Magi magic to hold the Roka in place. Leianna almost didn't recognize him as he chanted and sent the creature through a cloud of darkness. As the smoke cleared the Roka had disappeared, she turned back to look at Da'ragh who dropped to his hands and knees coughing. He looked up and waved his hand to indicate he was ok.

She called out to him, "What did you do?"

Da'ragh spoke with a roughness in his throat, "I cast it out of the Labyrinth. It was the only thing I could think of to keep everyone safe."

Leianna went to ask where it had been cast too when the realization hit her. This Zradsi was now free of its prison. She took a quick breath and hoped that they never ran into that thing again when she heard Dugan yell out in pain.

She looked over at Dugan, who was bleeding badly from his leg, and rushed to his side. She felt a sense of panic when she looked down at the deep gashes across the top of his right thigh. He was trying to tie a bandage around his leg, but he looked pale and there was far too much blood.

She threw her bag on the ground and pulled out one of her shirts. Quickly wrapping it around his leg and pulling it tight. Trying to stem the bleeding. She grimaced at the sight of the terrible wound. It was as if the Roka had sliced his leg clear to the bone.

Dugan was shaking and had a cold sweat dripping down his forehead, "Tha... thank you Leianna... I think it got... pretty deep..."

Leianna went to reassure him when she watched his eyes close, and his body slumped. She looked at the shirt she had tied around his leg, and it was already soaked in Dugan's blood. She heard herself scream, "NO! Dugan, you stay awake!" She reached into her bag and pulled out another random cloth and pushed it against Dugan's leg as she applied pressure.

She looked on the ground to see a deep pool of red that had formed underneath him. She gasped at the sight of so much blood. Leianna looked up at his face and he was barely breathing. His breaths were shallow and labored. Peter slid in next to her and took her spot on his leg, attempting to stop the bleeding.

She grabbed the sides of his face as she tried to get him to open his eyes, "Dugan, listen to me... we have almost stopped the bleeding... just hang on..."

Da'ragh leaned down next to her and put his hand on her shoulder, "He is dying, Leianna. There is nothing we-"

Leianna turned and yelled at him, "There is nothing you can do! But I can..." Leianna turned and focused on calling magic forward through her fingertips and down into Dugan's leg.

Da'ragh barked upon seeing what she was doing, "If you use Do'earee magic on him here and now, you risk all of our lives!"

Leianna had heard what he said but did not care. She would risk all to save her friends, and that included putting her own life on the line. As she felt the love in her heart, she focused on his leg. She focused that feeling into his wounds and the mending of the damage done. Soft yellow and white lights in the shape of butterflies fluttered about in the air overhead, all converging on Dugan's leg.

After just a moment, she had to close her eyes as the surrounding area grew so bright she could not bear to look at it. Her hands felt warm, and she thought she could hear faint voices in the distance. They sounded like they were singing and by the time the bright light around her had faded, she could no longer hear them.

When she opened her eyes, she could see that Dugan was wide awake and pulling the bandages off his leg to show the wounds underneath had completely disappeared.

Dugan looked up at her in shock, "I was... dead."

Leianna shook her head, "No, but you were about to. I used healing magic to keep you alive."

Dugan slowly shook his head, "No, Leianna, I was dead... you brought me back. You shouldn't have... not here."

She sat there stunned, staring at him as he again checked on his leg in complete astonishment.

Da'ragh was behind her as he spoke softly, "I fear you may have doomed us all..."

She turned to look up at him when she heard a sound that chilled her to the bone. A deep hollow, resounding chime rang in the distance akin to that of a great gong. The sound echoed around them as it slowly struck six times, then in an instant, the surrounding area amplified with a cacophony of the dead screaming.

Leianna lifted her hands to her ears, but the sound was horrendously clear in her mind. Peter was looking at her and saying something as he held her shoulders, but the sound of the screams drowned out anything he may have been trying to tell her. Her mind was on fire and the sound tore through her like a blizzard wind. She could think of nothing else but for the desperate need of the wailing to cease.

A loud boom shook the ground, and hot air blew past her. Then, as quickly as the dead had started screaming, the area fell into absolute silence. She looked at Peter, who was now staring off into the distance.

He looked back at her with panic in his eyes, "WE need to run... NOW!"

Peter helped pull her to her feet as she looked back behind them towards the direction of the Cathedral. Floating just above the ground was a figure clad in ragged and torn robes. Its hood was pulled down in front to conceal its face as it slowly made its way toward them.

She felt dread overtake her just by looking at the thing. Its arms were small and not unlike that of a child's, except that they looked withered and dry as mummified flesh. Its feet appeared atrophied and dangled worthlessly from under the robes. It made absolutely no sound as it moved toward her. She could not will her legs to move and could barely make out the voices of her friends crying out to her to run. She felt herself take a step towards the thing and felt her mind go numb. The overwhelming sensation of being drawn to it overtook her.

She felt the air rush out of her lungs as Dugan picked her up and slammed her on his shoulder as he ran. She could only watch as the forest flew by. Dugan was running through the dead forest with impressive speed. Everything seemed so distant and quiet as she watched the others follow behind.

Torin was clutching his chest, which was wounded and bleeding, while Hylon trailed behind him. Peter was helping Telgrid as she limped forward as fast as she could. Telgrid's face would wince every time she stepped on her left foot. She could faintly make out Da'ragh yelling for everyone to follow him.

Even though she had just healed Dugan, he seemed no less capable of carrying her and lost no momentum in his stride. She stared at the thing once again, as it made no effort to accelerate its pursuit. The robed entity merely floated towards them in the same creeping tempo. She felt lost, like she was somewhere else, as she stared into the darkness under its hood.

She was jolted as Dugan jumped from stone to stone across a chasm to the next floating island within the ruins. As they crossed, the group stopped as Da'ragh stood with his arms chanting and black smoke billowed from his mouth. The smoke covered the stones floating in the air like a fog. After a few moments, the rocks they had used to cross were nothing but dust as the black fog dispersed.

She felt Dugan take a deep breath and hold it as the robed being made its way to the edge. The thing just stopped short of the chasm and floated in place. She felt Dugan began to breathe again as everyone seemed to relax a little.

Da'ragh collapsed and began another coughing fit that did not last too long. Peter had walked over and began patting his back. Dugan placed her on the ground as she stared forward. Dugan looked her straight in the eyes as he spoke, but it just came across as gibberish to her.

She could not take her sight off the thing. It remained silent, but she could feel its call all the same. She attempted to get up and walk toward it, but Dugan had stopped and restrained her. She wanted to go to it, but her mind was still numb and she didn't know how to break free of her friend's grasp.

She was staring at it when Da'ragh kneeled in front of her. He reached into his bag and produced a small leather pouch, which he gently opened in front of her. The pouch contained a finely ground brown powder. Da'ragh took a pinch of it in his fingers and placed it under her nose.

As she breathed, her head felt like she had just been kicked by a horse. She could taste blood in her mouth and her head was pounding. Her ears were ringing as she looked up at Da'ragh, "What in all the realms was that?!"

She could hear as both Dugan and Peter let out a sigh of relief.

Da'ragh was chuckling softly, "That, my dear, was imp powder. It has a way of clearing the mind of unwanted thoughts and memories. In a way, it burns them out."

Leianna looked up at Da'ragh as she felt her nose begin to bleed. She quickly raised up her arm to wipe up the blood and tilted her head back. She couldn't believe that he would give her such a dangerous sounding remedy, "Why would you give me that?"

Da'ragh looked to Dugan and Peter, "The powder seems to have worked. Don't let her look back until we are clear of the sight of it."

She looked to Peter for answers as he helped her to her feet. Peter spoke but looked shaken as if he had just seen his grandfather's ghost, "Leianna, I need you to listen carefully to me. Trust me, whatever you do, do not look behind you and just follow me."

She reflexively went to look behind when Peter slapped her. She looked at him angrily, "Peter! Why would you do that!?"

Peter looked nervous, "Leianna, it's for your own good... trust me. Do not look behind you or I will slap you again."

Leianna could not believe what she was hearing. Why would Peter do such a thing?

She went to protest when Peter again mouthed the words, "Trust me."

She sighed and decided that if she was to trust anyone here that Peter would be by far her first pick. She grudgingly decided to listen to Peter.

Torin was completely bandaged and grinning at her like a fool. Telgrid was leaning against a broken wall. She had a splint tied around her ankle. Leianna looked down and could see where she had been laying on a bedroll.

She looked to Peter as she felt panic set in, "Peter what happened? Why can't I remember?"

Peter forced an awkward grin and looked very uncomfortable, "Side effect of the imp powder, I'm afraid. Da'ragh said that you would gradually get your memories back over time. But I can assure you that it was for your own good."

She reached up and held the side of her head. She had a headache that could kill an ox. The pain in her skull was making it hard to think. What was it that happened? She went to turn and sit down when Peter slapped her again.

She turned to him, ready to beat him as she scolded him, "Peter! This is not helping my headache!"

Peter shrugged as he held out his hands to his sides, "I am sorry Leianna, but under no circumstance am I going to allow you to face that direction."

She huffed, "I wasn't trying to look, I was trying to sit down."

Dugan walked over and helped her take a seat facing Peter, "He is trying to protect you, we all are."

She looked up at Dugan, "Trying to protect me from what? Looking that way?" Leianna unintentionally waved her arm behind her as she turned her head in the same direction.

Dugan reached out with startling reflexes and grabbed her hair, preventing her from turning her head. She winced as his hand had a firm grip on her hair that almost hurt. She went to protest until she saw the seriousness of the look on his face. She lowered her arm as he spoke, "You are so stubborn. If you can't keep from looking back on your own, I won't hesitate to blindfold you myself."

Leianna nodded in understanding as she swallowed timidly. Dugan released his grip on her hair and pointed a finger at her, "Blindfold." She watched as he got up and went to his pack and pulled out a length of black cloth and waved it in the air before putting it in his front pocket. She took a deep breath, knowing full well he was not joking.

Torin called out as he laughed, "And I thought I was the most stubborn one here."

Hylon chuckled, "You still are Torin."

Dugan and Telgrid both chortled in agreement when she heard Da'ragh behind her. She began to turn around to look at Da'ragh when she was met with a stern gaze from Dugan. He mouthed the word "Blindfold", and she pivoted her sight straight forward.

Peter was smiling, "See, I knew you would get the hang of it."

Leianna huffed. She very much disliked being treated this way. It was driving her mad with curiosity as to what was behind her. If it wasn't for Peter and his sincerity, she would seriously contemplate taking a quick peek behind her. For now, though, she would listen to her friends regarding their odd request.

Da'ragh was speaking slowly, "This thing will not stop now that it knows Leianna is here. It will forever be drawn to her like a moth to a flame and will stop at nothing to seize her. If it manages to get ahold of her... it will consume her."

Leianna watched as Dugan looked behind her, presumably at Da'ragh, as he spoke. Dugan sounded agitated, "What is it?"

Da'ragh spoke again, "I don't know for sure. It appeared after the fall of the Grove Cathedral. Once it arrived it immediately consumed all magic users in its path and was ultimately the reason Magi have abandoned the Labyrinth. They gave it the title of The Blighted One."

Peter scrunched his nose, "Why did it only come after Leianna and not you?"

Leianna could hear Da'ragh sigh behind her, "I am not sure. She is young and a Do'earee apprentice... I feel like I should know why, but ultimately I do not know why it would not pursue me as well."

Leianna interrupted the conversation about her, "I am right here guys. I would like to be part of the conversation involving an evil entity bent on devouring me."

Da'ragh cleared his throat, "Of course, we are just trying to devise ways of protecting you. The imp powder used to clear your mind was effective in stopping it from locating you. This makes me think it can only see itself through your eyes. In a way, I think it links to its victims. Without a clear image in your mind, it is currently lost, loosely speaking."

Leianna didn't like the idea of anything being inside her head, let alone something that wanted to devour her. Leianna bit her top lip as she thought about the thing linking to her again, "Da'ragh, this powder only has a temporary effect. What happens when I remember this thing?"

Da'ragh was dry in his response, "It will resume its pursuit of you. Our only hope is that we will be free of the Labyrinth by then."

Leianna did not like the thought of something chasing her through this place just because she knew what it looked like.

Peter chimed in, "Couldn't we just use the powder again to make her forget?"

Da'ragh was quick to reply, "No, absolutely not. Using imp powder even in small doses is risky. Using the powder on Leianna this soon after would most likely kill her."

Leianna felt her nose bleeding again, as if to confirm his statement. Her head was still pounding, and she was feeling nauseous. She closed her eyes and focused on her breathing.

After a moment, Peter nudged her and offered her a drink from his waterskin. She took a couple sips and thanked him, but it did very little to relieve the pain.

Leianna looked over at Hylon, who was staring in the direction of everyone else... everyone except her, that is. She noticed he had a worried look on his face, "Hey Hylon. What has you looking so worried?"

Hylon looked her way and forced a flat grin, "That thing... The Blighted One, I can hear it whisper, but I don't understand what it's saying."

Leianna felt a sense of momentary panic, "Is it just standing there? Is that what you guys keep looking at?"

Hylon nodded, "After Da'ragh gave you the imp powder, it just sort of stopped moving. It's kind of floating there... murmuring."

Torin chuckled, "We already talked about this Hylon. No one can hear it, except for you. I think the stress of this place is affecting your sanity."

Hylon shrugged, "It could be, I guess. It's just that... Well, I can hear it clearly, just not with my ears. If that makes sense?" He hid his face behind his hair again.

She was catching on that this was his defense mechanism for when he felt uncomfortable. Leianna gave Hylon a smile, "I believe you, Hylon."

Torin scoffed, "Just wait, he will be seeing things next."

Leianna gave Torin a dirty look. For caring about his friend so much, he was quite tough on him. She watched as Torin reached down and grabbed Hylon's shoulder to comfort him. She was confused. Maybe Torin was just acting out on his own concerns for Hylon.

Dugan was squinting as he looked at The Blighted One, "Now that Leianna is awake, I think we should get to moving again. We have been here far too long for my liking and we really don't know what is going to cause that thing to move again."

Telgrid spoke up, "I agree with Dugan. The more distance we can put between ourselves and that thing, the better."

Da'ragh made his way in front of Leianna as she looked up at him. He kneeled in front of her and handed her what was left of the imp powder. She gave him a puzzled look as he handed it to her.

Leianna was going to ask what good the powder would be if it would just kill her, when Da'ragh began to speak, "I have seen what that thing does to Magi and Do'earee alike. I will leave the decision up to you."

He stood up, and the others gathered their belongings when it hit her. The powder would kill her. It was a mercy. Da'ragh had given her the choice for if The Blighted One had caught up with them. She shivered at the thought and quickly put the small leather pouch containing the powder away.

Before long, everyone had gotten to their feet and took up a slow pace in the direction of the vault. From what Da'ragh had revealed, they were getting closer.

Hylon had mentioned something about his bad luck getting everyone into trouble, but she paid little attention to it. As far as she was concerned, this whole place was bad luck. She stared up ahead as she walked. Each footstep she took was like a drum banging in her skull. This made it rather difficult to think about anything at all, so she just focused on taking one step after the other as she followed the others.

She did notice, however, that both Dugan and Peter were being rather protective of her. Peter was holding her hand and guiding her on the path while Dugan was staying quite close behind her. Hylon was helping Telgrid with her injured ankle. She was still limping, but it didn't seem serious.

They had made their way through some particularly chilling buildings at one point where the dead seemed to be melted into the very walls themselves. She tried not to look at it as they passed by. The more she examined, the more she found her mind contemplating possible magics that would have caused such terrible results. Which just made her head hurt all that much more.

She realized that her headache was directly connected to how much she was thinking at the time. Leianna took a deep breath and tried to clear her head of any thoughts. She brought her focus on the here and now and found that the headache subsided. She smiled at her own cleverness. They had just passed across an uneven and narrow stone pathway across yet another chasm when she heard a crashing of stone up ahead.

She gasped as she saw Hylon holding on to Telgrid's hand. Telgrid was slipping through a hole that had formed underneath the walkway. Peter let go of her hand and ran to help Hylon lift Telgrid from the hole when a large portion collapsed, bringing the floor beneath them loose.

She went to run to help, and the headache shot an intense pain through the side of her head that dropped her to her knees. She was trying to focus on her breathing as blood dripped from her nose and created little red spots on the stone in front of her face. Her ears were ringing, and her vision was becoming blurry. For a moment, she thought she was going to pass out. She felt Dugan's hands on her arm, and he helped her to her feet. She looked up to see Torin yelling down into the hole.

Torin's voice was full of fear as he screamed into the darkness below, "Hylon! Hylon, can you hear me?"

Leianna stumbled over to the edge of the hole with Dugan helping her along the way.

They stood there in silence awaiting a response when she heard Peter yell up, "We are ok. Just a little scratched up is all."

There was relief on Torin's face as his shoulders slumped. Torin yelled again into the pit, "I am going to get you guys out of there!"

She could hear an echo of Telgrid as she shouted up to Torin, "We will not get back up the way we came! An iron grate of some sort covered the opening. Peter and I can't seem to get it to budge."

Dugan called down to them, "If we lowered a rope, do you think we could pull the grate free from up here?"

Peter was laughing as he yelled back up at him, "I never thought I would say this Dugan, but I don't think you are strong enough to move this."

Da'ragh leaned over the edge as he shouted down the pit, "Do you see another way out?"

Telgrid was quick to reply, "I can see a couple of pathways, and one looks like a possible way out of here."

Peter quickly chimed in, "It's worth a shot."

Da'ragh stroked his beard, "We will continue forward and see if there is another way to reach the lower levels."

Torin stood up quickly as he growled at Da'ragh, "We are not leaving them behind!"

Da'ragh shook his head, "Of course not, we are going to find another way down to them. These ruins are filled with passages and tunnels. I don't know if you have noticed or not, but they are also in a state of decay. If we can't find a way down, we can always make one."

Torin nodded and then yelled over the edge, "We will get you out, Hylon."

Leianna was relieved that Da'ragh was not trying to convince them to leave the others behind. She believed Da'ragh was right about the ruins. There was bound to be another way for Peter and the others to get out.

Dugan whispered to her, "I am sure we will find a way to get Peter out."

Leianna was not sure if he was trying to comfort her or if he was trying to convince himself. She peered over the pit at Da'ragh and Torin who had already moved forward and had begun searching the area ahead for a route down to the others. Dugan nudged her arm as he motioned for the two of them to join in the search. She followed Dugan the long way around the pit and through an opening in one wall that looked like it might have been a window long ago.

She began searching the surrounding area when she noticed a rotten wooden desk with the skeletal remains of a Do'earee draped over the top of it. The remains were long, decayed, but she could see something clutched in its left hand. She kneeled down to get a closer look and found that the skeletal hand was clutching a small silver chain with something still attached to it. She could not see what the chain was attached to, as it was obscured by the palm of the corpse's hand.

Her head was still pounding, and she was finding herself having difficulty keeping a clear thought. Her curiosity was getting the better of her, even with the headache. She determined that a quick peek wouldn't hurt anything as she reached for the chain.

Dugan called out to her and the sound of his voice had taken her off guard, "Hey Leianna, what are you doing? I wouldn't touch anything if I were you." The tone of his voice let her know he was trying to warn her.

She nodded slightly and stood up while still glancing sideways at the silver chain. She wanted to see what it held in its hand, but decided Dugan was probably right. Leianna turned and slowly made her way toward him.

She took a deep breath and tried to focus on the surrounding area instead of the pain in her head. She made her way over to Dugan, who was looking down at the ground. She looked down herself at two more bodies, these did not look like Do'earee or Magi.

She leaned on her staff for balance as she spoke, "We have seen so many bodies down here. I can't help but wonder how many people must have died during the war."

Dugan was flat in his response. It sounded like he was lost somewhere in his own mind, "To read about it is one thing, but to see it firsthand... that's something else entirely. We are seeing the aftermath of a war that caused the Cataclysm. The Labyrinth is just a speck of dust compared to the lives that were lost when the old capital and surrounding area was reduced to the magic torn Broken Lands."

Leianna nodded in quiet agreement. Dugan was right. It had reduced the whole western region of Auldryche to rubble during the Cataclysm. The old capital itself had been destroyed alongside the royal family.

She wondered if the Labyrinth was just the beginning of the horrors they would witness.

Dugan sighed, "We have no idea what actually happened. They have erased even places like this Labyrinth from history while they have kept the old races silent. The Magi have used fear and force in order to keep them from telling the truth less they suffer the same fate as the Do'earee."

Leianna hoped that what they were doing would help in revealing the truth to the people. She still had her concerns. Even if the people knew the truth, how would they even begin to oppose the rule of the Magi? She felt a painful twinge in the side of her head and took another deep breath. All this thinking was making her head hurt... literally.

Torin was waving his arms to get their attention, "Over here, I think I found a stairway that leads down to the lower levels."

Da'ragh was already standing next to him. He appeared to be staring down the stairway they had just discovered.

Dugan walked toward them when Leianna took another glance at the bodies. They appeared to have been bystanders in the conflict. Whoever they were, they died because of a power grab by the Magi. She thought of Oakbridge and for a moment she could envision the Magi wiping it off the map just like they had the Labyrinth.

If she was to continue this path, she would have to take full account of the Magi's capabilities and the lengths they would go to in order to realize their goals. For now, she was the only Do'earee left according to Da'ragh. If she had anything to do with it, she would make sure she was not the last. She made a silent promise to bring justice to the Magi. She would make sure they were held accountable for all of their wrongdoings. Her heartbeat increased, as did her anger. She hadn't realized she was letting herself get so worked up over all of this.

Da'ragh followed Torin down the steps when she realized Da'ragh was part of the Magi. When the time came, would she seek justice for the lives he took as well? She did not take any joy in the thought, but he himself had stated that he had played a role in the destruction of the Do'earee. She took a deep breath and decided that there would be time enough for those thoughts, but for now, she needed to focus on getting her friends out of that pit.

She followed behind Dugan as they descended the staircase in search of Peter and the others.

Chapter Eighteen

Peter brushed the dust and debris from his clothes as he observed the wide tunnel ahead of them. He could make out a faint light coming from deeper within and decided it must be coming from outside. He glanced back at Hylon, who was helping Telgrid limp her way forward.

Peter turned to face Telgrid, "I can help if you like?"

Telgrid smiled back at him as she nearly tossed Hylon to the side, "I would like that very much."

Peter noticed as Hylon shot her an eye roll of amused disbelief. Telgrid grabbed hold of his hand as he helped to support her wounded foot. Peter looked over to Hylon, "I will help Telgrid, Hylon, but will you keep an eye out for trouble up ahead?"

Hylon nodded, "I can do that."

Peter watched as Hylon moved quickly, but quietly, into the shadows of the tunnel. Peter raised his eyebrows. Hylon had practically disappeared. It impressed him at how adept Hylon was at staying out of sight. Hopefully, he could give them a heads up to any dangers that may lurk in the tunnel up ahead.

Peter thought of Leianna as they moved their way slowly forward. He hoped she was doing better after that encounter with the Blighted One. That thing gave him the creeps, but he was sure a good heavy swing of his sword would put a quick end to the creature.

Da'ragh had told all of them to run, so he did, but after observing it while Leianna was unconscious, it appeared rather feeble and frail. It looked like it was on the verge of collapsing into dust. He couldn't imagine it surviving a good hard swing of his blade.

The features of his face turned to a glower as he thought of the Roka. That thing, on the other hand, was clearly dangerous. Peter couldn't believe something like that even had a name. He could still hear its slimy, grating voice in his mind. It had called itself Zradsi.

Peter shook his head, who talked about themselves in the third person like that. If it had been olaumen once, it was nothing of the sort now. They warped this Zradsi mentally as well as physically.

Peter couldn't imagine what kind of magic must have been used to create such a being. He hoped he would never find out. He was thinking about how Dugan had almost died when it nearly severed his leg.

Peter was incredibly thankful that Leianna had risked using her healing magic to save him. He was playing the battle over in his head when he remembered something it had said. He had heard it say something that sounded familiar that pulled at his curiosity.

It had stated that it was looking for Madu Flesh. Peter didn't even know who or what a Madu was, but he felt like he should.

Telgrid squeezed his hand, "What are you thinking about? You seem to be engrossed by it."

Peter helped her over some loose stones on the floor, "I am just thinking about that Roka and what it had said."

Telgrid chuckled, "That thing was out of its mind. It may have been someone once, but now it's little more than a bloodthirsty animal."

Peter bit his lips before replying, "Do you know what a Madu is?"

Telgrid shook her head, "I wouldn't worry about it, Peter. For all we know, a Madu doesn't even exist outside the mind of that thing."

Peter hadn't thought of it that way. The Roka was clearly unstable. Who knows how long it had even been down here trapped in the Labyrinth. Peter made a mental note to ask Da'ragh about it when they caught back up with the others. Telgrid was smiling at him, and Peter remembered the talk he had with Dugan.

Telgrid clearly liked him, and he didn't want to string her along. Peter really liked Telgrid, but only as his friend. He was in love with Leianna. Peter let out a sigh as he tried to figure out how to tell her. He knew he shouldn't say anything until they were free of the Labyrinth, but it was killing him not being honest.

They came across a crack in the wall that was letting the red light of the sky through when he stopped and turned to face Telgrid.

She looked up at him quizzically as he tried to find the words to express his feelings.

When Telgrid spoke, he interrupted her and just started blurting out everything all at once, "Telgrid, I am in love with Leianna! I have been in love with her ever since we were little. I don't want to hurt you by trying to hide that from you. It's not that I don't like you. You are super strong and great at weaving. You always have great ideas and I like the way you handle yourself in a fight. I feel grateful to have you as a friend. It's just that I..."

It shocked Peter when Telgrid reached up a hand and placed a finger on his mouth to shush him up. Telgrid was laughing softly as she spoke, "I know you are in love with her. Everyone can tell that you are head over heels for her, but does she love you back, Peter?"

Peter stood there, staring at her in shock. He didn't know what to say. He was sure that Leianna loved him, maybe not in the way he wanted, but in time... maybe.

He felt doubt cross his face when Telgrid raised her eyebrows and gently grabbed his arm, "Peter, I think you are amazing, and no one has taken a punch from me like you have." Peter smiled as she continued, "Leianna does not look at you the same way you look at her. I know how you feel, but that will not stop me from showing you how I feel about you. Your positivity, determination and sense of duty are like nothing I have ever seen, and that is what I love about you. That is why I love you."

Peter wasn't sure what to say, but he could feel his face flush red. No one had told him anything like that before. He struggled at what to say when she smiled and pulled him down to kiss his cheek.

Telgrid was speaking softly, "If anything, we dwarfs are patient. I will wait until you decide what you truly want. It is only a matter of time until you realize that what you want is me."

Peter gulped nervously. This was not at all how he saw this conversation going. He forced a grin, "We... we can talk more about this later."

Telgrid shrugged, "Whatever your heart desires, Peter." She stuck out her tongue and winked at him. Peter knew that she just had to be teasing him now. Peter made himself chuckle, which sounded strained, even to himself.

Telgrid laughed and quickly covered her mouth to keep from being too loud, "Peter, you are so cute that I can't handle it sometimes." Peter was not sure if that was a compliment or not, but he decided not to think too hard about it.

Hylon coughed as he stepped out of the shadows and into the red light coming in through the crack in the wall. Hylon let out a snicker before speaking, "If you two are looking to get more intimate, I can just wait over there."

Peter was shocked at Hylon's statement and blurted out nervously, "No... no Hylon, that won't be necessary. We are ready to move now. We were just... talking about... things."

Both Telgrid and Hylon started laughing at him.

Peter didn't understand what was so funny.

Hylon inhaled sharply as he caught his breath, "Peter, I needed that laugh after everything that's happened." Hylon moved forward and held out his hand, "There is an old wooden door up ahead with light coming through the seams. It is partially rotted and is jammed shut. Do you think you could try to break it free?"

Peter nodded as Telgrid shifted her weight over to Hylon for support.

Telgrid winked at him as she spoke, "Peter can do it. He's pretty tough." Peter immediately spun on his heel and marched forward confidently. He could feel his face had turned a deep shade of red. He was convinced that the talk with Telgrid had emboldened her advances instead of dissuading her. Peter shook his head. Being handsome was difficult. He smiled to himself; this must be similar to what Dugan has to deal with back in Oakbridge.

Peter had not gone very far down the tunnel when he could see light peeking through the seams in the large wooden door up ahead. He stepped up to the door and gave it a shove, which gave him resistance. He braced himself and placed his shoulder against the door as he gave it another hard push.

The door moved ever so slightly inward, and he heard what sounded like chains rattle from the other side. He pressed his face against the door as he tried to peer through one of the seams to the other side of the door. He was having trouble seeing clearly through the seam because of how thin it was, but then it hit him as he slowly leaned back and looked at the light. It was not the same red as the outside sky, but had more of a turquoise hue. He bit his top lip as he turned to the others who had caught up and were waiting behind him.

Telgrid and Hylon had been giggling, but stopped when he turned to face them. Peter pointed at the light slipping through the seams in the door, "Why is the light coming through of a different color than outside?"

Peter watched as both the smiles faded from Hylon's and Telgrid's faces as they realized what Peter had told them.

Hylon nervously looked to Peter as he whispered, "What is behind the door?"

Peter Shrugged, "We could break it down and find out or we could backtrack and try the other way. What do you guys think?"

Telgrid narrowed her eyes on the large wooden door, "Break part of it free so we can see inside."

Peter grabbed the hilt of his sword and frowned; he would not be using this on an old wooden door. He began searching the area when he found a piece of stone that had broken free from the wall. Peter scooped it up and approached the door.

With the rock held firmly in his hands, he swung the rock down on a part of the door that looked more decayed than the rest. The wood made a cracking noise as he struck and gave way after a few heavy strikes. Peter tossed the stone on the ground as he pushed the broken portion of the door in. He took a breath as he leaned forward to peer inside.

Peter could barely believe what he was looking at. The room in front of him was large and circular, with a tall pedestal in the center. He could clearly see multiple doorways on the perimeter of the room's edges, including the one he was looking through. Floating just above the top of the pedestal was a turquoise stone glowing softly.

Peter could tell that this odd stone was the cause of the light that had been slipping through the door. Peter felt excited. This might be the Cipher Stone Da'ragh had been talking about.

Peter half whispered back to the others, "I think I see the Cipher Stone!"

Hylon and Telgrid both looked excited. Peter was sure that with a few more whacks with that rock in the right places, he could get this door to open for them. He searched the ground for the rock when he heard the jangle of chains from within the room. Peter was puzzled, as he had not seen anything that would give off such a noise when he examined the room. He turned and peered into the room just in time to see some chains pull up into the darkness of the room's ceiling. Whatever it was had just moved outside the glow of the orb on the pedestal.

Peter stared in disbelief for a moment as he watched another couple of chains dangle from the ceiling and drift about the room before disappearing back up into the darkened shadows of the ceiling. Peter was unnerved as this process happened a couple more times before it stopped altogether.

Peter could hear Telgrid speaking softly behind him, "What is it, Peter?"

Peter turned and looked at her, "There are these chains coming from the ceiling that look like someone is lowering and pulling back up again."

Hylon groaned, "I knew something like this was going to happen."

Telgrid was staring at him, "Peter, what is lowering and pulling the chains?"

Peter shrugged, "I can't see up that high. The ceiling is dark, and light isn't reaching it."

Hylon slowly raised his hand, "I can take a quick look if you like."

Peter could tell that Hylon was nervous. A little shaken by his description of the chains. Peter was not sure how Hylon could get a better look than himself, but decided there would be no harm in Hylon giving the room a look. Peter moved out of the way so that Hylon could look through the gap he had created earlier.

Hylon stepped up to the door cautiously as he peered inside. Peter watched as Hylon scanned the room, "Do you see anything, Hylon?"

Hylon gave a slight frown, "No, I don't see... Oh no..."

Peter watched as Hylons face turned to that of fear as Hylons gaze looked up at the ceiling within the circular room. Peter held his hands up, "Well, what is it, Hylon?"

Hylon frowned and shook his head, "We will have to find another way. There is no way I am going in there."

Peter wasn't sure what he was talking about, "What do you see?"

Hylon faced him eye to eye as he spoke slowly, "I don't know what that is. I just know it looks scary and dangerous to our health."

Telgrid limped over to look through the hole herself, "I don't see anything, Hylon."

Peter could hear her voice echo in the room ahead as he heard chains drop.

Hylon shuddered at the noise of the chains moving about the room.

Telgrid looked back with concern at Peter and then to Hylon, "Hylon, what is moving the chains?"

Hylon swallowed, "I don't know. It looks like a dead guy covered in chains crawling on the ceiling."

Peter winced, "That sounds terrible."

Hylon nodded, "You should see it yourself. Then you would know just how terrible that thing looks."

Telgrid was peaking through the hole again as Peter heard the chains stop moving. Peter went to ask her what she was seeing when she shushed him.

Telgrid whispered back to them, "I have an idea I want to try. You two stay quiet."

Peter closed his mouth and nodded as he watched her turn her gaze back to the hole in the door. They stood in silence for a few moments, with nothing happening, when Telgrid let out a sharp whistle. Peter heard the chains once again as they swung around the room. The only difference is that they sounded like they were being dragged about the room more hurriedly than before.

Telgrid turned to look at him with a smile as she wiggled her eyebrows at him. Peter gave her a puzzled look when she pushed her finger to her lips, signaling that they all remain silent. A few moments had passed, and the sound of the chains had fallen silent once again.

Telgrid held out a hand behind herself, gesturing to the two to wait. Peter waited anxiously when Telgrid whistled loudly and the sound of chains dragging about the room happened once again. Telgrid watched for a while as Peter listened to the chains. This time, the chains moved about the room longer than the last, but after patiently waiting, the sound of the chains disappeared once more.

Peter watched as Telgrid stepped away from the door. She had a cocky smile as she spoke. "It is using sound to look for us. Whatever it is, it is reacting to sound. I am not sure it can see at all." Telgrid looked over at Hylon, "Did you see where it had any eyes?"

Hylon shivered, "No, it has chains wrapped all around its head and through its body. The chains seem to weave through its flesh."

Peter could see that Hylon was disgusted by whatever it was he was seeing, and he could understand why. If it even looked half as disturbing as Hylon had described it, then his disgust was warranted completely.

Peter whispered to Telgrid, "So, what is your plan?"

He watched her purse her lips as she contemplated. She let out a sigh before speaking, "We could try to sneak past the thing as long as we stayed quiet. But we don't know if the doors are stuck like this one. Not to mention we don't have any idea what is behind any of them."

Peter nodded in agreement. That was a lot to consider and more than he would have thought of. He was thinking about running across the room to avoid the chains and picking a door at random. Peter exhaled sharply; this was going to be harder than he had expected it to be.

Hylon slowly raised his hand, "I have an idea. We could always go back and try the other path."

Peter shrugged, "That is an option, but I think we should try to get that Cipher Stone for Leianna. Once we have the stone and find the others, we can get out of here."

Telgrid nodded, "So that is what a Cipher Stone looks like."

Peter shrugged, "I guess I don't know what one looks like either, but if I had to guess, I would think that would be one."

Telgrid looked back at the two of them with a grin on her face, "Even if it's not the stone we are looking for. It still looks extraordinarily valuable."

Hylon sounded on edge, "I don't think we should risk it. I think we should go back and try to find a way out of here. Then we can come back with the others for the stone."

Peter thought the idea was fair, but he would like to take the opportunity to impress Leianna as well. If they could somehow get the stone and find their way back to the others, then Leianna would be bound to be grateful.

Peter had an idea, "What if I run in and grab the stone and come right back out? Then we can make our way back to that other path you are talking about."

Hylon was looking at him in disbelief, "If you want to go in there, I am not going to stop you, but don't expect me to follow you in there."

Telgrid was eyeballing him as he turned to face her. She looked him once over before she started speaking, "Do you think you can make it to the stone and back out again before the chains get you?"

Peter smiled, "If I am quiet and careful, I should be able to get the stone with ease."

Telgrid nodded, "Alright, you can give it a go. But I won't be able to help if you get in a spot of trouble." She motioned toward her ankle. Peter knew that if he went in there, he would be on his own.

He thought about it for a moment and decided it should be an easy enough task to get the stone. He would sneak quietly in, grab the stone, and sneak back out. If the thing with the chains reacted to the stone being taken, he would make a break for it and run for the door.

Peter nodded, "I can get it done. Help me with this door."

Peter took the rock and was able to break the corners loose that were keeping the door jammed. With the three of them working on the door, it didn't take long until they were able to get it free and moving. Peter watched as Hylon gathered some pieces of the door off the ground and sorted through them until he showed Peter what he was looking for.

Hylon was smiling, "This chunk of wood should work as a wedge if that thing decides to try to follow us. Once you are through the door, I will close it and jam this piece of wood under it. It may not stop it from getting through, but it may buy us time to get away."

Telgrid was smiling, "Just like that time in Markagra when you and Torin jammed the door to escape from that old grumpy merchant's estate."

Hylon nodded in agreement, "Exactly like that." Peter turned to Hylon, "Did the old merchant capture you like Mr. Sidestreets?"

Hylon shook his head, "No, we were being chased by his hired guards because we had broken in and stolen from him. It would have been a big payout if I hadn't forgotten the bag in all that chaos."

Telgrid let out a chuckle, "Hylon has a knack for getting the job done. However, he almost always loses the goods in the process."

Peter smiled nervously. He forgot that is how they had to survive on the streets. He couldn't imagine himself stealing from anyone. It wasn't in him to be a thief. He was extremely grateful that he had a family that took care of him.

Peter slowly opened the door and looked across the floor that had tiles laid out in a circular pattern. Each circle appeared to be a different color the closer you got to the stone. Peter couldn't make out what the colors would have been, as everything was shaded in a turquoise hue of the glow from the stone. Hylon and Telgrid were giving him a silent thumbs up as he turned to enter the room.

He took a step forward when he felt Hylon grab his arm. Peter looked back to see Hylon with a defeated look on his face, "I can't let you do this. I can tell already you are going to make a racket trying to sneak in there. Best leave the sneaking to me."

He was going to ask if he was sure about that, but Hylon had already stepped into the room. Peter was once again impressed by how quietly and gracefully Hylon moved. Peter was squinting. If he didn't know any better, he would have thought he was watching a slender, dark-haired girl step softly across the room. Peter now understood why Dugan had been mistaken the first time he had met Hylon.

Peter watched in awe as Hylon had already made it halfway across the room without making a sound. He was about to cheer him on when he caught himself. He had almost forgotten the thing on the ceiling was sensitive to sound. Hylon was steadily moving forward when Peter heard a loud click, followed by a low grinding noise coming from the floor.

Hylon spun to look at them in horror as the floor began spinning. Each row of colors spun in the opposite direction of the others parallel to it. The floor became a dizzying spiral of rotating patterns. He looked up as Hylon hopped to the side, just in time to avoid a swinging chain.

Peter watched as Hylon threw his arms in the air as if he were surrendering as he mouthed a panicked silent scream. Peter mouthed a sorry back to him as Hylon rolled, dodged, and tumbled away from the chains searching the room below.

Hylon looked completely frantic as he tried to gain his balance on the moving floor beneath him. The chains coming from the ceiling moved like that of an insect antenna that was trying to locate its prey. Peter watched as Telgrid reached down and picked up a rock. She watched the rotations of the floor in combination with the flailing chains and threw the rock at the opposite side of the room that Hylon was in.

The chains shot out and snatched the rock up with unnervingly fast speed, and pulled it up into the darkness of the ceiling. Mere seconds later, dust and pebbles fell from the ceiling. The thing up in the shadows had reduced the rock to dust in seconds. Hylon had noticed Telgrid throw the rock almost immediately. He had hopped from spinning tiles to the next almost all the way up to the glowing stone when the chains resumed their search of the area.

Peter quickly caught on as Telgrid threw another stone to distract the chains. Peter reached down and picked up a stone to throw it near where Telgrid had thrown her stone. The chains whipped about, picking up each of the stones and dragging them into the shadows of the ceiling. Only seconds would pass before the left-over debris of the rocks fell to the floor.

Peter watched as Hylon practically bounded from the floor and gripped the pedestal to hoist himself up and grab at the stone. Peter gasped as a chain whipped and nearly struck Hylon as he ducked. Telgrid threw another stone, but this time, the chains had ignored it. He didn't wait to find out why as he threw another rock into the room, only to see that this one was ignored as well.

Peter was desperately trying to think of a way to help Hylon when he threw caution to the wind and jumped into the room, yelling up at the ceiling. The chains immediately slashed into the air where Peter had just been standing. If it wasn't for the rotation of the floor, they would have hit him for sure.

Peter pulled his sword from his scabbard as he watched the chains whirl about the room. Peter could not anticipate their movements. The chains were so chaotic in their search for them.

He noticed out of the corner of his eye that Hylon had already climbed up the pedestal and was reaching for the stone.

Peter whistled as he saw the chains whip ever closer to Hylon. Peter was barely able to duck as a chain cut through the air. It swung dangerously close to his shoulder.

Peter heard Telgrid cry out, "Hylon, watch out!"

Peter watched as Hylon grabbed the stone and was attempting to jump out of the way when the tip of one chain caught his foot, sending him crashing to the ground. Hylon hit the ground hard. He could hear the air rush out in a wheeze. The stone was ripped free of his grasp and clattered across the ground.

The same chain that had struck him whirled as if it were alive and began wrapping itself around Hylon's left ankle. Peter was sure that Hylon would have screamed if it were not for all the air having been knocked out of him. Peter could feel the adrenaline surge through his system as he bounded across the shifting floor tiles in long strides and jumps.

Hylon was grasping at the Pedestal and fighting against the pull of the chain when Peter swung his sword with as much force as he could manage just above Hylon's bound ankle. The sword bounced off the chain with a loud clang. Peter did not know what he was doing, but he knew he had to save Hylon.

As if driven by an outside force, Peter jumped and grabbed hold of the chain and pulled for all he was worth. At first, both Hylon and himself were being lifted towards the ceiling. Then all at once, Hylon, Peter, and the creature clinging to the ceiling all came crashing to the floor.

Peter felt the full impact of the fall on his left side, making his ribs scream out in pain, but he gave no thought to himself as he reached for the loose chain around Hylon's ankle. Peter was able to yank the chain free as he tossed it aside. Hylon scampered backwards away from it in a panic. In one swift motion, he brought his sword up in a guard's stance. His eyes darted about the room, searching for the thing that had fallen from the ceiling.

He could barely believe his eyes. The figure on the ground was grotesque. The chain creature looked like some sort of twisted amalgam of body parts. It had five arms connected around a torso, its head was wrapped in chains so tightly that Peter could barely make out the mouth with a swollen tongue sprouting from it. It appeared to Peter that the flesh was lifeless, but it was clearly moving. This monstrosity was clearly the work of a demented mind.

The chained creature made no noise other than the clanking of its chains in an attempt to right itself. Peter was partly relieved to see that it was struggling because of the shifting directions of the floor. The creature also appeared to have broken one of its arms in its plummet from the ceiling. The arm hung limp underneath it as it shifted its weight to lift itself from the floor. However, in its attempt to get up, the spiraled movements of the floor were causing the creature to become tangled in its own chains.

Peter called out, "Hylon, get to the door!"

He wanted to make sure that Hylon was getting to safety. Instead he saw Hylon going towards the stone.

Peter could hear Telgrid from the doorway, "Hylon, what are you doing?! Just leave it!"

Hylon was not showing any signs of slowing as he hopped over the now lifeless chains scattered on the ground, "Not this time, Telgrid! I am getting that stone!"

Peter would not try to stop him, instead he refocused his gaze upon the chained creature who had managed to get itself up on its hands. He noticed that the chains had started to move and shift under his feet when he realized that now was the time to strike. He may not get another opportunity to do so.

He immediately ran his way across the room when he stepped on a chain, causing him to slip and lose his balance. Peter covered his face with his left arm as he hit the floor mid stride. He quickly turned over and took solace in not dropping his sword from the fall. As he sat up to regain his footing, he looked up and could barely bring his blade up in time to block the rush of the chained creature.

It pushed against the edge of his blade as the arms tried frantically to grab at him. The blade dug into the exposed areas of its skin that were unprotected by metal. Peter was pushed along the ground on his back by the force of it. It took everything he had to keep his grip on the hilt of his sword. The thing completely disregarded the blade edge digging into it as it thrashed about blindly, grabbing for him.

He lifted his left leg and began kicking at its face and shoulders to dissuade the thing from its attack. Peter kicked hard and caught the creature with the heel of his boot right in its mouth, nearly removing its bottom jaw. It shocked Peter that the creature was completely unfazed by the damage done to it. On top of that, there was not a single drop of blood. The chains were slowly beginning to untangle and wrap themselves around him. He knew he had to do something fast, or this thing was going to kill him.

Peter was being pushed all around the room as he strained to come up with how he was going to break free of this thing. The light from the stone was causing the room to flash as it bounced around on the moving floor, making it harder for him to get his bearings. He had an idea. Peter kicked out with both feet at once as he braced himself against the creature's shoulders, giving him just enough time to pull his sword free and thrust the point forward into the thing's neck.

The creature made no noise but seemed to lose some of its momentum and balance. Peter gritted his teeth and began slashing and stabbing at the thing's throat until he had nearly severed the horror's head entirely. Then, all at once, the creature fell to the ground. Peter kicked himself free as he stumbled backwards. He stood up and hurriedly finished the job until the thing had been fully decapitated. He was out of breath as he couldn't take his eyes off it. The room slowed in its rotations until it came to a complete stop.

Peter was still trying to catch his breath when he noticed Telgrid untangle herself from some chains that had wrapped themselves around her. Peter could hardly believe it. She had been braced in the doorway pulling the chains as the creature was attacking him. He had a grim realization that if not for her, he would have been in a lot worse shape. The thing was overpowering him, even with Telgrid trying to hold it back.

He stared down at the thing. Its flesh appeared a dull and lifeless gray. He frowned as he thought about the people who must have died to generate such a morbid creation. He couldn't believe the lengths that the Magi would go. They made this thing from at least three or four different individuals.

Peter wondered what the Magi would truly do if they finally got the total control they lusted after. Telgrid brought a rock down on the creature's skull, causing him to flinch. He hadn't even noticed her walk over to him. He was so lost in thought.

Peter found himself staring at her as she brushed her braid behind her shoulder. She turned to him as she exhaled in relief, "Just to be sure. I don't want that thing getting back up again."

Peter nodded, "I agree. It was hard to put down."

He searched the room for Hylon, who was peeking out from behind the pillar, his silhouette outlined by the glow of the stone he clenched in his hands.

Telgrid had caught sight of him as well, "It's okay Hylon, I think we killed it."

Hylon stepped out from behind the pillar and his voice was tense, "All the same, Telgrid, I think it's best we got out of here as soon as we can."

Peter had no qualms about leaving. He had gotten his fill of this room, and then some. Peter helped Telgrid as they crossed the room over to Hylon. The circular room had doors spread around it. He bit the corner of his lip as he tried to see any sign of where the doors lead, but to no avail.

Telgrid tugged on his arm, "So which door should we try first?"

Hylon spoke under his breath in response to her question, "How about we try to take a path that doesn't try to kill us this time?"

Peter wished he knew which path would be the safest. Ultimately there was no way to tell which door would be dangerous or not.

Peter sighed, "I guess we start checking the doors one by one. I don't know where any of these lead." He began walking towards one of the doors, not waiting for a response from the other two. No sense in delaying the inevitable.

Peter grabbed hold of the iron ring handle of the door furthest across the room, "Here goes nothing."

He took a deep breath before giving the door a pull. Unlike the door they had used to enter the room, this one opened with relative ease. He peeked inside.

To his surprise, he witnessed torches lit on either side of a long hallway, one after the other. Peter thought to himself that this had to be magic. Torches don't light themselves like that. As unnerving as seeing the torch's light themselves was, he was comforted by the fact that the hallway ahead was absent of anything threatening.

He opened the door all the way open and revealed the well-lit corridor to both Telgrid and Hylon. They both looked puzzled as they looked down the hallway.

Peter broke the silence, "So what do you think? At least we can see where we are going if we decide to go this way."

Telgrid shrugged and Hylon was looking worried as he spoke, "Not to be the one to point out the obvious, but a magically lit hallway wouldn't normally be my first choice. That being said, at least we will see whatever tries to kill us by torchlight." Telgrid chuckled nervously, "Hopefully, we won't run into anything else. Although, the way this excursion has turned out already, I wouldn't hold my breath. It seems this place just doesn't want to give us a break."

Peter scratched the back of his head as he turned to gaze down the lit corridor once more. "Well, I think you are both making excellent points. This hallway seems to go the direction we were headed already, so why change course now?" Peter stepped over and held out his hand to Telgrid, who quickly grabbed him by the arm.

She leaned up and whispered to him, "Thank You for saving Hylon like that. You put yourself at risk to help him."

Peter nodded but felt a little guilty, "If I had listened to him in the first place, he would have never been put at risk."

Peter almost jumped when Hylon spoke to the other side of him, "You know I can hear both of you, right? But Peter, if you had taken my suggestion, we would have backtracked all that way and... we wouldn't have this." Peter watched as Hylon pulled the turquoise stone up from his side and handed it to him.

Peter took the stone and looked at it. He really hoped that this was the Cipher Stone that they had all been looking for. He shoved the stone into his pack. Now the next step was to find the rest of the group and get out of this place. As hair-raising and wondrously scary as this place was, he hoped he would never have to return here ever again.

Peter took the first step into the hallway with one eye closed as he scrunched his face in anticipation of something bad. He exhaled as nothing happened and the light from the torches was pleasantly soft, as opposed to the dark chill from the circular room. Hylon had moved up front like before and cautiously walked forward. Peter could tell that he was on high alert and on the lookout for anything that might mean them harm. Peter hoped they wouldn't run into anything dangerous like the chain creature. With any luck, this would lead to a way out and back to the others.

They continued down the corridor for a while until Hylon stopped them by holding his hand out behind him. Peter looked around him to see the torches further up the corridor were dark and remained unlit. He let go of Telgrid's arm to examine one of the torches on the wall next to him, unexpectedly the torch came free of the wall easily.

Peter inspected and to his surprise it was not a regular torch. Instead it resembled those of the fairy lights from within the Soga Burrow. Peter held the torch out so that both Telgrid and Hylon could see, "It's like the orbs from the burrow."

Telgrid took the torch from him and held it in front of her, "Well, we better take them with us if we are going in there."

Hylon groaned, "I knew you were going to say that."

Peter reached up and gathered a couple more of the fairy torches for Hylon and himself.

Hylon stared into the light of his torch before exhaling sharply, "I will keep a lookout."

Hylon resumed his slow, cautious walk ahead of them. Once they entered the part of the corridor that was darker, Peter could see the torches were not completely out. Some flickered with embers of light and others still had a bit of glow left to them. They appeared to be dying.

Peter was busy staring at one light that was flickering when Hylon looked back at him. He looked like he was straining to hear something far away, "Peter, I think I can hear someone."

Peter listened but could only hear his own breathing, "I hear nothing."

Hylon raised a finger to his lips and Peter held his breath so that Hylon could listen more clearly. After a brief moment, Hylon lowered his hand, "I think it might be them, but I can't be completely certain that it is."

Peter understood, but the only way they could find out for sure was to keep going. Staying here wouldn't do them any good. He really didn't want to make their way back to the circular room on the chance it was them.

Peter looked to Telgrid and then to Hylon, "I say we keep moving forward and hope for the best."

Hylon gave him a nervous smile before turning around and walking slowly forward.

They had only taken a few steps when Peter thought he heard something. He listened closely for just a moment before immediately recognizing the sound of thrashing chains far behind them. Peter noticed that both the others had heard it, too. Hylon looked back at him with a look of fear and confusion.

He could think of only one thing to do, "Run!"

Hylon wasted no time in spinning around and going into a full sprint down the corridor.

Peter reached into his pack to grab the stone and threw the rest on the ground, even tossing his torch.

Telgrid looked at him with confusion as he practically yelled at her, "Ditch the pack, we need to go now!" Telgrid understood exactly what he meant as she tossed the pack and climbed onto his back so that he could carry her.

Peter stood up and was surprised at how heavy she was for her size. He thought that she must be made of dense muscle as he ran after Hylon. He held her legs looped in his arms while she held onto his shoulders. The chains were gradually getting louder behind them as they ran down the corridor. Peter wondered how far this hallway actually was. There didn't seem to be any doors or turns, it just kept going on and on in a straight line.

He focused on running as he followed closely behind Hylon with the bobbing of his torch, lighting the way. Hylon was showing signs of slowing down, and even he was feeling winded. He hoped that there would be a door or something else they could use to stop the thing from chasing them. The muscles in his legs were burning. Peter didn't know how long he could keep this pace up. He could really feel himself slow down when he glimpsed something up ahead.

He could see the faint red of the sky outside peeking in through a broken part in the roof of the corridor up ahead. They just had to reach that point, then even if they had to fight the chain creature again, it would have to fight its way up through the opening. Peter felt renewed energy as he pushed forward.

Hylon must have felt the same, as he was again sprinting so quickly he was putting distance between himself and them. He watched as Hylon turned back to look at him with dismay. He had reached the hole in the corridor's roof.

Hylon was clearly distraught as he yelled, "It's too high up!"

Peter was panting as he let Telgrid down off his back and looked up at the hole in the arched ceiling. He was pretty sure he could give Hylon a boost so that he could reach the top. Peter interlocked his fingers and kneeled as he heard the chains grow ever closer. Hylon had caught on quickly as he stepped onto Peter's hands. He was surprised at the weightlessness of Hylon as he stood up, lifting him towards the hole in the ceiling.

Peter watched as Hylon grabbed at the edge that was just within his reach. Hylon up and disappeared out of sight. Peter stared at the hole, hoping that this would provide them a means of escape, when Hylon peeked back over the edge and lowered a hand down.

He was speaking quickly and most likely full of adrenaline as he motioned for Peter and Telgrid to follow, "It looks like a stairway out. Quick, I will help pull you guys up!"

Peter locked his fingers again and kneeled to boost Telgrid up in the same way that he had just helped Hylon. Telgrid limped over and balanced her good foot in the palms of his hands. Peter couldn't help but let out a grunt as he began lifting her towards the outstretched hand of Hylon. She was incredibly heavy for her size.

Peter strained and lifted with everything he had; he could feel his arms shaking as he raised her. Just about the time he thought he was going to drop her, she grabbed Hylon's hand. With the combined efforts of all three of them, she cleared the opening. She had spun around so that both Hylon and herself were holding their hands out.

The clashing of chains and stone was incredibly loud now and Peter half expected to see the chained creature out of the corner of his eye as he jumped for the hands of his friends. His jump came up short. He was just barely out of reach. He attempted a few more jumps, but each time was just short of grabbing hold of Telgrid and Hylon's outstretched arms.

Peter wished he had the rope from his pack right about now. They had to leave the pack behind in order to carry Telgrid to safety. He looked around his feet for anything to grab hold of but found only scattered stone from the broken ceiling on the floor. The clamour of the chains were growing closer. He tried to peer into the corridor, but could only make out the pitch black darkness stretching out in both directions.

He attempted another jump but once again came up short of grabbing a hold of his friend's hands. He looked up as he held out his arms, "I can't make it up. It's too far!"

Hylon called down as he pulled away from the opening, "I am going to see if I can find something for you to grab hold of!"

Telgrid kept her hand lowered for him, "Peter, you can make it! Just try again!"

Peter took a few steps back and got a running start as he jumped in the air, reaching out to grab hold of Telgrid with his arm. He felt his fingertips brush against hers. He was still short of getting high enough to reach her hand. Peter looked back up at Telgrid, "It's too high, Telgrid. There is no way I can reach."

Telgrid nodded, "I am going to help Hylon and see if we can find something to lower down to you."

Peter watched as Telgrid disappeared from the opening above. The loud crashing of chains snapped him back into the predicament he was currently stuck in. Peter spun around and drew his sword as he looked down the long corridor. He could just make out some sort of movement in the darkness.

Peter steadied his breathing. If he could get another strike on it like last time, he could use its chains to help himself out of here. He was sure they had killed it. Telgrid had made quick work of the thing's head.

He strained as he stared into the darkness. There were three different figures moving through the corridor towards him. He realized with grim truth that this was not the same one, but three entirely new ones moving rapidly toward him.

Peter gripped the hilt of his sword tightly as he called out to the others, "Telgrid! Hylon! You better just run. There are a lot of those chain monsters down here!"

Peter took a defensive stance and mentally prepared himself. If he could use the corridor to his advantage, he would only have to fight one at a time. With any luck, they might get tangled in each other's chains.

Peter stood with determination and strength. If he was to die here, then he would die fighting. These creatures would feel the bite of his steel and the bravery that surged with every beat of his heart. He tuned out the noise around him and focused on the creatures bearing down on him. Time seemed to move at a slowed pace as he relaxed his shoulders. He would not pass up the opportunity to strike at any opening in the defenses of these grotesque and evil born creations.

Peter watched as the first of these creatures barreled down the corridor, picking up speed and leaving the other two behind it. Peter couldn't help but grin. This one would be the first to fall. Peter raised his sword above his head in preparation as he took a deep breath. He exhaled slowly as he pictured in his mind the exact location of his strike. Peter was ready, his mind was clear.

He jumped backwards in shock as a rope slapped him in the face. Peter looked up in confusion to see Dugan had lowered a rope down to him.

Dugan was chuckling, "You going to grab on or what?"

Peter wasted no time in grabbing the rope as Dugan and the others hoisted him up and out of the corridor.

Once Peter had his footing on the floor above, he quickly warned the others, "There are three of those chain things!"

Torin was tossing the rope aside when he looked back at Peter perplexed, "Chain things?"

Peter was struggling to find the words of urgency, "They are monsters covered in chains and... they might be undead or something... we gotta get out of here!"

Torin had already laid flat on the ground. Peering down into the corridor as Peter spoke. Peter went to caution him against his curiosity. Torin shot up to his feet in one rapid movement that made Peter think of a startled cat.

Torin now had the same look of urgency, "What in all the realms are those... THINGS!?"

Dugan looked at Peter, "How bad are they?"

Peter waved his arms outward dramatically to further demonstrate the gravity of the situation, "Really bad! Twice as bad as that giant skeleton we fought back in Oakbridge!"

Peter watched as Dugan's eyes widened in concern.

Torin waved his left hand at the hole, "There is no way we are outrunning those things. We are going to have to fight them."

Peter didn't like that idea. He scanned the area around him for the first time since exiting the corridor. He was hoping to find something they could use against the chain creatures. Peter looked over to see a crumbling pillar near the side of the hole leading to the inside of the corridor. The upper half was missing from the pillar and it was free of the ceiling. It's base looked almost completely disintegrated. The broken pillar crashing into the floor is what must have created the hole in the first place. If they could collapse the rest of the pillar, it could cover the hole and prevent the chain creatures from getting out.

He turned to see Hylon was helping Telgrid up the stairs to the side of the room. That must have been how they had gotten down to the corridor. Telgrid looked concerned, but Peter waved her forward with urgency. If they had to run from these things, he would feel better if Telgrid was already a safe distance away.

Peter turned to Dugan as he pointed at the broken pillar, "Do you think we could push that over and into the hole?"

Dugan looked at the pillar and nodded his head, "It is worth a try."

Torin was shaking his head, "I say we fight them as they try to come out."

Dugan was quick in his retort, "If they can't get out, there is no fight. Use your head Torin."

Peter watched as Torin got a sour look. He could tell he wanted to protest but gave in with a shrug. He followed in behind Dugan, who was already making his way behind the pillar. He rushed his way around so that all three of them were pushing against the pillar.

At first the pillar seemed solid and unmovable when Peter heard a cracking noise. The cracking was just barely audible over the sound of the chains coming out of the hole.

Dugan grunted as he spoke, "On me, we all push with everything we got on the count of three."

Peter nodded and watched as Torin did the same.

Dugan took a deep breath, "One. Two. Three!"

Peter slammed his shoulder into the pillar with every ounce of strength that he had. Dugan hurled his weight against the pillar like a bull, his muscles bulged as his shoulder contacted the pillar. Torin had hit with equal force, but his frame was dwarfed by that of Dugan's. The pillar seemed to hold just before it broke free.

Peter nearly fell to the floor as the pillar fell like that of a tree freshly cut. It toppled and hit the hole just moments before chains shot out like grasping tendrils. The pillar didn't stop as Peter watched it crash through the floor and collapse the corridor underneath.

The stones beneath his feet began to shake violently when he heard Torin cry out, "Run! This whole place is going down!"

Peter could barely maintain his footing as he tried to keep up with Torin and Dugan. They were all trying to run up the stairs as stones fell from the ceiling and the walls around them. Peter could not hardly believe his eyes as he watched the entire building crumble around them.

He nearly tripped a couple of times as the three of them made their escape. He followed closely behind the two as they zigzagged their way through doorways and rooms until they had made their way outside. Torin was already running across the floating stones that led to the next area by the time he cleared the last doorway. Peter stayed right on the heels of Dugan as he jumped from stone to stone on his way over the top of the chasm. He didn't look back until he was safely on the other side.

Peter hunched over and held his knees; his chest was heaving from breathing so hard. After taking a moment to catch his breath, he stood up and stared at the area they had just ran from. He watched in amazement as the building was collapsing, but parts of it were floating in all directions. Whatever magic had held the building together was losing its hold, resulting in entire portions of the structure floating off in random directions. The main ground where it had stood broke free and slowly drifted away from them.

Torin let out a sharp whistle, "Now that is something you don't see every day."

Peter couldn't agree more. This place was full of unexpected and unpredictable hazards. Peter looked down at Telgrid as she moved beside him. She was watching the building fall apart and drift just as he was.

Peter smiled, "I am glad we all made it safely out of there."

Telgrid nodded as she continued to look forward, "I am thankful you made it out, Peter. For a moment I thought..."

Peter looked at her as she trailed off, "You thought what, Telgrid?"

She just turned to him with a grim smile on her face, "Nothing to worry about. I am just glad you are safe."

Peter gave her a nervous grin, "I am glad that I made it out as well."

Dugan was watching the debris of the building disperse with fascinated interest. Torin was laughing as he gave Hylon a hug. He couldn't help but smile. They seemed to be the best of friends, just like him and Leianna.

Peter searched around the area in a panicked realization that Da'ragh and Leianna were nowhere to be seen.

Peter looked to Dugan, "Where is Leianna?"

He appeared to be only half paying attention to him as he mumbled, "She's back there."

He waved his hand halfheartedly behind him. Peter moved in that direction but was halted when Dugan started speaking, "That is interesting. The pathway stones are following the portion of the building were just escaped from. It's like this place is alive somehow... it's as though there is an intelligence to it."

Peter witnessed what Dugan was rambling about. The stones they had used to cross the gap between land masses were floating after the chunk moving away. Peter chuckled, "It's like a duck and her ducklings."

Dugan scoffed, "I suppose you're right with that one, it does appear that way."

Peter turned and started walking in the direction Dugan had indicated before hoping to find Leianna well. She seemed to be in a lot of pain after that blighted thing had afflicted her. Da'ragh had stated that the Imp powder would cause headaches and memory loss, but it didn't make Peter feel any better to see his friend hurting.

Peter clambered to the top of a large stone pile to get a better survey of his surroundings. Once on top, he could see clearly in many directions. Over to his left he could see the Cathedral they had fled from earlier and the dead forest surrounding it. Off to his right, he could see an area that looked just like the one they had arrived at. In fact, he was sure it was the same one. Were these floating islands of ruins moving around them as they tried to navigate them?

He couldn't shake the feeling that something was trying to keep them lost in this maze of wreckage. Peter thought of what Dugan had just been saying about the place acting like that of a living thing. Was the vast endless sea of ruins attempting to keep them away from the vault? Peter shook his head. He bet that his grandfather never had to deal with magic like this. He thought he would use his sword a lot more than his head. Peter smiled as he remembered one of his grandads many lessons.

His grandfather Lamar, when he was smaller than his younger brother Liam is now, had taught him that a battle is won in the mind and the heart long before it is ever touched by hand. Peter nodded. He had been approaching this place all wrong. They had tried using mindless strength to force their way through this labyrinth. Just like the others, he was intent on fighting their way through when in fact they needed to be using their minds to overcome this living maze.

Peter was reveling in his own sharp wit when he looked down at a rather small and damaged acropolis to see Da'ragh and Leianna speaking within. He could tell they were discussing something serious by the gestures they were making. Peter wondered what they were talking about as he rested his hands at his sides. He felt something from the outside of his pocket when he realized he had forgotten all about the stone.

Peter reached down into his pocket and pulled out the turquoise stone that appeared dimmer now that it was free of the darkness of the tunnels. He was sure that the finding of this Cipher Stone would cheer them both up. Peter made his way down the pile of rubble when he heard Leianna cry out and collapse on the ground. Peter was running before he even realized what he was doing.

As he ran up to her, he helped Leianna lean up against one of the acropolis's pillars for support. She was holding the sides of her head. She looked like she was in a lot of pain. He kneeled next to his friend as he looked to Da'ragh for answers.

Da'ragh looked concerned and spoke softly, "She is remembering. The imp powder is wearing off faster than I had expected."

Peter lifted the turquoise stone in his hand and showed it to Da'ragh, "It's a good thing we don't have to stick around then. I found one."

Da'ragh stroked his beard as he picked up the stone and inspected it in his hand. Peter had expected him to at least be a little surprised or thankful for his discovery. It didn't matter as long as he could get Leianna out of here.

Da'ragh moved his gaze from the stone back to Peter, "This is not a Cipher Stone Peter. It looks like something I should be familiar with, but unfortunately, I don't have any idea what it is." Da'ragh examined the stone before handing it back to him.

Peter was disappointed that it was not what they were looking for, but he could still give it to Leianna. Leianna groaned as she rubbed at her temples. Peter reached for his waterskin, only to be reminded that he had left his pack behind in the corridor.

Peter spoke softly as to not make her headache any worse than it needed to be, "Is there anything I can get for you Leianna?"

Leianna winced from the pain, "If you can get rid of this pounding in my head, that would be great."

Peter could tell she was attempting to smile, but struggling to do so. She was breathing deeply as she stopped rubbing the sides of her head, "I can't wait to be free of this place. How close are we to this vault?"

Da'ragh looked uneasy, "I am unable to determine our location. We should have arrived there by now, but by my approximation we are further than when we started."

Peter wanted to share his idea with them, "I think this place is alive just like the burrow. Dugan had noticed that the landmasses move like they are alive. I believe that this Labyrinth is keeping us from the Vault. It doesn't know that we are the good guys, and it is trying to keep us away from the Do'earee artifacts. It's like the burrow knows what you are looking for and the lights showing you the way. If we can just figure out how to communicate with it..."

Da'ragh started laughing so hard that Peter wondered if he had said something dumb.

Da'ragh shook his head, "All these years, the Circle of Magi had said that they had locked the treasures of the Do'earee away here within the Labyrinth. When the truth is the Labyrinth was keeping the relics away from the Magi all along. Since the Magi could not obtain the relics and artifacts for their own use, they instead locked away the entire Labyrinth."

Peter thought that made sense for the most part, "So how do we convince the Labyrinth that we are not Magi?"

Leianna seemed dreadfully quiet as she stared at Da'ragh, Peter couldn't help but feel like she knew something that he didn't.

Da'ragh let out a sigh, "I will need to leave before the Labyrinth will open itself to you. It is treating me like an enemy, and as long as I am near you, you will never reach the Vault."

Peter was confused, "But why would it consider you an enemy... you are a Do'-."

Leianna interrupted, "Peter, Da'ragh is right. We need him to leave the Labyrinth if we are to find the vault."

Peter furrowed his brow, "That doesn't make any sense. How are we supposed to find one of these stones without your help?"

Da'ragh stood up to lean on his staff, "Leianna will know once she sees it. I need to leave in order for that to happen."

Peter didn't understand. He was going to voice his disapproval when Leianna reached out and grabbed a hold of his shoulder.

She looked serious, and he listened carefully to her, "Peter, trust me on his. Once Da'ragh leaves, then the Labyrinth should reveal the Vault to us. Once that happens, we will get the Cipher Stone and get out of here."

Peter nodded, "If you say that is what needs to happen, then I believe you." Peter still felt like he was missing something, but trusted his best friend.

Da'ragh lightly brushed at his robe with his offhand. Peter noticed he did not like the idea any better than himself.

Da'ragh let out a slow exhale, "We will tell the others and I can take Telgrid with me because of her injured foot. You will need to be quick Leianna. The Blighted One as I explained to you will get more traction in your mind the closer it gets to you. Peter, don't let it touch her no matter what."

Peter could hear the severity in Da'ragh's voice and place his fist over his heart in a warden's salute. Peter spoke with candor, "I promise you Da'ragh that I will protect her with my life."

Da'ragh smiled, "I know you will, my boy. However, be cautious in the taking of oaths. Although this is a good cause in protecting your friend, oaths have a way of turning on you. Just take it from me."

Peter had no idea what he was talking about, but nodded like he understood. Da'ragh began making his way through the rubble toward the others as Peter turned back to Leianna.

She was staring at the ground when she noticed he was looking at her, "Sorry Peter, just trying to sort things out in my head."

Peter smiled, "Don't worry Leianna, Da'ragh told me about the effects of the imp powder."

Leianna gave a half grin, "Yeah, the imp powder..."

Peter stood up and helped Leianna to her feet, "How does your head feel?"

Leianna rubbed the back of her neck, "It's feeling better every moment, but I am not sure that's entirely a good thing. The more I remember, the more I am in danger of this Blighted One."

He stood up straight and thrusted his shoulders outwards with confidence, "Don't worry Leianna. If that thing comes anywhere near you, I will take care of it."

Leianna chuckled softly, "Let's just hope that it doesn't come down to that."

He just hoped that all of this would work out and they could get out of here safely. Peter walked beside Leianna as they followed in the same direction that Da'ragh had gone. He couldn't stop thinking about how this place was full of all sorts of terrible monsters. They had just escaped those chain monsters and this Blighted One seemed to really concentrate on Leianna. He hoped he was not underestimating how dangerous it was.

He looked up to see a large portion of a ruined structure float past. This place was fascinating. It held its dangers to be sure, but Peter felt lucky to witness such things as what the Labyrinth held. He wished he could show his family what he was looking at.

Peter grinned. Liam would probably be just as excited as he was about all of this. He took a breath as he thought about his younger brother. These Magi had to be stopped before their desire for control brought the entire realm to destruction. Learning that they were the ones responsible for the Cataclysm was hard enough to accept, but knowing they had caused the desolation of a place as wondrous as the Labyrinth was hard to swallow. If left unchecked, the Magi would twist the everything into a nightmare of their own design. If he could make any difference in all this, he would do whatever it took to provide a better future for Liam. Peter relaxed his hand on the hilt of his sword. Thinking about this was putting him on edge.

Peter looked up to see everyone gathering around Da'ragh. In his thoughts he had fallen behind Leianna. He quickly caught up and joined the others as Da'ragh discussed the next plan of action.

Da'ragh was leaning on his staff as he looked about the group, "Leianna and I have come up with a possible reason as to why we cannot find the vault. The Labyrinth may be reacting to me even in its current state. I believe it remembers me and is preventing us from reaching the Vault. If I leave the vault may reveal itself to Leianna."

Peter watched as Hylon slowly raised his hand, "But why would the Labyrinth hide the vault from you?"

Leianna practically shouted when she interrupted Da'ragh from responding, "We think it may be unable to determine who he is. Da'ragh was here before. It may be having difficulty remembering the difference between Do'earee and Magi. Look at the state of this place. It's amazing the Labyrinth has survived all this time. Especially after what took place here."

Peter nodded with the others. That made sense to him. This place was in a terrible state and if Da'ragh had been here before, it may not realize he was a friend. Peter thought it was just what a wounded animal would do. It wouldn't understand you were trying to help; it would only recognize the pain and attempt to prevent further injury.

Da'ragh tapped his staff, "I propose that most of us leave. The Labyrinth is more likely to respond to Leianna that way."

Peter chimed up, "I will not abandon Leianna. I am going to stay."

Torin was snickering, "Of course you are."

Da'ragh coughed to get everyone's attention again, "Telgrid, I would appreciate it if you came with me. Your injured ankle is slowing you down."

Telgrid scoffed, "I get it. My injury is not your concern, but my slowing everyone else down is. I will go with you, but only if they don't want me to stay."

Telgrid's gaze fell upon Peter, and he felt like her eyes were burning a hole right through him.

Peter smiled nervously, "I would feel a lot better if I knew you were safely free of this place. If things go right, we will be right behind you."

Telgrid returned his smile and her intensity softened a bit, "You better be Peter. Alright, it's settled. I will go with Da'ragh."

Torin grabbed Hylon by the shoulder and pushed him forward, "Hylon is going with you. I would feel better if he was safely free of here."

Hylon turned toward Torin to object, but Torin wasn't having it. "Hylon will go with you. I am not sure I can protect him down here. Not to mention this 'would be' Do'earee and her ginger idiot needs someone to look out for them."

Dugan took a step forward, "I feel the need to stay as well."

Peter instantly felt better. With these two coming with them, there was nothing they couldn't take out as a team.

Leianna spoke up next, "Thank you. Once we have our hands on a Cipher Stone, we will leave this place. Da'ragh, should I use the serpent wand to leave here?"

Da'ragh shook his head, "No, use the Skein Pathway to travel back to the Burrow. It is best you do not use any of the Magi tools for magic. I will use the Serpent Wand to get us out of here so that we do not draw unwanted attention with the use of Do'earee magic. By the time they detect the use of your Skein Pathway, you will have already left this place. We will all meet at the Burrow."

Peter watched as Leianna nodded in understanding.

Da'ragh faced the others, "I suggest we leave now. Time is of the essence and Leianna, please exercise caution in using your magic down here. The next time you use your magic, make sure it is to open a Skein Pathway and nothing else. The moment you use it, the Blighted One will come for you."

Da'ragh took a few steps back and smiled at Leianna, "It's up to you now."

Hylon turned and hugged Torin before standing next to Da'ragh. He was hiding his face behind his long hair again.

Telgrid limped forward and grabbed Peter by his shirt, pulling him down towards her. She kissed his cheek and whispered into his ear, "Just be sure you come back to me Peter... I will wait for you."

Peter felt his face turn red as both Torin and Dugan began snickering. Peter felt extremely awkward. "I... I will Telgrid. We will come back safely."

Telgrid winked at him and tossed her braid over her shoulder as she made her way over to Da'ragh.

Da'ragh held out the Serpent Wand and black mist swirled in front of him. Da'ragh turned back for just a moment, "Godspeed."

Peter watched as the three of them stepped through the black mist and disappeared. He assured himself that he would do his absolute best to keep Leianna safe.

CHAPTER NINETEEN

Da'ragh, Hylon and Telgrid stepped through the portal created by the usage of the Serpent Wand. After the blackened smoke cleared, Leianna realized they were gone and free of the Labyrinth. She glanced over at Peter, who was beaming. He seemed absolutely unfazed by all this pandemonium and darkness down here. In a sense, she was grateful that she had him to rely on. He never gave up hope.

Torin took a step forward, "What now, our fearless leader? I want to get this over with as soon as possible."

Dugan murmured as though he were in deep thought, "I think this place is alive. If you could somehow reach out and communicate with it, then it may reveal the Vault to you."

Leianna thought about what Peter had said earlier about this place being akin to Soga Burrow. She decided it was worth a shot. She would try to reach out to communicate with it. Leianna sighed, "I have an idea."

Leianna stepped forward past the others so that she was standing on the edge, facing the chasm of ruins below. She was distracted momentarily as she gazed once more across the expanse. These floating landmasses gave off an eerie semblance to that of lost ships at sea. If she could be the lighthouse through Do'earee magic, she could guide them back together.

Leianna turned back to the others, "Turns out that I may have a dangerous idea."

Torin got a giant grin on his face, "Now you are talking my language."

Dugan seemed less enthusiastic, "Does this dangerous idea of yours involve the use of magic?"

Peter went from smiling to a look of concern, "Leianna, you can't use magic. Da'ragh said that if you use Do'earee magic, then the Blighter will come for you."

She held up her hand, "Just hear me out. I think I can bring these landmasses together and that includes the vault. With the right focus, I think I can undo some of this chaos around us."

Dugan raised an eyebrow, "You are going to bring order... to this?" Dugan spread his arms out, trying to emphasize the formidable undertaking that she had suggested.

Leianna was not swayed, "I believe I can do it, Dugan. I have had success in talking with the Soga Burrow, and if I can reach the heart of the Labyrinth, I believe I can convince it to show us the Vault."

Torin raised his eyebrows and swirled his finger by his ear to imply that she had gone crazy.

Leianna glared at him, "I am not crazy Torin, I can do this. It is not unlike that of healing the wounded, it's merely on a larger scale."

Peter spoke up in her defense, "If Leianna says she can do it, then I believe her. We must keep her safe. She is the only one who can find the stone."

Dugan was smiling, "I think the twerp has a point. For now, that sounds like the best chance we have of finding that stone. I guess I should leave the magic to those who know how to use it. My skills lay elsewhere."

Torin shrugged, "I suppose you are right. Also, if she uses magic, then there is the possibility I get to stab something."

Leianna was glad they agreed with her. Even Torin was on their side, despite appearing a little unstable at times.

Leianna turned back to the ocean of floating ruins and gazed beyond the crumbling of remains of the once monumental structures. She slowly reached out with her heart in search of the Labyrinths. Leianna fixated on the belief of speaking with the Labyrinth and emptied her mind of all other thoughts.

Her head no longer ached as badly as it had before. After a few moments, she could not even detect its discomfort. She had the sensation of drifting in the breeze. She felt weightless as she felt the heart of the Labyrinth grow closer. Leianna called out across the ruins to the Labyrinth itself, and after a temporary silence, it answered.

Once connected to the Labyrinth she was immediately struck with a sense of pain, fear, and anger that brought her to her knees. The agony of the Labyrinth rushed through her body, equivalent to venom. She screamed as images of Do'earee being slaughtered flooded her mind. The Labyrinth was showing her all the devastation it had to endure. Misery it had dealt with on its own all this time.

Her chest tightened in response to all the sorrow that the Labyrinth had held for the Do'earee and at the same time she sensed the resentment of the Labyrinth in its inability to save them. She began weeping as the images played in her head as if they had recently occurred. This Labyrinth was in immense pain, physically, mentally, and emotionally. Leianna desperately wanted to help, but did not know on how to do so. She was made aware of how the Labyrinth was a long-lost friend and its suffering was breaking her heart.

After what equated to an eternity, she forced open her eyes to discover the spirit of the Labyrinth laying on the ground in front of her. Its image, not that different from Soga, but faded and barely visible. The light of it was a soft golden yellow. She immediately reached out, but found no solid being to comfort.

The spirit lifted its head off the ground, and she could hear its whisper in her mind, "Hope... you have brought us hope, young apprentice. We raised the Cathedral... to show you the way... to show the Reaper we live on..."

Leianna could feel the tears stream down her face, "What do I do? I don't know how to help you..." Leianna perceived warmth wrap around her heart. The sensation was identical to being hugged by her father.

The spirit sounded peaceful and calm, "You already have Leianna Braun, Apprentice of Da'ragh. You have given us hope. We had forgotten hope. We had forgotten love. We were dying. Only pain... only fear... only suffering. But now... only hope."

Leianna tried to reach out with her magic. She focused on trying to heal the labyrinth. She closed her eyes and concentrated, but was interrupted as she felt a warm palm on her cheek. When she reopened her eyes, she could behold the apparition clearly. Its light was brighter than that of even Soga's.

The apparition had no facial features, but Leianna could sense it was smiling at her, "We cannot be saved. You have saved us. Save the others, Leianna Braun. We go to rest."

Leianna cried out as the apparition faded out and disappeared from her mind. She detected what brief presence of the Labyrinth that remained fade out of existence. She fell to the ground, sobbing. There was nothing she could do to save it.

Familiar arms wrapped around her and when she peered up, she saw Peter was holding her. She was so very grateful for her friend as she hugged him back. After a moment she sat up, the pain of the Labyrinth and Do'earee still fresh in her mind.

She heard Torin let out a sharp whistle and turned to look in the direction he was facing. She could barely believe her eyes; a landmass had appeared out of nowhere and attached itself to the one they were standing on. The structure in front of them was untouched by the destruction that plagued the rest of the ruins.

It resembled a flower garden in the center of a forest meadow more than anything else. The landmass was so very small compared to the others around them. Leianna frowned; this must have been the last living part of the Labyrinth.

She stood up and stepped forward. She watched as the trees and flowers slowly began to lose all their color. The green faded to gray while the flowers wilted, their petals falling to the ground below, right in front of her. She covered her mouth to keep the tears at bay. She was watching the burrow die.

Dugan called out behind her, "I don't understand what is happening, but I think we should hustle this along. We've got company!"

Leianna viewed behind her to discern why Dugan was so concerned. All the dead throughout the labyrinth were stirring and rising. The corpses of the long deceased were moving towards them from the other floating landmasses that were all converging to the heart of the Labyrinth.

She hastily wiped her eyes and began moving forward, "The stone should be here. This is the Vault."

Leianna walked out into the heart of the Labyrinth and pushed all the emotions aside. She needed to keep her focus, and the overwhelming feeling of loss would overtake her if she let it. She glanced around her to regard relics of various sorts, but that was not the shocking part. Each relic was protected in the arms of a wooden statue. It was as if the wood itself had grown to hold these mementos within their arms.

Row after row of carvings of the Do'earee clutching artifacts, scrolls, and all manner of magical items stretched out in this small, dying forest. She scrutinized one closer and gasped. Each wooden being here resembled that of one of the fallen Do'earee the Labyrinth had shown her. The Labyrinth, in trying to cope with its mourning, had created a memorial for every single one of the fallen Do'earee.

She could not imagine what the Labyrinth had to endure by itself. It had hung on to life by a thread in protecting the Do'earee relics. It had been alone in its battle with the Magi after they had slaughtered everyone within. Who knew what atrocities the Magi had committed in their attempts to get the Labyrinth to relinquish its treasures? After the Magi had been unsuccessful, they had locked the Labyrinth away to be forgotten. Leianna took a sharp breath; she couldn't be thinking about all of this right now.

She quickly searched around, unsure of where the stone would be, when a wooden statue caught her eye. It was separate from the others and had its arms reaching out in front. Once she got closer, she could clearly identify a small, cloudy white stone in the palm of its outstretched hand. The statue was offering the Cipher Stone freely, unlike the others who clutched their relics tightly. She slowly reached out and picked up the stone and immediately knew that this was what she was looking for. She held it close to her chest and thanked the Labyrinth for its help.

When Leianna opened her eyes, she stared at the face of the wooden statue and nearly dropped the stone. It was her mother. Her mind erupted with questions; she thought that her mother had died in the village when she was young. How could she be here? She had a clear image of her mother in her mind, of when she was little. Had Da'ragh lied? Was he the one that was responsible for her death? Had Lorcan killed her mother...

Her thoughts were scattered to the wind as the sound of a gong in the distance resonated behind her. The horrid image of the Blighted One forced its way back into her mind. It was coming and she could hear it calling to her. She turned to shout after the others, only to discover that they were in the middle of a battle with the dead.

How long had she been standing there? The undead lay in crumbled chunks around the feet of her friends. Peter was yelling at her. He sounded comparable to being underwater and far away. Dugan was swinging a large club that appeared to have been ripped free from one of the trees while Torin spun through the dead equivalent to a bladed whirlwind. Their saving grace being that the dead were long decayed and sluggishly slow moving.

She stood in a stupor as she searched the surrounding area. The dead were shambling toward them from every direction. Each landmass that connected to the heart of the Labyrinth added to their number. She heard whispering as she glanced up to discover the Blighted One slowly floating over from within the ruins behind them.

She sensed the amulet around her neck grow hot as the staff grew warm in her hands. A familiar voice echoed in her mind, "Focus, child, use the light."

Leianna detected her mind becoming clearer and quickly reached into her bag to grab a seed for the Skein Pathway. She swiftly focused on the seed when something tackled her. The impact of hitting the ground knocked the air out of her. She lifted her head off the ground just in time to see the acorn tumble under Dugan and created a misshaped archway. Her inability to focus clearly on the destination had created a strange-looking Skein Archway that glowed with an odd orange hue. She panicked when she saw Dugan and several undead get sucked through it. She pushed for all she was worth and noticed that a few of the undead were blindly trying to claw at her. Leianna pushed her hand forward out of impulse, sending a shockwave through the dead, causing them to explode into dust in all directions. She jumped to her feet precisely in time to witness the Skein archway that had sucked Dugan through close. She experienced her heart sink. How would she possibly get him back?

Peter was screaming as he fought his way backwards. She was completely taken off guard, witnessing Peter swing his way through the bodies of the dead like a sickle through wheat. They surged in a mass, only to be reduced to rubble beneath his quick and forceful swings.

She stood awestruck when Peter yelled at her, "We need to get out of here... NOW!"

Leianna reached for her bag and grabbed another seed, only to drop it. Dead rushed her from her left side in waves, only to be held back by her frequent magical blasts. She was experiencing the toll of the repeated usage of magic. Her breathing was becoming labored as her heartbeat quickened.

Leianna had to think of something fast. She lifted her staff high in the air and slammed it down on the ground and reached out, with the thought of stopping in her mind. It felt as if the air was ripped from her lungs. She experienced a tide of fatigue slam into her body.

Leianna clutched at her chest as she attempted to catch her breath. Bright ribbons of silver and blue raced out in all directions from her and wrapped around the undead. It was as if time was halted. The undead stood motionless in place. She had engulfed the entire area in a haze of stasis.

She watched as Peter and Torin both ran towards her. Peter helped her up as they ran. They had to clear the edge of the undead horde. Leianna took a quick glance back at the statue of her mother before turning and sprinting with the others. Her magic was only temporary, and they had limited time to be free of this place.

They were all sprinting as she attempted to collect her thoughts. Using all that magic had left her feeling exhausted and her thoughts scattered. She squinted ahead at an oddly arranged stone structure absent of the dead when the frigid grip of an unseen hand wrapped around her neck.

She grasped at the air around her to grab hold of whatever held her, only to find nothing as it lifted her off her feet. She could feel the clarity in her mind fade as the image of the Blighted One appeared before her. Whispers in a language she did not understand filled her mind as the thing approached her.

She began to panic as it grew ever closer to her. Peter charged forward, screaming and plunging his sword into the phantom, as she couldn't comprehend what was happening. Her mind could barely comprehend the shimmering glimpse of Peter's sword glowing a bright blue upon striking the form of the Blighted One.

A terrifying screech filled the air that made her mind ache and scatter as she tumbled to the ground. When she finally came to her senses, she discerned they had pulled her to safety at the base of a strange stone structure. The staff in her hand hummed. This stone structure was a Dolmen gate. She didn't know how she knew, but she did.

She stood up shakily as Peter helped her to her feet. Peter had blood dripping down his arm and on his chin. The wounds that the dead had inflicted were beginning to take a toll on him. Peter held her shoulder, "Leianna, we need to get out of here, but we can't do it without your help."

Leianna nodded as she reached into her satchel, only to find it had been torn in their escape from the dead. She looked up at Peter in a panic. She had no idea how they would escape without the Skein seeds. The dead were slowly beginning to move as Torin pulled her behind him. Their backs were to the Dolmen Gate as they faced the horde of undead. The throng of corpses were now free of the haze and were now running and climbing over each other towards them in an unholy hunger.

Torin was chuckling, "Never thought that this was the way I would go, but beggars can't be choosers, I suppose."

Peter stood silently as he faced the dead, rushing towards them with his sword drawn. She could barely hear him when he spoke, "No harm will befall you while I still stand, Leianna. I promise you that."

Leianna felt disheartened. How would they escape now? She wished they could all be somewhere safe, simply somewhere far away from here. She fell backwards and caught herself on one of the Dolmen Gates' tall stones. After a flash forced her to close her eyes, dizziness overtook her. Hot air blew through her hair, and she could feel the warmth of the sun on her face.

When Leianna opened her eyes, it took a moment to adjust to the glaring brightness of the sun overhead. She gasped when she realized they were somewhere else entirely. The Dolmen Gate had responded to her and transported them somewhere else. She noticed that her hand was still touching the stone of the Dolmen Gate. It appeared exactly the same, but this one was constructed of a yellow and gold-colored stone.

Peter was trying to get her attention, "Hey uh, Leianna... where are we?"

She surveyed the middle of what appeared to be a great stone plaza, with numerous people standing about garbed in flowing white clothing. They all stood motionless and staring at Leianna and her friends.

Torin turned to look at her, as he spoke in hushed tones, "I sure hope that they are friendly."

Leianna watched as one figure approached them. The figure stood at least three heads taller than herself. Once they had stepped closer, she could tell that he was Elven. His long golden hair hung straight and loose over his shoulders. Leianna could barely believe what she was looking at. His skin resembled more of carved white marble than formed of flesh and his eyes were of a brilliant golden hue. He had a strangely decorated tattoo that was under both of his eyes and stretched across the bridge of his nose.

The elf bowed in greeting, "Welcome Do'earee. It has been quite some time since our Sun Gate was last put to good use."

Leianna stood in awestruck. She had never seen elves akin to this before.

Peter wasted no time in holding out his hand to shake that of the elf, "Sir, my name is Peter Finley, and it is a pleasure to meet you… uh, what is your name?"

Leianna watched as the tall elf smiled and took Peter by the hand.

CHARACTERS, FACTIONS, PLACES & RACES

Characters

Buska: A friendly stone dwarf and longtime friend of Opals. He is in charge of the mess hall within the Deep Halls. Has developed a keen ear and uncanny way of finding out well-kept secrets. There is more to this stone dwarf than just another cook.

Caldane Evanandur: One of the original Magi council members and cousin of the old king. Known by the Do'earee as The Betrayer during the great war. Uses dark and forbidden magics to extend his own unnatural life. A sadist that is very skilled at inflicting pain through magical as well as physical means.

Da'ragh: He has a mane of long gray hair with an even longer gray beard. He is an elderly man with a seemingly infinite wealth of knowledge about the arcane. He is a wanderer who seeks to undo the damages of the Cataclysm. Arrived in Oakbridge in search of Leianna to teach her the ways of the Do'earee. He has a tumultuous past that continually weighs on him.

Dugan Oslo: He is handsome with dark hair and an olive skin tone. Grew up in a prominent wealthy family in Oakbridge. Naturally strong, with a mind to match. He has a love of learning, particularly that of history. He has a pragmatic approach to life but also has a tendency to become impatient with others.

Grymsnar: So'Baka's Dragon brother. So'baka and Grymsnar have formed an Oathpact binding the two and their fates together. Black as midnight, with the only other color on his scales being an ivory white streak that runs from the left of his jaw down his neck to his chest. Favors speed and martial prowess over the magical aptitude of his kind.

Hylon: He has long raven black hair with deep emerald-colored eyes. Shows obvious signs of being half-elven. He grew up on the streets of Markagra with his friend and fellow orphan Torin. He is timid, shy with a low value perception of himself. He has a talent for sneaking into locked places but has a weak stomach when it comes to combat. He is a pacifist that wants the good for everyone.

Kerrungull: Xanaphia's dragon sister. Her coloration is a deep black with shimmering stripes of dull gold. She is a dragon that prefers to use offensive magic rather than getting her talons bloody. She delights in setting battlefields ablaze, then using magic to enrage the flames to terrifying temperatures that can melt rock. Known by the other Dragons as an Arcane genius when it comes to the crafting forms of magic used by the Dragon Elders.

Leianna Braun: She has deep brown skin with eyes to match. She is an attractive young woman with an innate talent for natural magic. She was aspiring to be a Magi until her encounter with Da'ragh. She is stubborn with a strong sense of justice. She grew up in Oakbridge with her father and brother. Her mother died when she was still very young.

Lorcan: A Magi during the Do'earee wars who was known as the Reaper King. Was one of the few who sought the complete annihilation of the Do'earee. Feared by both his Magi allies as well as his enemies within the Do'earee. Has not been seen since the ending days of the cataclysm.

Lord Kull of House Sher'Atul: Merciless ruler of the Dragon Isles. Brilliant warlord who seeks to conquer the realm in its entirety. He has established dominance over all Tal'Kor Houses through bloodshed and fear. Known as the most powerful Black Blood in all of Tal'Kor's history. He is cruelty incarnate with a lust to feed his hunger for even more power at any cost. He has mastered the dark arts of soul, blood, and oath magic in a single lifetime.

Mr Sidestreets: A ruthless entrepreneur with a lack of morality in pursuit of riches and self gain. He has forsaken his stone dwarf ancestry in pursuit of his own selfish endeavors. Values personal wealth above all else. His loyalties lie with coin alone. Current underworld boss of all illegal dealings within Markagra. He gets a cut of all unsavory deals done in the shadows.

Opal: She is an old stone dwarf with mysterious ties to the Magi during the Do'earee and Magi War. She is a wise and competent leader of the Deep Halls. Current acting embassy ambassador for the Crimson Massif. She cares greatly for her people. This results in her going to great lengths to prevent conflict with the Magi whenever possible.

Peter Finley: He has curly red hair with freckles covering his pale skin. He dreams of becoming a Warden just like his grandfather. Strong desire to protect others with a seemingly unwavering positive personality. He places the needs of others above his own. He grew up in Oakbridge with a large, loving family.

So'baka: Dragon Rider and chief ruler of the beast tribes. Has a short temper and is easily provoked. Smaller than the average Tal'Kor with many piercings worn in respect for the discarded Beastmen of the Dragon Isles. Has formed an Oathpact with his dragon Grymsnar that helps the two fight as one in battle.

Soga: A still living library of the Do'earee hidden in a secretive burrow. Sentient and instinctively helpful, it reveals itself to Do'earee as a blue ethereal spirit.

Telgrid of the Iron Hull Clan: She has long black hair usually kept in a braid with deeply tanned skin. She is a sea dwarf with a love of sailing. She joined both Torin and Hylon on the streets after a shipwreck left her stranded in Markagra. She becomes impatient with others when things don't go her way. She has a big heart with an endless love for those she considers family.

Torin: He has short blonde hair with sky-blue eyes. He has grown up alongside Hylon on the streets of Markagra without parents. He has a tendency for impulsive and hedonistic behaviors.

However, he never backs down from a fight, no matter the odds. Over time, he has honed his skills in the use of a half-spear. He believes in living for the moment and does not do well with long-term planning or prolonged goals.

Vilak: Lord Kull's son. Commonly known by the Tal'Kor as the Murmuring Prince. Sacrificed not only his own soul but that of his dragon's as well to form a pact with a powerful demon of nightmares. The two have become one, granting him unnatural abilities and powers that are foreign to most. He is both feared and loathed at his sacrilege for killing his own dragon. A master of blood magic even before he made his demonic pact.

Vondur: Head of the Magi, the Great Archon. Holds communion with the Madu in secrecy. One of the original Molcainan Magi who still desires dominion over Auldryche. His arcane abilities are beyond compare. He has an intellect that shames those who would consider him as their equal. Incredibly handsome with deep brown skin and silky black hair. There are few within the halls of the Magi who do not fear him.

Xanaphia: Kull's Daughter. Heiress and Keeper of the Dragon Oath Riders. A proud and noble paragon of what it means to be Tal'Kor. She embodies the heights to which the Tal'Kor may rise using their own strength. She formed an Oathpact to her dragon sister, Kerrungull. She is a master of oath magic and arcane forging. She has crafted many of the enchanted weapons used by the most powerful within House Sher'Atul.

Zradsi: A former Roka. Madu Eater and presumably insane. Was sentenced to death but due to his obsession with eating Madu was unable to be executed. Madu flesh gives the consumer a dark regenerative capability. Holds no alliances to anyone or anything. Currently trapped in the labyrinth.

Factions

Do'earee: Was commonly known for their pursuit of knowledge before their destruction at the hands of the Magi. They followed a code of learning natural magics for the betterment of all. During the height of their order, they actively sought the containment of evil beings and hiding away of dark magics. Now known as a deplorable order that sought the overthrowing of the throne and control over the people of Auldryche.

Greencloaks: A guild of thrill-seeking guides and eager explorers. Their main branch is located in Kronus. No two Greencloaks are the same. They offer their skills to the highest bidder but seldom take jobs that would be considered unsavory. They instead favor work involving adventure through experience within the dangers of The Brokenlands. Since the Cataclysm, they have developed a reliable reputation. If someone wishes to explore The Brokenlands, then they would be well advised to hire members of this guild.

House Calembrech: One of the great noble houses residing in the southeast of Auldryche. They outwardly show distrust and defiance toward the Magi. Wealth is derived from their governing of fertile farm ground and livestock. Their prowess is that of large calvary and a chivalrous order of knights. These knights are known as the Lions of Calembrech. The knights spend equal time studying philosophy as much as they do training in combat.

House Stronlind: Noble House residing at the base of the Crimson Massifs. Strong alliance with the dwarves and wealth derived from large mining claims. House is divided and at war with itself. One side claims allegiance to the Magi while the other half of the house holds true to the finding of the heir of the old king. They reside within the incredible mountain fortress known as the Sky Citadel. Stronlind Steel is known as the best when it comes to weapons and armor.

House Vonum: A smaller yet wealthy Noble House who claims loyalty to the Magi while simultaneously working against them in secrecy. They pay for and are allowed training within the tower. The House uses their cunning to keep themselves wealthy as well as out of the direct investigations of the Magi inquisitors. They utilize their skills of diplomacy and vast historical knowledge to keep the House in a position of influence. They have mastered the art of diplomacy as they have contracts and treaties with all of the remaining houses of Auldryche. Current ruling house of Kronus.

Magi: A powerful wizard order that rose in opposition to the Do'earee. They believe that magic should be used in the interest of their own desires. They are currently the acting stewards for the empty throne. They are working on the rewriting of history to fit their agenda. They have been corrupted and are being influenced be the Madu.

Stonespeakers: Stone dwarfs who practice the art of stone singing. A form of lithomancy that brings the stones to life. Viewed as sages and spiritual guides by other stone dwarfs. During times of conflict, the Stonespeakers will give life to stone statues by going into a trance and placing their own soul within. This creates stone golems with the heart and mind of a dwarf. Brutal and nigh invincible in combat. Former allies of the Do'earee who now maintain a tense peace treaty with the Magi.

Wardens: Protectors and Law Keepers. Although they were once a branch of the old kings official law enforcement, they are now little more than a shared ideal. They are almost always volunteers with a uniting desire for protecting others and the need to uphold the ancient laws of the time before the Cataclysm. Usually, they are self-funded while being managed by a loose network of regulating veterans. Overall, they are still recognized by most as an official law keeper of the old crown.

Places

Auldryche: A powerful and great nation at the heart of an infinite realm. This once thriving country was ruled by a noble and just king, now it has fallen into darker times under the rule of the Magi. The lands are at a tipping point as the houses loyal to the old kings bloodline seek to unseat the despotic Magi stewards.

Crimson Massifs: Large Mountain range spanning the northern border of Auldryche. Their peaks making travel across the tops essentially impassable. Mountains stretch from the edge of the Stardust Sea all the way across northern Auldryche to the Storm Straits. Home of the stone dwarves and their many underground fortresses.

Deep Halls: Large Dwarven hold under the city of Kronus. A Crimson Massifs embassy for stone dwarves. Currently kept free of Magi politics due to the efforts of Opal.

Do'earee Borrow: Hidden settlements and refuges contained within magical pockets of reality. Used by Do'earee to safeguard their collective knowledge and powerful artifacts. Most have been destroyed or their locations lost after the Cataclysm.

Isle of Dragons: (Tal'Kor Islands) Covered in rocky crag like mountains with nearly constant winds. Severe rainstorms from the eastern ocean are a regular daily occurrence. Several Tal'Kor houses wage a never-ending war of supremacy over one another. Their impressively large strongholds built from an age long forgotten, with methods lost to time. Now dragon forged molten glass structures have become more common place.

Kronus: The largest city in Auldryche. Serving as the current capitol of the nation while the Magi still hold stewardship. The city was founded under the guidance of House Vonum in the first age. Operates as a hub of information and trade within the interior of Auldryche. Seat of political intrigue and diplomatic relations between all the great houses. The towers of the Magi reside within the city, serving as the heart of the Molcainan Magi.

Markagra: Sizeable merchant trading city on the coast at the base of the tree of rivers. Contains a massive trade port that deals with the river settlements and Sundown Ocean shipments. Trade typically travels through Markagra before finding its way along the coast or up the rivers.

Oakbridge: Small town in addition to a large farming community. Has been the center of the Harvest Festival for generations.

Storm Straits: Storm ridden area of ocean between the lands of the Tal'Kor and Auldryche. Typically, raging waves and storms make the area almost uncrossable. Tales from before the first age talk of the first king of Auldryche severing the land with forbidden ruinous magic that connected the olaumen to the Tal'Kor. Thus, creating the first defense against the Tal'Kor and their dragons.

The Bourban Lady: Mr. Sidestreets establishment. Inn, brothel, and gambling hall all in one. Infamously known for its shady dealings, prostitution and local hangout for the ne'er-do-wells. Those seeking illegal dealings would most likely find what they were looking for here. Transactions ranging from petty theft all the way up to assassinations can be purchased within. No questions asked.

The Brokenlands: Former capital city and seat of the old king's throne before the Cataclysm. Now the area is uninhabitable due to magical storms and tears in reality, leaving the area in a constant state of chaos and destruction. Treasures from the second age lay hidden within, begging to be discovered once more.

The Brokenlands now serve as the last resting spot of many an adventurer seeking their fortune within.

Races

Amoraug: Giant troll like wolf-men with a tribal hierarchy. Their fury and hunting instincts held in check by their simpleminded shortsightedness. Focus on the edge of obsession while pursuing prey or while fighting in battle. Refuse to wear armor or use shields, as this is seen as a form of cowardice. Prefer to fight with a weapon in each hand. Wield crescent pendulum style blades known as the Fangs of the Amoraug.

Kluzke'memon: (Goblins) are known as Goblin's by the Tal'Kor. Pale green skin with a sheen of moisture and greasy hair. Viewed as little more that useful vermin. They specialize in poisons which they sell to survive. They originate in the harsh, frozen marshes on the eastern islands of the Dragon Isles. Inhospitable to other races, but a thriving habitat for the goblin tribes. Known for their coward like sneaky tactics where they employ poisoned arrows and toxic dart blowguns.

Madu: Dark magical shapeshifting beings, an evil that whispers in the dark. Associated with symbols of darkness and serpents. Self-proclaimed gods of the realm. They are an ancient race rumored to be older than all the other races.

Naga: The once great rulers of the Dragon Isles, or so according to them. They claim kinship to the dragons which is not reciprocated. Great seers, competent spell wielders, and tempered advisors. They seek whatever work they can find within the Great Tal'Kor Houses. Each scheming and vying for their rise back to power. They are open worshippers of the Madu.

Olaumen: (Humans) A race of people so varying in color, demeanor and size that no one remembers their true origin. Auldryche has been a great mixing pot of the people for millennia. All are recognized and accepted as one people within the olaumen. Given the title of "Children of Light" by the river elves.

River Elves: Elves that live with and off the land. They are found throughout central Auldryche. Recognized for their natural talent as extraordinary negotiators. Most are known for having noble bloodlines. These families can trace their ancestry back centuries. It is not uncommon for river elves to marry and produce viable offspring with Olaumen.

Roka: Long disbanded experimental branch of the Magi. Consisted of people magically altered for war and assassinations. No two Roka are alike, as the transformation process twists each individual differently. Roka proved to be unstable and uncontrollable after the war. Most Roka were put to death or banished to the Labyrinth. Some of the more intelligent ones fled to The Brokenlands.

Sea Dwarves: They have a natural inclination toward wanderlust, which makes them ideal explorers. They are shrewd merchants who have a knack for sniffing out a good deal. They are the primary sea traders along the coast. Most make their homes out on floating cities south of Auldryche upon the Sundown Ocean. Many have found their way to Kronus to find jobs as fishermen or guides to The Brokenlands as Greencloaks. It is rare, although not unheard of for sea dwarves to marry and produce viable offspring with olaumen.

Stone Dwarves: A humble and hardworking people. They make their homes in the mountains of the Crimson Massifs. They are the primary source of valuable ores and minerals for Auldryche. They have vast underground cities and flourishing mushroom farms. A very stout and hardy people who have a strong sense of hearth and home above all else.

Tal'Kor: Warring race of peoples that reside across the storm straits on the Isle of Dragons. They are skilled dragon riders and blood magic users. Typically, the houses war amongst themselves as much as they war against the western lands of Auldryche. The Houses of the Tal'Kor follow a survival of the fittest mentality, resulting in those with the greatest power becoming the ruling class. Despised by almost all the other races for their cruelty, superiority complex, and insatiable bloodlust.

About Author

I grew up in a small town in Utah raised by two incredibly amazing and loving parents who instilled in me the values I live by to this day. I have a great sister who has always been supportive of my many endeavors. I am married to the coolest and most ambitious woman ever. Without her dedicated efforts, I would not have been able to accomplish my goals. I also have two awesome children who are secretly mini clones of myself. (Don't tell my wife.)

I am a Free Spirit and Idealist. I have been blessed with an incredibly vivid and overactive imagination. I tend to get lost in my own mind quite often. Many times, I have been caught with my head in the clouds rather than focused on the task at hand. I took this imagination and decided to turn it into stories that can be enjoyed by others. I love telling stories to others in the hope of sparking their thoughts, ideas, and imaginations. I hope that through my writings you and others will be inspired to create stories of your own. Whether that be through living your own adventures or creating them such as I have. I believe everyone is capable of excellence if they truly believe in themselves and work hard to pursue their goals. Follow your path and the way will be made clear.

If you enjoyed reading Refulgent Eyre please leave us a review. If you look forward to reading more of the Soga Archives join our readers list at Eccentricgoat.com and/or follow me on social media.

www.ingramcontent.com/pod-product-compliance
Lightning Source LLC
Chambersburg PA
CBHW021408310726
48971CB00005B/1245